The Ascension of the Dead

Todd Andrew Sundell

ISBN 0-7414-2040-6

Michael J. Garrett	Editor
Chris Moreno	Cover Art
John Bliss	Inside Illustrations
Francis Tejeda	Inside Illustrations
Gabriel DeMaggio	Inside Illustrations

Published by:

INFINITY
PUBLISHING.COM

1094 New Dehaven Street, Suite 100
West Conshohocken, PA 19428-2713
Info@buybooksontheweb.com
www.buybooksontheweb.com
Toll-free (877) BUY BOOK
Local Phone (610) 941-9999
Fax (610) 941-9959

Printed in the United States of America

Printed on Recycled Paper

Published June 2004

Acknowledgements

A whole bunch of thanks to Mike Garrett for helping me put together this whole manuscript. A lot of appreciation goes out to Chris Moreno as well for designing such a wonderful cover for the book. Much gratitude goes out to George Romero for creating such an interesting universe, and on which this work is based. I would also like to thank Karen Aldridge and Deon Minnaar for the help they gave me with the Afrikaans. Judith Atiri, Joachim and Ramona Kausch assisted me immensely with the German dialogue, and I would like to express my gratitude to them as well. I would like to give credit to Mike McIrvin and Joseph Galanti for proofreading this work. Tons of thanks go out to Esther Slade for suggesting that I crank the novel out while I still have the chance.

Thanks to my mother, Doris Sundell, for raising me, and to my dad, David Sundell, for bringing me up to become the man that I am now. Thanks to Joseph "Jay" Gage for giving me the encouragement that I needed so many years ago. A lot of gratitude goes out to Rob DeMaggio who inspired me to write fiction that is well thought out and great to read. Lastly, I would like to express sincere appreciation to Yeshua HaMashiach who saved me so many years ago and gave me the idea that is now printed upon these very pages. God is so good!

Contents

Foreword

It was many years ago, in the summer of my 19th year, when I saw George Romero's *Day of the Dead.* I found the movie both interesting and entertaining, yet it painted a picture that was both bleak and filled with foreboding. The dim world that Romero created was one rife with destruction as the human race slowly gets annihilated.

In *Day of the Dead*, Romero constructed a universe where a contagion somehow infected dead bodies. The bodies revive to become slow-moving and dim-witted travesties of the people they once were, and they were on the prowl to turn the human race into copies of themselves. If one of these animated bodies bit someone, that person in turn would die and become one of these "undead things" prevalent in the Romero tradition.

All in all, it wasn't the threat of the undead in these movies that was so intriguing, but rather the interpersonal conflicts that were found in them. In *Day of the Dead,* we see scientists and soldiers holed up together in some isolated storage bunker in Florida. The scientists and the soldiers do not get along due to contrary agendas, and because of that difference, they deal with the impending crisis uniquely. The scientists use the power of reason to find a solution for the problem, and the soldiers resort to brute force. Neither approach seemed to work. Romero's movie concludes as an army of ghouls chase the soldiers through the bunker, where they are caught and dismembered. The movie emphasized the theme of cooperation. The more we argue, the less we get done, and the more humanity succumbs to the tide of the undead.

The same can be applied to Romero's *Dawn of the Dead*, which precluded *Day*. In this flick, the United States government, and other governments throughout the world, try to curb the threat of the undead by forcing citizens to hand over all dead bodies to be destroyed. Most ordinary citizens took matters into their own hands and dumped the bodies into the basements of apartment complexes, which only put everyone's life in danger. Police and National Guardsmen have gun battles against the citizens over the possession of the dead bodies. The problem occurs on such a large scale that the authorities are overwhelmed as the cities of our nation become haunts for the ghouls themselves. In other words, the subjects of the federal government and the federal government itself refused to get along, and as a result the human race started to lose.

Later on in *Dawn*, the same spirit of disunity is evident, as the motorcycle bandits rip through the shopping mall and fight for the possession of all the valuables within it against the occupants already there. Instead of joining forces to fight the ghouls, they spar with one another, wasting precious time and ammunition.

In *Night of the Living Dead*, the protagonists are trapped in a farmhouse in Western Pennsylvania. They squabble over who should be leading who. As a result, no one makes it out of the farmhouse alive. There was too much infighting, too much indecision, and no one can come up with an effective solution to deal with the crisis.

To sum it all up, the theme that runs through all of Romero's movies pertains to conflict. Everyone wants to take control. Everyone wants to do their own thing. There is no harmony and no cooperation. Authority breaks down and everyone just does what he or she wants. Egos and reckless pride stand in the way of any answer that would help deal with the situation. It is no wonder the ghouls overrun humanity and possess the earth.

Night of the Living Dead was released in 1968, *Dawn of the Dead* came along in 1978, and *Day of the Dead* followed in 1985. The movies spanned a period of seventeen years. It is unclear as to how much time had actually elapsed from the beginning of *Night* to the end of *Day,* and Romero leaves this to anyone's guess. However, I actually established a time frame for the crisis presented. *Ascension of the Dead* takes place in a period that lasts about two years. Society disintegrates in this little universe that I created, and does so quickly. Like the Romero trilogy, the cities are the areas with the biggest problems. A ghoul can easily infect a living person, since the two camps are in close proximity with one another. The whole process continues until the whole world is practically destroyed.

As the crisis grows in magnitude, order breaks down and conflict begins to brew. Southold, a suburban New York town, is infected by the contagion. Andrew Frank Goering awakes suddenly to find that he lives in a chaotic world where everything disintegrates and the benign universe he was familiar with vanishes. The laundromat is now a dangerous place, and the street that he normally drives upon is unsafe, as a place of refuge becomes hard to find.

Goering encounters some characters he does not get along with. One is Sasha Bernstein, a teenager who has a love for reckless violence, and the other is Robert Capasso, a police officer who seeks to put everyone under his heel. Goering hates both men, and this hatred festers within as he harbors the thought of killing Capasso, while society devolves into a state of primitive savagery.

The suburbs become too violent and uncertain. Goering, Capasso, and Bernstein flee to Upstate New York, where the primeval woods shroud the landscape. The forest symbolizes mankind's downward slide into havoc, and most seem to obey every momentary impulse, as lawlessness prevails. This decline is exemplified in Bruce DeVries, along with the Haley family. The humans seek to do nothing more than kill each other as they steal their neighbor's property and dignity. Capasso and Bernstein act as barbarians, giving in to primitive tendencies, although we never know quite to what extent until Goering and his group cross the Atlantic in a sailing vessel.

The story continues as Goering and company find themselves on the shores of Africa where they encounter both an Afrikaner nationalist and a dictator of German ancestry. The dictator tries to forge another society from the ashes of the one that has passed. The dictator borrows his methods of state-crafting from the defunct Third Reich. This leader, this *fuhrer*, is a man for all seasons, who seems to know how to survive and flourish. Although he is the protector of Western Civilization, he can't escape the prevailing lawlessness of the age and resorts to barbaric tendencies to keep order.

The protagonists begin to understand that the ghoulish plague has been planned and instigated by an ancient intelligent force that has wanted to decimate humanity for eons and now finally has the opportunity to do so. Circumstances spiral out of control as legions of the undead threaten and surround the dictator's utopia. The dictator himself looks around at the hopeless scenario and comes to the gripping realization that there appears to be no escape but death.

Romero's tradition in these movies implies that God is either not interested in the affairs of humanity or doesn't exist at all. The path I take follows another perspective. In my work, the Judeo-Christian God presents himself in a way that is painfully obvious. This process begins in a sort of hazy manner, wherein Goering is at first barely aware that there is a God at all. His character changes; he grows more aware of God's presence and comes to the understanding that the Deity is actually guiding and directing him. Finally, it is God who confronts and defeats the ancient evil force, and it is God who rescues humanity from their plight of hopelessness.

Ultimately, God, through the redemptive power of Jesus Christ, overcomes the inherent barbarism and hopelessness that plagues everyone on a daily basis. In a nutshell, this novel commemorates hope. If each individual person believes life will someday get better, then he or she can face and overcome the obstacles that are presented. The notion to create this work has been in my head for well over a decade, and it was just recently that I sat down to carry it through. It was an exhausting and grueling task that has taken months to complete, but it is finally finished. It has been worth all the blood, sweat, tears, and toil that I have put into it.

Regards,
Todd Sundell

Part I
Suburbia

Chapter One: Dream of the Gray Expanse

One cool October day, the destruction began. It is strange how you can wake up and go about your daily business, then come to the realization at some point that things have changed drastically. I got up, aroused from the escaping bliss of slumber, and it became apparent to me almost immediately that everything had been altered. The world of yesterday was not like today. Humanity has seen great epochs of human expansion and times where large numbers have died, alternating in concentric pulses. There was the catastrophic Black Death that annihilated the population of Europe, and there were the bloody wars of German aggression that destroyed many millions. Now I was in a new age of such darkness and spilled blood, a new age of death in which I was uncertain if I would make it to the next morning. For it was at this juncture in history that a plague came, supernatural in origin, that baffled our greatest minds, confounding the skeptics and the doubters, while our cities and towns became vast charnel houses for the men that refused to die.

Through the years, I have had strange dreams, but the one that I had on that fateful October evening was the most bizarre. I had just returned from a roofing job in Orange County, New York. After carrying one hundred pound bundles of shingles up a ladder for several hours that day, I was exhausted and in desperate need of sleep. I made the journey back home on the New York State Thruway and got off at exit 15 for Southold, the community where I resided. As I drove through the sleepy town, I remember that I passed a homeless derelict pushing around a shopping cart, wandering along the roadway in search of things that would enable him to survive. After driving for a few minutes, I returned to my Southold flat, which was on the second floor of a quaint old brown house that had been divided into three apartments.

After skillfully maneuvering my car and parking it under a gnarled maple in the front yard, I emerged exhausted, my legs feeling like lead. I walked across the dark green lawn in the cool afternoon air to the door that led up to my apartment. As I met that red door, I reached into my pocket and pulled out the keys, which jingled like chimes in the wind. The key opened the creaking door before me, and I stepped in, ascending the dissonant stairs to my abode.

Once in my apartment, I lay down on the sofa and turned on the dull television. I surfed through the channels briskly, and I caught some presentation from a young dark-haired woman who ranted about paganism on a raucous talk show. I quickly grew disinterested and continued to flip through the channels, finding an upstart railing about atheism and the inequitable distribution of wealth. The whole thing made me nod off because I was tired and television hadn't thrilled me for some time. In fact, I thought frequently about chucking the thing out the window.

I was exhausted. With two Masters' degrees and a flair for the conceptual, I found myself unsuited for doing physical work indefinitely, but I was young enough and strong enough to get by for now using my body like a machine. At age thirty-five, this work was beginning to get too hard, however, so there would be no way I could make a career out of it. Sleep overwhelmed me and I inevitably dove into its sweet happiness.

Sleep. I cannot easily find the words to describe what went on in my head as I fell into an unconscious state. The visions in my mind were entirely nondescript — almost as if my subconscious was trying to unravel a mystery I had been confronted with over the years. Certainly my mind was active, sensing a change that had occurred as I traversed the arid desert of mystery where sparse and undernourished vegetation grew.

Searching. My eyes fell upon something indistinguishable ahead of me, as I ran through this desert of the indecipherable riddle. There was a definite object up on the horizon of this dreamscape that kept its distance, as though it sought to prevent me from uncovering its identity. The dark unknown shape remained at that range in my subconscious, out of reach and persistently elusive. An event or conspiracy was afoot, and I looked up into the light blue sky above and a sun that sought to illuminate the circumstances before me. Through intuitive impressions, the sky and the sun reassured me that I would receive the answer and would one day be able to identify the mysterious figure in the distance.

Studying my surroundings, I looked down to determine the surface I tramped upon, and I could only see unclear matter made of an unidentified material. I knew not my own being, nor my destiny, nor the environment in which I stood. I paused, lost in perplexity as my head swam. Mercifully, the swimming stopped, and I again peered out across the empty gray, barren vista and could see nothing on the horizon. Whatever the dark shape was, I lost it as it disappeared over the forlorn expanse. I looked up at the warm sun as it continued to radiate promise. Who I was, and the purpose I was created for would no longer be a mystery. The identity of that black shape would one day be revealed, as would my inevitable destiny.

I understood that the cosmos had called me to a higher purpose, but the specifics of it did not belong to me at this point. For what seemed like eternity, I stood beneath the sun in the barren, unclear landscape, knowing that it was critical to uncover the identity of the object. There was nothing left for me to do but press on toward the figure as it crossed the sands of understanding. This was the first of many dreams wherein my mind walked backward in introspection, attempting to interpret the significance of the events the day before.

Chapter Two: The Rude Awakening

As I lay in bed in the middle of this panorama, something from the outside world intruded. BOM! BOM! BOM! It sounded. I was violently jolted out of bed! BOM! BOM! BOM! It rudely sounded again. Quickly, I threw on a pair of shorts and slippers to investigate the source of the disturbance!

My feet took me down the noisy staircase, which whined and creaked as they landed. I found myself before the front door that led to the outside world. Someone was at the door and wanted to be let in, but I could not see them through the windowless oak entrance. I waited for a passing eternity, the seconds ticking by incessantly. Sweating and my heart racing, a strange impulse prevented me from opening the door.

BOM! It pounded upon the door once again, demanding to be let in. A deafening and tense silence dominated the vestibule. In anticipation, I waited for another noise, dreading the whole event with nervous expectation. Sluggishly, laboriously, the figure on the other side of the portal turned the knob and rattled it. In response, I slowly backed away from the door, expecting the source to step in. However, the deadbolt was latched. The intruder outside could not walk into the house uninvited nor cause me harm. Often I would forget to lock the door before going to sleep. Thankfully, this time I did not; for all I knew that act protected my precious life.

Forever passed by as I sweated, sitting on one of the steps in my jogging shorts. My breathing grew heavy and I trembled nervously in the dark of the night, hoping for the visitor to go away and leave me alone. However, I also had to know the identity of the intruder that knocked at such an ungodly hour. I would not be able to sleep until I found out who the person was, but unfortunately I lacked the courage to investigate, caught between the push of insatiable desire and the pull of the fear of the unknown. I grew afraid, deathly afraid, realizing how abnormal this whole event was.

Devising a strategy to gain the necessary nerve, I thought it might be a good idea to count to one hundred and open the entrance once the count had ended. I enumerated, slowly and deliberately, as my life hung in the balance, making sure the countdown did not get dragged out longer than necessary. After what seemed like hours, I finished and knew it was time to go out, to step into the cold uncertainty beyond.

The door opened then cool gray air rushed in and struck me in the face, my consciousness lapsing for no more than a second. The sun was coming up over the Ramapo Mountains in the west. West? The sun never comes up in the west! It comes up in the east! Could it be that I had slept through the entire night and most of the day? Was I that tired from putting on those hot, steaming shingles?

I stepped onto the front porch, into the twilight of the evening, and peered down the dark street before my house. I heard no noise except for a dog barking somewhere in the distance beneath the streetlights of this suburban New York town. There was no sign of the caller who had tried to enter my apartment earlier; only silence and shadows of the unknown remained. To the left there were lights flashing and reflecting off the street, beyond the opaque buildings that occluded my view. An urge came over me to investigate the matter further.

I bounded back up the staircase, two at a time, to my apartment. I ran into my bedroom, slightly out of breath and noticed the clock. It read: 9:00 pm. It became obvious that I had slept for nearly twenty-four hours. I came to the realization that it was Saturday evening.

This area was usually filled with men, mostly Mexican, congregating upon the street corners, sitting on curbs, conversing in Spanish, and smoking a variety of cigarettes. The street was unusually vacant, too quiet, and I wondered why. Something was out of place and I had to find out what it was. I put on a shirt, grabbed my baseball bat for protection, and ran back down the whining stairs to investigate the source of the flashing light.

I headed left from the gravel driveway toward the rundown laundromat several buildings away. There the establishment sat in the distance, lit up in all of its persistence to survive. I saw a police squad car parked in front of it, its flashers rapidly turning in the night, casting out spurts of bright color. From the distant scene, I detected strange animal-like sounds drifting through the air, almost as if there was a pack of coyotes down the street surrounding the carcass of a dead deer. Curiosity burned in my breast, and I headed in that direction, seeking to understand.

I proceeded cautiously toward the laundromat, stepping into the solemn, cold air, my right hand tightly gripping the baseball bat. As I neared the squad car sitting in the parking lot, I detected a great deal of activity. There six figures had gathered, crouching around something that was vague and unclear.

As I got closer, I realized it was a body lying in the lot, and it was wearing dark clothing. The figures squatted around it, full of activity and vibrancy, preoccupied with the corpse on the pavement. I walked closer, in disbelief and shock, unable to understand all that my senses absorbed. I stood over the six crouching figures with their heads engaged upon the body as it lay upon its back on the cold, black asphalt.

Judging by their faces, which had a dark Mestizo look to them, they all seemed to be Mexican immigrants. Their race was not the important thing; it was the activity in which they were involved that disturbed me to no end. *They crouched around the carcass and actually ate bits and pieces of the corpse, dining upon it in a bestial manner!* They growled and made barbaric noises as they consumed the macabre feast. Before my eyes I beheld what must have been a case of 21st century cannibalism! This could not be! Not in the United States of America!

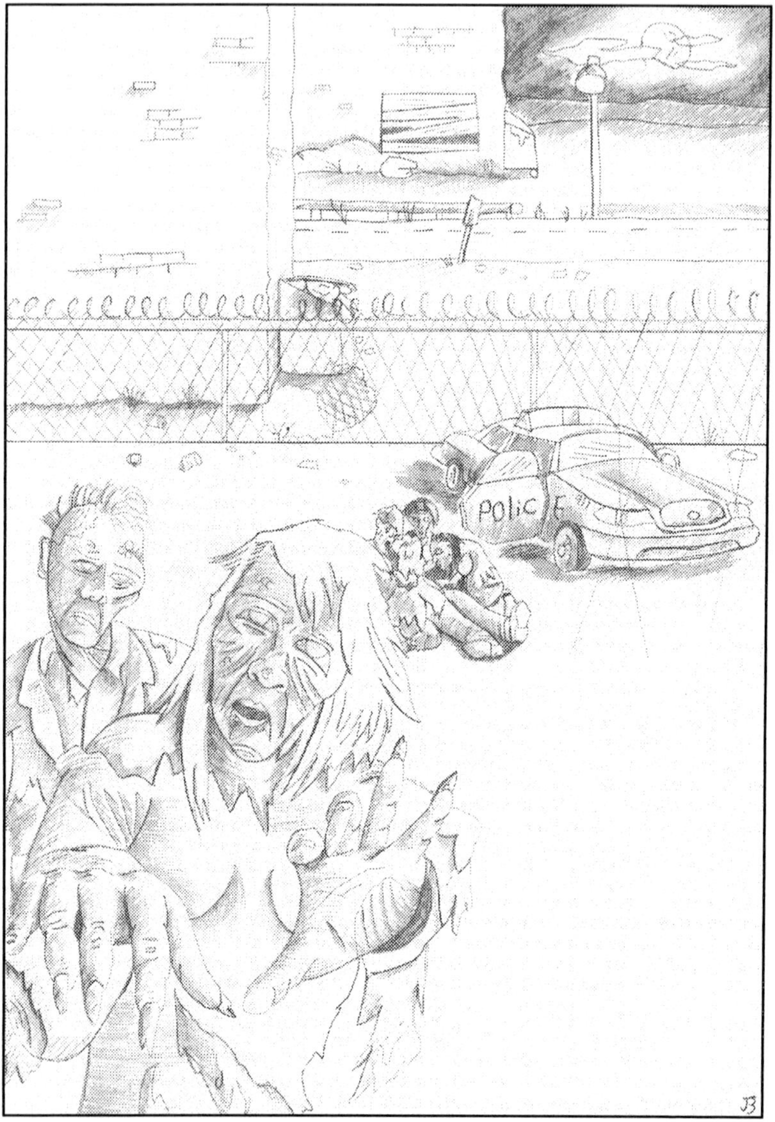

One of the women stopped her grisly feeding and slowly lifted her bloodied head to look at me. At first, there was no expression on the woman's face, but then her eyes caught mine. She let out a horrible animalistic hiss, and the expression became one of vicious savagery. All of the people crouching about the body turned their eyes to me as they hissed with that same bestiality. I came to the realization that the corpse on the ground belonged to the cop originally driving the squad car. I backed away from the terrible circle in horrific revulsion!

The people, or things, because I could not call them people anymore, laboriously got to their feet and struggled to move in to capture me. Their arms hung to their sides, occasionally stretching outward as they growled in an unclear manner! I continued to back up, not even sure if what I was seeing was real! They hobbled towards me, limping as if wounded, groaning so horribly, as the glow from the overhead streetlight revealed a discolored quality to their skin. There was something seriously wrong with them.

One of the females, with arms extended, emitted a savage ululation, and advanced toward me.

"What's the matter with you, lady? Get away from me! Get away from me!" I yelled at her, poised to swing the bat. She did not respond, pursuing me while sounding like an animal incapable of human speech. Frightened, I swung the bat furiously and caught the woman on the side of the head. She jerked back from the impact, righted herself, and proceeded towards me while the others followed.

Again, I observed the cop lying on the ground, his chest savagely ripped open. His body began to stir as he moved his head from side to side. Could he still be alive? The cop sat up quickly and turned his head toward me, letting out a horrible cry that was not exactly human! Cold, clammy hands reached out and clawed at my clothing, grasping my arms, seeking to immobilize me forever. Their mouths opened wide to eagerly consume my flesh. I pulled back and broke from the group, terrified, and ran into the darkness that I hoped would protect and obscure my flight back to my apartment!

Chapter Three: The People in the Street

I bounded up the steps to the porch and stood before the windowless door with that same set of jingling keys. I thrust the instrument nervously and quickly into the keyhole and turned the dead bolt back. I ascended the whining stairs, not worried if I disturbed my sleeping neighbors or not. Quickly, I ran into my room, sat upon my unmade bed, and pulled my slippers off while I slid into a pair of jeans. After putting on a pair of tennis shoes, I threw on a light denim jacket and ran down the stairs and locked the door as I left.

For a second, I stood on my porch and stared into the dark sky over the Ramapo Mountains before me. I looked down to my right, in the direction opposite to the laundromat, and saw movement. Three dark silhouetted objects walked with a stiff, clumsy gait, accompanied by inhuman growls as they made their way down the sidewalk toward me. My heart fluttered as I inhaled irregularly in a racing panic! From the opposite direction, I heard those same creatures from the laundromat getting louder, heading toward me!

Immediately, I ran to my car, which was parked conveniently under the gnarled and twisted maple. I unlocked the door. Once inside, I thrust one of the chiming keys into the ignition, and the engine sputtered to life! I noticed that the three approaching things were now on the front lawn; two were heading to the door and one towards the car. To my right, I saw the murderous group of Mexican cannibals approaching, oscillating ever nearer on the sidewalk and on the street. They were coming for me, and I could have sworn there was a taller figure in the middle of them that looked very much like the cop that had just fallen!

Without hesitation, I backed the car out of the driveway, turned it around and took off before they had reached me. At the next light, I made a right hand turn. It was my desire to find my nearest friend, Roger Scarpaci, who lived on the other side of Southold. I had to get there, and perhaps his company would make me feel safe from all of this madness.

I had met Roger several months before, outside of a grocery store. I found him very accepting and supportive, and I was quite comfortable in his presence. He would invite me over for dinner, and we'd spend the evening shooting the bull into the dark of the night. I felt that I would find a safe haven in his house.

As I raced down the main street of the town, sweat beaded on my forehead and trickled down my face. I drove the car through a series of lights, noticing that the streets were essentially desolate as I passed by the array of dark houses and silent shops. Up ahead was the crest of a hill, and somewhere beyond that would be Roger Scarpaci's secure apartment.

I went up the grade and passed over the crest. In my headlights, I saw several people on both sides of the road, perhaps seven or eight in total. There was something wrong with their gait, as they shuffled beneath the overhanging branches, but I did not have time to dwell on it. Driving on a little further, I spied the hospital looming to the right, with several windows still lit. As I approached the infirmary, a few obstacles rudely thrust themselves in the road before me. They were people moving about stiffly in blue gowns and green hospital scrubs, as if hypnotized or in some sort of trance. I slowed the car down long enough to get a look at them.

In my headlights, I could see them clearly, dressed in tattered garments and with bleeding wounds. Like the Mexicans at the laundromat, they moved slowly, tottering forward with extreme difficulty. As the car slowed, they all took note of me and lurched towards the automobile with arms outstretched, emitting strange growls. With contorted countenances, they raised menacing gestures with their hands, making them look as if they wanted to tear me apart. I felt like plowing through them, but I did not want to be charged with manslaughter. I swerved sharply to the left and lost control of the vehicle, colliding head on with a short stonewall in front of some woods.

I was not sure what happened, but I found myself sitting in the seat behind the steering wheel. The front windshield was cracked, indicating that something had hit the glass. I touched my forehead and felt warm liquid collecting in a growing bead. I looked down at my fingertips and realized it was blood. Groggy and stunned, I stepped out of the car and got to my feet with wobbly knees. I began to think I might need medical attention.

With bat in hand, I looked at the damage to my car. The front end had crumpled inward like an accordion. Clearly, I had totaled it and my means of transportation and freedom was now gone! This was the least of my problems as the moaning figures approached the car in a menacing way!

Their faces were twisted and they growled like animals closing in on their prey. Their unrestrained expressions horrified me and I found myself surrounded. I got a better look at them under the eerie glow of the overhead streetlights. Their skin had turned a pale gray, and some of them had chunks of flesh taken out of their arms, legs or abdomens! I wondered how these creatures could be alive.

They closed in with savage growls and furious expressions; their claws raked the air as they slowly limped toward me. They reached out to seize my arms and legs so I could not get away. As their fingers tightly encircled my arms, I found their hands cold to the touch and absent of bodily warmth. Thankfully, using all of my strength, I managed to break away from their grip! If I were a weaker person, I certainly would have been one of their victims! I swung the bat and hit one of the females in the torso! She stumbled and regained her footing, still trying to reach toward me!

I swung my bat again, and this time I struck her in the head, which flopped lifelessly to one side. I struck the woman yet again on the opposite side of the cranium, hoping to halt the attack. A blank look came over her face and her eyes swam for a second, losing their luster. She collapsed on her knees and fell forward on the ground! She did not move! I came to the stunning conclusion that I had taken the life of a human being! "Oh dear God, what am I gonna do?" I said to myself, realizing I was now a murderer!

The things continued to close in on me undaunted, despite the fact I had taken one of their own. I pulled away again and turned around, finding myself standing in front of the wall. Although I was groggy from the accident, I had the composure to lift my leg onto the barrier and pull myself over it. I landed on the other side and took off through the trees, leaving the growling things behind me.

I stumbled in the dark, my head hitting tree limbs which kept me from proceeding in the dead of night. I stopped to listen. At first I heard nothing, but then I paused again. I heard my pursuers groaning and growling, pushing away the snaking limbs and blundering through the underbrush. Somehow, they got around the fence so that they could continue the chase. I desperately held my pace, able to see a little, now that my eyes had adjusted to the darkness. Before me was a wooded decline, and beyond it, through the trees, I could see a road that traveled perpendicular to me. I ran through the branches toward it, hoping to escape the terror in the trees behind me.

Reaching the road, I found myself isolated near an abandoned factory. Across the street were a few two-story houses, partially hidden behind a number of evergreens and showing no sign of life. I ran down the driveway to one of the houses. It was dark and appeared empty, nothing moving within it. Behind me I heard the creatures growl in cold and slow pursuit, stumbling clumsily out of the woods. Panicking, I ran up the stairs to the porch of the dwelling and pounded frantically upon the door in an attempt to escape this ongoing nightmare.

"Hello! Is anybody there? Hello!" I yelled as I ferociously banged on the door. No one stirred from within and the door would not open from the outside. The occupants were either asleep or away on vacation, avoiding these horrid circumstances.

Due to the loss of blood, I was not thinking clearly, I left the house and ran into the next yard, making my way back to the street. My strange enemies persistently continued on with the chase, lurching into the road. I lost my footing as I ran over the tarmac, landing upon my knees! I struggled to my feet, realizing that my shins were most likely bruised and cut up. This was one hell of a night! If something did not happen fast, I would soon be dead! I stood in the road, confused, not understanding nor accepting everything that was going on around me.

Suddenly, a car turned down the street. The automobile drove toward me, while I hurried to it with bruised up legs, along with a head that swam. The vehicle came to a halt alongside of me as the brakes squealed. The monstrous humans behind continued to ululate and groan as they eagerly sought their prey, wanting nothing more than to destroy, and erase me from the dark world that I had fallen into!

I ran around to the driver's side, and the person within opened the door quickly with a loud creak of hinges that desperately needed oil.

"Get into de car fast, man!" The driver said. "Once dey catch you, dey will rip de skin from your bones!" I recognized the distinctly Jamaican accent of a woman. I climbed in as the things stumbled up against the hood, snarling and creeping towards the windows, seeking to immobilize the car.

Quickly, she backed away from the murderous mob, leaving them in the glow of the overhead streetlamps. She swung the car around so that it was back on the main road.

"I was drivin' home from de Tru-way, den sometin' made me wan' stop and I saw you runnin'."

"Thanks, I can't tell you how much I appreciate that. God knows what would have happened if they had caught up to me. My name's Andy Goering," I said, extending a handshake.

"My neeme Marcia," she said smiling. "Marcia Clarke, glad to meet you, man."

"Do you live around here?" I asked.

"Yeah. I do, not too far from here," she said.

"What're you doing out driving around in this chaos?" I asked.

"My modder in Brooklyn, and I wanted to visit her, but I can't."

"Well, why not?" I asked, rather surprised.

"Because dey shut down all de roads. You can't leave on de Paliseedes or de Tru-way. Dey shut dem to all traffic. Everyone stuck in deir homes for now," she said.

"What?" I asked, not understanding the whole situation.

"Dis been goin' on de whole dey. Where you been for de past twenty four hours?"

I was in complete disbelief.

Chapter Four: The Unacceptable Broadcast

"I don't tink dey human!" she said. My chest tightened and my claustrophobic spirit squirmed when I heard that. We went along one of the main county routes that pierced most of the large towns in the suburban counties just outside of New York City. For the first time since I awoke from my dream-haunted slumber, I felt safe and secure.

"Marcia, what the heck is goin' on?"

"I try to answer your questions as soon as possible," she said.

For a minute I studied this young and somewhat heavyset Jamaican woman, who had a braided weave and wore a brown dress. She was a sanguine person, with a tendency to laugh a lot, but she also seemed strangely insecure. Marcia drove me to a row of condos in the eastern end of Southold. She lived there with her mom, but her mom was trapped in Brooklyn with Marcia's two other siblings due to the ongoing crisis. Something had clearly happened as I slept, dreaming about that gray wasteland in the corners of my mind.

Marcia parked the car in the street, then we got out. She pulled out her jingling keys as she walked to her door and unlocked the condo. The portal opened up into the dark shadowy interior, but she flicked on the light switch, dispelling the soupy blackness. We stepped into a living room. There was a television set within a black laminated cabinet against the wall directly ahead of me. To the left of the TV were a large golden sofa, a cream-colored recliner, and a wooden bookshelf with little knick-knacks on it that sat against another wall. A coffee table was placed in front of the sofa. Above the recliner, was a tranquil painting of a Jamaican family reposing on the stoop of a stilted house. Somehow, that picture gave me the sensation that perhaps one day things would stabilize and work out in my life. I wanted to establish myself on firm ground.

"Have a seat, please," she said as she presented the sofa with her hand. I sat down and touched my forehead. She noticed the blood then.

"Oh, you've been hurt. Let me help you," she said in a concerned tone.

Marcia went into the kitchen, which was to the right of the laminated cabinet, emerging with a damp washcloth in her hand. The young woman placed it on the wound and dabbed it, removing the dried and clotted blood. The injury had drained my strength and I needed to recover.

She went through an opening at the rear of the living room then I heard her ascend the stairs. I detected some footfalls on the floor above me, which I assumed belonged to Marcia, but as she moved I thought I heard her speaking to someone. However, the voice, or voices, upstairs were so faint that it was difficult to determine anything. A few minutes later, she descended the stairs with a bottle of alcohol and some cotton swabs, along with some bandages, eager to serve and heal.

"Andy, please relax, man. Dis only teeke a minute," she said.

The alcohol stung a little, reminding me of a burning match to the skin, but it quickly disinfected the wound, and that was good. Marcia applied the bandages to my forehead. I should be as good as new within a few days, able to run again and go on with my life.

Marcia left the living room, and I heard her ascend the stairs again. Upstairs, she spoke in barely audible whispers, as if she conversed with someone in one of the bedrooms. I detected her footsteps once more as she descended the stairs, but I suspected I heard someone walking with her. She entered from the dining room and walked into the living room, smiling and her long braids swaying with each step. A somewhat short and lean man with dark hair and a beard followed her. I recognized the figure at once, both familiar and a relief to find here. It was Roger Scarpaci!

He walked toward me as I got up from my seat on the golden couch.

"Rog!" I said with a smile. "It is so good to see you!" We embraced. In a time of confusion like this, it was good to see a friendly face.

"You know this lady?" I asked, in the fog of surprise.

"Yeah, she goes to my church. I've known her for quite a while!" Roger answered.

Unlike myself, who was a lapsed Episcopalian, Roger was an Evangelical Protestant, and had a "born-again" experience some years before. He explained the "gospel message" to me several times, but I rejected it, since it required me to give control of my life to Jesus Christ. I had grown accustomed to being my own agent, and I was not eager to abandon my ideals. It was apparent that Marcia had known Roger for some time.

"What're you doin' here, Rog, of all places?" I asked.

"I was on my way to a prayer meeting when this whole thing unfolded," he answered. He could not go back to his home nearby, due to police roadblocks. He was cut off from both family and many friends at church, so he decided to stop at Marcia's for rest.

"Marcia, Roger?" I asked solemnly. "What the heck is going on?"

"That's what we are tryin' to understand," Roger said in his usual serious tone. "Maybe the TV will give us some answers."

Marcia took the remote control off the coffee table then gingerly woke the device up from its slumber. Nervously, I reposed on the couch, hanging by some sort of thread, trying to keep myself from falling into the abyss of despair. The picture of a test pattern materialized, and I found that my eyes were glued to the screen for many minutes, in both frustration and in fright. Roger stood silently on the living room floor, while Marcia sat uncomfortably in the recliner.

Finally a broadcast aired. An unfamiliar, somber man with glasses, suit, and tie appeared on the screen. He was not one of the evening news regulars. This was indication that the normal pattern of things had ceased. Seated before a blue background, he looked down at his script and read with a monotonous voice: "We urge everyone to stay in their homes until this crisis has passed." A shiver shot down my spine at this. Whatever it was, it was bigger than this town that I lived in.

"Once again," the broadcaster continued, "there have been reports that thousands of people are being attacked by unidentified assailants all around the United States. The government is uncertain as to why, but believes that it may be the work of terrorists. We beseech everyone to please remain in their homes. Cities and towns throughout the country have reported an unusual wave of attacks. Please stay calm until the crisis is over. We will update you as the situation unfolds." The broadcast concluded as the square test pattern appeared once again on the screen.

Chapter Five: Night of the Long Knives

"A wave of attacks?" I said, practically screaming from the sofa. Marcia gazed at me with a sorrowful look in her eyes, almost in confirmation. Could hundreds of thousands of people in this country have died in one day? This rash of violence must be occurring all over the United States. For all I knew, it may be all over the world. How was I supposed to remain calm while my mother and sister Upstate were in danger? I had to get out of this God-forsaken county and find them.

Chances are, the world was changing for the worse and the situation would deteriorate before it got better. Since I am a history buff, always comparing and contrasting, I began to think back to a similar context in the past. I remembered an event that occurred about seventy years ago in a country thousands of miles away. After he had become the chancellor of Germany, Hitler began to clear up resistance in his own party. Germans were then dragged from their beds and apprehended on street corners, and eventually murdered. The Nazi Party worked to alter the future of the planet.

At this present time, people were also being dragged from their beds, apprehended on street corners, and probably murdered, but at an unprecedented rate. These assailants were the same ones that attacked me earlier, I believed. I knew intuitively that, just like in the 1930s, the events of today would radically affect the course of the world tomorrow. There would be casualties, but how many remained to be seen.

"What wrong, Andy?" Marcia asked, sitting on the sofa with an anxious expression while staring at me. I refused to answer her question, as my eyes glared at the wall to her right. She looked downward nervously, a usually jovial woman, who was now scared and threatened. Roger let out a heavy sigh. None of us knew what to do. The test pattern on the television ceased then the somber man appeared again. He peered down at his script, wincing, as if he was uncomfortable with the information that he was about to relay.

He faltered for what seemed to be a difficult eternity, then uttered something unintelligible, hesitated, and then spoke again. He could not get the words out. They just hung on his stammering lips, refusing to let go. He found the clarity and the courage to read the terminology, and they shot forth, shattering the tension like a stone through a glass window.

"They have found that all unburied corpses are rising from the dead and they're attacking living people." This can't be. This is inconceivable! *He just told everyone that the dead were coming back to life, and they were attacking the living!*

I wondered at what I heard. Marcia sat there on her recliner with her braided weave disheveled, looking exasperated and in disbelief. She sobbed, covering her face with her hands, and said, "No. No. No. No." Immediately, I found myself denying that this information could be true, and I thought I must have been watching some science fiction flick. However, I was wrong. This was an actual broadcast, telling the world about a crisis whose origins were rooted in fantasy. Roger did nothing but stare blankly at the empty wall before him.

"Just this morning," the somber man, whose name was Michael Burnside, said, "a cadaver in a Washington university returned to life. Eventually, they had to find a way to destroy it. They found that placing a hard blow to the head stopped it permanently. They concluded that a ghoul, a resuscitated corpse, can be rendered inactive by hitting its head with a heavy object or by firing a bullet into the brain. Once again, please stay indoors until this crisis has passed." Burnside's broadcast concluded.

This was horrible! The dead could not be coming back to life. Could they? Mankind had withstood all sorts of disasters, including world wars, rampant contagions, and the Cuban Missile Crisis, only to be subjected to a wave of unexplained and unacceptable phenomena. Could this be stopped? My head spun in circles as my mind raced to the corners of my skull, trying to find an answer. These were the things that had attacked me earlier. I was relieved to find out that I really didn't take the life of a human being; I took the life of some netherthing that wasn't exactly human.

Dusk had now clearly fallen. Marcia went upstairs to pray with Roger and then went off to bed. Roger came down to the kitchen and got something to eat. As he passed by, I noticed that his face was blank and expressionless.

"Roger, what are we gonna do about this?" I asked.

He stood there in the kitchen doorway, leaning against the threshold eating a slice of cold pizza. "I dunno," he said with his mouth full. "I just don't know." His eyes were upon the floor before him. "Wish I could tell you." He walked through the living room into the dining room, without looking at me. I heard him ascend the stairs, as he avoided furthering our discouraging conversation. He went off to sleep in the other room that was on the second floor.

It was my turn to get some shuteye, so I slipped into slumber once again. I dreamed that I found myself walking along that vague gray expanse, where a few tufts of grass shot up through the nondescript soil. On the horizon, that elusive shape continued to move ahead into the distance. Hopefully, a day will come when I would unravel this cosmic mystery that had befallen the entire earth. The sun shined bright and hopeful. My slumber steadily concluded, and I awoke.

Chapter Six: A Little Radioactivity Would be Nice

Morning came and I heard the birds chirp joyfully. It seemed like a typical, cool October morning, as if nothing had changed, but everything had changed and I knew it. I wanted to return to the world of yesterday absent of this pervasively destructive threat. Now peril lurked in every corner, and there was not even the promise that I would make it to see the sun go down. The world was laced with so much uncertainty.

The three of us wandered the townhouse during the course of the day, cleaning nooks and crannies and pacing off all the nervous energy we had stored up. Marcia managed to place a call to her mother and her siblings in Flatbush.

"How's your family?" I asked her.

"Dey okey. My sister doin' alright and so is my brodder, but everyone a little unnerved."

"Where's your dad?" Roger asked.

"He in London at de moment. I guess he doin' okey too." I found out that her father was recuperating from his separation from Marcia's mom. It is strange how difficult male and female relationships can be. For a second, I wondered how my own mom and sister were doing up in Rome. I hoped that they had kept safe from harm. Maybe I should impose upon Marcia and see if I could use her phone to find out.

I wondered also if Rome was inundated with those dead "ghouls" that were attacking fragile humanity. It looked as if they were everywhere in the country. I knew that they were in New York City, Detroit, Pittsburgh, and with this in mind, fear shot through my heart, like a burning spear from the dark rainforests of Africa. Was it all over the world?

A subconscious buzzing filled the back of my skull, indicating something was wrong. Another broadcast interrupted the square test pattern. Marcia and I stood before the set in eager anticipation. Burnside appeared once again.

"We want to remind you that taking a heavy object to the head will kill a ghoul. We also would like to inform you that government agencies have detected a rising radiation level throughout the entire domestic atmosphere. There has been speculation that this radiation was carried to earth by a space probe that landed upon the planet Venus several months ago. Some authorities believe that the National Aeronautics and Space Administration may have something to do with it. Let us turn to an interview with NASA scientist Dr. Robert Cummings, earlier today."

The somber man finished his script as the cameras switched to a clean-shaven man in a dark suit and tie briskly walking along a street that passed the front of the Capitol Building, chased by reporters.

"Dr. Cummings, is it true that you are partially responsible for ordering the destruction of the probe before it could reach the earth?" a determined woman reporter in a dark blue dress asked.

"I decline to make any comments until an investigation is launched," Dr. Cummings said.

"Once again, are you working with the military, Dr. Cummings? Did you order the destruction of the probe?" she asked.

The man in the dark suit stopped and looked at her. "ONCE AGAIN, I REFUSE TO MAKE ANY COMMENTS UNTIL AN INVESTIGATION IS LAUNCHED!" he said angrily. He resumed his hurried walk in front of the Capitol Building. The segment ended, and once again we were all staring at the TV which aired a phrase stating: "Please stay tuned for more instructions." I guessed that the newscasts would be more frequent now.

A little worried about the crisis, I wondered if I could call my mom to see if she was okay. As Marcia moved around in the kitchen preparing food, I thought it might be a good time to ask if I could use her phone.

"Marcia, could I call my mom?" I asked politely.

"Yes. Go ahid, Andy. It important, I know," she said.

I dialed once, got a busy signal and dialed again. I got another busy signal. Was everybody and their grandmother trying to use the phone? Finally, I got through to my mom. Her sweet voice echoed through my mind, placating the anxiety in my soul.

"Mom, how're you doing?" I asked.

"Oh Andy, it is so good to hear your voice again. Are you okay?"

"Yeah, I'm okay, but I can't get outta here. I just wanted to know if you and my sister are doin' alright."

"Everyone is fine. Your sister and her kids are okay. Your brother-in-law is staying home from work to make sure everyone is safe," she informed me.

My mom, however, spoke very little about the worsening crisis. She told me that the next-door neighbors were all intact, but nobody was going outside and no one knew where the attackers would strike again. The conversation concluded without incident.

The three of us remained in the condo for the entire day, sitting at the dining room table, playing bridge along with some board games. It made me feel stifled, claustrophobic, as this townhouse became my prison, with walls that seemingly contracted. After playing a losing game of chess, Marcia got up from the kitchen table and went to the refrigerator.

"You guys wan' spaghetti? I cooked it several naights agoo. We better eat it up, because it spoil soon," she said.

"Marcia, that would be great if you could. I'm famished," Roger responded. The two of us hadn't eaten all day, and our empty stomachs growled in anticipation.

Marcia took the food out of the fridge and warmed it up on the stove, the smell of oregano filling the downstairs of the condo. She put the meal before us on plates, then Roger and I eagerly devoured it. I wondered what we were going to do when we started running out of food. Hopefully, by that time, the crisis would have abated.

Around 6:30 that evening, a loud knock sounded at the door which felt like a bullet going into my brain, shattering the false sense of security we had in the condo. Marcia got up from the table to look through the little peephole to identify the stranger. She opened the door to let in a police officer clad in a navy-blue uniform. A big man, a little over six feet tall, stood in the doorway. He was poised in an arrogant fashion, with a .45 sitting firmly in his holster, and he was obviously prepared to use it. He was a stocky man in his late thirties with a crew cut, and I sensed that he liked being in control of situations.

"Come in," Marcia said, appearing a little uncertain about the nature of the visit.

"My name is Officer Robert Capasso. I've been serving the Southold Police Department for about six years now," he said. The rest of us introduced ourselves, shaking his large, burly hand.

"Where were you before?" Roger asked, standing in the middle of the living room.

"I'm originally from Brooklyn, and I was in the NYPD for about nine years," he answered.

"How can we help you?" Roger asked.

"I'm recruitin' people to take out these ghouls. D'ya wanna be a part of it? If you have guns, you can pahticipate," Capasso said.

"We don't have guns, but my parents do. They live about a mile away, and I think they have a pistol and rifle," Roger said to Capasso.

"Technically, you're not supposed to leave the house," he said in an authoritative tone. "Just don't let anyone catch you. We're meeting tomorrow at the Southold Fire Depahtment at 9:00 am. Be there." He turned around, walked out through the front door, and disappeared into the early evening air rounding up as many armed citizens as possible.

Roger and I sat down with Marcia in the living room.

"Y'know, if we could get your parents' guns, we could be part of this thing," I said.

"It might give us something to do," Roger replied. We were bored, and destroying a few ghouls sounded like an inviting thing to do, giving us excuse to leave the claustrophobic confines of Marcia's condominium and to escape the monotony. I remembered that many of the recruits for World War I and II were lured by promise of adventure that would be waiting for them. We had the same desire and were no different than they. We had to go to get the guns from his parents' apartment. We would need them to defend ourselves in case things got out of control.

Chapter Seven: Journey into the Night

Roger tried to call his parents up, but there was no response. The phone kept on ringing and ringing into infinity. It seemed as if they were not there. "Maybe we should drive over," I wondered. I passed the idea by Roger.

"Look, if we get caught, we're gonna be in a lot of trouble. They could fine us," Roger said.

"So, then we'll have to walk over," I suggested. "How far away is it?"

"I'm guessing it will take about twenty minutes, since they are about a mile away."

We agreed to do it and take the bat as an effective weapon. Roger would do the same with a rolling pin that Marcia kept in her kitchen drawers.

"Marcia, we're going to leave to get Roger's guns."

"Guys, don' leave me here. I don' have anyone to protect me. Dose tings could get in here!" she said, distraught. It was obvious that she did not want to be alone.

Both Roger and Marcia sat on the couch and took her by the hand.

"Dear Lord, please watch over Marcia and make sure that she gets through the night safely, without any harm," he said. Hopefully that would allay her fears, and the two of them hugged each other.

We opened up the front door and went into the thick, dark swill of the night. I looked back and noticed Marcia standing in the doorway and staring after us; she went back inside and closed the door firmly behind her, shutting out all danger that may be moving through the evening.

The moon hung in the night sky as Roger and I tried to make sense of our surroundings.

"We want to go to the back of the row houses," Roger said, pointing to our left as we faced Marcia's condominium.

Cars were parked in their designated spaces on the street. Marcia's townhouse was part of a group of row houses, and Roger knew that the direction behind the townhouses would lead to his parents' home. We found the end of the row.

"This looks like the place," Roger said as we took a right into a backyard. Behind the row houses was a line of conifers that sat in what must have been the rear of someone else's backyard. We stepped through the cold autumn air, over the green grass of the lawn, and passed through the thick line of firs. The branches scraped and scratched us as we went by. We pushed aside the boughs, making the way to the clearing ahead.

We emerged in a fairly spacious backyard leading up to a dark, ranch-style house. There was a single light on in one of the windows, but I was not sure if anyone was there. Both of us headed to the left of the quiet, unresponsive dwelling that seemed not to acknowledge our existence, and we entered the silent street beyond the yard.

The street was dark as well, and few lights were on in the houses. Another ranch-style house sat across the road from us, and we approached it. The backyard was enclosed in a chain-link divider.

We stepped onto the lawn, getting closer to the fence before us. I saw a flash of white fangs as a large Rottweiler barked at us from the other side of the chain-link barrier, threatening to attack and push through the fence if we got too near.

"Let's try another house," Roger suggested.

"Guess we'd better," I replied, gripping the bat.

We walked down the street before the rows of monotonous suburban homes. We had to find a yard that we could walk through, not wanting to remain on the street where we could easily be detected by the authorities. However, I wagered that the local constabularies had their hands full with all of the problems the bizarre circumstances had brought to this town.

There was a split-level home on the right, surrounded by evergreens. We thought cutting through the yard might take us to the areas beyond. Looking at the split-level that was cooperatively silent, we entered the yard, noticing that there was a wood full of trees in the distant back. After ambling by the house, we walked into the wood, which was populated by both firs and deciduous trees. The deciduous trees were falling asleep, losing their foliage, dying as the days wore on.

"If we continue, we should find a road that leads to my parents," Roger said. We went up the hilly area toward where their condominium was located. It would probably take another ten minutes to get there from this point.

We entered the forest, pushing the branches out of the way under the cold moonlight that cast hopelessness and despair to the earth like rain from the sky. Our breath hung heavy in the frigid air as the lifelessness of winter approached. Without warning, we heard the sound of a woman's scream come from the house behind us, shattering the temporary despondency.

We looked back in the night, not able to see what was happening, trying to determine if we actually did hear a woman cry for help. It was tempting to continue on our way, but I found that my conscience would not easily allow that. Both Roger and I had to stop and turn around.

Roger kept insisting, "Jesus would want us to help her."

"I don't care! We're putting our lives in jeopardy. Let's go on and let her fend for herself," I said, worried about my own safety.

"Andy, I don't believe you can be that cold. Jesus would want us to help the girl, and that is exactly what we have to do," he insisted.

I looked into my heart and came to the clear realization that there was another person in need nearby. I really did have to lend my assistance in some sort of fashion.

"Okay, let's walk over," I said. We decided to go back towards the house.

The cries split apart the night and wore on my mind as we made our way through the branches. We emerged from the wood and saw what was happening. On the wooden deck in the back of the structure, there was a young woman dressed in dark clothing struggling with a larger figure that leaned over her. It growled and grabbed at her clothes like an uncivilized primate. I did not like that! I shot like lightning towards the wooden patio with my bat ready to go to war. Roger followed me with his savage rolling pin.

The woman on the deck struggled against her attacker, flailing her hands at the assailant, hitting his arms and torso, trying to defend herself. She rolled around and screamed on the floor of the deck, doing anything she could to escape. I stepped up on to the platform and the monster heard me. He paused and extended his hand in my direction, seeking my flesh like an animal while still awkwardly bent over the woman. It was one of those dead things and I knew it.

"YOU GET AWAY FROM HER!" I shouted, saliva shooting from my lips.

I took the bat in hand and swung it with all of my might, striking the thing in the head. It fell to the floor of the deck, but it struggled to its feet! I hit it in the skull with the bat for the second time, and the creature stopped entirely, falling like an oak to the ground. The ghoul was obviously deceased.

Roger helped the young woman to her feet. "Are you okay?" he asked.

"No," she said. "It came into my house and bit me on the arms several times."

"Does it hurt?" I asked.

"Yeah," she answered matter-of-factly.

"What's your name?" I asked.

"Sue Greenberg."

"My name is Andy Goering. This is Roger Scarpaci," I said, pointing to him. She did not bother to shake, and I noticed that there was quite a bit of blood on her hands. She was badly injured.

"What are you doin' here?" I asked.

"My parents live here."

"Where are they now?"

"I dunno. I hadn't heard from them for many hours. I don't know if they're coming back," she said distraughtly.

"My arms are going numb," she added. The sensation she experienced came from the wounds themselves. We would eventually have to bring her to a hospital, but I suspected that the doctors were not accessible and that the staff had their own problems to deal with. Maybe once we got the guns from Roger's parents, we could take Sue back to the apartment and have Marcia dress her wounds. She fixed mine well, and she could probably do the same for this woman.

The three of us made it through the silent and dark trees, nearing a road up ahead. After stepping through hostile briars that violently snagged our clothing, seeking to stop us, we got to the lane. That street was lined with trees and wound up into thicker woods that concealed a number of houses.

"This is so uncomfortable!" Susan said, nursing the bites upon her arms. "I'm losing feeling in other parts of my body." She might need some sort of painkiller, like morphine, I thought, but I was unsure where we could get something like that.

Like before, the area was silent. Nothing stirred on this stretch of street, and no cars moved by in the prevailing desolation. We all walked up the winding road and heard a raccoon chatter in the dark as it ran through the branches overhead, lost in its own pursuits. There were no streetlights in this part of the town. So we were thankful for the hopeful light of the white moon that shined through the night sky. The moon seemed to hang there distantly, not offering a hand to help us.

"Where's their apartment?" I asked.

"It's up ahead someplace," Roger answered. After passing several houses, we saw the large, three-story apartment complex surrounded by defoliated trees. It loomed with a single lamp shining from one of its corners. I ran up to the building beneath the dark New York sky and approached the door. On the outside wall, near the door, was a metal panel that contained a number of buttons, and next to each button was the name of a tenant. Roger found the buzzer for his parents' condominium. After receiving no answer, he rang it again as a stubborn reality began to dawn upon me. There was something wrong.

"Where are they?" he asked with a distressed tone in his voice.

Roger took a set of keys from his pocket and opened the door. The foyer was lit, but there was no activity. Surely people lived here, but I guess they did not bother to venture outside as they tried to hide from the gathering storm of intolerable circumstances. We helped the girl in, then Roger located a stairwell that would take us upstairs.

"It's up here," he said.

We ascended the stairway, coming to the second floor, then walked down the dismal poorly lit hall.

"This is the place," he said as we stopped at the door. I hesitated and listened carefully before contemplating entering, detecting a faint sound of something fumbling around on the other side of the door. Intuitively, I knew that the noise was made by something without intent or direction. "What was it?" I wondered.

"Hello, Mom? Are you there?" Roger asked.

Something approached the door from the other side, producing a shuffling sound. I heard the doorknob rattle.

"Mom? Dad? It's me, Roger. Is everything okay?" The door creaked backwards into the dark unknown, and a face suddenly appeared – a horrible and contorted face that hissed in dire anticipation! It was an evil and revolting countenance, which made me shudder and want to vomit!

It was the face belonging to his mother! She, or it, was an undead mockery of what she once was, and it stood there before us in a blouse, a skirt and an apron, with horrible malice burning in its eyes! "GRAAAAAAAAA," it said, hobbling forward trying to capture Roger. "Mom. It's me. It's your son, Roger," he said to the figure that was once, but no longer, his mother.

The thing grabbed his wrist and opened its maw, attempting to fill its inhuman stomach with unholy nourishment, threatening Roger's life. With the bat still in hand, I hit it against the side of the ribcage. It stumbled against the wall just inside the doorway, and came to, crawling on the ground towards me with a horrid, demonic look upon its face!

"What are you doing to my mother?" Roger screamed.

"Roger, she's dead! She's not your mom anymore!" I tried to reason with him. It reached out and grabbed Roger's ankle. He lost his footing and fell backwards into the overcast hallway. Sue Greenberg screamed as the creature that was once Mrs. Scarpaci tried to take a bite out of its son's leg! Realizing that Roger's safety was at stake, I struck the thing against the side of the head with the bat. I hit the monstrosity again and again in the cranium until it crumpled to the floor, lifeless, inactive and no longer functioning. It was dead, but in truth, it was never really alive.

"What did you do to my mother?" Roger sat on the floor of the hallway, crying.

"WHAT DID YOU DO TO MY MOTHER? I OUGHT TO KILL YOU FOR THIS!" Roger screamed.

Part of me wanted to hit him, but I restrained the urge, realizing that he was just upset. It was obvious that his parents had died some time ago, long before we got here. The girl sat against the wall of the hallway, covering her face revealing large red wounds on her forearm. She cried in violent distress in the dark hallway, storm clouds swirling around near the ceiling.

The apartment was dark, except for the kitchen lamp, accompanied by the flickering glow of the television set. I was scared. Was another one of those things here in the apartment? Where was Roger's dad? I heard footfalls that slowly passed along the floor in my direction. Something in the hallway moved, the corridor illuminated by the ghostly flickering of the television set at the rear of the corridor. It came closer and the figure finally emerged from the obscurity of dark shadows.

It looked at me with what I could only describe as bloodlust in its eyes, and it sounded horribly like an animal! "GRAAAAAAAARRRRRRR!" it said. It was Roger's father! As the monster groped towards me, it became clear that his father had become a damnable creature! I hit it in the head with the bat!

"No!" screamed Roger, as he sat in the hallway bawling, his deceased mother in his lap. I struck the abomination in the head again. The thing faltered in its tracks and slumped to the floor with no life or direction present within it anymore. Roger sat in the hallway, crying and sobbing his brains out. It was hard. It was real hard; I know.

"Andy, what are you doing? Those are my parents! Don't you care about me?" he cried, still on the floor with his dead mother.

"Roger, he would have killed you! I had to do it!" I said, defending myself.

This place smelled of death and suffocated me as danger lurked in the nooks and crannies of the unknown, and I wanted desperately to leave. After managing to free it from Roger's grip, I dragged Mrs. Scarpaci's body into the apartment and left it there in the gray atmosphere of the hallway to decompose. Roger and the girl stayed in the corridor, while I began to search for firearms. I uncovered them in the closet of Mr. Scarpaci's office. After taking the box of rounds next to them, I picked up the shotgun and revolver then brought them out into the hallway. At least now we had a fighting chance.

"Roger, we have to get going. We can't bring them back from the dead, and we can't stay here. We have to go," I said to him, admittedly without emotion.

"Then let's at least bury them in the backyard!" he said, still upset at the scenario.

"We have to get back to Marcia's apartment now, and maybe we can do that later. Sue's sick and she needs medical attention," I said.

"My whole body is startin' to get cold. I'm scared," she wailed, her back against the wall of the depressing hallway. I helped her to her feet, and finally, Roger got off of his backside and began to walk again. We loudly shut the door to his parent's apartment, leaving two corpses behind in a resounding echo that went on for infinity. We found the stairwell, descended it to the first floor, and stood in the foyer to collect our heads. Weapons in hand, we left the apartment complex and went down the long, winding road that led us back to the woods. The girl continued to complain about her entire body going numb as we walked through the naked and skeletal trees. Roger and I realized we were going to have to take her to the police, so that she could get the attention she needed.

I began to think a bit about the law. It is interesting that a form of martial law ruled the land, even though we were not fighting against an actual invasion. However, an invasion was not too far from the truth. This was a kind of war where dead corpses rose only to destroy the living. Society had to resort to drastic measures in order to preserve itself. It seemed as if tough times warranted the tactics of an iron fist.

Sue Greenberg was starting to get weak and finally collapsed. We had to grab her by the underarms and pull her along, through the lifeless trees that offered no assistance.

"Sue, we're going to get you to an ambulance soon. Hang on, honey. Please hang on. Just a little further," I said.

The woman let out a faint groan. Could she have lost that much blood from wounds? Her body got heavier and heavier as her legs dragged along the ground. We got to that same house we had found her at earlier. By that time, her body had stopped moving, as if she became extremely lethargic. It went totally limp.

"Roger, I think she's dead."

"Then we have to drop her here!" he said, somewhat short-tempered.

"We have to make sure she's dead, if we do that," I said calmly, with little emotion.

"You didn't do that when you killed my parents!" he screamed furiously.

"I didn't kill your parents. They were already dead," I explained.

We continued to argue for several minutes, remonstrating into the night like little children. We arrived at Marcia's condominium, knocked on the door and it opened slightly, just a crack. I could see her brown eye peering at us through the narrow space with cautious hesitation.

"Roger? Andy? Dat you?" she asked with an uncertain tone.

"Yeah. It's us. Marcia, open the door. We have someone who needs medical attention."

Realizing it was just the two of us, she unlatched the door.

"Oh, you guys come in," she said smiling.

Roger and I dragged Sue Greenberg's body into the center of the room, proceeded to load the weapons with several rounds of ammunition, and then laid them on the couch. The body did not move; it became deathly cold, her pink skin turning a pallid shade of depressing gray.

"What are we going to do with the corpse?" I wondered.

Marcia bent over it to see if it was still alive.

"She dead?" she asked.

"Think so," Roger said, all traces of emotion fleeing from his facial expression.

The body did not move; just lying there, pale as death, turning a strange out-of-place color. We watched the corpse for several long moments. Then a shudder passed through the entire cadaver and the hand twitched! All of us backed away from the corpse that had been dead for about fifteen minutes as it clearly returned to life, defying the natural order of the universe! It turned itself over upon its back, and its eyes stared blankly up at the ceiling, as if it was trying to understand its surroundings! It sat up straight while a horrible expression came over its face, hissing like an animal and growling savagely as barbarism began to reign!

Clearly, this was not Susan Greenberg, but rather some sort of joke of what she once was. The creature that was once human struggled to its feet, and it looked around the room, taking note of the three humans that stood before it. Marcia, in a panic, let out a loud and piercing shriek! The monster, with a stiff gait, reached out for her with its right arm, seeking to make her its first victim. Marcia did nothing but scream, lost and hopeless, panicking frantically to no end.

"Andy, do something! We have to do something, quick!" Roger said.

"Do what? What do you expect me to do, Roger?" I asked, alarmed.

"She's become a ghoul! Hit her in the head or something! Don't just stand there like a bump-on-a-log!" Roger said.

"I'm not standing here like a bump-on-a-log, and don't talk to me like that!" I said. Marcia continued to scream, paralyzed by fear and unable to move.

I spied the revolver on the sofa as I awoke from the cloud of the argument. Quickly, I picked it up and took aim at the thing's head, just as it closed in on Marcia. The gun went off when I pulled the trigger, and the bullet plowed through the skull and lodged in the creature's head. The thing that was once Susan Greenberg was now dead, and it collapsed to the floor. Marcia put her hands over her mouth and cried loudly for several long moments, trying to regain the composure that had left her during the attack.

"We have to get rid of the body. We sure as heck can't keep it here!" I said.

Roger grabbed its arms and I took its legs. We carried it out the front door and placed it in the vacant street against the curb. It would stay there, decomposing amongst this dull assortment of bedroom apartments and become fodder for insects. We went back inside. Roger grabbed Marcia's hand and tried to comfort her for a while with a gentle and soft embrace.

"It's okay," he said over and over again.

She finally calmed down, and her equanimity returned to her.

It was clear from this experience that once one of those things bit someone, an infection spread. Once the infection had spread, the person would die, and after a short period of time they would become like one of those inhuman things. They would wander around aimlessly, wanting to destroy the rest of humanity, spreading far and wide to the very ends of the earth unless the whole outbreak was ruthlessly kept in check.

Chapter Eight: The Meeting on the Hill

The next morning, after Roger and Marcia had their devotions at the dining room table, the test pattern ceased on the TV once again. Burnside, the monotonous man, appeared before the light blue backdrop on the set.

"We want to inform you that the United States is not the only country that has been subjected to this strange phenomenon," he said, reading from his script.

"There have been similar outbreaks of this disturbance in Nigeria, Argentina, and the United Kingdom." Roger and Marcia left the dining area and joined me in the living room.

This terrible outbreak was taking place all over the world. Would humanity finally be able to clean up the mess? I did not have an answer for that question, and it bothered me.

The camera angle shifted then centered upon a man with a beard, long straggly hair, and a pair of glasses. He also sat at the table, before the blue screen. A caption below him read: "Dr. Neil McIntyre." He was a scientist.

"Just want to remind everyone that the ghouls can be destroyed with a sharp blow, or a gunshot, to the head. Once they are rendered inoperative, they must be taken to the street and be disposed of by burning them. This terrible invasion leaves no time for funeral arrangements," the scientist said. Judging from Roger's response to the death of his parents, I wondered how well the public would accept this. I paid no further attention to the broadcast and dismissed the suggestion as hogwash.

Roger sat in the recliner, expressionless and silent, almost catatonic. I sensed that he was in a dismal state of mourning.

"Roger, I'm sorry I yelled at you last night," I said.

"Apology accepted," he mumbled. He seemed to be hardly aware of the words I had spoken. He paused, and then replied, his tone strong. "My father kept on complaining of incidences of heartburn the day I left to go to the prayer meeting. They were probably heart attacks. The whole crisis hit us, and I ended up stuck here at Marcia's," he said. "He probably died later that day and became the creature that killed my mother." His eyes blankly stared at the space ahead of him. "Can't believe that they're both dead. Wish I could have spent those last moments with them."

A little while later, Roger and I started to get ready to meet with the police at the firehouse, making sure that our weapons were cleaned and in good working order. Amidst it all, I had this growing desire to check up on my family Upstate.

"Is the shotgun working?" I asked.

"It was the last time my father used it," Roger answered.

"How long ago was that?"

"'Bout three weeks ago."

I stopped for a moment, realizing that I had a few minutes to call my mom. I stepped into the clean white kitchen and rang the number. Surprisingly, she picked up.

"Hi Mom, how's everything going up there?" I asked.

"Everything's okay. Your sister and her kids are doing fine," she answered. "They're all up in the mobile home, safe and sound as can be. Little Davey is playing video games, and he keeps beating his father," she said.

"Swell, are the police having a lot of 'problems'?" I asked.

"Not so much," she answered. I realized that the plague of ghouls could not spread as fast in the country, as it had in the crowded metropolis.

"Some incidents occurred in the City of Rome, though. It lasted for several hours," she remarked.

"Did the police take care of it?" I asked.

"As far as I know."

Although, the rural areas fared better than the cities, the effects of the plague were everywhere, and there was no place that was really "safe." A few minutes later, I said "goodbye" to my mom and hung up the phone.

Roger apparently had gone upstairs to catch a little sleep. I could see Marcia through the doorway, sitting at the dining room table in the back. She was sipping hot coffee from a white cup with a brown teddy bear on one of the chairs joining her. She did not acknowledge me but stared off into space. This whole crisis probably weighed on her mind heavily. The sun in the sky shined through the doorway, glowing off of Marcia's brown skin as she nervously drank the black liquid. She was beautiful, and I wanted to know her more. I looked at my watch, noticing that it would be 9:00 am soon. Roger and I would have to start moving.

It was about 8:50 when I heard Roger rouse from his sleep and descend the stairway, seemingly charged up to vanquish the enemy despite the despair over losing his parents.

"You want the pistol or the rifle?" he asked.

"I like rifles," I said.

"Then the rifle it shall be!" he said in a good-natured sort of way. I picked up the shotgun and he took the pistol from the couch where they rested, one beside the other. We left Marcia, still anxiously sipping her hot coffee, who gingerly waved goodbye. The two of us went out to the street and we walked to the right. Across the road, I detected Sue Greenberg's displaced body decaying in the gutter of refuse. Passing by several of the bland houses, the inactive street took us to the main road, where we noticed two more corpses stinking near the curb. Apparently, someone had killed the reanimated bodies of their loved ones and dumped them in the street, leaving them in cold neglect. I wondered how many of them actually followed through with the instructions given them by the authorities.

"Rog, I hate this," I said.

"I know," he answered.

We turned the corner and went to the right up a short grade to the firehouse on the left. There I could see a group of armed men, probably about twenty altogether, standing outside of the building. Between the armed men and the firehouse were two police cars with four officers in blue uniforms standing about them. As we got closer, I recognized one of them as the domineering cop who had come to Marcia's to recruit us, Robert Capasso.

"There's the big man himself," Roger said with a grin.

Roger and I drew nearer to the gathering. Capasso stood there, wearing a small pair of black sunglasses, trying to dictate and rule over the rag tag group of civilians before him.

"Boys," he said to Roger and me, "sign here. We want to keep tabs on all you people who help us out." I sensed he was a mean man who would step on people to get what he wanted. We took the pen carefully from his hand and signed the sheet of paper on the clipboard. I took a look around and noticed that more men had joined us with weapons at their sides. They were a motley assortment of guys, wearing plain everyday clothes with unshaven faces. They banded together to rid this town of these inhuman things that were spreading all over the suburbs.

Capasso then briefed the group that consisted of about thirty armed men.

"Okay, fellas. There are a number of ghouls that have been spotted in recent days. The key is 'co-op-er-a-tion.' If we don't have it, you have problems with me. Let's work togethuh and mop up town. There are some ghouls down the main county route near the hospital. There are others near the retirement home. Does anyone wanna tell me why there are so many at these two places?" Capasso asked, in a boisterous and condescending tone.

"Have no clue," a man behind me wisecracked.

Capasso just stood there for several long moments, appearing very serious as no one said a word. He then approached the man.

"You are addressing an officuh of the law. I don't want to hear something like that from you again," he said very softly. "Do I make myself clear?"

"Yessir," the shorthaired man said.

"Because a few people died in both," another man said confidently, answering Capasso's first question.

"That is correct. There are a lot wanderin' down by the funeral parluh, and they broke into a few boarding houses, where the Mexicans are stayin'," he said.

Capasso went on to say that all of the ghouls in the boarding houses took out a small number of officers. I realized that the funeral home was near my apartment, which explained the ruckus I experienced a few nights before. A ghoul from the funeral parlor attacked someone and killed him. That person was, in turn, corrupted and killed others, and they in turn corrupted more. The contagion spread down the street.

Capasso divided the group in two. My group would take the retirement home, and the other bunch would head to the hospital. All the ghouls would be shot in the head and taken to the street to be properly disposed of, without any respect for their remains.

Roger went with me.

"You guys ready to go?" some man asked who was ahead of me, walking backwards.

"Yeah," I answered.

Everyone turned to the right, down the county route that was lined with houses and business offices. The whole area, despite the fact that it was heavily populated, was deserted and without activity, and the landscape looked bleak and dejected. The people had either fled or shut themselves inside, not wanting to bother with anyone. In front of us was a grade flanked by a number of trees. We approached the hospital that was on a hill to our left, a silent monument to this suburban death that ran rampant.

While standing on the street, Capasso took a bullhorn and cried, "COME AND GET US!"

In response, we heard these animalistic and savage growls. About fifteen or so of those shambling and stiff monstrosities appeared in tattered garments as they converged on the street. They had gray skin and dark shadows beneath their eyes, and they would try to turn us into mockeries just like themselves. They emerged from the hospital and other locations in slow motion, in a way that was surreal and not acceptable. People never move in such a manner. Capasso drew his gun as a group of armed men approached the things first.

"All right, take aim."

Everyone pointed their weapons at the inhuman mob.

"When I give the signal, fire!" Capasso ordered.

"FIRE!"

The men let loose upon the seven that emerged from the hospital. They fell down like trees hit with chainsaws. The other eight or so came over the grade in the direction of the retirement home. They got closer and closer with their slow gait and groping claws. The men all took aim with their rifles and pistols in response, ready to send them to an everlasting destruction.

"Okay, FIRE!" Capasso dictated. The guns pumped out a volley of lead then the creatures fell to the ground. Capasso had the men lay their weapons down and take the dead ghouls by the hands and feet and put them in a pile. One of the men had a can of kerosene and doused the corpses with it. Capasso lit a match and the flames went skyward with a rush of air.

"Okay gentlemen, we're doin' so well today, but we have to go on. My superiuhs believe that there are about two hundred of these things in this town, so get ready 'cause it ain't gonna be fun!" Capasso barked, seemingly not caring how he was perceived by the men.

The group split in two again. My group went with Capasso to the retirement home below the grade, while the others went towards the silent hospital up on the hill to the left. Everyone in my group walked along the street, approaching the crest of the grade, breathing in the still and polluted atmosphere. As we climbed over the grade, we could see the retirement home below, a relatively modern-looking building made up of red bricks and a roof covered with black tar.

According to the police reports, one of the residents there had died. The person's resuscitated body began to take victims accordingly, kind of like the thing that attacked Sue Greenberg. Eventually, several of them became infected and in turn infected the others. The surviving staff had to evacuate the residents as quickly as possible and remove them to safety. Many got lost inside and became casualties of this war, though no numbers had been figured yet.

The retirement home was isolated, surrounded by trees on three sides. My car was still down the street, the front end crumpled with a green tag tied to the side mirror, and I realized that it would eventually be towed. I would have to get a new car somewhere along the line, but that fact was inconsequential and I cared little about the matter. Next to me was a young man, a teenager, wearing his baseball cap backwards. I got bold and decided to introduce myself to him.

"My name is Andy Goering. What's your name?" I asked.

"Alexander Bernstein, but I prefer to be called Sasha," he said, speaking in a tone that was a little different from the people in this area.

"You have an accent. Where are you from?" I asked.

"From Ukraine," he answered.

After talking to him for a few moments, I noticed that he had something of a flair for violence. Brandishing a shotgun, he seemed to be looking forward to the coming carnage.

"Can't wait to blow these rotten things away," he said with a smile. I didn't really care for him at that point.

The group of seventeen approached the brick one-story building; many of the windows had broken panes of glass in them. The front door was left hanging open and inviting us to possible disaster. Behind a bush next to the open door was a moving shadow. Bernstein proceeded slowly towards the bush, one hand on the trigger of his gun and the other wrapped around the barrel. Capasso yelled something undecipherable to him, and then I saw it. From behind the bush, a shambling creature rushed out, its arms outstretched. Bernstein was ready for it, pointing his weapon at the thing's head and firing! As it went down in a flash of blood, Bernstein smirked as if he enjoyed the whole thing.

"One down," he announced with an exaggerated grin.

Capasso joined Bernstein and scrutinized the handiwork eagerly. Below us was an old man in a set of striped pajamas and buckshot now in his head, destroyed with rude disregard and contempt. I think Capasso liked the fact that Bernstein was prone to violence. He patted Bernstein on the back like they were the best of buddies, and both of them walked in through the open door.

Capasso looked back and said, "Let's go!" The rest of the men followed, including me. We found ourselves in a white office that had a large counter with plastic chairs behind it. Windows were mounted in the white walls and more plastic chairs sat up against them. Sheets of paper were strewn about the room as if someone had ransacked the place, hunting for something that remained forever elusive. The fluorescent lights overhead still hummed eerily since no one had shut them off.

There appeared to be nothing here as our footsteps echoed in the vacuous corridor. We walked on through a hallway that took us into the bowels of the complex, the fluorescent lights giving off a ghostly glow. All of us proceeded, with Capasso and Bernstein leading the way into the iridescence. The hallway curved to the right and took us into another wing of the complex. I noticed that the walls of the corridor were an off-white and the hallway radiated an air of despair. Dining trays were haphazardly on the floor of the hallway, and food was smeared on the walls. The place was an absolute mess. We all moved carefully and slowly, cautious in our advance. Detecting some sort of clatter down the corridor, Capasso motioned with his hand for everyone to proceed in silence. We did, no one uttering a word.

Up ahead, an open door led to a brightly lit room. Capasso, pistol drawn, placed one foot in front of the other and walked towards the entrance, the rest of us in tow. He stood there before the room and peered into it for a few moments as Bernstein joined him. Apparently, both men silently observed an event in the chamber that they could not take their eyes off of.

The rest of us gathered at the entrance. Capasso and Bernstein walked into the room and we all followed them, finding ourselves in utter amazement. In a room used for physical exams were ten senior citizens gathered in a crouching position around a body in the middle of the floor. The senior citizens were engaged in some sort of activity that was out of sorts. I looked closer and I could not believe my eyes. *The senior citizens were eating the corpse!* This was just like the situation at the laundromat. Some of the men started to vomit. Bernstein reacted by cocking his shotgun and holding it up to the head of one of the creatures. He pulled the trigger and just shot it right there, the thundering blast reverberating throughout the room, shattering the spell of shock and unacceptance!

Bernstein created a reaction. Some of the senior citizens got to their feet and took notice of us. They let out their horrid growls as they stiffly walked toward us. The rag-tag bunch just responded by shooting them point blank in their chests, and the senior citizens fell to the ground, still groping around. However, shooting them did nothing to discourage the attack as the corrupted things got back up with stubborn resilience.

"Go for the brains, guys! GO FOR THE BRAINS!" Capasso shouted.

Roger fired his pistol into one's torso, causing the creature to stumble. It regained its footing and lunged for his neck! I took the butt of my rifle and struck it on its temple. The thing stopped in its pursuit and faced me with a murderous look in its eye, a hateful expression coming over its countenance! It growled and lunged forward, trying to end my life! I held the barrel of my rifle up to its skull and pulled the trigger, blowing away half of its cranium and sending the creature to the floor. The other men around the room were firing like mad. Some of the creatures were stopped by the excessive fire and were reduced to dust.

One man, McDermott, was bitten in the arm by one of the creatures and howled in pain during the confusion. One of the other men knocked the creature away from McDermott with the barrel of his gun, and then fired into its skull in a rush of vengeance. It fell to the ground like the others. The smoke of the battle began to clear, and we could see that all ten of the senior citizens around that corpse were stilled. Their bodies were all over the floor, lying in pools of red blood like refuse to be thrown into the street and burned.

"Who is that?" Bernstein asked, concerning the man whose body was originally lying on the floor.

"Never seen him," stated the same insubordinate man with the short hair.

We all decided to take a closer look at that corpse that was in the center of the room. I recognized the body. It belonged to the derelict whom I saw push the shopping cart a few nights before. He was an endless wanderer and must have drifted into this place looking for something to take, or maybe he walked in for other reasons unknown. We noticed that his chest was in shambles and his skin was turning a shade of gray. Dark circles beneath his eyes became prominent. It was not certain as to how long he had been dead. Maybe for half-an-hour or more I guessed.

We looked at the corpse's eyes. They had been closed for several long moments and the face remained still like a department store mannequin. Suddenly, they opened! The derelict sat abruptly and emitted a horrible growl, shocking us all into panic. It tried to get to its feet while making an extremely loud ruckus. It lashed out wildly with its hands as it attempted to grab some of the men who were too close. Roger walked up to the creature and pumped two rounds into its chest cavity, which had no effect as the thing began to rise to its feet. Capasso then put his black .45 to its head and fired. The vagabond fell to the floor on its back. It was killed.

This little battle was over, but not without a casualty. Those things had bit McDermott and another man named Amodio. William Masterson, another member of the militia, was found lying on the ground outside of the retirement home. He was dead, apparently after emptying a round into his own head. I guess he couldn't take this whole thing any longer and laid there in unresponsive resignation.

Chapter Nine: Bad Public Relations

We all ended up meeting at the firehouse again. An ambulance took McDermott and Amodio, along with another fellow from the other party, to a special rescue center. Those things had bitten the three of them and hopefully they would be dealt with accordingly. The police dismissed some of the men to go out and get their autos, which were parked in various parts of the neighborhood. Roger and I waited around for about an hour with our hands in our pockets, not knowing what to do next.

"Andy, you really need to know Jesus. Things are too chaotic and you have to be in his will," he said.

"Not now, Roger, not now," I said in disagreement. Capasso stood near with his imposing presence, listening to the nature of the discussion. His face was without emotion, like steel that did not move.

After nearly a whole hour, a number of the men returned in their cars, ready to embark upon the next mission. Capasso stood up in front of us bellowing orders.

"Okay, get in line. Make sure your weapons are loaded, or we can use you for something else," he said condescendingly. He gave as little respect to us as possible, kind of like a kid kicking a doll down the street.

"There are some problems ovuh by the funeral home, and we have to clean it up. Some of the local Chicanos told us that there were some distuhbances."

We all climbed into eight cars, including some squad vehicles, and drove, twisting and turning through the streets of Southold, until we finally arrived at the forbidden area near the funeral parlor. There we saw a large three-story brown house that had a number of gabled roofs on it. All of the autos were parked in front along the tree-lined street, and they opened up and vomited forth the men ready to do battle. The guys sported their weapons with confidence, feeling so sure of themselves.

Roger and I checked out the lawn of the house. A tricycle sat on its side, neglected, while some garbage from a nearby trashcan was scattered all over the premises in abandonment. I did not like what I saw; the place looked as if someone had wrecked it with no respect for the occupants.

I had heard earlier that the police force took over the area after Mexicans filed complaints in the local precinct. Some officers got lost in the darkness and never made it back to the station. Remembering what I had seen at the laundromat, I could attest to that. I had no idea how many people were killed in these attacks, but apparently it had been going on for over an hour before the police were finally notified.

"Don't go through the front doah. They'll be able to see us," Capasso said while standing in the lawn under a large tree.

"Sasha. Lead the way around the back of the house," he said.

Bernstein found the back door –one with a four-paned window in it. All of us followed him like he was the pied piper of our destruction. He opened up the door, then he and Capasso walked through it. The rest of us filed in with our guns to our sides, following suit, trying to be good little soldiers. We found ourselves in an off-white kitchen with a laminated table and some padded chairs that had been knocked over. More garbage was strewn on the floor, as if this place was little more than a sewer hole.

"Hello!" Capasso called. No one answered.

We next entered the living room. There were toys thrown about the chamber in disregard amongst a number of recliners, two brown couches, and a large television set that sat upon the floor. To our left was a stairway with a wooden banister that led up to the second story.

"A number of you go up theah and check the situation out!" Capasso demanded.

Roger and I, along with a few of the others, went upstairs, while Capasso dispatched men to locate the cellar. We ascended the brown staircase and found ourselves in a dark hallway lined with wooden walls. There were no lights on, and it was difficult to see in the thick blackness. We noticed that some of the dark wooden doors to the rooms were shut. What terrible surprises lurked behind them?

"There's something movin' around behind theah," a young, clean-cut man named Roberts stated.

We gathered outside that room in the hallway, a little uncertain as to what to do next. Roberts got daring and threw open the dark portal. Inside, slowly moving around, was a Mexican male dressed in blue jeans and a tee shirt, fingering through a pile of dress shirts as if he was trying to find out what they were. There was something wrong with him as he went about slowly and stiffly. His skin was not colored right. It was wrong, deathly wrong.

"His skin's gray. He's one of 'em," Roberts said as the creature made these inarticulate grunts. Whatever sentience he once had was now gone. The corrupted man only had the desire to investigate the immediate world around him. He was clearly and unmistakably a ghoul.

Learning the lessons of earlier today, I walked up to the walking corpse with my rifle. The thing stopped its groping and noticed me. It grabbed my wrist and opened up its mouth, seeking to take a bite of my flesh! Revolted, I put the barrel to its head and pulled the trigger, wanting to lash out at it for violating me. The beast that was once a man jerked backwards from the impact of the bullet and stumbled, falling down face forward. That which was "dead" was now truly and permanently "dead."

"What are we gonna do with the cohpse?" Roberts asked.

"Guess we'll have to burn it," Roger answered.

We all went back down to the living room and waited for Capasso's men. As we sat around in the chairs and couches amidst the broken toys, we heard gunfire from the cellar.

"Do you think theah in trouble?" Roberts asked.

Immediately, we ran to the basement door and opened it. Before us were wooden stairs that descended into a dark and musty cellar with a stone foundation. We heard a tumult of voices rising up from the shadows, but could not tell who was speaking. We heard this savage growling as if there were animals down there feasting in bloody carnage. Below us, on the wooden stairway, was a shambling Mexican male making his way up the steps with arms extended outward. He was seeking to make us his victims as he emerged from the black depths.

"Guys, get down now!" a voice from behind the ghoul said. Everyone at the top of the stairs dropped down with their faces to the floor to get out of the way. Gunshots were heard from below. The thing on the stairway fell backwards and tumbled down the steps. It was dead.

"Are you guys okay?" we heard a voice ask.

I told him, "Yeah."

"What's your name?" I asked.

"Frederick Sorensen. You?"

"Andy Goering. What happened down there?"

"We had a fatality. Seven or eight of these things attacked one man. They were wanderin' around behind stacks of boxes and hot water heaters. One of them jumped out from its place and killed him. They had to shoot the man in the head to make sure that he was...," Sorensen paused.

"Was what?" I asked.

"Dead," he answered coldly.

"Sorry to hear that," I answered. That was a lie. My heart was not going out to these people.

About ten bodies were found in the poorly lit basement. Roger, Roberts, and I lifted out the corpses, mostly Mexican laborers, but I noted that three were police officers originally dispatched to investigate the situation. We took them out of the basement by the arms and legs. We dragged them over the lawn to the street where they would be burned and consumed. The Mexican from upstairs was laid to rest upon the pile.

As we applied gasoline and kerosene to the mound of dead bodies, I took a look at what went on in the streets around me. People stood in doorways and the windows of the nearby houses. They just silently waited, watching from their dwellings as spectators, lost in some sort of fog and not knowing what to do about the panorama before them. I gathered that they did not like what they saw and were silently protesting.

Later on in the evening, Roger and I returned to Marcia's, emotionally spent from the horrid carnage of the day. Marcia, heartily greeted us with a smile, her long braids dangling.

"So glad you guys back," she said.

She was lonely, stuck in the house by herself all day, and happy that she had some company. Roger and I did not have the enthusiasm to return the greeting adequately. We were exhausted and hugged her in a limp sort of manner.

"Yeah, good to see you too," I said lethargically.

Roger went upstairs to take a shower, while I sat on the sofa. I started to nod off, to enter a place where there was neither time nor space.

I went to sleep and had no dreams I could remember. I woke up feeling restless as anxiety gripped my soul. To pass the time away, I turned the television on. As the screen materialized, I could see that same scientist with the beard and glasses being interviewed by Burnside. It was Neil McIntyre again, here to appeal to the good side of New Yorkers and get them to follow through with the unreasonable instructions.

"Just to remind everyone, in order to destroy these creatures, you have to put a bullet through their brains and take the dead bodies out to the street. Here they will be disposed of by dousing them with gasoline and setting them ablaze. We know that doesn't give anyone time for funeral arrangements, but you have to follow these instructions. It is imperative that you do this," he said.

I realized that this whole method of disposal allowed little time to give proper respects to the dearly departed. I began to think. Perhaps this policy would work well in a population of secular humanists who did not care about the dead, but most societies do care about the dead and are not made up of secular humanists. I realized that this posed a problem, since these traditional populations may not go along with official policies. Through the recent ages, tradition quite often butted heads with secular humanism. Only time would tell how the people at large would react.

After the interview was finished, the networks televised a list of "rescue centers," which were stations placed out in rural areas. Here people could receive food, clothing, and take shelter from the gathering storm of abominations that hung over the land. There were some out in Jersey and more Upstate, but it made no sense to leave since we were safe right where we were. Most of the roads were closed in the county, so there was really no escape route per se. We were trapped like rats on a sinking ship, scrambling for survival. The networks eventually told the viewers that the local police were now acting in tandem with the federal and local governments, and that they would continue to keep us abreast of the carnage.

Roger woke up from his nap and came down the stairs in a rush.

"Gotta pray with Marcia," he stated, his hair disheveled.

"Yeah," I said unenthused. I could care less who he was praying with.

After getting a glass of water from the kitchen, he went back up stairs and entreated with Marcia. I sat on the couch, letting the mental dust settle into the natural crevasses of my brain. He came down later, practically running into the living room, and told me that the two of them had asked God to clear up the enigmatic crisis. This bothered me; if God were alive and well, he would not have allowed this to happen in the first place. Surely he would have intervened if he knew about it. If God did not intervene, it was simply because he does not care about the affairs of humanity, or perhaps that he just did not know, or maybe didn't exist at all.

Marcia came down the stairs, her braids swinging as she carried a teddy bear, a timid look upon her face. The three of us stared at the test pattern for long moments without exchanging a word. We had nothing to say to each other, like gravestones poking through the grass.

We heard the sound of a siren wail outside in the suburban New York air.

"What goin' on?" Marcia asked as Roger and I opened the front door. There we saw a police car with its flashing red lights parked in the street. We watched the two officers leave the car and knock on the door of a neighbor somewhere across the street. A man opened the door and faced the officers. The two cops said something to him we could not hear, and the man answered back angrily, seething with discontent, but we were still unable to determine what the whole situation was about. The two cops pushed their way into the apartment and disappeared for several long moments. We heard a gun shot from inside the still condominium. The two police officers emerged from the townhouse with a limp body in their hands. The man who had met them at the door again argued from behind the threshold, his face turning red all the while. One of the officers turned around and said something to him, remonstrating with the same intense hostility. The officers took the dead body and dumped it into the street. They also took the body of Susan Greenberg and another corpse and placed them together in one pile. One retrieved a can of gasoline from the trunk of the squad car and doused the bodies with its contents. A match was lit, and the flames eagerly licked up the corpses.

The two officers remained there until the cadavers were entirely consumed. The odor saturated the Rockland air as the smoke wafted above the rooftops and into the clear blue sky. Marcia looked on, silent and sullen. Roger gaped at the panorama and muttered, "where's God?" That was the big question all along.

Chapter Ten: The Sweep

Looking behind me, I noticed that Marcia was no longer there and I sensed that something was wrong. Roger was in the clean white kitchen to the right, standing over the dark wooden table, seeking comfort in a cold piece of fried chicken. I decided to walk through the dining room and up to the second floor. After climbing the stairs, I knocked on Marcia's bedroom door to find out how she was doing.

"Come in," she said. I opened up the door, stepped in to find a room full of stuffed animals on the dressers and on the light wooden rocking chairs. Marcia was lying on the double bed in fetal position, sobbing to herself in remorse.

"What's wrong?" I asked with as much compassion as I could muster.

"I don' tink I ever goin' see my parents ageen," she responded. "I can't get in touch wit dem by phoone." Apparently, the device seemed dead most of the time, indicating that the phone lines were not working, hanging in permanent malfunction.

"Maybe Roger and I can get you back to Flatbush," I said reassuringly as I could. Remembering what had happened to Roger's parents, I could only imagine what was going on in the City. Hopefully, her relatives were still alive and she would be able to see them again. I hugged her, the only thing that I could do to give her comfort in the time at hand. I wished that I did have faith. Maybe I could offer something more to people than a hug, like the inspiration that says things would one day get better. I shut her door behind me, leaving her with the stuffed animals, which tried to comfort her with their lifeless smiles. It was time for her to go to sleep.

I went downstairs to join Roger. He was watching the TV munching on the same piece of fried chicken. Another discouraging bulletin flashed across the screen. We did not see the usual newscaster, Burnside, with the glasses and somber demeanor. This time it was an attractive woman with black hair, brown skin, and a red outfit, reminding me of a runway model in a fashion show. Her name was Lucretia McLean.

"We want to keep you updated on the situation as it develops. Right now we are switching to local coverage of the progress made in the suburbs."

The screen changed as the network televised the sweep that local police, civilians, and National Guard units were making, working in tandem throughout Orange and Rockland counties. In one clip, a group of six men with rifles stood on a decrepit street that looked like Spring Valley. It was lined with despondent three-story brown buildings marred by the graffiti of disrepute. Their backs were turned towards us as they aimed their guns.

Ahead of them some distance away, a few corrupted and feeble creatures wandered towards the camera. This group of six men pointed guns at these tottering figures and fired their rifles upon them, releasing a volley of lead. All of the hobbling figures fell immediately like a row of dominoes. Don't they realize that, this could make all of them look like butchers or Nazis? The thought immediately came to my mind and I dwelled on it for some time.

The broadcast changed to another sequence. We could see a group of police officers pushing a cart of dead bodies down a street and dumping them into a larger pile in some remote and corner of Spring Valley. Uncaring men doused the heap of corpses with flammable liquid. Like the earlier scenario with the cops, the accumulation was set on fire. The flames voraciously consumed the ghouls that had once been men. They were disposed of as if they were martyrs, burned in the destructive ovens of Auschwitz.

The camera panned the crowd that had gathered to watch the spectacle, to get a look at their expressions. The mass was mostly Haitian, and their faces seemed slightly agitated, like those of the people I had seen earlier near the funeral parlor. What were we doing to ourselves?

Another man appeared on the scene, a clean-cut, cookie-cutter reporter with a tie and brown suit jacket.

"My name is Kieran O' Connor, and I'm here to ask Police Chief Wendell Annunziata about the progress being made. How are things, Chief Annunziata?" he asked a uniformed middle-aged man with a mustache.

"Well Kieran, things are progressing very well. The police, local posse, and National Guard units have killed ovuh four hundred of these things right here in Rockland alone. These things aren't human, and we uhge total cooperation from the public until the conclusion of this crisis," the police chief said.

If four hundred were found, how many more were there? How many nooks and crannies were they hiding in? How much cooperation would my fellow suburban dwellers offer? These questions reverberated through my head and nearly split apart my skull, and I realized that the answers had to be found but seemed forever elusive.

Once again, the model-like woman, Lucretia McLean, appeared. She interviewed Neil McIntyre, the same scientist we had seen earlier. I took note of his lengthy beard and wild, somewhat long hair. He reminded me of Rasputin, the monk of lawlessness who spelled out the doom of the Russian Czars.

McIntyre was a scientist working for the Center for Disease Control down in Atlanta.

"We urge everybody in the New York City area to continue to stay indoors until the crisis has abated," he said.

The scientist reviewed the methods of extermination as well as the connection between the radiation from the space probe and the resurrection of the dead. They tried to find explanations from the fount of secular humanism that advocated that humanity itself held the keys to all crises, yet could locate nothing that helped the situation.

A knock came at the door, ungraciously shattering the fortress of isolation and despair the two of us fell into before the TV. Roger answered it. It was Capasso, with Bernstein faithfully in tow. Both stood in the doorway to Marcia's townhouse.

"If things go well, they may lift the cuhfew," Capasso said arrogantly without thanking me for the work I did. That was a hopeful report. I looked at my watch and noticed that it was 11:00 at night. Don't Capasso and Bernstein realize that most people are asleep at this time?

"Gentlemen, if we have fuh-thuh need of your services, we'll contact you. Ciao." Capasso rudely left with Bernstein, who was grinning maliciously. Roger went upstairs to bed and sailed off to sleep.

I stared out of the living room window at the dim outline of the Ramapo Mountains, which I barely made out in the darkness. The mountains had been around for eons and would not be leaving any time soon, remaining forever. How much of the human race would be left after this whole thing had finally subsided? Would any of us be alive? Would God, this being I had so much trouble believing in, allow the human race to turn upon itself? Where was God anyways? Did he care? Maybe he just left the human race alone, occupied by the busy affairs of a remote corner of the universe. Unable to find answers to my questions, I laid down on the sofa and drifted off to sleep.

The gray expanse appeared once again and I floated in the air, my feet searching for a place to land. Footing eventually came as I touched down upon the barren soil. As I traversed the awareness, the sprouting vegetation increased as the crisis in the waking world seemingly unfolded. On the horizon, I could see the dark figure ahead, still unidentified. The sun above continued to smile and promised me I would someday know what that shape was.

My dreams had run their course, and I awoke a few hours later before the dawn. I left Marcia's townhouse and walked out to the street despite the curfew. I turned and faced the sky behind the row houses and noticed a faint light that appeared somewhere out beyond the suburban cesspool of Rockland County. A new morning arrived, and I hoped it would help me see the human condition for what it was.

Bathed in the golden light of the dawn, I stood in a pair of shorts and soaked up the warmth of the rising sun as it came up over the rooftops, despite the chill of the autumn air. Hope. The promise of the danger ceasing was sure as the sun coming up over the Hudson River Valley. I knew my sensations were unreliable, and many times they did not indicate the real truth, which is often obscured from view. Circumstances, I found, robbed one of promise. The situations can be cruel, building a prison around a person, leaving no escape save for death. Conditions can alter though, and one cannot rely upon them heavily, for there is always hope and life beyond them.

Momentarily, I felt trapped by the county I lived in. I couldn't see my family. Marcia could not get to Flatbush to see her family, and Roger's parents were dead. Technically, we could not leave this townhouse. For one second, everything became extremely claustrophobic. I had to trust and believe there would be a way out one day.

Bars seemed to form around me, and I wanted to get out of this confinement so badly, but some impulse shot through my soul which told me to be patient. I felt that, if I waited, the time would eventually arrive. I stepped back inside and sat on the floor with my head down, letting out a long sigh in exasperation. Somehow, I was being forced to believe in a higher power above me.

After laying several hands of cards on the table and engaging in board games by myself to occupy the time, my mind drifted. In my thoughts, I hoped that this curfew would soon be lifted. All of us would be running out of basic amenities, and there wouldn't be any food left. Soon, I would have to do my laundry, since Roger and I were both forced to share Marcia's brother's clothes that were kept in the closet. Thankfully, the faucets still dispensed water, so at least we could bathe. It reminded me of living under an enemy siege. This is probably what the people of Leningrad felt like during World War II. When the Germans mercilessly cut off all transportation into the city, the inhabitants had to forage like animals to live. In this case, we were dealing with a siege that had expanded and taken the whole world captive. I wondered what came back from Venus on that probe. What was the source of this mysterious radiation, and what did it do to the multitude of dead bodies?

Chapter Eleven: The Crisis Abates?

During the course of the day, the networks continued to air the news, which was censored and monitored by the federal government. Everything was now regulated by the iron influence of the state. The state dominated all, and none of us had a choice. Our society was at war against a savage enemy that subverted everything from the inside out. It was a siege, and I wished this new war were as tangible as the Germans banging on the gates of Leningrad, but it was not. Another day had passed, the orange sun setting upon the Ramapo Mountains.

We all got up the next day. Roger opened the curtains to the dining room and stared out towards the distant eastern sky. I could tell by his facial expression that something had occupied his thoughts and burdened his spirit.

"Rog, what's wrong?" I asked. I received only silence as he continued his purposeless vigil over the rooftops. He had just lost his parents. Maybe he was mourning and needed his space. Marcia, on the other hand, managed to reach her mother and siblings.

The broadcasts continued throughout the day. Burnside read some of the reports and the dark-haired Lucretia McLean took the rest. Even the president gave a speech telling everyone that this crisis would soon pass. Intuitively, I realized that it would only get worse before it got better. Something did not sit right and a piece of the puzzle was out of place. I knew something was still very wrong, but I could not figure out what it was. The numbers of corpses piled up. More than 8,000 were counted in Brooklyn. 13,000 were counted in the other four boroughs. This was probably the deadliest period in New York City's history. There were another 18,000 tallied throughout the metropolitan area. They were casualties of mankind's bloodiest and most expansive war.

Other reports existed too, where the efforts on behalf of police, local militia, and the National Guard did not fare so well. Police could not get into parts of certain neighborhoods, such as Haverstraw, and Spring Valley. They were more traditional; the people came from the Caribbean, where the legends of Voodoo and Santeria proved to be strong. Furthermore, such people respected the dead greatly and didn't want them disposed of, so the locals fought back in these communities, using the small number of weapons they had to deter the authorities. Many of them were killed in successive gun battles with the police, but the cops lost numbers too, and the casualties continued to mount across the board. It was like a war zone, comparable to Iraq or Vietnam. No one knew who the next enemy would be.

Repeatedly, throughout the day, network authorities urged viewers to cooperate with the police, by handing over all the corrupted bodies to be burned. Perhaps things could reach some blissful state of normalcy, maybe, just maybe.

Marcia sat on the couch, fidgeting nervously and holding the same brown teddy bear, its arms opened wide as the news aired. It had been several days now since the crisis began, and time seemed to stretch on forever.

"I'm so sceered. I wan' be wit my family," she said.

She was insecure and desired to be with the people she was the most familiar with as she continued to clutch the toy.

"You can't go back there, Marcia. You'll violate the curfew," I said. She just sat there on the couch, looking upset and disappointed.

Our sense of loneliness was bad and it suffocated all of us. I supposed I could sneak out at night and go back to my home on the other side of Southold, but that would be suicidal, foolish as well. I would be alone in my apartment again, and I had no desire to remain in that situation. At least here I was with other people. The isolation of my own apartment brutally choked me at times, and I did not want to return there.

We all became weary from the day's developments and our heads became heavy, growing more tired by the minute. As I fought off exhaustion, I wished for my normal life to return. It meant a lot to me to establish myself by getting a job teaching history, having a wife, and getting a house out here in the suburbs. It was the American dream, and it seemed to be constantly withheld from me, especially in light of the current situation. Perhaps once the crisis let up, we could all come back to a sense of regularity. Exhaustion eventually found the three of us, and we all shuffled off to bed.

The next day came, which may have been the seventh. I had lost track of time due to the surreal nature of the situation that could not be happening. Later in the day, I dialed the phone in Marcia's quiet and lonely kitchen and got in touch with my mom.

"Mom, how's everything goin'?" I asked.

"As far as I know, everyone is okay. Your sister is okay, her husband is okay, their kids are okay. We're all okay," she said.

No one had lost their lives in the crisis that she knew of, although there were scores of deaths in Rome. The police got together with the locals and annihilated almost every walking corpse that was about. The country boys did well out in the rural areas. Real well. I was actually proud of them.

Although we hadn't heard from them directly, we believed that Marcia's family held out too. The police went through Flatbush "killing" (if you want to call it that) every ghoul they could find. In some cases, the locals did put up resistance and some Brooklynites took the lives of a few National Guardsmen. In a crisis like this, it was a good idea to obey authority, since only law and order could save us from impending doom. This was the rational thing to do, but people aren't always inclined to rationality in extraordinary circumstances.

Roger phoned his aunts and uncles and told them what had happened to his parents, tears welling up in his eyes as he did so. Eventually, they would have to go to the condominium, collect the dead bodies, and make funeral arrangements. Roger was not sure what had happened to his parents' corpses, but hopefully they were there.

We watched reports of police and their allies sweeping through Rockland, Westchester, and Orange counties. This time, they only killed a few dozen of the things. It looked as if this whole crisis would end quite soon and our lives would return to normal. I began to fantasize about how great it would be to earn some sort of income, get a new car and live life with a degree of regularity. There was a need in my soul that was not met. I wanted to believe in something that would help me realize my dreams, but there was nothing I could trust.

After several boring hours of playing more board and card games, we ate the rice and beans left in the refrigerator. Roger and Marcia prayed a bit in dense despondency as the sun sank down below the Ramapos. The uneventful day provided me no stimulation, however, and I began to doze off. Dreams did not come to me as they had the previous night, but it seemed as if I spent eternity in slumber. Sleep offered the only refuge from the storms of reality, and the reality still seemed as unacceptably horrible as ever.

The next day, I got up to get out of Marcia's condo, to beat the suffocation of being indoors for too long. I stepped outside to drink the light of day and inhale the cool suburban air. The temperature was beginning to drop; autumn was almost over. Soon, the area would be blanketed in virgin white snow, concealing the evil so prevalent in the world. Walking across the street, I noticed the area on the sidewalk where Sue Greenberg's body was placed. There was nothing there and it was obvious that she never got the funeral that all human beings deserve. When all is said and done, we want respect and the situation warranted just the opposite.

"How's it goin' buddy?" A slightly accented voice said.

I moved my head toward the source of the question, and I noticed a teen standing in the doorway of a nearby townhouse, holding a plastic garbage bag in hand. He wore a blue sweatshirt and sported a baseball cap backwards. It was Sasha Bernstein. I had to brace myself.

Chapter Twelve: Basic Training

I walked over to him, trying to be as amiable and polite. I didn't like the man. There was something about him that made me nervous. He seemed to be very shallow and destructive. He certainly was not an intellectual and probably did not ponder about life as much as I did. I couldn't help but think he was the type of person who would try to get ahead in life no matter how many people he stepped on in the process. I shook his hand firmly as I greeted him.

"You lookin' for some work?" he asked me.

"I suppose," I answered.

"Bob would like to put together a group to take care of any rebellions," he said. In other words, Capasso wanted to train men to put down any little revolts that occur during the "ghoul hunts" that have been going on from day-one of this whole thing.

"They'll pay you several hundred bucks per week," he said.

"Who will?"

"The state of New York," he answered. "If you're interested, Capasso is holding a meeting at the fire department today at noon. Be there! It's kinda like what we did the other day," he said.

He was controlling. I did not like that in him, or any man for that matter. Nevertheless, I thought about the suggestion. Serving in this "militia" would give me steady employment, enabling me to replace the car I wrecked. Above all, it would satisfy my love for adventure, which was at times insatiable. Hopefully, it would allow me to help Marcia with expenses, or perhaps my own when I eventually got back to my apartment.

"Sasha, dude, I'll think about it, okay?" I answered.

"Okay," he answered in a barely tolerant sort of way. He speedily placed the garbage at the curb and went back to his flat, quickly closing the door to his apartment.

I turned around, took out the garbage from Marcia's household, and put it at the curb. I went back inside. I sat down in my usual spot on the sofa and turned on the television set. Neither Roger nor Marcia were up yet.

The morning was filled with broadcasts that continued to advertise the rescue centers in both the suburban and rural areas. I managed to use one of Marcia's blank videotapes to record the reports as they aired, since I felt the information was pertinent. Although the plague did not spread as rapidly in the country as it did in the cities, some communities such as Evans City, Pennsylvania and Brownsville, Texas were entirely devastated. According to estimates and body counts, Detroit lost nearly 4% of its population to this plague. All in all, over 2,000,000 bodies had been "resurrected" and later "killed" all over the United States. That meant over 2,000,000 Americans had lost their lives and similar ratios were common in most countries overseas.

Many of the nation's most prominent scientists were interviewed by news personalities throughout the day, along with an array of intellectuals including the familiar Rasputin-like scientist, Neil McIntyre.

"I have been informed that the Center for Disease Control down in Atlanta is studying the tissues of ghouls and working to find a cure. We think this is nothing more than a virus. If we can nail it down, we can reverse the process and make sure dead bodies stay 'dead,'" he said to the somber and monotonous man, Michael Burnside.

Others addressed the problem as being the result of harmful radiation from some unknown source. After all, the space probe did return with some sort of fallout from its journey to another world. Scientists in NASA were thinking about sending another probe up to Venus to investigate the area where the first one had landed. Another think tank was working on developing new forms of radioisotopes in cyclotrons to counteract the radiation now prevalent in our atmosphere.

According to the broadcasts, there were others who believed this epidemic was the result of supernatural manifestations. One happened to be a young woman with long dark hair who believed this whole phenomenon was the result of ancient paganism. She sat with a panel of scientists in front of a live studio audience. The spectators and the scientists scoffed at her explanations as she sat there, one leg crossed over the other. Maybe that was the case, but I found the idea foolish as well, and didn't take it very seriously. There had to be a scientific explanation for this whole thing. The supernatural could never be that powerful, if it existed at all. Marcia was finally up and she took a break from cleaning the kitchen to listen to the young woman on the screen.

"I tink dat dis has sometin' to do wit Caribbean magic," she suggested. "Some islands believe in deir own brands of spiritualism, like Voodoo and Santeria." She was Jamaican and therefore subjected to many Caribbean folk explanations. It was interesting to note that I had seen this young woman on the screen on TV before.

I realized that it was almost noon and that it might be a good idea to leave and hear Capasso's proposal. I thought for a while about the whole opportunity of working for the local government. Yes, I would be gainfully employed, but the job entailed putting down any resistance to the authority of the state. In other words, there'd be a lot of lead flying through the air. I could be hit by a bullet, or worse, die. If I died at least I could say that I did it for God and country and would even have a hero's funeral.

Picking up the shotgun I had used the other day, I left the condominium, stepped out to the street, into the cold air. Since Halloween had just passed, I wondered how the supernatural world responded to this whole scenario. Maybe the supernatural world did not truly exist, and perhaps gods, demons, and hobgoblins only lived in the imagination.

On the other side of the street, I saw Sasha Bernstein, wearing the same dark blue sweatshirt and baseball cap, still sporting it backwards.

"How's it goin' buddy?" He asked that same irritating question. The man bothered me to no end. As he approached me, I wanted to hit him.

"Okay, I guess," I responded. I wanted to leave him and get to the meeting as fast as possible. There was tension between the two of us, and I knew we did not get along.

"Are you goin' to the meetin'?" he asked.

"Yeah," I answered.

"We have to take care of all the problem people and I'm glad I can be a part of it," Bernstein commented.

"Good," I said.

He seemed to have a lot of zeal for this whole mission, where I seemed kind of disheartened, particularly over the fact that people were going to die. I needed the money and a little adventure, but this may be too extreme. I did not feel comfortable with Bernstein, and did not speak to him very much. He had a tendency to trump his own accomplishments, which I thought was a type of arrogance and self-absorption I found quite difficult to tolerate.

"You know what city I'm from, Andy?" he asked. I knew I was going to be sick.

"No idea," I answered.

"I'm from Kiev. We're really tough people," he boasted. I was tempted to hurl everything in my stomach.

He went on to tell me that he was raised Jewish in this city, and had to fight other boys for his belongings growing up. His parents had to leave that ex-Soviet republic to escape the rising tide of anti-Semitism that reared its violent head. Bernstein told me that he thought about working with the Russian mafia that operated stealthily out of Brighton Beach in Brooklyn. He decided against it, however, and didn't want to tangle with the law. He was used to violent pursuits and gravitated towards these opportunities.

We walked up the hill, past a few houses and office buildings, to the firehouse on the left. There we saw Capasso, standing with his fists on his hips, ordering people around without mercy or respect. This time he wore a light blue shirt along with dark blue pants and dark boots. He reminded me of a member of the Nazi Gestapo, and the description fit his personality like a glove.

Bernstein and I found our way up to the top of the hill, looking out upon the massive mortuary of New York City. Along with Capasso, there were three other officers and about fifteen other men dressed in plainclothes. They were nothing more than volunteers like Bernstein and myself, wanting glory, excitement, or just plain money. Using his commanding presence, Capasso had us all line up in partial formation in front of the closed overhead doors of the firehouse, which was hard to believe since we were civilians. The guy had colossal gall.

"The puhpose of this whole thing is to form a local militia that will work with federal and state authorities. You are employees of the state and will listen to and serve the state. If you don't like it, you can get out!" he said. He then added that this militia would work to put down any possible internal rebellions.

"Listen up. You're gonna have to wohk with me so that you'll become an effective fighting force. You'll undergo some basic training. We will give you firearms and we'll teach you how to use 'em. You will also be given survival training so that you can live in the woods for a short period of time. If you don't like it, then get out. I don't wanna hear any whinuhs," he said. I felt like I was a Green Beret lost in the jungles of Vietnam, desperately trying to shut down the Ho Chi Minh Trail.

"You guys are gonna have to be trained to kill, or you'll be killed," he stated bluntly.

Looking at his demeanor, it was clear that he enjoyed the dictating and the directing. The man liked to lead, and I bet that he would do it at all cost. I met a younger man, about thirty, whose face was unshaven. He introduced himself.

"My name is Milano. Harry Milano. What's yours?"

"My name is Andy Goering," I said and shook his hand.

Milano lived a few blocks away. He informed me, in a boastful sort of way, that he liked to fix things and repossess cars. Milano was a man with a great number of skills. He told me that his mother had been killed by those things and he had to bring himself to put a slug right into her brain. She was a casualty of war, and we were undoubtedly at war. He wanted revenge on the creatures, caricatures of God's own creation.

For a second, I wondered about the events of the other day. What had happened to McDermott, Amodio, and the other man who helped take the hospital? I decided to ask Capasso. He stood there in front of the police cars, not bothering to look at me as I presented my question.

"Goering, wait till after the briefing. Not now. I'm busy," he said.

Once it was over, I walked up to him and stated the question again. He stood there, lost in paperwork set on the hood of his squad car, making no eye contact. I would have to press it again to force an answer. So I asked the question, somewhat intimidated.

"What happened to them?"

"They died this mornin'," he said. Still, he refused to make eye contact.

"And that's it?" I asked.

"No," he said.

"What happened to them?" I insisted.

"We had to shoot both in the head and we buhned their bodies outside of the rescue station in Sloatsbuhgh." Now I knew. These were clearly casualties of war indeed.

"Report back here tomorrow morning at 8:00," he ordered.

I left windbag Capasso and returned toward Marcia's townhouse, the eye of this storm. I plodded back down the hill in the gray, sullen, still air. I walked into her place and heard activity in the kitchen. Marcia stood over the stove, the weave tied in a tail in back of her head, while she fixed something in pots and pans. It turned out to be chicken flavored in jerk seasoning. Roger and I ate it and found that it was good. After supper, all the blood went to my stomach and I found myself exhausted. There was nothing I could do but go to sleep and stew in my own juices.

The next morning, I got up and left the house to walk down the street in the heavy and still atmosphere that was so eerily silent and dead. I pondered my fate and that of all of mankind. Up ahead, I could see Bernstein walking with his baseball cap sported backwards. He turned the corner, onto the county route, proceeding up the hill to the firehouse amidst the residential houses and office buildings. I followed him at a distance. There was no desire to subject myself to his speech that was laced with arrogant boasts that elevated his importance.

Both of us joined the group that was there already. Milano was present as well. Capasso stood there with his arms folded, looking quite tough and inconsiderate. There was something about Capasso that I did not want to mess with. He had a commanding presence that made me deal with him in a no nonsense type of approach. You could not joke with the man, for he might kill you as soon as he looked at you.

He started the meeting off.

"Okay, sign here," he said as he distributed some sort of document.

"This is the contract. Sign and you'll get six hundred bucks per week."

That wasn't bad. I could certainly pay my rent with it and buy a cheap used car.

"Okay. Gentlemen, line up. You're gonna get govuhnment issued firearms. These have to be returned. Got it?" he said coldly. Everyone got in line as Capasso and the other officers passed out two firearms to each person, a shotgun and a black .45. A few boxes of rounds came with each firearm. Capasso walked around in a commanding, intimidating manner, speaking with words well thought out.

"Behind this firehouse is a yard. It has tah-gets on it. You're gonna play 'Hit the Tah-get.' Got it?"

Capasso led us through the firehouse, past the large red engines and into a yard that terminated into a hillside. The yard was about fifty feet long and sloped upward into the woods. It was here where we would learn how to fire the weapons and become serious marksmen. On the green hillside sat a few targets. We fired our shells at the objects for several hours, and I do have to admit that my marksmanship dramatically improved. However, at times I found myself afraid of the recoil and the sound the rifle made as it was fired, my reaction obvious to those around me.

"What's the mattuh Goering? Afraid of some loud noises?" Capasso asked, rubbing me the wrong way. I hated him for breathing down my neck like that.

I sweated a lot under the pressure, but I had made my commitment, signed my contract, and had to follow through with it even though at times I wanted to pull out. Sometimes I wondered if my sense of adventure was strong enough to take me through all of these upcoming raids. Looking at Bernstein and Milano, I noticed that both men hit the targets accurately and with unusual joy. I think they relished the very thought of the bloodshed and the armed combat that we would eventually partake in.

Capasso made an announcement before we were dismissed.

"Just a word before you go home. You will be on call every day of the week. If you don't show up, you violate the state. If you violate the state, you violate the law. Do I make myself clear?" I nodded in agreement, hating this man with a passion.

The next day I woke up and continued to watch the grim broadcasts that aired on the TV. McIntyre, the somber man with the glasses, and the McLean woman told us the same things about the crisis. They included the whereabouts of the rescue centers, how to kill a ghoul, and how much progress the state, local, and federal authorities were making. It was the same stuff over and over again. Marcia and Roger got together to pray in the dining room as the light from the outside poured in through the window. I overheard them pray for me.

"Dear Jesus," Roger said. "Make it clear to Andy that you're out there." They hoped I would one day give my life to Jesus Christ. I didn't scoff at the idea this time. Roger walked out to the kitchen and fixed some toast. He brought it back into the dining room where he and Marcia devoured it.

Chapter Thirteen: Heat

The phone rang. It was Bernstein on the line.

"How's it goin' buddy?" He asked. It was that same irritating question again, raking across my cerebrum.

"Okay. What's up?" I answered with little enthusiasm.

"Bob wants us up at the firehouse, now. You gonna be there?" he asked.

"Do I have a choice?" I said.

"No."

"What's going on?" I asked.

"There's trouble in Spring Valley."

We had to quell a disturbance that blew up over there. The conversation ended, and a few minutes later Bernstein stopped by and knocked on the door, shocking me out of my fog. I opened the door and let him in.

"Ready to go buddy?" Bernstein asked with an exaggerated grin.

I answered his question with a nod of my head.

"We're praying for you Andy," Roger said from his seat at the table. "Andy, you'll get through this. The Lord is watching out for you."

I reluctantly left the house with Sasha Bernstein, listening to his mouth exalt his own magnitude.

"Bob told me that I was the best shot yesterday. I hit the bull's eye five times!" he ranted.

The whole thing sickened me, but I found I was beginning to develop the stomach to put up with it. We went all the way to the firehouse through the stale and uneventful air, joining Capasso, Milano, and twelve others to find out about the latest situation. Bernstein's tongue was wagging long and hard all the while.

Capasso stood in his normal, no nonsense manner, pacing back and forth like a drill sergeant (and I bet that was what he had in mind).

"Today, we have a group of men in Spring Valley who are hidin' cohpses. They have locked a bunch of ghouls in the basement of their apahtment buildin' and they will not give us the bodies, violating the law. We are gonna have to hit 'em hard with tear gas, and then we'll go in and soften 'em up," Capasso said.

After hearin this I realized I would actually have to storm a building and fire a gun. A burning sensation materialized in my chest as I came to the conclusion that I could be killed. Three police wagons showed up at the firehouse with flashing red lights that spun and spun into infinity. Most of the civilian force, including me, entered the largest vehicle. All wore gasmasks over our heads so we could easily pull them down to protect ourselves from the tear gas that would be used. Milano informed me that the police officers were seated in the other wagon. About thirty men would participate in this raid, and Bernstein expressed his jubilance and enthusiasm over the promise of conflict.

"I can't wait to put a few slugs right between their eyes," he said as he craved bloody excitement. I, on the other hand, craved a paycheck, my love for adventure having waned.

The three vehicles drove along the county route that led to Spring Valley. Since there were no windows, except for the ones on the rear doors of the wagon, I could not tell exactly where we were. My heart burned, and I felt as if I wanted to urinate. Lead was going to fly, and I could be killed, which meant that I would never see my mother, sister, Marcia, or Roger ever again. Insecurity abounded in waves, and I had to stifle it to maintain the appearance of being in control. If I didn't look like I was in control, everybody would think that I was weak.

The wagons stopped somewhere in Spring Valley. Two officers opened the back doors of the wagon and everyone subordinately got out.

"Fall into formation now!" Capasso ordered with his booming voice. We all got behind several cars that were parked in front of the three-story apartment complex sitting next to a basketball court.

Another officer stood in back of the line of armed men squawking through a bullhorn. He was a black man, dressed in a dark blue police uniform, and he spoke in a language that sounded like French, which I guessed to be French Creole. The people in the complex were mostly Haitian, and I could see their faces and the barrels of their guns in the windows. I felt the urge to vomit and urinate.

"Turn over the bodies and no one will be hurt. Turn the bodies over now!" The Haitian officer said in English. The Haitians in the windows did nothing. Tension continued to burn in my breast.

Milano was on one side of me, and Bernstein was on the other. "They think being dead is sacred. Too bad being dead is just being dead," Milano said with a smirk. Apparently, the locals were stashing ghouls in the cellar of the complex. One of the neighbors learned about it and tipped off the police. The authorities believed that the building had about fifteen armed men in it, men who had nothing left to do but stand and fight.

"Turn over the bodies or we will not hesitate to use force. At the count of ten, we will ask you to come out with your hands up and you will lay down your weapons. No one," the Haitian officer continued, "will be hurt or arrested. Just cooperate. That's all we ask."

He counted from ten downward. Every number fell from his lips and spilled on the green lawn in front of the complex.

"These guys are idiots. Don't they realize that we outnumber them?" Milano said.

"They're too stupid to let live," Bernstein laughed. I said nothing. The countdown continued. Everyone pulled their masks down over their faces to prepare for the eventual assault.

"Three," the Haitian cop said.

"Two," the tension hung in the air with the nervous expectation of the coming conflict. The men inside showed no signs of cooperating. The tops of their heads could still be seen in the windows, reminding me of unmoving stones.

"One!" the Haitian officer said through the bullhorn. We fastened our masks as tear gas canisters were launched into the windows, shattering the panes. The police and militia waited only about a minute to let the gas take effect.

"Okay!" the Haitian officer said. "Take the building!"

Bernstein and Milano got up from their positions with their firearms. I followed them with the nagging thought that I could die at any second! At this point, I felt like I was in the French trenches of World War I, storming the German lines.

Shots rang out from the windows of the apartment building. It was less than I expected, and I guessed that the tear gas immobilized most of the men inside. To my right, as we rushed the complex, one of our militia went down in a hail of bullets. I fired my rifle at one of the windows in response. Some of the men took the front entrance and smashed the casements with the stocks of their rifles. I followed about ten men into the entrance of the building. We ended up standing in a large vestibule, trying to get our bearings. Ahead, through the smoky haze, I saw a dimly lit stairwell that seemed all too inviting. A shot rang out from the dominating clouds of confusion. Bernstein took aim with his weapon and fired it. A man, who was hiding inside of the stairwell, collapsed in the entryway. He was either dead or wounded.

A number of us went over to investigate the body. We found that it was a black male, most likely Haitian, hit in the neck by Bernstein's barrage. His eyes were coated with a lifeless glaze, and it became obvious that the man was deceased, but we had to make sure that he did not revive. I pulled out my .45 and fired it into his skull, looking away as I did so. Blood splattered across the walls.

Another shot rang out from above, somewhere in the stairwell that ascended into the dark unknown. I looked up and saw a Haitian fellow standing over us two flights up, holding a revolver and a handkerchief over his mouth. Milano, Bernstein, and I discharged our weapons at the man. He fell over the railing and landed with a dull thud on the stairs in front of us. Like the other man before him, he was also dead and completely out of our misery. We had to put a slug into his cranium to make sure that he did not become a ghoul. I was beginning to loathe this.

The group I was with went up the three flights of stairs. At the top of the stairway was a door leading to a hallway. Bernstein opened it. Five of us stood in the doorway, trying to determine if the murky corridor was clear. There was no sign of activity. Then, a child's rubber ball innocently rolled out from an open doorway into the cloudy hallway. The silhouette of a man's head and torso appeared out from behind the opened door. In the haze, I could see the man raise his rifle in blunt defiance!

BOOOM! A shotgun went off. We ducked down into the stairwell. Bernstein kneeled to the side of the doorway that led to the hall, crouched down and stuck his gun into the corridor. BOOOM! Another shotgun blast discharged! Bernstein withdrew into the stairwell. I took my pistol, went to the doorway, and extended my head slightly into the corridor, tear gas still floating about. I let off two rounds at the attacker behind the door, unsure if I hit my mark or not. Milano pointed his rifle at the door and opened fire upon the attacker. Bernstein joined in, and we all filled the door with bullets. The man fell out on the floor lifelessly. He was dead.

We ran up to the corpse and realized we had hit him in both the torso and in the side of the cranium. There was no need to put a bullet through his skull, since there was one already there. The five of us had to now make sure the apartment complex was not harboring any more problem people.

We checked out the flat where the man was hiding. We found a twelve year-old-girl with cornrows sitting on the kitchen floor with her back up against the cabinets, looking dazed and uncertain. The man, whose body was now dead in the hallway, may have been her father. There was a baby lying in a crib in one of the bedrooms, asleep. She must have been the man's other child. There was no mother here. We left the children alone and abandoned. Milano, Bernstein, two others, and I investigated the rest of the apartments in the hallway, but we encountered no resistance. A single barking dog stood in the doorway to one of the apartments, causing a ruckus. Bernstein wanted to put a slug in its brain, but I told him we had seen enough bloodshed for the day.

Later, all of us met in front of the complex. The raid proved to be a success. All fifteen of the suspected perpetrators were either captured or killed. Seventeen ghouls were found confined in a storage area in the basement. All of them were shot in the head, and their bodies were taken out and destroyed in an all-consuming bonfire inthe street.

It was not all fun and games though. Two of the men were killed in the assault. Also, the ghouls bit two more of the men as they were being rounded up in the cellar, and their wounds bled severely. It seems as if most of the people who had been bitten could expect to live no more than three days before the infection got to them and completely shut them down. Once they died, they would return as undead corpses. This whole experience was not pleasant by any means whatsoever, and the expressions on the faces of the Haitian population were ones of solemn loss. A gut feeling told me that this reaction was not good and there would be problems later on.

The next week, things began to return to normal as the crisis wound down a bit. I finally had the money to buy a cheap used compact, and did so, enjoying my newfound mobility. We only had to stage one raid, near the Mahwah, New Jersey border. It was not quite as involved as the one in Spring Valley. We surrounded the two-story house and fired a few tear gas canisters into the windows. The young couple inside, of Italian-American extraction, walked out with their hands up, throwing their guns to the ground. After the investigation of the house we found four ghouls in the basement, and all were destroyed. I wondered how they could constantly put their lives in danger like that. Perhaps it was due to the irrationality that lurked deep within the human subconscious, something refusing to listen to reason that confined their reaction to absurdity.

Chapter Fourteen: The Days Gone By

The day after the raid near Mahwah, New York State decided to lift the curfew. Everybody could go back to his or her home and the buses would run again on a regular schedule. Things were returning back to normal, but with some constraints. People had to be in their homes by dusk. Roger returned to his apartment to mop up the situation with his relatives and bury his parents. For him, it was an end of an era. Marcia's mother came up from Flatbush and moved in again. I called my mom and my sister, telling them about my adventures here in Rockland.

"I'm so glad you're okay," my mom said.

"Thanks," I responded.

"Andy, I don't want you putting your life in jeopardy all the time. I want you to quit."

"Mom, I can't do that. I'm thirty-five years old and I have to live my own life. I appreciate your concern but I have to make my own decisions. If I can't make my own decisions, I feel incompetent. Besides, I need an income. What else am I gonna do?"

"You can learn how to drive a truck. They still need drivers," she said.

"I have no idea how to do that, and I don't really wanna do that. I'd rather just do what I have been doing for the past several weeks. Whether my life is in jeopardy or not." She didn't push the matter anymore. I wished my dad were here in times like these. He passed away over ten years ago, just after the end of the first Gulf War. Perhaps he could have dispensed some much-needed advice, but I guess we were all on our own.

I had been on my own for over ten years, since I had finished my undergraduate studies. After graduating with a history degree, I had moved away from Rome, hoping to find more promise in Rockland County, near the New York City region. Finally, after passing in and out of jobs, I decided upon getting a Master in history, which I earned at CUNY.

Periodically, I had been teaching at a local community college, but only as an adjunct. Nevertheless, I decided to take a semester off and work on house construction, in order to strengthen my ability to work with my hands and become a well-rounded individual. For the past several weeks I had done that, and now I wondered, in light of the present chaos, if I would ever teach again.

The crisis seemed to have let up. There had been no reports of ghouls attacking anyone in the county for the past few days. Perhaps our lives would revert back to the state of normalcy I craved. Still, I had a nagging suspicion that this was only the calm before the storm. It was almost as if this problem would blow up once again, in a way worse than ever before. When the problem hits, it would be difficult to stop — extremely difficult.

For some reason, the dreams I had about the gray expanse ceased. However, in one dismal phantasm, I saw the human race eliminated by hundreds of millions of souls; it was represented by a dark shadow that enveloped the globe. I awoke from this dream disturbed, scared. I found myself kneeling before God and praying, unusual since I regarded myself as an agnostic. Who else had the power to change this situation? Who else could I rely upon? If that dream were to come true, I wouldn't want to face the reality it pointed to.

Normal network television had returned. Periodically, the stations would give us reports on how the authorities were doing at finding a solution. They also covered the progress other nations were making. It appeared that China and the Russian Federation had the worst problems. The North Atlantic Treaty Organization was putting together a force to help the Russians deal with the crisis, but I wondered how successful the whole thing would be.

One day, I sat down in front of the television in my usual spot on the sofa. Roger stood in the kitchen doorway eating a bowl of cereal. The somber man with the glasses appeared once again and told us of a development in an

African country called Namibia. Something unusual was happening there.

"Namibians of German ancestry have barricaded themselves into a nuclear complex near Windhoek and will not let anyone in. The United Nations has asked them to leave the complex for several days now to no avail. Namibians have erected a wall around a number of buildings that make up this research facility and have defended it heavily with machine guns. It has been rumored that some Russian and South African nuclear physicists have taken up residence there and many fear that they may be manufacturing nuclear weapons. The secretary general is now trying to make a decision with the help of the Security Council whether to use force," Burnside said.

"I had no idea that there were Germans in Africa," Roger remarked.

"I learned that in my undergraduate years," I quipped with smug astuteness.

Somehow, I believed that the U.N. would be able to do nothing about the situation. They were working on too many resolutions and had their hands full. If the Namibian government couldn't do anything about their own crises, then the United Nations would have no power over them.

McLean went on and gave us another dismal report without emotion. She stated that a number of villages and small cities in Vietnam had been irrevocably eradicated and had become haunts for ghouls. The government had to abandon vast tracts of the country and withdraw to protect itself. It seemed that many nations had trouble organizing effective fighting forces to deal with the crisis. If there was organization, perhaps they would have been able to control the problem. No one, it seemed, could establish any sense of cooperation. The governments of some nations had even gone so far as to discuss the use of atomic weapons to wipe out the cold and unfeeling creatures that wandered their cities.

Another couple of weeks passed by, and I packed up and went back to live in my apartment. Thanksgiving rolled around, and I celebrated it with Roger and the Clarke's. Marcia's mom, who happened to be tall and overweight, cooked us a turkey as well as stuffing, rice, peas, and fried plantains! There were many prayers expressing gratitude to God that evening.

Thanksgiving came and went and I strolled back to my apartment, constantly ascending and descending the discordant stairs, pacing off the lonely energy I had. The snow had covered the hard green ground several times in the space of a few days. Over time, I felt a bit lonely in my flat and found myself calling up Marcia, going over to her townhouse and joining her for dinner. Roger also partook with us, as we devoured another jerk chicken supper. It was great, but I still missed my family Upstate and desperately wanted to see them.

One day, near Christmas, I approached Capasso at the Southold Police Station to see about taking next weekend off. It would have been good to visit my family, so I stepped into the office to find Capasso sitting at his desk lost in a mound of paperwork. He endlessly filled out forms, and he hardly noticed someone had walked into the room.

"Officer Capasso?"

"Yeah," he muttered, his eyes still on his work.

"I need some time off," I stated.

"When?" he asked. Still he would not look at me.

"The weekend before Christmas."

"Can't do it," he said. My heart was sinking.

Capasso never bothered to look at me the whole while. He sat there at his neatly arranged desk, inundated with forms. He was a cold man who never married and was satisfied with having sex with a few live-in girlfriends. He did not communicate with his immediate family much. Bob Capasso was a man who lived his life unattached to anyone but himself. It was a form of selfishness, or arrogance; however, I wasn't going to take "no" for an answer.

"Look, I may never get a chance to see my family again. I would like to have the time off," I demanded. Capasso looked at me for a second with a stern expression.

"You know we might need you. Can't let it happen."

"If you don't give me the time off, you're gonna have serious problems with morale. You know that," I insisted.

"Goering, if you continue to be insubohdinate, you will be on my list. I'm not going to put up with your mouth much longer. I'll give you forty-eight hours off and that's it." True, he coldly granted my request, but he did give it to me. I got what I wanted and was happy.

The next Friday, I left Rockland County before noon in order to get to Rome before darkness fell. The traffic was light now, but I knew it would get heavier around 3:00 pm and choke the Thruway. Businesses were forced to let their employees go before the fall of night, in accordance with the dusk-to-dawn curfew. Looking at the scenery from the Thruway, I noticed that not much had changed since the crisis began.

The clouds hung heavy in the early winter sky, indicating that snow was most likely coming tonight. It would blanket the gray and brown landscape in a virgin white carpet, hoping to make the world clean and harmless. Everything looked so cold and expressionless as the wind whipped up the autumn leaves that laid upon the ground. After a couple of hours I found myself on the banks of the Mohawk River, where I noticed the community of Amsterdam sitting on a hillside, motionless without activity; it was a monolithic mill town determined to die. I wondered how much the contagion had spread in that community. It was funny how I once knew a girl who lived there, who had long since moved away to the Deep South to get married and have a new life. It made me wonder how she was doing now.

The open space along the Thruway proved to be devoid of life, except some blackbirds circling in the still gray skies above. Depression hung in the air as the surroundings had little to offer, save for impending death and destruction. It was almost as if the heavy gray iron sky was descending to the earth, threatening to crush all beneath it.

I arrived at my mom's home, nestled in the rear of a housing development near the edge of a small woods. I parked in the driveway. Darkness had crept up on me, and I found myself staring into the setting sun behind me. I climbed out of the car and walked into the garage where my mother affectionately met me at the door.

"Andy, I'm so glad you're home!" she said.

"Love you, Mom. Good to see you," I said as I gave her a hug and kiss. She was happy to see that her son was safe and hopefully sound.

"There's some food in the kitchen, waiting," she said.

She led me through the door and into the kitchen, where a dinner of fried chicken, rice, and salad was set upon the table against the wall. I was hungry from the long trip that took me away from the crisis near New York City, and I ate the meal eagerly.

"Andy, I really am so glad you're home," she said with tears in her eyes as she sat across the table from me. Since she had lost my father, I had become very precious to her.

"What would your father do now if he was still alive?" she asked. I had no answer for that.

Being brought up in this house, my memories began to drift back to my childhood, particularly to the times when I attended the little Episcopalian church that was down the nearby highway. Those were the days I used to believe that there was a God above me and my future was full of hope. I had gone through too much inconsequence since then to believe that. I wanted to return to the days when I did believe. I needed to trust in something greater than myself. I went to bed that night, staring at the ceiling with no answers to this great enigma of life.

The next morning, I got up and read the account of the Great Flood in the Bible and wondered what its significance was. Could God choose to eliminate the human race again, like he did so many thousands of years ago? The question haunted me as it attached itself to my heart and mind. I got my clothes on and strolled around the woods behind the house, staring at all the dead leaves protruding through the blanket of snow that covered the earth.

When I was younger, I had played "guns" with the neighborhood kids here amongst these trees. We formed armies equipped with plastic machine guns and fought each other in endless battles of great fun and laughter. Those days were gone, and the innocence of childhood had left with them. The surroundings depressed me and I decided to go back into the house.

Once I was in the house, I phoned up Marcia's place to see how things had transpired.

"Hello?" A man's voice asked. It was Roger.

"What's up, dude?" I said.

"Andy, how's it goin' brother?"

"Everything's cool."

"How's your mom?"

"She's glad I'm home."

"Do you think you'll give up the force?" he asked. My mother was in the next room. This was not the time to talk about this.

"Roger, I can't speak about this now. This isn't the place." He dropped the whole subject right then and there.

"How's Marcia?" I asked.

"Guess she's doing okay. You wanna talk to her?"

"Please, it would be great."

There was a pause and I heard some stirring in the background, then I heard her footsteps over the phone.

"Hey Andy, how you?" she asked.

"Everything's going great," I said to her. "How's your mom?"

"She okey and doin' fine."

We went on to discuss the affairs of our siblings and extended families, and the tone of the conversation began to wind down.

"Andy, take ceere of yourself. Come back soon. Can't weet till you get back," she said.

The gab session ended as we hung up the somewhat reliable horn. I was sad for some reason; maybe it was because I didn't really want Marcia to leave me. After talking to her, I wished so badly to have my own family to hold and protect. In some ways, Roger, Marcia, and her mother had become my family. Perhaps someday the circumstances would change and things would move in my direction.

Later on in the afternoon, as the sun began to near the horizon, I went to see my sister, who lived up the road with her husband in a despondent trailer park. Walking into their home, I decided to play video games with my niece and nephew who were both sitting on the floor in front of the TV before the large bay window. A Christmas tree was in the corner of the living room, covered with sparkling tinsel. I enjoyed it immensely, losing myself in both their laughter, and in my own.

For several minutes I talked to my sister, who sat down at the kitchen table that was more like a countertop, layered in formica.

"Davey and Sarah are doing well. They have a lot of school to make up. We lost time because of the crisis." My sister went into no more details about the circumstances at hand. She just told me how well both of her kids used to perform in school and how smart each of them are. Guess she dealt with the whole thing by not bringing it up. My sister loved denial.

I left the inside of the mobile home to find out how my brother-in-law was doing. As I noted the surrounding mobile homes in the park about me, I located Pete, my sister's husband. He stood there in a light jacket, wearing a baseball cap tinkering with his car, drinking a cold beer, seemingly content in the circumstances.

"Hey Pete, how're you doin' on the car?" I asked.

"It's goin' real good. Will have her runnin' in an hour," he said. He apparently had lost himself in an incessant number of car repair sessions. All of us coped with the crisis differently, hoping it would one day go away.

Eventually, I said "goodbye" to everyone and embraced my sister just outside of the mobile home. She started to cry.

"Andy," she said as she began to sob. "Do you think they're going to find a way to stop this?"

"I dunno. Not sure. Have no clue. Sorry Missy, I have to go. Have too much to do," I told her. Not able to deal with her emotions, I just walked away, got into my car, and drove off, leaving the rural trailer park. I wasn't used to coping with feelings.

The next day, my mom and I went out for Sunday brunch at a restaurant near a golf course. The food ran over, stocked to the brim, filled with sausage links, pancakes, and sliced melons, all displayed on an aluminum buffet table. It was a feast before a famine, and I ate like a homeless man in a soup kitchen. My mom just continued to talk about everyday occurrences she had with her friends, denying the crisis like my sister had done.

"How's horseback riding?" I asked.

"We've been out only twice since this whole thing began," she said, appearing very solemn as she ate a piece of sliced melon.

"How's Barbara Stuyvesant doing?" I asked, referring to a woman my mother rode with often.

"She's okay, but her husband beat her a few times in the past couple of weeks," she said.

"Is she thinking of getting a divorce?" I asked.

"She might file papers early in the coming year," she answered, downing half a glass of orange juice.

If I were married to a guy that did that, I would want a divorce too. My mother and I continued to banter about friends and personal developments for the rest of the meal amidst the noise of the eating-place.

Both of us went home and hung out in the kitchen, sitting at the table under the overhanging lamp, sipping coffee. We heard a knock on the door. It was one of our neighbors, George Ambrose, a balding forty-something year-old man who wore glasses. My mother opened up the door and let him step into the kitchen, where he leaned up against one of the cabinets.

"Did you hear what happened last night?" He directed the question to both my mom and me.

"No. What's happening?" I asked.

"The cops broke into a house just north of Lee Center. Dey kept some of the bodies in the basement and there was a number of arrests, but that's not all."

"Yeah?" I said. My mother was seated down at the kitchen table, looking at a magazine, not participating.

"Dere were reports that some ghouls were wanderin' around in the hills and the country folk weren't disposin' of them. Dey were sick of the poor treatment that the authorities were givin' those zombies, like shooting them up and burnin' up their dead relatives, so they started to protest. The police were wanderin' around in the hills up there for several hours, shootin' those things and burnin' them up," Ambrose went on.

"Did they finally take care of the whole thing?" I asked.

"No. Some of the locals fought back with their guns. There were a number of gun battles that went on up there. Some of the police were killed and all the cops had to withdraw. It was pretty bad," Ambrose answered. "Well, gotta go. Have to blow the drive." Ambrose turned, left the house, and went back out to the empty street, his bald head disappearing from view. I was reminded that I had to go soon as well.

In order to observe the curfew, I would have to leave before the sun went down.

"Mom, I have to go to work tomorrow. I'm on call. I gotta leave."

She looked rather sad as she sat there at the kitchen table, sipping black coffee. She stood up, her face turned downward. I didn't know what else to do but embrace my mother as I had done my sister. Mom began to cry, appearing slightly agitated.

"Andy, I want you to stay to protect me and your sister!" she demanded.

"Mom, I can't. I have a life to live down in Rockland. All of my friends are there, and I have to go to work," I responded.

She continued to resort to weeping.

"Mom, I love you. I'm sorry, but I have to be on my own. It's important. I feel inadequate living under you. If I live with you, I will feel as if I can't make it on my own."

My mom looked at me silently and waved goodbye; I returned her wave. I got into my car and noticed her staring at me rather woefully. Turning the key in the ignition, I started it up to make the long journey back to my other home. As I drove back to the hazy metropolis, more of that dark snow fell from the heavy iron sky, darkness descending like a curtain upon the land. As I got home, I found Rockland County devoid of activity. Everyone was resolutely shut up inside, trying to keep safe from the dangerous world around them. As I walked up the creaking staircase to my apartment, I began to think about the God that I had so blatantly and adamantly denied for years. I needed to trust that someone would help me understand and categorize the insane cascade of events around me.

Christmas Eve had now arrived. The strain of not believing in anything but myself began to take its toll upon my restless and lost spirit. I wanted so badly to be part of a community of people who believed in a little bit more than the material world. Clearly, I was searching for something supernatural to get me through this storm.

I got a phone call that night. I picked it up to find that it was Roger.

"You got home alright?" Roger asked.

"Safe and sound," I answered.

"You never know in times like these," he calmly stated. "Marcia and I are going to church. You wanna come along?"

I had nothing better to do, and it might keep me occupied.

"Sure. What time?" I asked.

"In about forty-five minutes, pick you up?"

"Yeah. Sounds good."

Just like that, Marcia and Roger invited me to church. From the front window of my apartment of isolation, I saw the headlights of Roger's car pull into the driveway next to the gnarled maple. I got into his car and the vehicle wound through the suburban snow-covered streets of Rockland County. They took me to an independent charismatic church, located somewhere in New City, and I noticed that all the pews were filled. I guess I was not the only one looking for meaning in life today. Maybe there are really no atheists in foxholes after all.

I spent Christmas Day with Marcia and her mom, and we laughed under the false boughs of their decorated Christmas tree. Roger came over and made a cameo for a few minutes, then left to spend some time with his relatives. I found myself laughing but still insecure in light of the crisis at hand. It was time to go, and I did not want to leave the company of the young woman and her mother. I hated the suffocating loneliness of my apartment, and I wanted to avoid it so badly. I disliked the seclusion and the isolation it provided, as it gave me no one to connect with. I was on call for the latter half of Christmas Day, and there was nothing that I could do about it.

I walked up the stairs, back into the dismal apartment, and turned on the light, finding that illumination chased the dark shadows, reducing the blackness of isolation. Not having anything concrete to accomplish, I sat down on my sofa and turned the television set on to allow my mind to vegetate.

The phone rang, shattering the inherent despondency of the apartment. It was Capasso on the line, and I had to prepare myself for his discourteous conduct.

"Andy, we need you tonight."

"Okay. What time?"

"In about an hour, can you be there?" he asked.

"Of course," I said. Did I have much of a choice?

"Be there," he said.

He did not seem to care if I was having a good time or not. Capasso let me know that the police got wind that a group of men were taking dead bodies and placing them in an old cannery. The cannery was located near the abandoned railroad tracks in Southold. It was imperative that I go to the station to be briefed about the development. Agitation in my chest stirred around and around.

Chapter Fifteen: Terror at the Cannery

I got in my car with my police-issued shotgun and proceeded over to the station. I showed up to find Milano, Bernstein, Roberts, and several others present, standing there outside in the parking lot of the firehouse with their hands in their pockets. It appeared that our ranks had been growing smaller as time went on.

Capasso came to the front of the group, striking his pose of dominance. "They're takin' ghouls and puttin' them in the back of a truck and transpohtin' them to the old cannery, hidin' them in the cellar there," Capasso explained.

"Who's doing this?" Roberts asked.

"Some guy named Bill Lafayette, he owns a moving business." Capasso instructed that we would first visit Lafayette's home, and if he was not there, we would have to wait near the cannery for him to show up.

A number of us piled into squad cars and journeyed to Lafayette's home in the southern tip of Southold. Once we arrived at Lafayette's house, Capasso pounded on the door, stirring the people within, a number of us rag-tag individuals standing behind him.

A thin, diminutive woman with long straggly hair answered the door. I assumed she was Lafayette's wife.

Capasso blurted rather bluntly, "We're lookin' for William Lafayette. He's been smuggling bodies around."

"He's not here," she said.

"Wheah is he then?" Capasso asked.

"I donno," she answered.

"Your husband is in violation of federal laws for leavin' his home," Capasso said. Lafayette's wife looked nervously down at Capasso's finely polished shoes and said nothing.

Capasso scanned the yard and checked down the street. Lafayette's truck was not in sight. It was clear that Lafayette was gone, in violation of the curfew. With that,

Capasso ordered us into the squad cars to wait for a new game plan.

"Okay, we're goin' to the old cannery," Capasso firmly stated, not letting anything move him.

Six of us drove several blocks to the northern end of Southold, where the cannery sat in a wooded area by abandoned railroad tracks that skirt the town. We took the county route that runs through the center of the town, finding another road that cut to the left and disappeared into the trees in front of the cannery. Here, the road terminated at an old building. We had to park the squad cars some distance away so Lafayette would not see or suspect anything.

The group of men whom I was with walked down the road which led to the unused cannery. I realized that I had been here before, when the ghouls first chased me through the grove of trees. There were six of us on this lethal adventure, and the others were either sent back home or were waiting at Lafayette's house, hoping that he might show up and make this whole thing a little easier. He thought half a dozen would be enough.

I took my flashlight out and turned it on to make sure that it was working.

"What're you doin' with that Goering?" Capasso asked.

"We need to see," I said.

"Use that and the whole neighbohhood will know that we're back here," he stated. I handed my flashlight to Milano. His own was faint and almost dead.

We had to stumble in the dark, unable to see exactly where we were going. Ahead was the old factory that was once a productive food canning plant. Back in the early 1900s, this plant was the mainstay of the economy in this village. It was a square, four-story building whose windows were filled with panes of broken glass, the paint peeling from the outside walls. It was deserted except for the possibility of ghouls confined to its cold, empty basement.

Since trees surrounded the area, Capasso had Milano, Roberts, and me wait on one side of the road, under the cover of the naked snaking branches, where we remained trapped by the frigid black sewage of night. Bernstein, Capasso and an officer named Vega were on the other side in the trees closer to the old cannery.

We waited for at least an hour in the bitter cold, and still there was no truck. All of us just stayed in the lifeless woods, our eyes fastened upon the old brick building that seemed to emanate nothing but death and despair. The three of us stood with our hands in our pockets, watching our wisps of breath materialize in the chilly night air. Another half-an-hour had passed, and still nothing. We heard an animal pattering through the woods, traveling low to the ground.

"Maybe we should walk into the mill ourselves and check the whole thing out," Milano said.

"Nah. Capasso gave us specific orduhs. We can't do that," Roberts answered.

He was right. We could do nothing but sit and wait behind the bare trees which were firmly rooted in the soil. Milano, leaning up against a naked maple, lit a cigarette and took a drag. I drifted into thought about some situation comedies I saw when I was younger, and laughed to myself to pass the time away. Roberts began to sneeze but quickly stifled it. The thought of putting your life at risk did not help ease the tension.

Finally, the sound of a truck rumbled down the isolated road. The glow of the few streetlights enabled us to see its shadow as it approached. We heard it accelerate as it sped through the area we were guarding, and then brake to slow down, parking in front of the brick building.

A minute or two later, a tall, thin man got out of the truck that was conspicuously marked: "Lafayette Moving." That man must have been William Lafayette himself. Two other men in heavy jackets got out of the cab to assist him in what most likely would be a breach of the law.

They opened up the rear overhead door that led to the bed of the truck. The two men immediately climbed in and pushed four objects out through the open portal. The objects sat on the snow-covered ground but weren't stationary. Something was inside each of them, and they moved around, practically rolling about. I came to the realization that there were four ghouls sealed up in those bags. They were the undead, struggling to get out and destroy their benefactors without appreciation!

One of the men got on top of the loading docks and opened up the overhead door that led to the inside of the mill. He pulled out a large metal ramp that was lying on the floor and fastened it to the edge of the loading dock. The ramp led to the ground. He walked through the doorway and into the shadow-laden interior. A few seconds later the man emerged from the darkness with a cart that had two tires and wheeled it down the ramp to the truck. It would serve as an unlawful tool.

The three men picked up the struggling bodies as they groaned and growled underneath the bags and set them in the cart. Then, that same man disappeared, accompanied by the tall, thin man, leaving the last person with the truck alone. The solitary figure stood there with his hands in his pockets, almost as if he didn't know what to do. The other two emerged about five minutes later and picked up the last remaining body, placing it into the cart. Once again, the tall, thin man disappeared within the shadows of the cannery, leaving one guy alone near the truck. The lone figure leaned up against the vehicle, smoking a cigarette and exhaling fumes into the air, not suspecting anything. I predicted they would be back in a couple of minutes.

A cigarette lighter flashed on and off in the trees where Capasso and Bernstein were. It was the signal we were waiting for. While the man stood preoccupied with his smoke, Roberts, Milano and I ran across the road to the side of the building, totally avoiding detection. We stood against the decadent and silent structure, waiting to take the men that would be near the truck in a matter of moments.

"Okay! Freeeeze!" Capasso ordered.

The three of us walked out with guns drawn to find Capasso, Bernstein, and Vega pointing their guns at the men, their hands up in the air in submission. The men who had been taken prisoner looked nervous and frightened.

"Okay, where are the cohpses that you took? They are the property of the United States govuhnment. What you did is un-American," Capasso declared to them.

"We put the bodies downstairs," the tall man said.

"Where are they?" Capasso demanded.

Lafayette had no choice but to show us. Capasso had Vega, Bernstein, and Roberts watch the other two, while Lafayette led the rest of us through the garage and into the shadows of the cannery. We turned on our flashlights and the light illuminated the dark interior of the building, enabling us to see. We saw old rows of abandoned machinery amidst dirty cobwebs that obscured the filthy ceilings. Lafayette led us over to a conspicuous rectangular hole in the floor. As we neared, we found it to be a stairway lined with walls made of cinderblocks that led into the antiquated cellar that housed those forbidden things. At the bottom of the wooden steps was a solid metal door that was locked, serving to contain the living pestilence beyond it.

"They're in there!" Lafayette said as he pointed to the closed door.

"Unlock it, scumbag!" Capasso ordered.

Lafayette took the jingling keys from his pocket and descended the stairs. He thrust the keys in through the slot in the doorknob.

"I have no idea what's on the other side of this," Lafayette said nervously.

"Open it!" Capasso dictated.

He opened it and the door swung away from us into the forbidden darkness. Lafayette backed away up the stairs, trying to avoid what was on the other side of the solid barrier. We heard shuffling emanating from the black void beyond. I began to sweat again and perspiration trickled down my temples despite the chill of this forsaken building.

In the middle of Capasso's beam was a horrid gray face with unkempt white hair! A thing in a tattered dress made its way up the stairs with its arm outstretched. It let out a horrible growl from a bloodied, twisted face that disturbed me. Capasso unholstered his pistol, aimed it and fired. The creature fell to the floor and then ceased all of its activity.

"Goering, you come with me. Harry, you guard Lafayette," Capasso ordered.

Both of us stepped into the tomb-like cellar. We found it dark and windowless, full of dusty boxes and old hot water heaters, a resting place for the discarded. The two of us suddenly heard a clamor to our right. Capasso was the only one with a flashlight, and he panned his beam in that direction. We found three of the gray-skinned things limping towards us in the darkness, bearing hideous expressions, seeking our annihilation!

"Milano!" Capasso yelled. "We're gonna need backup. ON THE DOUBLE, MILANO!"

I heard Milano say something, but I was not sure what. The creatures continued to make their way towards us, surrounding us like vultures around a corpse. We heard more noises from a room or passageway in back of the stairway. A number of the things were in this basement and were converging upon us from all different sides! I pointed my weapon at the ones that were closing in to neutralize the threat. Both Capasso and I discharged our firearms into their torsos, just wasting what little ammunition we had. They continued on, groping for us, groaning and growling, trying to turn us into their demented nourishment. Capasso took his pistol and fired it into the nearest one's skull, sending it to the ground, but there were too many of them.

In the ensuing chaos, one managed to knock the flashlight from Capasso's grip. He loudly let out a curse that echoed into the emptiness of the cellar. The flashlight illuminated the boxes in the corner. I heard them around me, moving in, groaning and shuffling. My chest burned as I tried to figure out where they were in the enveloping darkness. I could hear them, perhaps only a few feet away, growling and making horrible noises, reaching out for me, trying to rip the flesh from my bones! One extended its hands and took my neck, emitting a bestial sound. Another approached me, hobbling very close, seeking to take me apart. I still had my rifle in my hand, and I held it by the barrel, swinging it wildly like a club, trying to hit the creatures that attacked me! The cold hands released my neck as I struck one of them in the chest with the stock of the rifle.

The beam of Capasso's flashlight was still frozen upon the stack of boxes, and I realized that he could not pick it up. I heard him shout at the top of his lungs, cursing loudly like a truck driver in overwhelming fear. He fired his gun, and the echo resounded in this empty tomb-like chamber.

One creature grabbed my throat from behind with disgustingly cold claws. I swung my rifle with all my might and sent it to the floor! In the glow of Capasso's beam I saw another advancing forward! As it neared, I aimed my rifle at it and fired. The head seemed to shatter as I hit it point blank, sending it to its knees. It fell forward and did not move.

Capasso fired off another round.

"MILANO! WHERE ARE YOU?" he shouted.

I heard more of the ghouls growling in the darkness, starting to surround us like sharks moving in for the kill! It was here where I knew I was in the struggle of my life. Capasso swore again as he shot another of the things. Finally he managed to pick up the flashlight. The light's beam swung wildly as Capasso tried to figure out what was going on in the smothering chaos. One of the creatures came up on my left. It grabbed my arm and growled as it tried to take a bite out of it. There was no shred of decency left in the ghoul!

"Where's Milano?" Capasso yelled.

I took the rifle and hit the creature that grabbed my arm, freeing my limb! Two were behind me, and I swung around to face them. I could see them well as Capasso's beam illuminated the walking nightmares before me. I took my rifle and fired it again. The one nearest to me jerked suddenly as I emptied a shell into its chest. I had wasted a lot of rounds, and I did not know how many more I had.

Footsteps bounded down the steps as two men rushed into this forsaken death trap. It was Milano and Bernstein. They had flashlights, and their beams permitted me to determine that there were nearly a dozen of these things down here. They fired their weapons at the creatures, and they hit their marks, the remaining creatures falling everywhere.

Milano stood near the stairs, firing towards my right, swearing in a panic. The beam of his flashlight suddenly pointed to his feet and found a gray-skinned creature on the floor grabbing his ankle. It widened its maw to rip into his flesh. I walked over and hit it in the head with the stock of my rifle while Milano yelled in a fit of rage. He walked up to the nearest ghoul and put a shotgun to its head. He fired and the ghoul ceased functioning, bone and blood splattering about. I took my rifle, aimed it at the cranium of the one at Milano's ankle. I pulled the trigger and its skull broke apart into nothingness.

One approached me on my left and tried to reach out and take my arm. I fired my shotgun. Nothing happened. There was no loud sound and my gun had no power. I was out of ammo! The thing lashed out with its claw. Bernstein had his shotgun and fired two shells into it, screaming at the top of his lungs! The thing ceased and went to the dark, cold ground. All in all, there were thirteen of the creatures down here. Milano and I threw up after the whole thing was finally over, realizing that three of us almost lost our lives in this wretched place.

The next day we took a team into the cannery and hauled the bodies out to be burned in front of the factory. Lafayette and his two henchmen, Sikorski and Zimmermann, were arrested and taken into custody. This was getting to be a little much, and rumors told me that not many of the guys wanted to deal with this abhorrent mess.

Chapter Sixteen: Shades of Totalitarianism

Roger came over to my apartment a few times, and we talked about the limitless subject of God. He told me that he thought God might be destroying humanity because it was too evil, just as he did in the times of Noah. I wasn't quite sure if I could believe that. Despite his comment, I did mark the surge in pagan practices after that horrible Islamic war that began with the American invasion of Iraq, which pitted the Muslim world against most of the West. Tens of millions had died.

In lieu of that, while Roger was reposing and vegetating in the cold and gloomy afternoon, I flipped through the channels and found a talk show. The host interviewed a woman who sat discussing the significance of Middle Eastern paganism. This woman, who happened to be young and held a Ph.D., gave an unbelievable presentation on the effects of paganism on American society. Why it was being broadcasted or what it had to do with the present situation was beyond me. Nevertheless, I found it entertaining and informative, so I taped it.

After the talk show had finished, both of us left the television playing while the phone rang incessantly. People were always trying to reach me. I guess this whole crisis wore on everyone's nerves. It would have been great if the enemy we faced could be defeated through a military conquest, or by dropping an atomic bomb as in World War II. However, this time, the adversary was intangible and its nature could not be easily determined. Everything was so vague and nebulous, and answers would not present themselves.

From the successive newscasts, we gathered that Vietnam was still having problems and so was Russia. A force of 100,000 would soon go over there to help the Russian army contain the growing chaos. It became obvious to me that people were not cooperating with the standing rules and regulations and were protesting with their triggers.

Everyone did their own thing, and they refused to dispose of the ghouls properly. Intuitively, I knew we were all in a lot of trouble.

It had been several weeks since my horrible experience in the old cannery. It is funny how I have come so close to death several times already. Will I die as a young man, before my time is due? With each successive raid upon a ghoulish haven, there were less militia members and police officers to deal with it. The whole scenario took its toll on everyone's mind, heart, and soul as law and order melted away.

I had participated in an average of two raids per week and it was gruesome. The insurgents, who did not want the bodies to be destroyed, had shot some of the men. Many of our people were also bitten and would die of the horrid and corrupting infection. The ghouls themselves would kill others outright without conscience. I recalled when one National Guardsman was bitten in the neck by one of those things in a house in New City, dying within minutes from the loss of blood. We had to put a bullet through his brain and burn his corpse before it changed.

Several months had passed, and the snow was beginning to melt, revealing the dirt and filth from the year before. Because of my commitment to the state, I was unable to visit my family, and the evening curfew made it difficult for anyone to travel anytime after dark. Periodically, I would visit Marcia and Roger, going over to her house for dinner where her mother would prepare a succulent Jamaican feast of beef patties, curried goat, rice, and fried plantains.

It was strange how the state was now in control of things. People were able to go to work, but they were not allowed out of certain "zones." They had to place a colored sticker on their car to identify the "zone" they belonged to. There were other restrictions as well. The larger grocery stores were open only on certain days of the week because food, although raised and prepared in other parts of the country, was now rationed.

Convenient stores were open at all times. Places that sold computers and office supplies were open only on certain days. The state had taken over the nation's financial facilities and issued everyone's weekly paycheck. Once again, we were in a state of war. Things were not functioning right and drastic measures had to be taken as we moved closer toward dictatorship.

Weeks went by, and spring had yet to break through the frozen cold. The earth had yet to return to life. My mom seemed to be doing fine, as was my sister. However, they told me that the police kept on shooting the wandering ghouls in the countryside around Lee Center. The poor white country folk no longer obeyed the federal ordinances. People were arrested and were sometimes killed. The whole scenario reminded me of the anarchy of the French Revolution. There were more incidents in downtown Rome as well. The town's inhabitants stubbornly placed the ghouls and the dead bodies in private homes, just as they were doing here. The Rome police were busy every six or seven days with a shootout and a body-burning session. I wondered how much more the human race could take.

The Rockland authorities were not doing so well either. Time and time again, ordinary citizenry would not cooperate with them. They converted private homes and old abandoned buildings into charnel houses, no one wanting their former loved ones to have bullets fired into their brains. No one wanted to see the bodies incinerated out on the street. It seemed this whole situation violated our humanity; something that made us all hope death was really sacred.

I ended up taking human life again, just as I had done in Spring Valley. The incident took place in one of the apartment complexes in the Hispanic district of Haverstraw. There was a group of Guatemalans who, assisted by a number of strict Catholics, were housing some ghouls in the basement of a flat, lost in a notion of rebellion.

A number of us, including Milano and Bernstein, plowed into the complex led by the police and National Guard. After a shootout with some local residents, we confirmed they were hiding the bodies in the basements of those buildings. Some of the armed men took refuge in the cellar, lurking behind the piles of junk, and fired back. One man took cover behind a stack of cardboard boxes, shooting his pistol. I opened fire upon the stack and my shells cut right through the flimsy material that served as a poor protective barrier. I watched him die, quickly. By the end of the whole thing, I just stared at his corpse and realized that I was getting used to this. My heart hardened as it moved closer to the primitive earth.

This was becoming like Vietnam. More and more people lost faith in the government's ability to control the crisis. The federal authorities could no longer check the spreading of this plague. Lawmakers in Congress did everything they could to give the police the power to raid suspected houses without warrants, but the guardians of civil liberties forbade it.

Talk shows aired, allowing ordinary folk to express their feelings towards McIntyre and the other government officials designing these policies. There was a lot of talk, lots of red tape to cut through, and not much action. They debated and accomplished very little, while people were dying in the streets of every town and city, the body count mounting as lead flew through the air daily.

Eventually, the authorities made it a crime for citizens to own their own homes. People were shuffled around and relocated to places where the ghouls had not taken over. Some people were moved into the apartment downstairs, and some were put into the apartment next door to me. This was done on a similar scale all over the country. Most of the industrial and Western countries adopted similar policies, while the Third World continued to collapse.

Parts of Rockland County were now uninhabitable, or pretty close to it. There were thousands of ghouls in a band that stretched from Haverstraw, through New City, to Spring Valley. The authorities were trying to get the population away from these places since they had the highest concentration of ghouls.

Through successive meetings with Capasso, I found out that the population of ghouls might number about 12,000 in Rockland, too great of an enumeration for the diminishing police force to handle. There were additional pockets of problems in Nyack, as well as sections of Pomona. People were not destroying the bodies like they were supposed to. They were dumping them into the cellars of complexes where they became the undead and eagerly killed some more. Morale had steadily declined and the population went into the doldrums.

They announced on a news broadcast that the full curfew was in effect once again. Citizens were not allowed to leave their homes anymore. The police and the militias, however, did enjoy some freedom. Thanks to my special status as a militia member, I could go over to see Marcia and her mother periodically. Roger decided to move in with them, and the town board approved of the action. I thought about drifting in with them as well.

The state had arrested all freedom of movement, and few could go to work. In some places, the government took control of farms to make sure the food sources were heavily guarded and well protected. The state also dominated all healthcare services in addition to the freight and shipping industries. Drastic measures were needed to preserve society and keep it from disappearing altogether. It seemed as if a downright dictatorship was evolving, reminiscent of Nazi Germany. Still others clamored for the preservation of individual liberties. I found this outright stupid. Couldn't they understand that these harsh measures were necessary in times of war? We must harmonize with one another and consider each other's interests, or *we will all be eliminated and the human race would disappear from the earth forever!*

One day, I decided to venture over to Marcia's to find Roger sitting at the dining room table. He had moved into the bedroom upstairs, and must have felt quite at home. Marcia gave me some news that was very sad and it tugged at her soul.

"My mom gone to Brooklyn. No one knows wheere she," Marcia stated, looking somewhat upset.

"She wan' go back to Flatbush for some ta-ime. She wan' see my brodder and my sister."

Marcia went on to say that she drove down there illegally, running bridges, away from the eyes of the authorities. There were ways of obtaining false passes and so forth, and Marcia suspected that she got down there in an unlawful manner. Earlier, Marcia called her brother and her sister to see if she was okay, but they informed her that her mother never arrived. There were over 150,000 ghouls in Brooklyn alone, and anything could have happened to her. The outlook did not appear so good. Marcia cried several times over the heavy worry and loss, constantly cuddling the brown teddy bear. I looked into my own heart and found what little emotional strength I had left had begun to fly away. Despite Marcia's sorrow, I asked if I could set up shop here, living with this cozy little family, some warmth in the midst of so much cold. I did not want to be alone. Marcia very nicely allowed me to come in.

I told Capasso that I was living here so he could call me if there needed to be any more raids. He knew where I was, as did Milano and Bernstein. One night, after watching a broadcast that covered the usual topics of legal developments, ghoul destruction, and corpse rising, we heard a familiar knock upon the door. It was Bernstein in a light jacket and with that worn-out baseball cap placed backwards on his head. Harry Milano had accompanied him, smoking a cigarette and still unshaven with the same growth of beard.

"What's up buddy?" Bernstein popped that annoying question once again.

He continued, "Bob would have been over here, but he had to take care of some last minute paperwork."

We let them in and they stood on the living room floor, with Milano's cigarette fumes filling the apartment. Bernstein reposed and fidgeted a lot.

Marcia served them smooth, cold water with the utmost of grace.

"Bob is getting sick of this whole operation. These tactics are not working. If this keeps up, there will be no one left," Bernstein said, still fidgeting as his right leg vibrated up and down rapidly, while still sitting on the couch.

"Sasha, what are you saying?" Roger asked.

He appeared a little impatient at Roger's question.

"We are thinking of getting out of here. *That* is what I am saying."

There was only silence. The situation was becoming hopeless. The only chance, it seemed, was to try to get out of the metropolitan area and carve out a new society somewhere else where the population was thinner.

"Bobby is thinkin' of skippin' out on the force. He's gonna get himself killed someday and he knows it," Milano added, taking a drag from the cigarette. The smoke burned my lungs.

Capasso was considering abandoning his job. I realized that he could get himself into a lot of trouble for that, but it was obvious there were more ghouls than reliable men to deal with them. The military was still functioning, but it was plagued with desertions. The police force had dwindled down to a skeleton crew. The citizen militias were rarely responding to calls anymore. We were in a lot of trouble, and the estimated ratio of humans to ghouls was nearly nine to one. The odds were getting bad and chaos was descending upon the world.

Chapter Seventeen: The Incident Across the Street

"We're thinking of doing it in two days. You wanna join?" Bernstein asked.

Roger and Marcia were uncertain of this, and I was not sure either.

"We'll let you know by tomorrow evening," Roger answered.

Life was not safe, and every turn appeared fatal as security proved precious and elusive. I discussed this insecurity with Roger and Marcia after Milano and Bernstein had left. I felt extremely claustrophobic; there was no place to run and nowhere to turn. I looked up at the painting of the Jamaican family posing in front of the house, the one that captured the tranquility of Caribbean life. I wanted to have faith, to believe that life would someday get better, just like in that picture on the wall. The current circumstances offered only doom with no way out.

"Maybe it is time for you to know Jesus, Andy," Roger said, sincerely looking me straight in the eye. Marcia sat there, staring at me with concern.

"Maybe you're right," I said believing that only God could help me find a way out.

It was at that moment in time when I decided to open up my heart to Jesus Christ and have him forgive me of my past sins. I prayed eagerly with Marcia and Roger, turning my life over to the Saviour. I experienced a very warm sensation in my heart, and it became apparent to me that something had changed there. I went to bed hoping things would one day work out and that the future would someday arrive.

When I woke up, I drew back the curtains and the incoming sunlight brightened the living room with hope. Society was falling apart, as all foundations crumbled beneath my feet. This left me with no solid ground to stand on, save the rock of Jesus Christ. Why was God allowing this to happen? He had the power to stop it, but why didn't he use that power? There were no answers, but I prayed something would present itself soon.

Roger stood in the doorway of the kitchen once again, stuffing his face. I sat on the usual sofa, lost in thought, trying to listen to the newscasts that told me of the same thing. It was different this time, however.

"We want to bring you the latest on the current situation. There have been reports of widespread looting all over the Tri-State area," Burnside said in a sluggish and boring voice that practically lulled me off to sleep.

He went on to say stores were being broken into and plundered, law and order were beginning to break down. There were riots near the Brooklyn Bridge, incited by the restrictions upon personal mobility. Thousands were angered and took action, but the whole thing was broken up by tear gas from the New York Police Department (what was left of it). Eventually, the lawlessness was suppressed and Brooklyn was under control.

"Some of my buddies told me that bandits are breaking into the local shopping malls, and some of the department stores in Nanuet had stuff taken from them," Roger said matter-of-factly while he ate a slice of cold pizza. He seemed to take comfort in food, as his beard-covered jaw went up and down, processing the piece of dough.

He went on, telling me there were cases where some men had broken into a few shops in the ghoul-infested region of Spring Valley and taken the cash left in the tills. The looters even broke open some safes and stole their contents. I misplaced myself in contemplation as society unraveled and men resorted to barbaric tendencies. What was going on?

Roger and Marcia sat down and prayed for a good forty-five minutes or so. After prayer, Marcia went upstairs in the condominium, occupying herself, lying down with the stuffed animals in her room. Lately, she had been doing that a lot. I thought I detected her gentle sobs filtering through the floor, indirectly pleading for comfort.

Roger and I heard a commotion outside in front of one of the townhouses. We stared out the bay window, only to see Sasha Bernstein and Harry Milano with a group of fifteen men milling around the condominium across the street. They were armed with guns, bats, and shovels, wearing jackets in the chilly winter air. Roger and I went straight over to investigate the matter.

"We found out Nicky Rourke's mothuh just died. He won't give up the body and the police haven't responded to the call," Harry Milano stated to both of us.

The group of men wanted to destroy the ghoul, but Rourke would not allow them in.

"Nicky, if you don't let us up there, we're gonna break into the house. She's dead and she'll kill you. Now let us in!" Milano shouted. One of the men pounded on the door of the townhouse. In response, the second story window swung outward and there appeared a young man with sandy brown hair and an unshaven face, ready to address the crowd.

"She's my mothuh and we are gonna give her a proper funeral!" he retorted.

"Then put a bullet into her head. It's going to take a long time for her to stop movin'!" Milano shouted.

"No! She's my mothuh! You're not gonna take her away!" Rourke said.

Rourke pulled his head back into the window and shut it, disappearing inside. Milano and Bernstein banged on the front door of the townhouse. There was no response.

"Nicky, we're comin' in!" Milano shouted. The house produced nothing but silence, the tension mounting with every passing second, as everyone nervously waited for Rourke's reaction. The upstairs window exploded with a loud noise as shards of glass flew outward and fell into the street below! Rourke had just fired a gun at the group. Another blast of lead came forth, this time hitting one of the men in the hand!

Some of the men below had guns, and they fired into the upstairs window, pumping slugs into the casement without end. Another blast came from the house, this time striking one of the men in the rib cage. This whole thing was getting out of hand! The men on the street continued to fire endlessly into the windows. One of them took a baseball bat and broke the front bay of the townhouse. The shards of glass were cleared from the window, and a handful of armed men entered the condominium through the opening. The sound of gunshots being fired on the upstairs level could be heard for just a minute, then ceased altogether.

In a few minutes, the men who had just entered the house walked back out through the front door dragging Nicky's dead body behind them. They had killed him and now they would have to put a bullet through his head. A man suddenly screamed from inside the house. A moment later, he appeared in the doorway, clutching his wrist in pain. Behind him, with its arms outstretched, was a short, stiff figure growling in anger. It was Nicky's mother, and her humanity had faded away. Milano pulled the wounded man out of the way and raised his gun toward what was once Mrs. Rourke. He fired a round into its head, and it dropped to the ground where it had once stood, stopping permanently.

I looked behind me. The locals had put bullets through the heads of both Nicky Rourke and the man he had struck with the shotgun. The wound was fatal, and he had to be disposed of properly. The man who had been bitten by Nicky's mother was taken into someone's home. They would eventually send him to one of the rescue centers to get treatment, but most likely he would die as all the rest had done. The bodies of Nicky, his mother, and the man who got shot were all dragged into the street and subsequently burned, smoke pouring into the depressing iron sky. The smell of burnt flesh in the air sickened me as it wafted this way and that.

"I think we'd better get out of here," I said to Roger.

"Yeah," he replied.

Chapter Eighteen: A Time to Fly

Later that evening, Roger and I went over to Milano's townhouse, which was a little ways away. Bernstein showed up, along with Milano's girlfriend, a dark-haired female named Rachel Negron. We all sat at Milano's laminated wooden kitchen table, amongst his brown cabinets as he poured us coffee and soda. We heard Capasso pull up in his squad car. The door opened, slammed shut, and he walked in, his face as cold and unemotional as ever. Capasso joined us at the table, and he sipped refreshments while we discussed our hatred for the "killing" of these corrupted corpses.

"I've heard that some people are stahting to leave the area," Milano stated.

"I'm not sure if I wanna be here either," Rachel said. "Thing's have gotta get better."

"But where's everyone goin'?" Roger questioned. No one had an answer for that. Perhaps it was easier to survive in the rural places than in the densely packed urban ones. Patrols were becoming less frequent, and the police had too many problems to adequately protect the citizens of Rockland County. The days of late seemed long, like years, as time crawled to the pace of a snail. I wondered if we would ever make it to an age where things would be normal again.

"There's a way to get out of here. We can sneak out on a bread truck. It will take us up to the Catskills," Capasso said. We all agreed to do just that. Capasso went on, informing us that the truck would leave tomorrow at sundown, taking us into the obscure wilds of Upstate New York, where farmers were common and mountains were about. The meeting concluded, and Roger and I traveled back through the dead night air and entered the warmth of Marcia's condo, where she had buried herself in her stuffed animals.

That night, I again drifted into the land of slumber. Grass, flowers, and trees rapidly pushed themselves up through the soil and began to cover the vague, gray landscape. I could still see that same figure up on the horizon, off to accomplish some objective out of place and out of mind. Suddenly, a jeep with no driver in it pulled up alongside of me. It stopped, the motor gently idling. After contemplating whether or not I should get in, I climbed aboard. The jeep took off and I felt a peaceful presence in the driver's seat, though it sat empty. The sun winked at me favorably as it hung in the sky, and I knew that eventually I would catch up to that object on the horizon — it was just a matter of time. The jeep sped on.

Abruptly, I woke up. Marcia came down to the living room, half alive with a teddy bear in her right hand, and turned on the TV. Her hair was disheveled, but she did not seem to care; she was probably wondering where her mother was. I remembered that, when my father had died, I was not concerned about a lot of things. If my hair was out of place, it did not bother me. It was the least of my worries. There were more important things to occupy one's mind with, and she probably felt the same.

She sat upright at the end of the sofa and digested the news report being broadcast. Burnside and McLean both now appeared on the screen behind the blue backdrop. They told us that platoons of National Guardsmen were being airlifted into Brooklyn to restore order after another riot had broken out. I found it funny how the authorities never sounded confident since this whole thing began. Perhaps they knew the situation would grow cancerous and eat humanity from the inside out.

Many hours later, as the sun began to sink in the sky, there was a knock at the door. I pulled the curtains back for a moment and found Robert Capasso, Harry Milano, and Sasha Bernstein standing in front of Marcia's condo. We let them in, and the three of them sat down at Marcia's white kitchen table on the cushioned chairs, practically taking over the place.

"Time to go," Capasso said. "Almost ten puhcent of Rockland is wanderin' around wantin' to eat us."

I knew Rockland County had a ghoul population of roughly 27,000. For New York City, the number was almost 800,000. Spring Valley, New City, and Haverstraw were now entirely abandoned, all three towns evacuated by the authorities. It was going to get worse, and humanity had been pushed to a defensive stance rather than the usual offensive one.

"Moscow is overrun by those things. The government has removed almost every living inhabitant from the city," Bernstein said.

The group went on to discuss the fact that Beijing was decimated, and how the Chinese government had to be relocated further into the hinterlands to escape the inside invasion. The northern half of Vietnam began to fall to the dead at an unprecedented rate. Hanoi was also destroyed and the capital had to be relocated to the south. I guessed Ho Chi Minh finally lost the war — too bad Ngo Dinh Diem wasn't alive to see it.

We collected quantities of food, clothing, blankets, portable kerosene stoves, and firearms to get ready for the long ride north in the bread truck. We were setting out for the remote wilds of Greene County, for a small isolated village called Barrett's Hollow. The three men engaged in coarse joking and went out into the cool evening and left us by ourselves. Marcia caressed the usual brown teddy bear in the recliner.

Roger and I packed all of our provisions into a pushcart. Each of us went over particular lists to make sure we had all that we would need so it would last us for about two weeks. It was time to go. There was no future for us here, and it was questionable if there was one anywhere else.

Milano, who made the arrangements, told us that the bread truck would be pulling up to the back of a small supermarket several blocks away. We could hide in a small cluster of trees until the truck stopped to make its delivery.

He told us it would cost a thousand apiece. The price of the journey did not bother me one bit, and in a few months, I thought, the money wouldn't be worth a single cent.

We loaded all of our gear in the cart and made sure our guns were loaded. Before we left, Roger and Marcia joined hands with me and we prayed intimately to God for his protection. It is strange how none of the other people from the church wanted to go, having no desire to leave. It is very hard to leave everything behind, but for us it had to be done. We had to survive. I stared up at the painting of the Jamaican family on the wall. It captured a sense of peace and stability, one that seemed to slip through my fingers, remaining forever elusive. Roger and I left the condo and turned around facing it, waiting for Marcia. She walked through the entrance and locked the door, one of her hands still gripping the stuffed bear. We left Marcia's condominium as the sun sank down beyond the hills, casting orange rays into the sky of the fading day.

The three of us made our way down to Harry Milano's. I found his townhouse and we knocked desperately upon the door. Milano met us at the open door sipping coffee from a Styrofoam cup, cool, calm and collected.

"Ready to do this?" he asked.

"Yeah," I said.

We walked inside and found Bernstein wearing his baseball cap backwards, arms folded across his chest at the kitchen table. For the first time, I saw Capasso out of uniform, also sitting at the kitchen table with white sneakers, a pair of blue jeans, and a light blue buttoned shirt. I was not used to seeing him dressed so casually. The dark-skinned Rachel Negron was also at the table, eating bagels and drinking coffee. There were two carts in back of them, chockfull of provisions.

"Ready to blow this joint, Andy?" Rachel asked.

"Yeah," I answered.

"Time to go," Capasso ordered, as he put a small knife into his belt. "This will come in handy," he said, referring to the knife. "It's a good idea to be armed to the teeth." He probably had fantasies about using it.

We wheeled the carts out to the dead street. No one made a sound as Milano turned around and locked the door to his condominium. Who knew if he would ever return? He certainly had no idea.

The group walked down a side street under the cover of the twilight evening. We hoped that no one would catch us, though it was unlikely. The diminishing police force could no longer support and regulate affairs as the ghouls took over the county. Our expedition strolled through the lots in Southold. Most of them were unoccupied. Their occupants had either fled or died, gradually turning this place into a ghost town.

The procession approached an old wooden shed next to a tree line in back of a large house with gabled roofs. In front of the shed was a figure with unkempt gray hair and dark blue clothing. The figure scratched at the padlocked door, grunting and growling, as it tried to claw up the ground before the shed. Due to the animal-like noises that it produced, I knew it was not an actual person, but a ghoul.

As we neared it, it stopped and took note of us, sensing the "warm" flesh that came close. It stood up and hobbled towards us, letting out animalistic ululations. Capasso walked up to it and struck it on the head with the butt of the shotgun he carried. He was a strong man, and his action destroyed the creature immediately. The things have been known to act like curious animals, with little more intelligence than the average house pet, which is not considered sentient by any definition. They exhibited very little ability to make choices and respond to their environment. In any case, this one had no time to do either.

We went on, wheeling our paraphernalia through the different yards. Up ahead, the silent houses sent dark shadows across the lawns in the sinking sun. We would finally be able to escape this all-encompassing suburban nightmare that widened its reach, pulling everything into it like a black hole, consuming all human flesh. Behind me, to the west, was my apartment with the discordant stairs. It still had some of my belongings in it, but I was now leaving it all behind, and I would probably never come back to it again. I wouldn't miss it much, and I cared little to return to that place of suffocating isolation.

We spied the small supermarket nearby. Neon signs still lit up its windows advertising different types of beer. I had no doubt there was someone inside, probably armed to the teeth to protect his life from looters and ghouls. Capasso led the group behind the structure to the patch of trees where we patiently waited for the truck that would bring us to some sort of Promised Land.

Once we were all behind the store in the trees, I took off my backpack. I found it extremely cumbersome, and it felt like murder on my spine. I pulled out my pistol to make sure it was loaded and dependable. Bernstein began to take apart his rifle on the ground of the little wooded area, where he proceeded to clean the weapon like it was his favorite toy. We all took out our money and handed it to Milano. Marcia, exhausted, leaned back against the carts, held her teddy bear in her arms, and began to nod off, seeking to shut down and escape. I, on the other hand, was unable to sleep. I needed to know that there was a hope and a future, and there was no guarantee of either.

The sun continued to sink into the twilight evening sky when we heard a large vehicle approaching. With a squeal of the brakes, a big truck turned into the back lot of the store, a truck large enough to hold a load of bread and possibly human cargo. It stopped. A man of average build wearing a white shirt and having a mustache under his nose, hopped out of the cab, eager to accomplish the mission that was before him, or so I imagined.

"You're Milano?" The man spoke as Harry walked towards him.

"Yeah. Patrick McMahon, right?" Milano asked as the man nodded in affirmation.

Milano handed over the cold cash. The man counted it with zeal and walked to the back of the truck. We stepped out of the trees and followed him, and he rolled up the rear door to reveal stacks of plastic bread racks. Capasso stepped in and we followed suit, trying to make ourselves as comfortable as possible. The driver of the truck pulled the door down and sealed us in the rear compartment. I hoped to God that we were not left in here to suffocate and die, shut up in the dark. I also hoped that the trip would be short and we would get to our destination soon. The truck should take us up the county route and onto the New York State Thruway. The truck started up, rumbling to life, and I prayed that the carbon monoxide would not asphyxiate us.

The driver pulled out of the parking lot and onto one of the main streets. We were leaving Rockland County behind, closed up in this windowless dark compartment as human cargo smuggled over the uncertain frontier. We would fare better in the rural freedom of Upstate New York, leaving this suburban death trap far behind us.

Part II
Upstate

Chapter Nineteen: Police Brutality

There wasn't much light filtering in through the back of the bread truck. Air came in through the spaces around the rear door, so I did not worry about suffocation. As my eyes adjusted to the lack of illumination, I could see all of my traveling companions sitting around the inside, on both sides of the bread racks. No one talked, everyone brooding in the silent solitude of uncertainty. I hoped that life would be better Upstate than in the suburbs, but there was no guarantee of that, or anything else for that matter. The truck rumbled on, the sound of the engine lulling me into a half-complete sleep that was laced with the distorted faces that I had seen over the past several months. It was difficult knowing that you were trapped in a small space, unable to get out. It was also difficult depending upon someone outside to release you from such a suffocating prison. It would take about two hours to reach the secluded safe haven in the Catskill Mountains. The area was originally settled by a group of Dutch pioneers, and I imagined us as pioneers of a sort, trying to conquer a brand new yet lethal world.

After about half-an-hour, the driver pulled the truck over. He got out and opened the door about six inches, just high enough for us to see his mouth and nose, while keeping his eyes from view. Capasso made his way to the slightly opened door and whispered something to the man. The door rolled shut and Capasso spoke into the darkness: "He just wants to know if we're all okay."

Almost everyone, to my knowledge, was doing well. We heard the door bolted from the outside. Soon the truck started up and proceeded northward.

An irritating sound could be heard over the rumbling of the engine, in fact it sounded like sirens wailing on the Thruway. Could it be the cops?

"What goin' on out deere?" Marcia asked, awakened from her slumber.

"I dunno. We have to keep real quiet," I said.

We felt the truck pull over to the side of the Thruway. The vehicle remained stationary for about five minutes or so. As I strained my ears, I could make out the sound of voices coming from outside the truck. I detected the sound of the driver's voice with the presence of two others. The tone of the discussion sounded like one of domination and subordination, and McMahon's voice started to waver out of fear. My heart began to beat and I felt the urine press on the inner walls of my bladder. If the cops were truly outside, we were going to be in a whole lot of trouble!

Suddenly, the metal door to the back of the truck rolled up, revealing the dark and foreboding night sky interrupted by flashing red lights. I could see shapes that bothered me and frightened me, moving around just outside the truck. My pupils adjusted to the lack of light again, and I could clearly see who was in front of me. There were two state troopers in light brown uniforms, firmly gripping pistols in their hands and ready to use them! Both were staring at the cargo in the back, and they stared in disapproval! McMahon appeared saddened, as if he did not want to turn us over to the police.

"We heard people were being smuggled out of New York, and now we're gonna do something about it. No one is supposed to leave their homes," one of the state policemen said.

"If we stay down there, we're gonna die. We can't go back there," Capasso sharply responded.

"Orders are orders," the other policeman said.

"Everybody get out!" the first officer shouted.

We all had to leave the truck and line up on the highway. We stood on the side of the road, the police vehicle parked behind us, its red lights oscillating endlessly. The two cops forced us to throw all of our weapons into a pile at the side of the road and had us fold our hands behind our heads.

"Folks, you can't just leave your homes like this," one of the state troopers said. "We're going to have to take you in for questioning."

I could not believe this. The police were overworked as it was and they were actually going to bother with us! Maybe these two guys were still wholeheartedly committed to enforcing the law, just plain in love with doing their job. They were probably going to take us to the nearest substation, keep us for questioning, and then ship us back to Rockland County. Maybe they could beat us, making us pay for violating the laws, rules, and regulations. I had no idea what these men would do at a time like this, and it scared me.

Capasso did not look frightened at all. He, of all the people here, had the most to lose. Since he was skipping out on the force, he certainly would be stripped of his badge. They might even try to execute him before a firing squad or hang him from tall gallows for his abandonment.

"We're tryin' to get out of Rockland. We can't stay there. It's gettin' really bad and we're all gonna get killed," Capasso said calmly.

"The law is the law, buddy. Either follow it or pay the consequences. Okay people! Let's see all your wallets!" One of the cops ordered, whose nametag read "Welch."

We had to take our wallets out and throw them into another pile at our feet, the police wanting to know with whom they were dealing. Rachel and Marcia had to go back to the truck and get their purses. Rachel looked frustrated, scared and hopeless, while Marcia said nothing.

"We'll go. We'll go. We'll go," Rachel said quietly to the troopers. "Just don't shoot. Don't shoot. Just don't shoot," she exclaimed with her hands extended, moving them up and down very slowly in a gesture implying obedience. She walked to the rear of the truck with Marcia.

The rest of us continued to stand with our hands locked together at the backs of our heads, in partial subordination.

The tension mounted to the point that I began to hyperventilate. I realized that I could be in a lot of trouble as well. I was definitely violating my contract as a member of the militia, as were Milano and Bernstein. Roger and the two women would be in a lot of hot water for just associating with us. We all would face serious charges for varying degrees of desertion, and we could all pay very dearly. I had to urinate so badly that I nearly wet my pants.

The two cops began to look through the wallets. One found my card that read I was a temporary employee of the local government.

"Goering, you're really in for it!" the other officer, whose name was DiNapoli, said.

Welch looked at Bernstein's wallet and repeated the same to him. As he moved on to Capasso, the tension really began to build, and I could feel every molecule generated from the brewing conflict.

Trooper Welch studied Capasso's identification. He fingered it in his hand and slapped it on the opposing palm several times. He eyed Capasso in a confrontational manner. Capasso only returned the glance coldly and without mercy. The guy was obviously going to challenge him.

"Mr. Capasso!" Welch said.

"Yeah," he responded, not respecting the man.

"You're in a lot of trouble. YOU ARE IN A WHOLE BUNCH OF TROUBLE!" Trooper Welch bellowed at Capasso. "WE SHOULD KILL YOU FOR THIS!"

The tension mounted to the proportion of a large hill. Capasso stood with his elbows out, his hands still behind his head. I looked at his eyes, and I believed that he expected this sort of thing to happen and was prepared to do something about it. What he would do was beyond me, but there was a deadly surprise coming in his repertoire. I could feel it.

"Robert Capasso, are you aware that the United States is under martial law?" Welch asked, looking him in the eye.

"Yeah," Capasso answered in an antagonistic manner.

"What you have done is treason," the cop said. "What do we do with traitors, Bobby?"

Capasso said nothing.

"We shoot them, Mr. Capasso. We shoot them with no trial. Nothing," the trooper answered smugly. "We shoot them right there on the spot. We don't have time for due process of law." The cop looked down at the black .45 in his holster. He was getting ready to use it.

"Law and order are really poor. We could shoot everyone here and dump the bodies in the swamp. No one would ever know. Maybe some of your family members would eventually launch investigations, but by the time they did, it would be way too late. There may not be a court of law left to try the case anyways," Trooper Welch said, looking coldly into Capasso's eyes. He was definitely going to kill him. I guess the stress of being a lawman was starting to get to him, particularly in tough times like these.

All of a sudden, Marcia stumbled backwards as if she was drunk, losing her balance out of sheer clumsiness, I assumed. Both officers turned to look at the commotion and Capasso took action. Welch, alarmed, tried to draw his gun, but Capasso was faster. He reached into his belt and withdrew the knife, plunging it into the cop's torso. Trooper Welch gurgled in pain as he put his hand over the blade, bleeding profusely! He bent over and tumbled to the ground as crimson blood gathered on the tarmac.

Milano, seizing the opportunity, cupped his fists together and hit DiNapoli in the side of the head. The trooper, momentarily stunned, tried to pull his gun out, fumbling with the holster. Bernstein dove and took one of the pistols from the pile on the ground and smoothly fired it into the cop's chest. DiNapoli's body lost all of its strength and fell backwards onto the gray asphalt. Two more dead corpses now lay on the side of the New York State Thruway, two belonging to the police, the caretakers of law and order.

We looked around. There was no other traffic on this stretch or road, deserted due to the restrictions that were imposed upon everyone. We had to get out of here, before officers were sent to investigate the matter. Capasso lifted the guns from the officers as well as the keys from the ignition of their car. With seemingly no fear of reprisal, he walked over to the trunk of the vehicle with definite intent and purpose.

"We may need what-evuh's back here," he said.

I walked to the trunk where Capasso was standing to find an automatic rifle that looked like an M-16, as well as two boxes of ammunition. We took all of it and placed the items in the rear of the truck. The driver of the truck appeared pale. This whole incident bothered him, leaving him insecure, I imagined.

"E-E-Everybody get back in the truck, now!" McMahon ordered, with a voice that wavered with lack of confidence.

We listened and prepared to do what he said. We would leave the bodies there, since they would eventually revive and wander off into one of the cattail-infested marshes that lined the Thruway.

"Not so fast, whinuh-boy!" Capasso stated. "I'm going to make sure that you take us to our destination. Get back in the truck," he insisted. Capasso took one of the pistols lifted from the police and pointed it at him. Patrick McMahon looked down at the gun anxiously and began to perspire at the temples. He was clearly frightened, his hands jittering and shaking as he got into the cab and Capasso boarded from the other side. We all crept into the back of the truck except Bernstein, who shut the rear door. Apparently, Capasso did not trust the driver anymore.

We took our positions in the back of the truck, absent Bernstein and Capasso. I could see the others as my eyes adjusted to the lack of light. Marcia was next to me, holding her bear, and Rachel, Roger and Milano were on the far wall opposite the bread racks. I could barely see Rachel's face, but I caught her hopelessly gazing upward toward the ceiling of the metal prison we sat in. She was a woman with a melancholic inclination.

I tightly held the assault rifle Capasso lifted from the cops. Capasso and Bernstein had just taken the lives of two law enforcement officers. They were cold-blooded killers, and I should have seen the tendency a long time ago. If

Capasso and Bernstein were heartless killers, I knew things would eventually come to a head, and I dreaded the very thought of confrontation. The truck continued north on the Thruway. Once, the driver stopped and Bernstein opened up the back of the truck a little bit to make sure that we were all okay.

"Hey buddy, how's it goin' in there?" he asked.

"A-okay," I answered.

He shut the door, latched it, and the vehicle fired back up, rumbling further into the green. After what felt like hours, the truck began to slow down and I felt it turn to the left, practically coming to a dead stop. I suspected that we approached an unmanned tollbooth. The vehicle did not stop for long and went on unimpeded by the revenue-generating device.

For about another half-hour the truck rode along what must have been a bumpy rural road. My hunch was that we were now either in the Catskills or we were approaching its foothills, and I wondered how much longer this journey would take. I could see Marcia's face next to me, her eyes closed in the dark, leading me to believe she was asleep, seeking solace in a little slumber with her teddy. She was too tired to keep awake any longer, despite the mayhem that had just occurred.

In the fullness of time, the bread truck did come to a stop, although it felt as if I would be trapped in this vehicle forever. Several moments went by, and I wondered what was going on out there. Curiosity burned in my breast, and I could have sworn that I heard the weak-looking driver shout about something, but the nature of the shouting match could not be determined from inside the truck. A loud crack suddenly split the night and rocked my little world. What the heck was happening out there?

The rear door rolled up about half way and Capasso peered in.

"Thought you might want some aih," he said.

Behind him, beneath the twilight sky, were a number of green deciduous trees whose leaves were just beginning to sprout, spring arriving early up here in the Catskills. I was stiff from being cooped up so long, and I wanted to get out and walk around in the crisp, clean atmosphere.

"Bobby. I need to get out of here. My legs are gettin' cramped," I said.

"Okay. Come out," he said calmly. "But you're not gonna like what you see."

I crawled out of the truck, a little hesitant at his remark, and I stood on the soft damp leaf-covered ground, taking note of my surroundings. The road before us was much more narrow than the Thruway we were previously on, isolated, and far from the throng of New York City. I noticed something lying on the ground next to the truck, on the side of the road. It was a body, more specifically, one that belonged to the timid truck driver, Patrick McMahon. He was dead.

"What did you do to him?" I asked Capasso, shocked, offended, and a little scared.

"I killed him. He was too nuhvous, and I thought he might take us to the police station. Couldn't chance it," he said without remorse. He put a slug right between his eyes, right in front of me, blood splattering about. I was appalled.

"What're we gonna do with his body?" I asked Capasso.

"Leave it here," he said calmly.

"Let the body rot," Bernstein said. This inhumanity was starting to wear on my already thin nerves.

"This is a man. We should at least drag the body off the road into the woods," I insisted.

"Goering, you're really stahtin' to irritate me, and I don't wanna listen to you whine! Go ahead. Move the corpse!" Capasso said. I was growing more afraid of the man all the time, hoping that I would not have one of those bullets buried in my brow someday.

Roger and I dragged the corpse over the moss and old leaves that blanketed the ground under the gray morning sky. I insisted that we have a short funeral for the man that had just been killed. I found out from Milano that Patrick

McMahon was raised Catholic, and that he had an ex-wife who lived out in Levittown. She would never see him again. Roger officiated over the ceremony that lasted a total of about fifteen minutes, giving the man one last ounce of dignity, one that most of us sorely needed. While the service was going on, Capasso and Bernstein disappeared. They were the types that wanted nothing to do with spiritual matters. They were men of the primitive soil, who didn't want to bother with what they could not measure or see.

Chapter Twenty: Beer and Lederhosen

Milano knew how to drive the truck, so we got him to man the thing. We knew we were south of East Durham, somewhere in the Catskills, but unsure precisely where. I wondered, as I sat in back of the truck, if Capasso should have shot McMahon later, perhaps sometime after we arrived at our destination, or maybe not at all! He was an impatient man though, and had the inclination not to think things through, acting in the heat of the moment. He guessed that the community we had to find was roughly ten miles from here, lodged in the middle of nowhere.

The more I thought about Capasso, the more frightened I became. He was the type of man who did whatever he wanted, without restraint or fear of reprisal. We could not go to the police with this. We would be in a heck of a lot of trouble if we did. Besides, we were now fugitives from the law.

We climbed in the truck and the door was shut again. I tried to relax for the ride, not wanting to think about our situation, or about Capasso for that matter. I had never felt so insecure in all of my life! I wished that my dad was still alive, whom I thought of as a protector and a provider. He was gone, and I was now on my own. Now, I had to believe that God would get me through the muck and mire my life had become. I wondered how my mom and sister were doing.

We went on for about ten minutes over the bumpy road, upsetting my delicate stomach. It was obvious that the lane needed to be repaired. The dwindling road crews probably had not been out here for weeks. The area was becoming more isolated, and the thought of being cut off from society scared me. There was no law and order to restrain Capasso, who was becoming more uncivilized by the day.

The ride stopped. Capasso twisted the latch open and rolled up the back, letting us out. I found myself stretching with a .45 in my hand, trying to flex my stiff limbs. The rest of the group clambered out of the truck onto the primitive dirt road in its prevailing dustiness. I looked around, combing the area with my eyes. There were a number of houses with low peaked roofs, not much more than summer cabins. In fact, that is probably what they were, the famous Catskill bungalows owned by people yearning to escape the uncivilized ways of the urban jungle. There were several of them, maybe fifteen or sixteen up and down the road, nestled in the trees and hidden from prying eyes. There were more off to the side, down the long driveways and under the cover of the blanketing deciduous foliage.

To my right and set back in the trees a bit, was a large, green two-story house with an overhanging roof, reminiscent of German architecture. The house had a light on over the doorway, like a beacon in the gloom. In the front hung a sign that read: Office. Capasso walked in through the black door of the green building, an innocent bell ringing as he passed through. We all followed him, our pistols safely tucked away under our jackets, ready to be used. A balding, overweight man sat behind the counter, running his fingers over his mustache. He took note and studying us, seemingly trying to size us up to see if we were friend or foe.

"Welcome to Barrett's Hollow! What can I do for you?" He greeted us with a suspicious smile.

I noticed that he had two revolvers in holsters at his side. No wonder he had no fear of us. He walked up to us and confidently pulled out one of the pistols and laid it on the countertop. I guess he wanted to show us that he was a force to be reckoned with.

"We need a place to stay," Capasso said in a jovial manner.

"We have them, but they'll cost you thirty dollars per night," said the man.

"Thirty dollahs a night?" Capasso questioned. "We can't affohd that!"

"No. Each cottage is thirty a night. If you don't like that, there is a place about seventeen miles down the road.

They may have a place for rent, but, then again, they may not. Who knows?" He smiled somewhat maliciously.

"By the way, where is Mr. McMahon? He was supposed to stop in before he left. He came with you, right?" the man asked.

"He had to skip out. He had business to take cahe of," Capasso answered.

"I was looking forward to seeing Pat this morning, and I hope we'll be seeing him again," the other man exclaimed. He would never see Pat McMahon again, and I knew why.

"If you want to, we can work out a deal in order to pay for the rooms," the man said.

"Yeah. What?" Capasso asked.

"We need a lot of help around this place. If you work for us, we'll give you food and lodging, and you won't have to pay for it!" he proposed in a boastful manner. He had us over a barrel and he knew it. I suppose that was fine, and what else were we going to do for that matter?

We found out that the man's name was Garrick Handelsman. He had a certain sparkle in his eyes that indicated that he liked to dictate and force people to do what he wanted them to do. He went on to explain that down the road was a large pavilion, which conveniently sheltered benign picnic facilities that cooked ethnic food. The curfew was not adequately enforced up here, and there were thousands of people trying to get out of the suburbs and wanting to live in this general area. Some would settle down here, or go further Upstate or out to Pennsylvania, passing through this place like a way station to an imagined utopia that existed in some netherspace.

Not far from the picnic facilities, there was a large farm used to raise livestock and grow green vegetables. Handelsman said we would have to work in both places throughout the duration of the summer. After the summer was over, we could go to wherever our hearts would take us. He mentioned that the whole population of Barrett's Hollow, all seventy-eight of them, were armed and could literally force us to leave if we got out of hand. The seven of us agreed to stay here as indentured servants, trying to live in this little refugee camp that housed ethnic Germans and inbreeds of Dutch and Anglo-Saxon descent.

As it turned out, it was not a bad place to be. Handelsman gave Roger and me a one-roomed log cabin that had two beds in it, two wooden rocking chairs, a large pine dresser, a kitchen area and a full bath. The spaces between the logs were filled with white mortar to keep out insects and other pests. Thin red curtains covered the windows, and a lone light bulb mounted in the ceiling gave us the illumination to see the interior clearly. It was rather comfortable. The others lived in similar facilities.

This little isolated community saw no ghouls. The authorities didn't seem to bother this place either, maybe because it was too hard to get to, or perhaps the diminishing police force did not want to tangle with an armed populace. Handelsman told us that about thirty or forty miles away, in Delhi, there was a large compound set up by the U.S. Army. It was surrounded by barbed wire and remained heavily guarded to keep the ghouls out. However, not everybody had gone to this place. There were still people who lived about the wilderness, trying to eke out an existence like hunters and gatherers, scrambling for a living in order to survive.

The experience at Barrett's Hollow proved interesting. Sometimes I worked on the farm up the road in the gardens, muscles aching and perspiring heavily. We had working tractors and a gasoline supply network that would periodically drop off a few drums. The drums of gasoline were expensive, and I wondered how long this whole arrangement would last. We worked hard, and I found myself exhausted at the end of the day, in desperate need of a shower. The work was good for the soul as we thrust our fingers through the same soil that would provide us sustenance. Everyone labored, including Capasso, who was mostly confined to the barn, taking care of the animals and constantly feeding them bales of hay. Sometimes Capasso and Bernstein went out into the woods to hunt deer or wild pheasants. The animals would be brought home, dressed, and butchered to become nourishment for this isolated pocket of humanity.

Although the community of Barrett's Hollow had only seventy-eight souls within it, in the evenings it would get larger as families from the surrounding area joined us for dinner. The meals were spectacular, German beer served along with roasts and German knockwurst. Musicians dressed in Bavarian costume, complete with Lederhosen, would dance and play music for hours into the enchanted evening. I found life here a joyous celebration, not the monotonous drudgery that I had expected.

Not everyone was German here in this little community. There was a peculiar contingent of Orthodox Jews whose last name were either Stein or Dubitsky, and they lived in a couple of log cabins. They insisted upon eating kosher food, which was barely accessible, but always managed to procure something to ingest. Another twenty were part of the old Dutch element that had been here for over three hundred years, intermixed with the English that later settled in this region. Perhaps we could weather the storm here until they come up with a cure to reverse the tides of bad fortune hanging over the land.

One day, Roger and I fervently prayed after dinner. Marcia joined us, crying with the bear in her arms while kneeling upon the warm wooden planks of the floor.

"Don' know wheere my mum. Wheere she? Wheere my brudder? Wheere my sister? I wan' go back home," she said, while holding the bear.

"Honey, you can't do that. Chances are, you won't make it back. Can't you give them a call?" I suggested as I sat in a rocking chair, swaying to and fro like a pendulum.

"I try dat, but I can't get trough," she cried, the tears continuing to roll down her face. I hugged her for several long moments, Roger looking on. After a few minutes, he got up and stared out the window. Eventually, Marcia left to go back to the cabin she shared with Rachel.

The next day I got Handelsman's permission to use the phone. Lo and behold, I got through to home.

"Hello," a woman's voice answered. It was my mom.

"Hi. How're you doin'?" I asked.

"Andy, it is so good to hear from you!" she said, almost overjoyed and exuberant.

"How's Pete and Missy?"

"They're doing well. They and the kids had to leave their trailer and move in with me. Government regulations," she said.

"How d'you feel about it?" I asked.

"I hate it. It's too crowded for a three-bedroom house," she answered.

"There's nothing anyone can do about it," I said.

"Andy, I want you back. I want you back here to protect us. We can find you a place to sleep. I may even be able to give you your own room!" she begged. It was clear that she wanted me back where I would be safe.

"Mom, I can't go back now. There are just too many problems!" I said.

"What type of problems?" she asked.

"I can't share that with you now," I said a little defensively.

"WHAT TYPE OF PROBLEMS?" she shouted.

"Mom, I told you I can't share that with you. Maybe later."

She acquiesced and changed the subject. She informed me that the woods above Lee Center were now infested with ghouls that crawled and groped through the clusters of trees. The authorities thought that there might be as many as five hundred of those things in the tangle of trees and underbrush, wandering about in search of warm flesh.

I wished I could see my family, but that was not an option. The situation rendered me a fugitive, an outlaw, and I dared not tell them about the experience that I had with the state troopers. My mom also informed me that there were some problems in the city of Rome. The police found out that someone was harboring those things in a run-down hotel in East Rome. Eight cops raided the place, but there were a number of armed collaborators in it and lead was thrown through the air. By the time the whole thing was over, two cops were dead and five men in the hotel were killed. The ghouls numbered in the thousands down there, but it was confined to certain areas of Rome, although many people had to be relocated. My mom refused to speak about the situation anymore.

"'Bye, son. Love you," she said.

"'Bye, Mom. Love you too," I responded. Our conversation then abruptly concluded, the phone line cutting out again.

It looked as if no one would survive this plague, that the human race was to be wiped out. I prayed with Roger and Marcia on the floor of this cabin about this terrible conjecture. After the petitions went up to the seemingly brass heavens, a thought hit me. God could easily recreate the human race and repopulate the globe. He formed Adam from clay, and he could always make a second Adam and a second Eve. Maybe he gave up on this race and decided to make room for a better one, one that was more righteous than the former. However, the idea of letting the entire human race slip into oblivion did not sit right with me. It violated something inherently good and wonderful in God's character. Perhaps there was a solution, but it evaded me.

As spring fully bloomed in this little community, I met an Orthodox Jew named Baruch Dubitsky while working in the gardens. He and the Stein's (the other Orthodox family) were getting ready for the Passover Feast coming up. He wanted to share the whole experience with us, so he invited Roger, Marcia and me to fully participate and witness the wonderful custom.

"We'd love you to join us tomorrow," he said smiling under his black hat.

The next day Roger, Marcia and I came to their cabin, which was filled with a loud multitude of children. A plate was prepared for each of us, and we partook in an actual *Seder*. We ate *matzah* sandwiches with horseradish and chopped apples, which made my eyes water. We dipped our pinkies in grape juice and cast the drops onto a plate, in commemoration of the Ten Plagues that were mentioned in the book of Exodus. Although the Jews here didn't look at it the same way, I found the feast to be a great reminder of what Jesus had done. Just as God had taken the Israelites from the bondage of Egypt and into the liberation of the wilderness, Jesus Christ took me from a place of sin and into the liberation of knowing God. It also served as a little escape from the tumult of the outside world that was gradually closing in on us.

A few weeks later, I had this desire to take a wife despite the craziness that was going on, and naturally my thoughts took me to Marcia. One spring day, while laboring in the large garden that was ringed by forest, I saw the lovely Jamaican woman before me. The late afternoon sunlight played on her features and made her skin glow. Her brown skin turned beautiful and highlighted her character, making her more inviting. I desired her almost more than anything else. For the rest of the evening, as I ate under the pavilion and conversed with Roger in the log cabin, I became consumed by the thought of knowing her more intimately.

The next day, I got up from my little sanctuary after having my devotional time in the Bible and proceeded to the farm. I noticed the other residents of Barrett's Hollow walking in the same direction like laborers hiking to a textile mill. Marcia was conveniently up ahead of me, on her way there as well. I felt that this was the time to begin to converse with the young lady, and perhaps I could find out if the two of us were compatible as life-long partners.

She walked down the road to the barn. It went through the woods, but there were trails that led from that road into the trees on either side of it.

"Marcia, do you mind if I tag along?" I asked.

"Why not?" she said. I took that as an open door.

"Let's go down here," I said, pointing to one of the trails that was overgrown with weeds.

"You tink deere might be a better pleece?"

"Let's see what we can do," I answered.

The trail was so choked with weeds and branches that I practically needed a machete to hack through it. Finally, we passed through all of the stubborn obstacles. It was at this moment that I began to talk to her about things.

"Have you heard from your mom at all?" I asked.

"No, nuttin' so far," she said, with her eyes staring forward at the blanketing Catskill vegetation, not even looking at me. I sensed the conversation made her uncomfortable, and I wagered I had better shut up or change the subject.

"So, how's Kingston?" I asked her.

"King-ston? Why you wan' know aboot King-ston?" she asked, kind of puzzled and looking quizzically.

"Well, you were born there, right," I affirmed.

"Yes," she responded, laughing and enjoying the moment.

"Do you want to go back?"

"Meybe somedey."

"How did you end up in New York, of all places?" I asked.

"I came here after high-school to go to col-lege. I study very hard to get an economics degree. I wan' to teach it, so I look for job after I graduate. Nuttin' came up. The city was dry. I got dis job at a laundromat and been deere for over a year. De crisis came along and messed tings up," she explained.

She then asked me about my career aspirations. I told her that I wanted to pursue a Ph.D. in history, but did not have the money to follow it through, shelving my career plans. As we continued down the trodden path, I wondered if we would ever be able to pursue any of our dreams. They seemed to be going nowhere but down at this point.

The path up ahead grew wider and the runaway vegetation began to thin and sputter out. The sky overhead turned a dark gray and looked as if it was going to rain. The woods dropped away from the course as a clearing presented itself on both sides of the trail. Within that clearing were many mounds of dirt, and the green grass grew over them like a fur coat. Beyond them we could see the wandering hills of the Catskills rolling off into the hazy day. Around the various mounds in this flat green area were puddles that had formed in the mud from all of the rain that fell. We walked over to one. Quite often, in rural collections of water, snails and white worms would congregate there, forming a world within a world, but I did not see any creatures moving about this time. If there were any, they escaped our notice.

Both of us stared into the puddle without making a sound and could see our reflections staring back at ourselves. My beard, I noticed, was getting long, since I rarely shaved at the present time. Looking nice wasn't a priority in this little community, and there weren't too many razors available. Marcia still kept her weave, but her hair continued to grow. In fact, it was almost down to the middle of her chest. We did not have access to basic services like haircutters and beauty salons any longer, but our little enclave was lacking in a lot of amenities. I wondered what would happen if one of us got sick. Would we have a physician available? What about dental care? There were so many uncertainties. I wondered if life would ever flow the way it had in the past.

I looked into her eyes, brown, warm, and inviting. They were moist, longing for intimacy. Her large, pink lips appealed to me, and I wanted to kiss them several times. I put my hands up to her cheeks and stroked them with my thumbs. I wanted to lose myself in her lips and in her eyes. I was nearly in heaven…

"Stop…," she said. "Do we know what we doin'?"

Immediately, I felt frustrated as the urge for intimacy was suddenly stifled. Romance would be good. It would help us both forget the current situation around us like a drug, but the promise was violently interrupted by protest.

"Marcia, what's your problem, honey? There's nothing wrong with a little romance on a dark afternoon," I said, a little short.

She went on to tell me that there is no guarantee there would be a tomorrow. Besides, if there was, what would the quality of life be like in the next few years? Could we actually raise children in these circumstances? So many questions presented themselves, and we did not really have any of the answers.

"I'm lonely, Marcia!" I said.

"Yeah, me too, but I don' tink we should be foolin' aroond like dis. If we find we can't be together for years to come, we will just frustreete ourselves," she said emphatically.

She was right. There is no sense in getting all wrapped up with one another like the fabric of a woven sweater, just to end. We agreed that we would have to pray on it and seek God's will about the whole thing.

Instead of losing ourselves in romantic pursuits, we walked towards some of the mounds that sat in the thick and stifling atmosphere. The sky overhead turned a darker shade of gray, and once again I could see the distant Catskills rolling away like a river into some unknown basin. We peered down into another puddle again and saw our reflections staring back at us. Then we realized that the puddle was not a naturally occurring depression in the earth; it was manmade!

"These are tire tracks!" I said.

"What?" she asked.

"Someone's been out here."

Chapter Twenty-One: Big Trouble in Little Germany

Both Marcia and I looked at the tire tracks that must have been made by an all-terrain vehicle, which indicated that someone had been out here recently, tearing up the ground. They were fresh and cause for some alarm. Marcia and I hurried back to the farm, realizing that we would have to report what we had seen. They may have been made by harmless teenagers, but then again, maybe not. It was best to be safe rather than sorry.

We went to Handelsman's office in the green Bavarian-style building with the black door. The two of us found him behind the counter, seated in his chair, poring over paperwork. His shiny revolver on the table before him, he checked his documents over and over, heavily absorbed in their content. I told him about the tire tracks and he looked up.

"No, there are no three-wheelers here. What were you doing down that path, anyways? Hmmm? You're supposed to be working, not fooling around." He was a man that wanted to keep control at all costs. For a second, I wondered if he would fire one of those revolvers and put me out of my own misery. After all, we lived in times of decaying law and order and everyone did what they pleased.

I told Capasso and Bernstein about the tracks at dinner under the pavilion, while the beer flowed and the Bavarian band mechanically played on. Capasso told me he could hear motorcycles revving through the mountains before one of the storms, sounding like approaching thunder.

"Maybe we should get outta here," Capasso stated.

"Maybe he's right," I said to myself.

Right after dinner, Capasso, Bernstein, Milano, Rachel, and I got the bread truck ready with provisions, in case we had to make a hasty exit. Someone was out there all right, wandering around the countryside, and Handelsman was not going to listen to any of our warnings. Handelsman,

I suspected, believed that his little kingdom was impregnable, too isolated and well protected to have anything happen to it. Rachel lifted the boxes quickly. She had a frightened look in her eyes. We all worked hard for a few hours and stopped when the night fell from the sky.

Roger and I got up the next day and prayed. Both of us diligently read the scriptures and tried to hear God's still small voice, but we could not since the times were so muddled with confusion. As we got ready to go to work, Marcia knocked on the door, and we both stepped out to join her. The three of us walked to the farm down the road together, where we worked hard in the garden surrounded by wilderness. We kept our guns with us all the while, in case of a sudden attack from an unseen angle.

It was dinnertime at the picnic facilities under the sheltering pavilion. The Bavarian band played their accordions loudly, and their tubas blared as some of the men and women decided to dance and lose themselves in the festivities. Even Rachel, who was usually depressed, smiled and clapped her hands to the beat, a cigarette wedged between her lips. The music sounded, the beer and wine flowed. I just laughed away the hours, hardly concerned with the threat of a doomed tomorrow. Marcia, Roger, and I did not get intoxicated, however; we had to remain alert in case of the possible danger that may be lurking about.

The sun sank out to the west over Delhi as darkness began to stretch itself over this little German *Dorf* in the Catskills. Our armed tyrant continued to award his people with beer and circuses telling them that everything was "okay." However, socializing in a party atmosphere did give me something to look forward to each day. It was much better than the society we left behind Downstate, where every person lived a life disjointed from the others.

After dinner, things got a little rocky. Handelsman called Capasso, Milano and me into his office and led us back beyond it to a dark room that had a lone window in it. Capasso was quiet the whole time. I could swear he was contemplating the situation heavily. There was a clean-shaven armed guard here, wearing a baseball cap and holding a shotgun against his light green jacket. Through the conversation I found out that his name was Schilling. Handelsman sat down in a folding chair in front of a bookcase that spanned across the whole wall, and I knew this whole situation was not going to be good. The atmosphere was sullen, and I felt Handelsman was perturbed to say the least.

"I haven't heard from Patrick McMahon for several weeks. From what I can tell, you were the last ones to see him. He's been missing. Come clean. Did you kill him?" Handelsman asked.

"We have no idea where he's been. Maybe one of those things got him. Maybe he was arrested. How're we supposed to know where he went?" Capasso stated.

"Bob Capasso!" Handelsman said as he sat on the small chair in front of the stack of books. He played with one of the silver revolvers in his hand, pushing the cylinder in and out of the gun, the light of the sinking sun shining off of its polished surface. I began to sweat. I wanted to vomit and urinate.

"Did you shoot Pat McMahon?"

"No," Capasso said.

"Bob Capasso, did you kill Pat McMahon?" he asked again.

"No!" Capasso said more emphatically.

"Bob Capasso. We haven't seen Pat McMahon for weeks. You shot him, didn't you?" Handelsman accused. Somehow, Handelsman knew.

Then I heard it. It was the sound of all-terrain vehicles and motorbikes rumbling outside the building, tearing apart all semblance of security we had. They ripped up what little peace the situation imparted. It could barely be detected above the remonstrating between Handelsman and Capasso, but it grew louder.

The guard, Schilling, picked up his gun and got ready to fire it.

"I should have shot you dead a long time ago!" Handelsman said in a rage, fury in his eyes. He pulled the revolver on Capasso and raised it!

We heard the sound of motorcycles and the three-wheelers in the air, getting closer as gunshots could be heard. Bullets flew through one of the windows in the other room, breaking the fragile glass. Handelsman, who was about ready to fire a bullet into Capasso, suddenly got up from his seat, rushed by us, and left the small room. We followed in reckless curiosity. Handelsman ran around the large room that had the counter in it, shouting orders at Schilling.

"Who are these people? What's going on?" Handelsman asked in a panic, racing to all the windows with his revolver still drawn. More shots were fired through the casements that had already been shattered. All of us got down with our faces to the floor, trying to take cover from the incoming lead. What was happening?

It was tense for the next few minutes. Outside we could hear several guns being discharged, and it sounded like a small war was being fought out there. It lessened in intensity and then stopped altogether, giving us a chance to come to our senses. As I picked my head up, I detected a number of footfalls across the wooden porch outside the door. The black door swung open and three dismal men stepped in, all wearing dark jackets, dark pants, and dirty motorcycle helmets.

The three of them stood at the entrance, observing their surroundings, taking them in. One of them happened to be a large and stocky man, exuding a great deal of power and a callous disregard for the human race. The big man took his helmet off and revealed a bearded face with long wiry hair that looked like a lion's mane. I imagined most of the others had a similar appearance. They were some of the local country boys, of that Dutch-English stock, out to have a good time, raping, pillaging, and burning.

"Okay, this looks like the main building alright, and I would like to get your money. All of it," the stocky man said.

Handelsman looked up at him from the floor. "What do you want?"

The other two men, who still had their helmets on, stood with pistols drawn, looking a little jumpy, as if they were ready to use them at the smallest sign of resistance. The stocky man smirked with malice. He seemed to be a sadist who did not care about bullying other people to get what he wanted.

"Everyone who has a gun, put it on the floor now!" The big man ordered. Schilling and Handelsman yielded up their weapons and placed them in a pile at the bandits' feet.

"Okay gentlemen, let me find out who's in charge of this place," the big man said, extending his hand towards us.

Handelsman got up and walked near him, unarmed.

"Good. We've got a player here! Sir, it is such a pleasure to meet you. I hope we can do a lot of business together. My name is Bruce DeVries. Pleased to meet you!" he said with a wide beaming smile, full of sarcasm, extending his hand for a shake.

Garrick Handelsman refused to take it, as the glistening sweat beaded on his forehead.

"C'mon, man. Shake my hand. C'mon, if you don't shake my hand, I'll consider it very, very rude," DeVries said.

Still Handelsman would not shake the man's hand.

"What is your name, sir? Sir, I asked you very nicely. Now what is your name?" DeVries asked. "Y'know I am not taking this very kindly. When I get mad at people, I shoot them. Stu, Dave, when I say 'fire', LET 'EM HAVE IT!"

"My name is Garrick Handelsman," he said with a weak handshake.

"Good," DeVries replied. "Now we can get down to business."

The boards creaked as DeVries walked across the wooden floor. He stopped at Capasso.

"Who're you?" DeVries asked Capasso, his face still to the floor.

Capasso moved his head sideways and replied, "Bob Capasso."

DeVries' creaking footsteps made their way towards me, and then stopped. My heart started to flutter. The man stood in front of me, and I could see the cracks in the tan work boots that he was wearing. I could feel his imposing presence that threatened to topple upon me.

"And you?" he asked.

"Andy Goering," I mumbled.

"Couldn't hear you," DeVries said.

This time I lifted my head off of the hard wooden planks. "My name is Andy Goering," I answered.

"That's more like it," he said.

Milano laid there with his face to the floor, scared and unmoving.

He took the heat off me and began to speak to Handelsman. DeVries told him that he wanted all the cash in the building. The big thief let Handelsman know that he had known about this haven in the Catskills for some time ago and he badly wanted to raid it. The large man was nothing more than a rural tough who led a gang of hoodlums around the Catskills, looting various places during the crisis. Since there were raiders in Rockland, what would make Upstate New York any different?

"Gary! May I call you Gary?" DeVries asked.

Handelsman nervously nodded.

"Y'know Gary, I was a poor farmer once, a little guy. But things have changed. Since all hell has broken loose, I'm a big man, and big men like big money. There's gotta be a safe here," DeVries said, stroking his bearded chin.

"I'm gonna have a lot of money and a lotta power. Ain't that great! Say 'yes,' Gary."

"Yes," Handelsman said nervously. Sweat broke out upon his bald head again.

DeVries asked Handelsman to take him to the place where the money was. Meanwhile, I heard the all-terrain vehicles start up again, letting me know that the three-ring circus had resumed. Handelsman and DeVries went up the stairs into the shadows. The four of us were just lying there on the floor, our guns nearby. The two helmeted men continued to watch us, making sure we didn't do anything rash. Long minutes crept by. Handelsman finally emerged from the darkness and walked back down the stairs, his hands held up high in the air. DeVries was right behind him, pointing a pistol at his back, a safety deposit bag in his free hand.

Once down the stairs, they went over to the counter and dumped the contents of the bag out upon its surface. They counted it out, and DeVries did not look too pleased.

"Where's the rest of it? There's only 15,000! There's gotta be more. Where's the rest of the money, Gary?" DeVries asked.

"That's it," Handelsman said weakly.

"I risked my neck for a lousy 15,000 dollars? You've gotta be kiddin' me!" he said practically screaming.

"I want the money, Gary. I want the money! If you don't give me the money, this is what will happen," DeVries said.

DeVries raised his pistol and then turned the barrel down upon the man named Schilling. As he picked up his head to understand what was happening, a look of horror came over the man's face. DeVries pulled the trigger, shooting him twice in the back and once in the head. His head went down, brutally murdered before me as blood accumulated and flowed across the floor. I wanted to vomit at the cruelty I witnessed. This is what happens to the human race when law and order are long gone!

"I don't have any more money. I sent it to some connections near Delhi. I just don't have any money!" Handelsman said nearly in tears, as Schilling lay dead, blood running onto the floor.

"Come on old man, there has to be more somewhere!" DeVries said.

All of a sudden shots were fired and lead sailed through the windows again! It seemed as if DeVries' bandits did not know when to stop.

"Those idiots! Don't they realize we're in here?" DeVries said, trying to take cover.

Handelsman, sensing the pervading confusion, reached down and grabbed one of his revolvers from the pile on the floor! Quickly, he fired at one of DeVries' men, who immediately fell backwards onto the boards he stood upon. DeVries pointed his pistol at Handelsman and fired it, hitting him in the chest. Capasso and I jumped up and went for the weapons on the floor. In the confusion, DeVries and the remaining man fled through the door. We heard the sound of two three-wheelers rev up amidst the continual revelry outside.

Capasso, Milano, and I stood on the front porch as the darkness gathered and threatened to crush the landscape around us. Men on three-wheelers passed by firing their weapons. We had to duck down while the barrage of bullets passed. It continued for about five minutes more as the last of them finally left. A few minutes later, about ten men showed up on the front porch, brandishing pistols and shotguns. One of them happened to be Baruch Dubitsky with his wide-brimmed hat and black and white clothing.

"We lost a few people," he said to us.

"How many?" Capasso asked.

"There are three dead and three wounded," Dubitsky answered. "What happened here?"

"Their leader tried to take every cent Handelsman owned," I answered. "They killed him."

No one spoke as the party walked into the main room where the office was located. They had to know about the demise of their leader. Dubitsky and the others stood over Handelsman and Schilling with solemn expressions. They were both dead. One of the men drew his pistol and shot Handelsman in the head so that he wouldn't come back. There was another body in the room with us, one of DeVries' men. We looked at his driver's license and identified him as Stuart Nuyver. Then, Dubitsky took the helmet off of the man's head and it revealed an unshaven face with dirty blond hair. The corpse was subsequently shot in the head so as not to cause us more problems. Dubitsky and the others dragged all of the men out to the dark street and burned their corpses after a quick eulogy was said. They were incinerated in a pyre that reached for the skies. Some tears were shed for Garrick Handelsman, the guardian of this little community. Although he was tyrannical at times, he was still loved by his subjects.

The next day, we gathered our belongings, preparing for the exodus. We had plenty of weapons and supplies thanks to Dubitsky. Dubitsky, acting as an authority, released us from our state of indentured servitude and told us we were free to go, like birds from a cage.

"Let me give you a van in exchange for that bread truck. You'll need better transportation," Dubitsky said. He was now the new leader of Barrett's Hollow.

By 12:00 that afternoon, our group of seven was about ready to leave for the unknown with a van stuffed with provisions. None of the people in Handelsman's settlement wanted to go with us, happy in their insulated little paradise. However, we knew it was dangerous. DeVries was still at large and would return someday to enact his revenge or suck the settlement dry of every last piece of dignity it had. I shook Baruch Dubitsky's hand and held it for several long moments. He waved "goodbye" as I boarded the vehicle. I looked back, and he disappeared as the van sped away into the tangled wilds.

Chapter Twenty-Two: Sarkill

My group found an old road that led us through the twisted woods into the knotted hills of the Catskills, taking us into Delaware County. Due to the pervasive military presence, we had to avoid the major route to Delhi. There was a population center there of more than 100,000 people, and the law enforcement agencies were still in operation. We were fugitives and had to live on the margins of a society gradually falling apart.

Although we had officially left the Catskill Park, the area still proved hilly, wooded, and remote. We had driven for over an hour through the hills, our progress slowed due to the disrepair of the roads. The local municipalities were in disarray, and some of them probably did not even exist as government entities anymore.

Quite often, we would see a stream or marsh on the side of the road, wooded hills in the backdrop. The area was quiet, isolated, and serene, and I thought about staying here for a while in these little valleys, soaking up a little sun. I was not sure what Capasso wanted since he was so silent and moody, driving the van without expression. I dared not ask him about taking little leisurely excursions. I sat in the back, reposing with Roger, Marcia, Milano, and Rachel, trying to stay out of the man's way. Roger seemed to be relaxed and unconcerned, and Milano was also nonchalant. Marcia gripped her bear, and Rachel stared out the window at the trees, spaced, not looking at anything else. She looked so cold and hopeless, her face a monument to the great goddess of despair.

Another hour went by, and the trees began to thin, green pastureland becoming common. I looked out on the horizon and could see the hills undulating into the sun that would soon set. Up ahead was a small community of old houses where the paint peeled off the outside walls and the shingles flaked from the roofs. All the structures were located on either side of the road. Some were set back into the hillside, practically out of sight. We approached a sign that read "Sarkill," which must have been the name of the community that we were nearing. There was a two-story house up ahead that looked like a general store with gas pumps in front of it. On the side of the road there was a woman walking vibrantly toward the store; she appeared to be alive and having definite intent. She was young, had dark brown hair, and wore a dress decorated with earthen colors. This little place seemed to be safe. We pulled up in front of the gas station and an older man, who was thin and wore a baseball cap and a tank top, approached the van.

"You need gas?" he asked without a smile.

"Yeah," Capasso said. "Fill it up."

The older man placed the dispenser into the gas tank as the dial on the pump started to rack up the bucks. I got out of the car, and walked across the gravel into the two-story building that served as the general store. A bell jingled as I opened up the door with curtains drawn across the window. As I entered, I sensed that strangers were not welcome. The clerk, a young man wearing shorts that went to his knees stood behind the counter absent of a smile. Food and supplies like plastic ware and lighter fluid sat on white wooden shelves. I picked up some canned soups that would be good for the duration of our stay, wherever it would be.

I noticed that the young woman, the one I had seen earlier, was now here in the store, standing and looking around at the items. Remembering my failure with Marcia back at Barrett's Hollow, I thought about trying to kindle another relationship. Although I doubted she was an evangelical Christian like myself, I thought it might be worth a shot to find out.

"You like this little place?" I said to her, trying to start up a conversation.

"Yes, I do, but it is not like I have much of a choice," she responded, in a happy-go-lucky sort of way. I really did not know what to say, and realized that we would need lodging, so I quickly changed the subject in order to save face.

"There are six others with me. Do you think we can find a place to stay?" I asked the young woman.

"I'm not sure. I can ask my dad. He may have some room at the house." I was grateful for the possibility. I took the girl out to the van and introduced her to all of its occupants. We found out that her name was Angeline Davies and her father was a retired professor from one of the state universities in the area.

"Could you guys give me a ride?" she asked Capasso.

He looked down at her coldly and nodded his head. She climbed into the back of the van and began to converse with Rachel, who followed her in.

Capasso turned around on the same road that brought us to the store, but made a left at the "Sarkill" sign that we saw earlier. The road took us into another part of the little hamlet populated by two-story homes and a few modern ranches. Angeline told us that most of the places were inhabited, despite the fact that so many ended up in the population center near Delhi. The people in this settlement actually banded together, patrolled the area, and destroyed any ghouls that wandered in.

We saw a quaint two-story home on the left-hand side of the road, smothered in a coat of green paint. A spacious backyard sat behind it, leading out into the tree-covered hills.

"This is 'our' place," she said. Capasso turned into the driveway and parked the van behind a tan station wagon that was falling into disrepair.

Angeline led the way as the rest of us piled out of the van, pistols tucked within our belts. The young woman led us into the house to a living room with a cream-colored sofa, a few blue recliners with wooden armrests, and a wall full of books set upon two sets of dark oak shelves. Maybe they were Angeline's, but I figured the man who lived here liked to read, and their presence indicated that he had intellectual pursuits. We could hear noise coming from the back of the shadowy house somewhere that slowly made itself more distinct. The footsteps grew louder as the person making them drew closer, echoing off of the walls. An overweight balding man, complete with a beard, appeared in the doorway, roughly about sixty years old.

"Daddy, these are some strangers who are new in town," Angeline said.

"My name is Arnold Davies," the man greeted us.

Angeline went around the room and introduced everybody to her father, a retired philosophy teacher from SUNY New Paltz. He was an eccentric man, seemingly absorbed in the realm of ideas more so than in the here and now.

"Where do you hope to go?" he asked.

"Someplace safe," Capasso grunted, somewhat facetiously.

"There is no place that's 'safe'," he retorted, looking at both Capasso and me. "But you can stay here for awhile," he said with a smile.

"I wish there was someplace safe," Rachel said quietly and so sadly. The woman looked as if all of her expectations flapped their wings and flew out a window.

I found it peculiar how the man opened his house up to strangers. He seemed to lack fear or apprehension of any sort. He just insisted upon having us relax in his living room and offered us tea and coffee. Davies was quite a host to us. I sat on the floor grateful, cross-legged, and thinking to myself. Rachel sat blankly next to Milano, who did not seem to pay much attention to her.

Davies spoke, rambling off a long soliloquy. Roger and I listened intently, as did Marcia and Capasso, but Milano and Rachel began to nod off as Bernstein fidgeted. Davies did not mind. He just continued speaking. I got the impression that he was a lonely man despite his daughter living here with him. He probably loved the fact that there were visitors here to entertain. Now he had someone to toss around concepts with.

"Where is your wife?" I asked a little boldly.

"She's dead."

"I'm sorry to hear that," I said. "What happened, if you don't mind me asking?"

"No, not at all. She contracted an infection while working in the backyard some time ago. I could not get her to a rescue center on time, the infection spread quickly and she died. I had to bury her body in the backyard after shooting her in the forehead," he said.

I didn't pry any further.

He explained to us that ghouls periodically wander into the community. Davies mentioned that some of the people here have died, and he had the opportunity to observe their behavior after their "resurrection." The ghouls acted like animals, almost as if their ability to reason had been stripped away. They can use simple tools, like a baseball bat or possibly a crowbar as a club, similar to what primates do at times.

"Traces of rational thinking seemed to be evident because many of them return to the old haunts. They were familiar with these places back in the days of their old 'lives'," he added.

Davies had apparently been studying the whole phenomenon as it ate away at humanity like a cancer.

"Why do you know so much about this?" I asked Davies.

"I am a naturally curious person," he said

Davies went on to say he was an avid philosopher who had many contacts with academics around the nation. He had friends in Atlanta and Washington who were biologists who had tried unsuccessfully to come up with a cure for this radioactive plague.

"They have found no solutions," he said.

"Why do you think they can't come up with any answers?" I asked Arnold Davies. Davies paced back and forth, his bald head reflecting the glow off the dim light that hung from the ceiling. He continued to walk the floor, totally consumed in the matter of my question.

"Because scientists are stupid. They think they know everything. They try to come up with rational explanations for phenomena, but life and existence cannot always be explained by reason alone. So solutions may always evade them. Unless…"

"Unless what?" I asked.

"Unless they consider other options." I noticed that sweat began to trickle down his cheeks. He was afraid of something and it made him apprehensive.

"What other options?" I asked in a very slow and serious tone. Capasso said nothing, sitting in the living room watching Davies without expression, Bernstein loyally doing the same. Milano and Rachel stirred almost as if they could feel the solicitude in their sleep. Roger stared at Davies intently, and Marcia appeared nervous, vulnerable. There was something significant about what Davies was going to say, and most everyone knew it subliminally.

"They look too much to the physical world. Maybe this contagion does not have its origins in the natural as they so believe," Davies stated. "Maybe it has been caused by the supernatural, or something extremely powerful." Capasso and Bernstein chortled at the comment. Milano, awakened from his sleep, stared groggily at Davies.

"I have studied *Voodoo,*" Davies said.

"Where are you goin' with this?" I asked.

"Just give me a second." I shut up. "Voodoo is a syncretism of Roman Catholicism and African animism that is or 'was' very prevalent in parts of the French Caribbean, Cuba, and the Dominican Republic. Everything is so uncertain now, but there have always been cases in Haiti where dead bodies started walking around, indicating some power had animated them. This has confounded the Haitian police on several occasions," he said. "Is there a connection?"

He continued, "Are you familiar with the story of Exodus?"

"Yeah," I answered.

"If you recall the story, Egypt's sorcerers turned the Nile to blood with their arcane arts. There were ancient magicks afoot back in those days that have been here with us for centuries," he said. "And they still have effect."

My ears perked up at this. Perhaps this reference was a reminder that the Almighty had not forgotten about the human race, and that he had not forgotten about me.

In the course of Davies' bizarre explanation, Roger looked at me without uttering a word. I could tell by the expression on his face that Davies' suggestion made sense to him. Marcia appeared scared and insecure, holding the bear. Part of me still wanted to comfort her, but I think it was too late for any romantic interludes between us.

"I think you all are tired, and it would be a good idea to disperse for the evening. We can continue tomorrow. Discuss it among yourselves in your rooms," Davies gently ordered.

Capasso, cold as steel, glared at Davies with seething hatred. I don't think he appreciated Davies telling him what to do. For a second, I yawned loudly.

"Let's go to bed," I said to the group.

Capasso now glared at me in anger, probably over the fact that I gave orders to everyone. He wanted to dominate and despised me for what I had just done. Capasso was an enemy, in spite of the fact that the real adversaries were the ghouls.

Angeline escorted Roger, Marcia, and me down the dark hallway into a large white room that had a lot of brown wooden bookshelves in it, all filled with tomes. It was his library, a collection of Roman and Greek law and thought, philosophical works of Kant and Rousseau, along with biological treatises. "Perhaps it might make good reading," I thought. This was a place that I could lock myself in for days. The three of us sat down on the floor cross-legged, trying to digest and understand Davies' explanation.

"Maybe he's right," Roger said.

"Well, that is the big question," I admitted. "What he said makes sense though. We are just wasting time trying to work on a conventional cure for a disease that is not conventional."

Roger fidgeted, got up, and paced around for a little bit. He sat back down on the floor and held his head in his hands, mumbling miserably, and again admitted that Davies was most likely right. For a moment, my eyes wandered off to the bookshelf. There I saw something most peculiar, as if there was some book there that may actually hold the key to this whole elusive mystery. I decided to put that off for tomorrow, since I was tired and in need of sleep. We all needed it. Marcia lay on the couch with the teddy as Roger and I sacked out on the floor, drifting off.

I began to dream of the same landscape that had haunted me so many times before. I was in the gray expanse, and I could see the vegetation growing as my subconscious became aware of the order that took shape around me. That same jeep without a driver approached me, and it slowed down long enough for me to get in, which I did. The sequence began to alter, and something different happened. This time, bony talons pushed through the gray soil as the dead unburied themselves! The dead were here and they twisted their way upward, hissing, as that same character loomed on the distant horizon. The vehicle picked up speed, driven by an unseen presence, and went on trying to catch up to the elusive figure.

The sun pleasantly winked in the sky at me, providing the sunny warmth that sustained me in this realm of phantasm. I looked out in the distance upon the sandy gray dunes, taking note that the object got larger and larger. I drew closer, and I knew I would eventually overtake it as the menacing corpses struggled to get out of the sand, moaning in pursuit of my warm flesh. They did not want me to understand the answer to the riddle of the living dead.

The object on the horizon grew larger as I gained upon it, seeming to move in a peculiar manner, galloping. I concluded that whatever it was it rode upon the back of a horse! The creature was a sentient being of some sort, and if it was sentient, then it could probably speak. If it could speak, I would get answers. God was and is good.

As the dream ended, I awoke to the day's light streaming through the windows and stirring me from sleep. As I sat up, I found myself unafraid, eager to understand more. Looking around me, I noticed that Roger was asleep on the floor and Marcia was still on the couch with her eyes closed, snoring lightly. I was now alive with excitement, and I knew that I was on the verge of unraveling this whole thing.

I wandered into the bathroom down the hall, changed my clothes and brushed my teeth. I walked to the bathroom window and stared into the backyard that led up the slope. I saw nothing but the green woods bristling with movement as birds sung and squirrels scurried across the lawn. I wondered if they were aware of humanity's plight.

As I looked out at the activity in the backyard, I began to think about the current situation. I had heard that ghouls are not interested in eating animals. Once in awhile, you may hear of them devouring a dog or a cat, but that was a rare instance. Usually they went after living humans, and that was it. Their goal was to completely annihilate the living and leave no evidence of our existence, to erase mankind. I left the bathroom and sauntered over to the kitchen.

Angeline was sitting in her white bathrobe and sipping coffee. I looked at her face and found it very appealing.

"Good morning, Andy," she said. As soon as she spoke, it shattered my intoxication.

"You're an intellectual, aren't you?" she asked.

"Yeah, I guess," I answered.

"So am I," she said. "I like intellectuals. I find them to be great people to throw concepts around with."

"Did you go to college?" I asked.

"Yeah," she said.

"What was your major?"

"I was goin' for a Masters degree in psych up in Albany," she answered.

"You want to continue with it someday?"

"God only knows, Andy. When this whole thing hit, classes were cancelled. Maybe once it subsides I can go back to school."

Angeline had nothing to do but to go home and try to pass the time away. She divulged to me part of her private history, since we had both brought up the delicate past.

Her mother, Sini Rajashakara, came from Bombay and married her father in the early seventies. Angeline came along in 1976, born into an unconventional household. Her father was an unusual philosopher, with a flair for mythology and the metaphysical. He believed in unusual concepts yet gravitated towards secular humanism. Consistent with his beliefs, he adhered to the Unitarian faith, which sought to serve humanity and offer no salvation. Her mother was originally Hindu, but she became a Zoroastrian, embracing the faith of the Parsees. Angeline was caught between the two systems and accepted the belief in nothing as a compromise. I wondered how she fared with men.

"Do you have a boyfriend?" I asked.

"Not at the present time," she answered.

"Why?"

"I had a bad experience in the past," she responded rather coldly.

"Maybe you can share that with me. You wanna now?" I questioned.

"Please Andy, not now," she said.

I dropped the whole subject immediately. Angeline was warm, like Marcia, but a little more inviting, similar to an advertisement in a department store window. Perhaps we could have a marriage, maybe even have kids, but I did not think she was a good one to marry. Unless she shared my faith, it would just bring me down, straining our relationship and tearing it apart at the seams.

It was enough of a struggle for me to believe that God was even out there, how would Angeline ever believe that God loves people at this point? I hoped to the Almighty that there would be a definitive answer soon.

Chapter Twenty-Three: Venus

Davies and the rest of the crew got up as the house stirred with activity. Capasso and Bernstein were cleaning their guns, something they were fond of doing. They took great pride in their weapons. Marcia took a shower that she sorely needed; most of us hadn't bathed for over a day. Rachel ate a bowl of cereal, absorbed in it as if she was trying to kill some sort of pain within her. Bernstein, Milano, and Capasso later stood around in the kitchen, engaging in coarse joking, another one of their favorite pastimes. The three of them were like peas in a pod, losing themselves in sexual innuendoes. Rachel sighed in worn-out exasperation. It was if she was taking things too seriously.

Davies announced to the group that he was going to have a conference in the living room and discuss the origin of the crisis. I was intrigued at this. Davies took the stage amongst the furniture and the wooden bookcases, continuing on with the same topic that he discussed the previous night. All of us were staying put to listen except for Milano and Rachel, who managed to skip out somewhere to avoid Davies' seemingly endless prattle. Milano seemed not to care too much about the crisis, as if it hadn't hit him that the human race was crumbling into dust. I think Rachel left because she had little hope, and maybe the conference would destroy what hope she did have. Davies continued the discussion undaunted, noting the significance of the supernatural and how departed spirits may linger on in a particular area for some time to come. He entertained the idea of supernatural entities trafficking with humanity.

"But what of Venus?" he asked suddenly.

"What do you mean, 'but what of Venus?' What's the point?" I questioned. The other inhabitants in the house grew inattentive except for Roger, who was absorbed in Davies' philosophizing. Angeline sat in the nearby kitchen, still in her white bathrobe and seemingly unmoved.

"It is the second planet from the sun," he said.

"Yeah. Well I know that. So what?" I blurted.

"It is certainly the second planet from the sun, and where did the crisis originate?" he asked.

"The probe went to Venus. That's where the radiation came from," Roger answered.

"Precisely, Mr. Scarpaci," Davies stated. "The key may not be on this earth, but rather on that planet up there in the sky. Since I do have an interest in physical science, I have connections with others who knew what happened to that probe."

Roger and I froze, a tingle going up my spine. Perhaps Davies had a clue to the mystery as he laid the subject on the table.

"Venus is our sister planet," Davies said. "Earth and Venus are similar in size and in mass, but the similarities stop there. For the most part, Venus is uninhabitable."

Davies continued on, Roger and I listening with all earnestness. It was interesting to allow the older man to "ramble on," although when all was said and done it wasn't really rambling. He was an eccentric person who had information that I believed was vital to unlocking this convolution of circumstances.

"The surface of Venus is cloud-covered, and for centuries, no one knew what was under that canopy. At one time it was thought that swamps and jungles, due to the belief that the clouds created a hot-house effect, covered Venus's surface. According to theories, the hot-house effect lent to a vociferous growth of vegetation. This idea gave rise to science fiction stories, wherein men made trips to the planet and lived there, such as in Edgar Rice Burroughs' *Carson of Venus*. Have you heard of this, Andy?" he asked.

"Yeah. I think I read a comic book about him once."

"Do you remember what the comic book was about?" he asked.

"Yeah, I do. It was about an earthman born in India, who journeyed to Venus to battle monsters and the strange beings that live there, right?"

"Andy, you are correct," he stated, smiling.

"Do you think anything can actually live on Venus?" he asked.

"Not that I know of."

"Right again, Venus is far from 'habitable.' The cloud cover traps incoming solar radiation and makes the surface underneath unbearably hot. In fact, the temperatures average about 900 degrees Fahrenheit. Any life form without protection would end up with boiling blood and its physical body would burn up. The intense heat, lack of water, and the absence of oxygen would make it impossible to support life, at least as we so know it. The atmosphere is composed of carbon dioxide, nitrogen, hydrogen, along with some water vapor, and it all combines to make the atmosphere on the planet unbreathable."

"Where are you going with this, Davies?" I asked.

"Just be patient young man, and you will see," he said sternly. "Due to the intense heat, the surface is dry and dusty; fierce winds whip over the surface, picking up sand as they go, wearing the surface down. It is more of a lifeless desert than anything else; the world of Edgar Rice Burroughs is most likely dead. Perhaps though, something really can live in the prevailing conditions of Venus, but if life exists there, the American and Soviet probes did not find it," he continued.

"What is life?" he asked.

"What is life? What d'you mean?" I pushed, a little annoyed.

"Young man, please be patient," he went on. "Life is something that can be difficult to define." This was becoming interesting.

"Once the spark of life has left, the creature cannot be revived. This is unlike a machine with a broken part. If the part on a machine is replaced, it can function normally, but with a living creature, one cannot do that." Davies paused. This was clearly taking a lot of his energy. The man was tensed up for some reason.

"A life form must have an independent consciousness that gives rise to independent action. A rabbit responds to its environment. A rabbit also has emotions, although they are not as complex as those of a human being. A machine does not have emotions at all. Nor does a rock, or the wind for that matter. Perhaps there is life on Venus. I think that there are life forms that science cannot easily explain," Davies said.

"Davies, what is up there? What did the probe bring back?" I insisted.

Davies hesitated and stared out a nearby window, lost in thought, looking toward the trees. He did not want to answer that question.

"What is up there?" I asked again, nearly losing my temper. Davies peered with his head half-turned towards me.

"There was something that was picked up by the camera mounted on the probe. The probe had spent several hours going over the dry sandy surface, collecting samples that would be brought back to earth and examined by NASA scientists. The reddish surface did not change and did not yield activity of any sort," he said. Davies paused again. This was very difficult for him to explain.

"However, there was a variation that could be detected during a gathering dust storm. Movement was seen in this disturbance..."

"What is this? A science fiction novel?" Bernstein mocked.

"Shut-up and let the man finish!" Roger insisted. Bernstein continued to snicker.

"And whatever it was in the distance walked to and fro, seemingly without definite purpose. As it got closer to the diligent probe, it no longer wandered around aimlessly, taking towards the device. Gusts of sand blew and periodically obscured the object, but it became more pronounced as it neared. The vague figure took on a humanoid appearance, walking upright through the chaos of the surrounding storm. It got closer, perhaps only thirty yards off, it passed by a small drift. As it passed by the drift, it could be clearly seen. What was in the probe's camera was something unnatural, that shouldn't be there and shouldn't exist, but it did exist!" he said.

Now all of us listened intently, hanging on Davies' every word.

"What was it Davies? What was up there?" I asked.

"*It was the shimmering form of a woman in a dress, gracefully walking towards the machine.* Then, the camera just sputtered out, stopped working, and that was it. The rest has been history, and now we're paying for it."

Roger and I fell into silence. Davies stood with his back up against one of the bookshelves. He had an uncomfortable expression upon his face. I'm sure all this made him feel very strange and kind of foolish, but the whole thing made me think. Davies believed the plague was created by the supernatural and not the natural. I remembered something in my possession, in one of the duffle bags that I had brought with me.

Later on, I went outside and down the street, and I met an older man who had glasses and a bald head. He owned a large garden. His name was Pierce, and I labored in his garden for several hours. It seemed as if I had been working on a lot of farms lately, reminding me of the experience I had in Barrett's Hollow with Handelsman and his people. It was interesting how all the communities that we have encountered had become little self-sufficient entities, almost like farm communes or Israeli kibbutzim, and I wondered why. It was my guess that, when there is a crisis, people band together in order to survive. No one can go on without knowing his neighbor. Times like these warrant the strengthening of ties.

Chapter Twenty-Four: Mesopotamian Myth and the Grim Conjecture

That evening, as we all ate the dinner that Roger, Angeline, and Davies diligently prepared, I began to really ponder the conversation of the morning. If there was something up there on that planet, what was it? At that point, the impulse to go back to the reading den took over. After supper, I returned to the library and found Marcia on the couch snoring lightly. She stirred, then sat up rubbing her eyes and muttered something, but I was too preoccupied to ask her what it was. She gave up consciousness again and fell back into the black pit of slumber. My blue duffle bag was lying on the floor next to where I had slept. I picked it up and started rummaging through it. Out went the socks, out went the shirts, and everything else until I had found it. In my left hand I held a videocassette composed of black plastic. I studied its surface and savored the object. Somehow, the information that was on there contained another piece of this abominable puzzle.

I found Davies in the kitchen desperately drinking coffee. "Could I use your VCR?" I asked him.

"Yes, but why?"

"I think I have another key to this whole mystery here in my hand," I said.

"Maybe I should join you," Davies said.

Davies and I went into the living room and placed the tape in the drawer of VCR, which greedily sucked it inside. Roger and Angeline were nearby and decided to join us, curious as to what was showing. We played the tape and saw the young dark-haired woman who was named Michelle Ramadan. She sat calmly in a brown leather chair, seemingly unconcerned about people's opinions; she was interviewed by a well-dressed host wearing a suit and tie.

"Before the war, Iraqis were starting to embrace ancient Mesopotamian paganism, pushed by the Baath Party," she said matter-of-factly, despite the jeers from the audience.

"Saddam Hussein and his cohorts wanted to emphasize Iraq's pagan past in order to instill a sense of pride within its people. Pagan cults were revived despite the tendency of Islam to absorb all other religions." The audience continued to heckle her unsuccessfully.

She went on to explain that the influence of paganism was stronger immediately after George W. Bush invaded Iraq, more so than at any other previous time period. We stopped the tape right there. Could it be that Michelle Ramadan had another crucial segment to this mystery? Was there a connection between that humanoid figure on Venus and this resurgence in ancient Iraqi paganism?

I spent the rest of the day walking around the woods behind Davies' property. I was joined by Angeline. We discussed both psychology and philosophy on the trails that led through the tangle of trees. Although she was an agnostic, she loved to toss around concepts and found it a great source of entertainment. The two of us wondered how to reconcile Aquinas's *Summa Theologica* with Christian and Jewish thought, and discussed the adverse revival of Iraqi paganism that had hung over the Middle East like a bad storm. We continued on under the summer sun, walking paths that twisted and wound their way amongst the birch and elm into the coniferous forest of Upstate New York. From Angeline, I sensed only warmth and peace.

"I've been alone for too long and I don't like it. I'm getting sick and tired of the whole thing," she said.

"You alluded earlier to the fact that you had a lot of bad experiences. Am I right?" I asked.

"Yeah, but not a lot. Just one," she said.

"What happened? Were you engaged?" I asked.

"No. I was living in this guy's apartment a few towns away. We got into a seriously heated argument one evening and he just kicked me out."

"He kicked you out just like that?" I asked.

"Yeah, just made me get out all of my stuff and leave. Then he admitted that he never loved me in the first place," she explained.

"Do you think that was true?" I questioned.

"Yeah, he never seemed to be too passionate about anything he did with me. It only took one argument and that was it. I've been really careful about getting into relationships since then, but since the crisis began I don't really wanna be alone."

She was lonely and insecure under these uncertain circumstances, and so was I. Her warm and gentle hand brushed up against mine, and I took it with apprehension. We approached life from two different angles, and I wondered if this was the right thing to do. After all, she was a secular humanist and I was an evangelical Christian. Our world-views clashed, but maybe that would change over time.

"Angie, you have beautiful brown eyes," I said to her.

Her pupils expanded to get a better image of my features as she smiled. We sat down in front of a birch next to the path that ran through the tangled and primitive wilds.

"You have beautiful lips, too," I told her.

"Thank you," she responded.

We kissed several times, my lips moving up and down her neck, passing over her forehead. I enjoyed the company of a woman, and it warmed my soul very much. It made me forget about this cruel world that I lived in.

Suddenly, I heard something stumble within the trees, stepping over broken branches on the ground and shaking the boughs as it jarred us both from the wonderful moment. I broke away from Angeline and turned around. There it was, a distorted thing with brown hair and a tan dress shirt that hung from its torso in ripped shreds. It was a ghoul! The thing, with its gray and distorted animal-like face, let out an inhuman growl as it clumsily walked out of the trees. It moved somewhat faster than expected and was upon us in no time, even before we had a chance to stand up.

It tottered towards us and grabbed Angeline by the head, threatening to take a bite out of her neck. In reaction, I seized its wrists to remove its hands from the back of her head, but it just looked at my own hands and positioned its mouth to bite them. I took my fist and hit it in the face without restraint, and then again out of sheer anger. It growled loudly in response.

The ghoul let go of Angeline. I joined both fists together like a demolition ball and hit it in the face as hard as I could. The thing stumbled back a little toward the primeval wood. I picked up a fallen branch that was on the ground and swung it madly, out of control. I drove the twisted mockery towards the edge of a little shelf that overlooked some brush. I hit it once again, causing it to fall backwards down the hill and skid into the trees. I could not allow it to get away, I had to kill it and make sure its body remained still and inactive.

I found a half-buried rock a little bigger than my fist and ran down the hill with it. I attacked the thing as it crawled around on its hands and knees underneath the large bushes that grew outward. It started to get its bearings and grumbled through its decrepit jaw, reaching out with its hand to take my ankle. I lifted the stone and brought it down upon its skull several times.

"That will teach you to never take me away from a woman again!" I said in rage.

Down the stone went, again and again, and the skull was soon crushed under the onslaught. The ghoul stopped moving and went silent, ceasing to function altogether, its machinery now in total disrepair.

Angeline showed up at my side and looked at my handiwork. She gazed down at the blood that oozed from the crushed skull and winced. The dead body disturbed her, and I didn't blame her. This thing was once a man who breathed and lived and enjoyed his life, just like I was doing a few moments ago.

"That thing almost killed me!" she said in anger. She calmed down and put her head on my shoulder. I placed my arm around her to provide the comfort she needed.

We ventured back to the house and sat down in the living room with Roger and Marcia, as Davies moved about his house sipping coffee. There was a little tension floating around in this home as the television played, everyone a little insecure. On the TV, the balding Burnside and the lovely McLean had been replaced by a black man who wore a black tie and a white shirt. Maybe the old ones died or had left like so many others had done, blown away by the winds of pestilence and destruction.

McIntyre, the guy that looked like Rasputin, reappeared and began to address the viewers.

"Things are going very poorly. If we don't start co-operating, we're all going to be in a lot of trouble!" McIntyre said condescendingly. "We're almost at the point of no return. By our estimates, the dead form about 40% of humanity, if you wanted to classify ghouls as being that!" Someone from off the set heckled him with words born of a foolish heart.

"Would you listen to me? WOULD YOU JUST SHUT UP AND LISTEN? By our estimates there are over one hundred million of these things in the United States alone, in addition to the hundreds of millions that are in other countries around the world!" McIntyre shouted through his long beard, his face turning beet red in frustration.

Angeline stared at the set, as did Marcia and Roger. No one said a word, the situation grave as death hovered over the land. There was no longer any hope that we would obtain a cure by chemical or nuclear means. The cities, for the most part, had been abandoned, and the squads of national guardsmen and police could no longer contain the plague of ghouls.

"Maybe we should drop nuclear bombs on New York, L.A. and Miami. Most of them are in our cities, and maybe that would take care of the problem. Just destroy them in a blast of pure atomic energy! BURN 'EM TO A CRISP! YEEHAA!" McIntyre ranted as he shook his clenched fists. It appeared as if the guy was at the end of his rope.

"That's preposterous! We can't decimate our own cities! That's self-destruction!" the black man, with the white shirt and dark tie, suggested.

The camera shifted from McIntyre and the black newscaster to a panel of scientists. The scientists brought up the idea of appeasing the ghouls by raising people like cattle and feeding them their body parts. With that, I knew it was finished. The solution to the crisis descended into the black pit of overwhelming circumstances. Marcia vomited on the floor and Davies nervously sipped his coffee. Angeline rubbed her eyes in weariness, almost as if this was all her fault. This whole matter was crazy, and I realized that the human race was going down the tubes and nothing could stop it. It seemed as if God had somehow turned his eyes from humanity, his ears deaf to our pleas. Where was he?

"God, where are you? Did you forget about me? Did you forget about us?" I asked in prayer that very moment.

There was no definite answer, but I sensed something tugging at my awareness. Thoughts went through my head, and they told me not to pay attention to the circumstances. For a second, I detached myself and got lost in thought. Circumstances are fluid and are not rigidly fixed. My thoughts implied the human race would somehow manage to survive. "How?" I wondered. Perhaps Andrew Frank Goering would be influential in some sort of fashion. I hoped my time was coming. We shut off the TV and the raving McIntyre to clean up Marcia's mess.

The dim report had passed, and I shut myself inside the library. There were books about science and astronomy along with classic works by Dante, Shakespeare, and Dostoevsky. Davies even owned treatises by Enlightenment philosophers like Rousseau and Locke. He was an intellectual who pursued knowledge for the sake of understanding alone.

I discovered a section of books that dealt with a particular theme: mythology. Mythology was a collection of tales where humanity tried to explain away its environment with no scientific understanding. Natural forces were described as being the works of powerful beings referred to as gods and goddesses. Perhaps gods and goddesses really did exist, living in the shadows throughout the ages, indirectly influencing human conduct. This whole concept made me shudder for a moment, and I sneezed in response.

I combed over the mythology section of Davies' library and stumbled upon the subject of Mesopotamian legend, which echoed Michelle Ramadan's theories. I began to peruse through but paused, unsure of what to do. Once more, I left the den and watched the videotape, afraid and apprehensive of that young, dark-haired woman.

She expressed the resurrection of paganism in Iraq without fear of reprisal from the audience. They picked on her without mercy, but she remained nonchalant and unconcerned in response; she believed in something that was greater than the opinions of the masses. The woman readily admitted that she knew pagan deities did in fact exist and still sought to carry out their will in the modern age. Davies believed that the plague was started by a supernatural manifestation of some sort, and her spiel began to make me think he was right. Supernatural entities could possess abilities to reconstitute matter and perhaps reanimate dead corpses. Perhaps these entities could still be out there, wandering around like restless spirits screaming through the night, existing for nothing else but to relentlessly consume.

Later that evening, I went to sleep and abandoned the waking world. Again, I found myself in that bleak and vague landscape, the vegetation more plentiful as my understanding grew. The sun bore down on me with its hopeful rays, and the jeep without a driver stopped at my left. I boarded it as the talons shot up through the dry and gray soil, desiring warm flesh. The peaceful presence was still there in the driver's seat as the jeep gained on the silhouetted figure on horseback.

As I approached him, I could detect his outlines. He sat on the back of a dark horse, wearing an old tunic with a sword hanging from his waist. His hair and beard were most peculiar, long and with multiple braids, very much like an ancient Mesopotamian nobleman. His dark horse sped away as he realized I was right behind him, but the animal could not match the jeep's velocity. I looked behind me and noticed that the gray corpses were still in pursuit. Nonetheless, the jeep sped on with a mission in mind.

The chase continued over the gray sand. The vegetation began to thin as I approached the mystery looming ahead. The bearded figure on horseback neared the sandy hill, running out of room to run. Peering behind me once again, I saw the army of ghouls stumble out of the vegetation-ridden area in slow pursuit. It was clear that if I stopped too long they would catch up to me and remove me from my existence in the realm of phantasm, and who knows, I might even die in the waking realm. The figure on the horse stopped on the crest of the acclivity and I could see that there was another landscape out in the distance, beyond that. The bearded figure on the horse slowed and so did the jeep. The sun shined down and gave me confidence. The bearded figure stopped and turned his horse around to face me as the wails of the dead were heard from behind. Suddenly, I awoke with a gasp!

The sun was coming up somewhere outside the window, shining through the trees with hope. Roger was not on the floor next to me, and Marcia was still asleep on the couch fully clothed, snoring lightly as usual. I moved quietly toward the large bookcase against the wall, careful not to disturb her. Perusing the variety of manuscripts, I once again found the section Davies reserved for mythology.

There was something I had read many years ago while an undergraduate in SUNY Oswego, and I felt it was crucial to this whole mystery. It was an ancient epic written in an equally ancient language called Akkadian, spoken in ancient Mesopotamian. I ran my fingers over the spines of the books on the shelf. Then I stopped and hesitated. There it was, nestled between the two larger tomes that flanked it. I pulled out the smaller book and read its title. It was *The Legend of Gilgamesh.* I opened the book and voraciously read a tale of a Sumerian king who wanted to live on forever.

I read it and read perhaps too much. What I had gleaned from it sent chills up and down my spine and disturbed me to no end. In it, Inanna, or Ishtar, the ancient goddess known for erotic tendencies, wanted to make love to Gilgamesh, the ancient Sumerian king. Gilgamesh refused, enraging Ishtar. She resorted to childlike tendencies and threw a tantrum when she could not get her way. She was mad to the point (and here was perhaps the crux of the matter) that *she threatened to let the dead out of the under-world where they would eat the living unless she got what she wanted.* I paused and began to think. What I had just read bore a certain similarity to the current crisis we were now in. This may have been the whole issue all along!

Chapter Twenty-Five: The Looming Shadow of Thieves

I took the book once again and watched the videotape of Ramadan making her spiel about the resurgence of Iraqi paganism, playing it over and over again. Was Michelle Ramadan still alive? I believed that I would have to find her, or at least find her office and notes. How would I do that? Despite the unanswered question, I felt confident that this whole mystery would become clear and praised God for the clarity. Perhaps Ishtar was real and had some sort of power over the dead.

Excited by my discovery, I barged into Davies' bedroom finding him lying in the sack, practically comatose, with closed curtains and heaps of clothing resting on the floor.

"I think I know the answer!" I exclaimed.

He looked at me with his mouth agape, as if he had just gone through some sort of shock. He stuttered while lying in bed, "I-I-I think I just had a heart attack!"

I apologized earnestly, and rapidly explained to him my discovery with thin patience. He began to laugh when I finished.

"Somehow I knew there was an answer. It just hadn't gotten to me yet. What can I do to help?" he asked.

We had to draw up some sort of plan. We called Milano, Capasso, Bernstein, and Roger to a meeting in the living room, and all of the men relaxed. Milano sat smoking his cigarette, while Capasso reposed expressionless. We explained the entire matter to men who seemed resolutely unsympathetic.

"This is really rich, Goering! Where'd you get that idea from? A science fiction movie?" Capasso said.

"Bob, this is a science fiction movie. Shut up." Capasso just glared at me in response. I knew he hated me for my disrespect.

The concept of an ancient goddess raising the dead sounded ridiculous, yet at the same time no one could come up with a better explanation. There was nothing for Capasso and Bernstein to do, and they sealed their mouths for the time being.

According to the information on the videotape, we knew that Ramadan taught at a local college within driving distance of this place, about forty miles away. We would have to load up Davies' station wagon with fuel and some provisions, as well as a number of firearms. Roger, Davies, Milano, and I would proceed to the college itself, locate her office, and try to wade our way into the middle of that ghoul-infested place.

Ghouls would be crawling throughout every nook and cranny of that campus, but we had to find Ramadan's office and see if she had any notes there; it was imperative to uncover her documentation. We would leave tomorrow night under cover of darkness to avoid detection by the authorities, as well as any ghouls, since they too relied upon sight.

On the day of our trip, we had to work in the gardens and try to straighten up the town. Some of the ghouls began creeping into the community's outskirts and had to be hunted down appropriately. All of the men in Davies's house went out to do so, as well as about twenty other fellows from the village. The group divided into two and took a few hours to comb through the primeval woods in the surrounding hills. Some of the guys actually found a few ghouls, subsequently killing and burning them. My group actually found something more alarming, tire tracks from an ATV dug into the earth and freshly made.

Later on, I walked down the road to the garden and brought it up to Pierce.

"We found fresh tracks. I think it's trouble with a capital T," I said, standing in front of his large garden.

"Yeah, a few guys heard the sound of motorcycles in the hills last night," he responded, as he took off his glasses and examined the lenses.

I remembered the whole affair in Barrett's Hollow, and I did not care to go through it again. I recalled the gunfire and carnage, watching three lives taken before me. The farmer-turned-looter will most likely come and would victimize this place as he had done to all the others before, leaving destruction in his wake.

We hung out in Davies' house for the duration of the day. Bernstein smoked a couple of cigarettes, and Marcia sat around looking somewhat insecure. Rachel stood silently at one of the windows in the den that looked out into the back-yard.

"Rachel, are you okay?" I asked.

She turned around and looked at me for a moment. She smiled.

"Yeah, I'm okay," she answered. Rachel resumed her vigil of staring out into the backyard.

A few minutes later, I went out there and started to walk around. Angeline left the house a few minutes later and joined me.

"Where do you think we're going –you and me?" she asked.

"It is hard to say," I told her.

"What do you mean?"

"This is what I'm sayin'. You believe one way and I believe the other. We're not really compatible. Doesn't look like there's much potential," I answered.

"Well, we could marry and you could do your thing and I could do mine," she said.

"Angeline, honey, it's not going to work. We believe in two completely different systems. Your system will take you in one direction, and my system will take me in another. We can't live together, and that little difference would rip the relationship apart. We'd be divorced," I told her, wondering how active divorce courts would be during the pervading mayhem.

"Andy, it's the end of the world," she said with a look of sadness in her eyes.

"We don't know that," I said softly.

She slowly turned around and said nothing as she walked back into the house with a downcast face. I was sad. There was an eternity between the two of us, and only God could bridge it. Maybe things would change, and I hoped that they would.

Chapter Twenty-Six: The Dismal Campus

I got a chance to phone my mom that afternoon to find out how things were going. Thankfully, I got through, which was rather surprising.

"Hi, Mom. How's everything at the homestead?" I asked.

"Things are fine. Pete and Missy are playing video games with the kids. Sometimes we get out of the house and walk around, even though we're not supposed to," she said.

"Is Missy there? I'd like to speak to her."

"Hang on a minute. I'll see if I can get her."

My sister eventually came on the line.

"Hi Andy. How's everything?" she asked.

"Hey, Miss," I said. "Things are A-okay!"

"Andy, we want you to come home. When are you coming back?"

"Someday soon, it's hard to get up there. The roads are really bad." Missy and I talked about her kids and discussed the fact that she was going through government issued school textbooks with them. Some places that were directly controlled by the government still received sporadic mail service, and the feds sent the books a few weeks before. There were no educational alternatives other than home schooling, so Missy had no choice but to follow through with the orders. We ran out of things to say and the conversation started to die.

"Miss, can I speak to Mom, now?

"Okay. Love you, Andy," she said.

"Love you, Miss."

My mom got back on the line.

She informed me Rome was almost a ghost town, most of the survivors were starting to abandon it. They moved out to the rural villages south of the town where it was safer. We changed gears and talked about ordinary things that happened during the course of the day. The oration subsided and the call concluded.

"I love you, Mom," I said.

"I love you too, son," she said. The words reverberated in my head as I hung up the phone.

Later on, I began to get ready for our trip to the college and prayed with Roger and Marcia in preparation. We would have to determine where we were going, and we would have to move quickly. Davies had been to the campus before, and in fact had taught some courses there as an adjunct. I figured that his knowledge would prove to be invaluable.

The time was approaching and we discussed a plan. We would go over the back roads, so that the authorities would not see us. Milano, Davies, Roger, and I would make the journey together, realizing that we might not make it back. At dark, it was time to go, and the sky turned an overcast gray as the sun receded. Marcia and Angeline both kissed all of us on the cheek outside of Davies' house with affection and appreciation. Rachel was there in front of the door and waved "goodbye" with her fingers. Her face was very heavy and it sunk to the ground. I got in the car while taking one long look at Angeline. She waved and walked back with a sad, disheartened face.

As the station wagon meandered over the countryside, I fell asleep and dreamed my usual dream. Everything was the same; the jeep picked me up on the gray terrain as the talons shot through the dry soil. The vehicle went over the dunes as the distant figure on horseback rode on. Eventually, I was close enough to see his long braided beard and hair that were blown by the wind.

The man stopped his horse and the jeep came to a halt at the crest of the acclivity. He turned his mount around to face me while the "presence" urged me to step off the jeep. Momentarily, I turned around to find hundreds of the dead advancing up the grade. They stumbled and groaned, with grayish-green skin, half-rotting faces and flesh, groping with hunger to consume my being. I got back in the jeep, but it refused to move. I had no choice but to get out again and face the problems both ahead and behind me, feeling like I was caught between a rock and a hard place.

The man with the braided beard and hair was a large figure, over six-feet tall. He dismounted, looking at me condescendingly. Dressed in black and sword at his side, he beckoned for me to walk over to him. We approached the edge of the hill together and stared out over a large plain of gray sand. Where was God and what was I going to do?

We looked out over that vista and I noticed small mounds in the gray sand. The mounds grew larger and more prominent as they rose from the earth. The winds came about and blew the dry soil off of the structures, revealing an ancient terraced city. The man looked at me coldly and said, "Babylon is rising." I got the impression he was the epitome of the ancient world that threatened the fragile present. The things moaned in hunger, slowly advancing behind me. I was in deep trouble with no avenue of escape. Only God could help me, for I could no longer help myself. I looked up into the hazy blue atmosphere, the sun continuing to shine. I woke up abruptly.

We drove into the expanding darkness, the sun setting in the west, passing a number of abandoned villages that exhibited no human activity. Nothing moved. The dark landscape exuded death and destruction as our anxiety built up. We approached the college and the roads proved to be additionally treacherous due to the abundance of potholes present.

As we continued into the night, there were no other motorists on the road save for a rusty white pickup truck going in the opposite direction. Sitting in the back with Roger, I took my pistol out and made sure it was loaded, ready to fire. I had never been a violent man, but a war will do that to you. This was a war between the living and the dead, and I realized that brute force was sometimes necessary.

We passed intermittent buildings and forests on the side of the road. The journey seemed to be a dragged out, arduous task. Everything was enshrouded in the ebony depths of night, concealing dead monsters that sought to destroy the living. The car traveled the tarmac, dodging the potholes that plagued the rural route. We continued through the darkness, noticing a few scattered lights here and there. Either people were present or the government hadn't killed the power yet.

"Mind if I have a cigarette?" Milano asked. I shook my head, not really caring if the acrid fumes burned my lungs or not. Perhaps I would contract lung cancer at a later time, but it made no difference to me; I didn't even know if I was going to live to see tomorrow.

I thought back to my childhood, when I used to run through my parents' house, enjoying little toy cars and multi-colored blocks stacked upon one another. I remember laughing as my mother tickled and how my father would chase me through the house. Those days of innocence were now long gone, they had slipped into oblivion.

Milano took out a smoke and lit it, holding his hand out of the open window. The winds threatened to extinguish the glowing embers as he took a drag from it periodically. Davies cut through the night like a cold knife through a stick of butter. The surrounding darkness had the consistency of a heavy soup, whose only ingredients were uncertainty and death. Davies drove transfixed, hands glued to the steering wheel as Milano stared blankly ahead into the enveloping night. We passed old abandoned vegetable farms that once prospered but now yielded no good fruit.

On the side of the road, we could see a small green sign colored in reflective paint. According to it we were in a community named Middletown, where the college was located. We entered the town proper as the ranch houses grew in frequency along the way. The architecture of the structures changed as we neared the center of town, the buildings here tall, flat-roofed, about three stories high and more antiquated. This was Middletown, abandoned and rejected.

The town was empty and dark, no lights blazing within it at all. We stopped to see if there was any life in the middle of the main street, only to behold the dead and quiet community full of rats scurrying about. Old used-up autos sat on both sides of the street. Paper and litter were thrown everywhere, as if the town had been used up and tossed away by its residents. As the car sat in the silent and dead street, Milano got out and lit another smoke. Davies just sat in the driver's seat, allowing the engine to idle while he contemplated the desolation, or so I imagined.

"There's no one here," Milano said as he inhaled the smoke and blew it out through his lips into the black atmosphere.

We heard the clattering sound of an aluminum can rolling away in the breeze. Then we heard a commotion coming from the surrounding lifeless buildings. The four of us listened closely, trying to determine what was going on. A moan came forth from across the cluttered and dejected street. A dark figure in torn clothing stumbled out of one of the buildings, groaning as it faltered towards us with its pallid undead face! It was a ghoul. Three others hobbled out of a building across the street in response to our presence. More wails were heard down the thoroughfare as I made out their cloudy and malignant forms in the hazy darkness. In no more than a minute, dozens of them began to surround the car, attracted to our living and breathing bodies!

Milano got in the station wagon quickly, slamming the door. Davies immediately gunned the throttle. The creatures stumbled out into the darkness with a stiff gait, reaching out for the vehicle to keep it there. Davies managed to evade them, leaving the ghouls behind us as they slipped into the distant darkness.

We could make out suburban-style homes in the blackness around us on both sides of the decaying roadway. The streets, like before, were vacant and lifeless. We saw a road sign that told us that our destination was nearing. It read "Middletown College 5." We went up over the crest and could see nothing but deciduous woods that disappeared into the shadows. As we approached the campus, Davies shut his lights off so we would not attract attention. He proceeded very slowly, with only the light of the moon to guide him. I looked up at the nocturnal orb. It winked at me but offered no assistance, cold-hearted and uncaring about our fate.

"The campus is on the left," Davies claimed.

It was hard to make out, but I detected a group of buildings immersed in the darkness of the vista. He pulled over to the side of the road and parked just before we reached the campus. We all got our gear out of the trunk and left the vehicle in the open space in front of the college.

Up ahead, I could see the buildings that numbered a little more than twenty altogether. It was so very difficult to tell. We had flashlights, but Davies insisted that we use them as little as possible. The ghouls might take notice and swarm around us, creating a carnivorous tempest. We took the paved road that cut through the field in front of the campus. We advanced in whispers, saying almost nothing, realizing that craftiness was the key to our survival; if only one of them sees or hears us, it would somehow get the others to join. They had some sort of ability to communicate, though none of us could understand exactly how.

We stood at a sign, a map of the dead campus. Davies turned on his flashlight on for about two seconds. Any longer than that and they would be able to pick us out in the darkness and home in like beacons. We could see from the diagram that there were about two-dozen buildings total, the residential cluster on the left side of the campus and the academic cluster to the right.

Davies led us through the campus, practically hugging the buildings. Trash, as in the town, was tossed everywhere. Cans were tipped over, and the grass was up to our knees. It hadn't been maintained for several weeks, if not months. The place had been abandoned, and the dead most likely overran it, chasing the living far into obscurity.

We walked in between an unkempt hedgerow and a white building. Under the eaves, set in the structure's outer wall, was a dark object that emanated a sinister impression. As I got closer I noticed it was a crouching figure that moved and growled. The thing put its feet into the high lawn and stood up. The creature let out a long moan and reached out towards Davies, seeking to send his shade to the afterlife. Milano took the .45 out of his belt and held it up to the creature's head.

"Harry, if you shoot it, they'll hear you and this place will be swarming with those things," Davies said.

Momentarily distracted, it put its hands around Milano's wrist. He pulled it free after he tucked his pistol away. Roger took the stock of his shotgun and struck the creature in the head, knocking it into the grass. The thing continued to moan and writhe as it struggled to get to its feet. Roger hit it on the cranium several times, rendering it forever silent.

We continued to a park in the center of the campus. Up ahead, were fountains made out of concrete, but no water came forth, stagnant with inactivity as death incubated within the campus. Across the park were dark buildings that loomed in the night. Davies believed we would find Ramadan's office there.

"The administration building is up ahead," Davies whispered, pointing to the cluster.

We heard something moving through the grass on the other side of the fountains. We stopped dead, totally still. Walking over the lawn were two of the creatures, pursuing something in the long shoots, groping around for some unknown entity. I wanted badly to shoot them and send them to oblivion, but we left them there and continued on to the first structure.

"This is the administration building," Davies told us in a quiet whisper.

We tried the front doors but they would not yield, locked. Roger took his shotgun and rammed the butt up against the window, shattering it, then knocked away the remaining shards. I wondered if any of the creatures heard it.

Milano went in first and pulled himself up through the window. All of us could nimbly follow, except for

Davies who was a little too portly to get through it quickly. We helped him through, Roger and I, by lifting him up. The two of us followed and wriggled our way in. We stood in a foyer with a lone desk in it, probably used for security purposes. We walked over to the desk and found a list of categories printed on a paper in a clipboard that sat on its top. The paper revealed a convenient list of departments. We had to find the office where they had a record of academic programs.

"It's on the third floor," Davies said after perusing the paper with his flashlight.

With a little hunting around, we found a stairwell down the hall to the left. We entered that stairwell, flashlights blazing. I cautiously walked in, having flashbacks from the days of the militia. There seemed to be nothing above us on the stairs, no vehement Haitians with pistols now, only darkness. We ascended the stairs to the third floor and opened up the door to the hallway, finding it littered with trash from months of neglect. I wondered if we were going to find what we were looking for.

"Remember who is in control," a voice said, cutting across my thoughts. I thought it was God.

Davies shined the flashlight on the walls so that we could read the tags that identified each office. We found the correct room number and walked into the dark, windowless chamber where I counted seven desks complete with overhead compartments, all neatly placed against the wall. In the center was a table with magazines spread about on its surface. We started going through the desks with our flashlights. After about fifteen minutes, Roger found what we were looking for in a file cabinet against the wall. Davies read through it, smiling and completely absorbed.

"Ramadan's office is across the center of the campus, in Markowicz Hall," he said.

Davies had a rough idea where that was. He grabbed a set of keys from one of the drawers in a desk to the right of the file cabinet, which jingled as he put them in his pocket.

The four of us left the building, helping Davies through the window once again. We could see no ghouls in the immediate vicinity but knew they were there, wandering around, eager to devour warm flesh. We took the same route between the overgrown hedgerows and the building, avoiding detection. I could see some figures shambling around in the distant darkness. They must not have known what we were. If they did, they would be right on top of us, wanting to irrevocably erase us from existence.

The four of us slinked with the utmost stealth along the side of the building. Markowicz Hall was in front of us. Milano ascended the steps to the building and tried the front door. Surprisingly, it was open. We walked in, unsure of what to expect. The insides were dark and we could see cushioned benches that sat in what appeared to be a student lobby. Magazines and newspapers were everywhere on the floor, and I decided to pick up a newspaper as Roger shined his flashlight beam upon it. The headlines read: "Ghouls Take The Bronx." It was dated about six months before and the odds were that no one had been here since then, except for the dead that moved over the breadth of the earth.

There was a body in this lobby, its face to the ground, and I wondered if it belonged to a ghoul or to a person who had died of a head injury. I decided to walk up to the corpse to investigate it and determine if it was a threat or not. I approached and rolled it over. Strangely, rigor mortis had not set in and the joints were still pretty flexible. Did this person die only recently? For the body to lie here inactive, it would have had to suffer trauma to the head. The corpse belonged to a young black male of about twenty-five, and the skin had turned a pale gray. Black circles formed under the eyes and the dermis was cold to the touch. I continued to stare at the corpse, studying it, looking it over from head to toe. The eyes suddenly snapped open! It bore its teeth at me like an animal and let out a hostile growl, almost as if it was a trap. I let the thing go as it struggled to its feet. I kicked it in the ribs, trying to immobilize it.

"Let me put a slug right where it counts," Milano said as he held the barrel of the pistol to its head.

"If you do that, they'll hear it and they will all be here in minutes!" Davies said.

Roger, sensing the urgency of the moment, took the stock of his rifle and rammed its head. The thing stopped moving, destroyed. It was almost as if it was feigning death.

We paused for a few moments. "Can they think now?" Milano asked. None of us had an immediate answer for him.

We found the nearest stairwell and took it to the second level. After ascending the stairs with the resounding echoes of our footfalls, we stepped into the hall and found it littered with papers, just like below. Davies led the way down the corridor to an office with Ramadan's name on a plate next to the doorway. Davies tried a few of the keys and eventually unlocked the door. The portal opened up to an office that was essentially neat, except for a jumbled pile of papers on the desk. We all took a step into the chamber and found two bookshelves about four feet high nestled in the corner. In the other corner was a potted plant that appeared strong and healthy, as if it had just been recently cared for. The only window in the office looked out over the dilapidated and haunted campus, filled with the specters of lost and tired souls. The room appeared as if it had been used on a regular basis.

I curiously approached the table as Davies illuminated it with his electric torch. The notes on it were mostly typed and easy to read. Davies and I began to pore over them, trying to make sense out of the information printed. Thankfully, they were dated and organized chronologically. Michelle Ramadan must have been very concerned about the documentation of her thoughts. Perhaps she believed everything that happened to her was somehow relevant or cosmically significant.

We looked at the ordered stack of documents. The first entry read: "There seems to be a remarkable interest in the ancient Sumerian legends amongst the Iraqi people."

The rest of the entry went on to describe the old pagan rituals that had been revived after falling into disuse for hundreds and hundreds of years.

There were other journal entries present that dealt with the current crisis. One entry actually documented the capturing of a ghoul by Ramadan and a few staff members, which they caged in an academic office. Ramadan and another associate incessantly asked it about its identity, day in and day out. Eventually, it told them its name, and it was clear that they had made some progress in restoring the ghoul's consciousness. Ramadan had captured a small number of ghouls and brought them to the basement of this building to subject them to a barrage of questions. She tried to revive their minds through brainwashing techniques. If this was the case, maybe these creatures were locked up in the cellar of this very structure, subjected to an obsessed woman's inundation.

That was our next stop. We took all of Ramadan's notes and put them in a valise that Davies had carried with him. We left the office and located the stairwell down to the dark and foreboding basement. As we reached the bottom, we found ourselves in a hallway made of gray monotonous cinderblocks. We walked down the corridor until we were in an open room with high ceilings. It was the boiler room, and within it stood a large brown circular structure that must have been the hot water heater. We looked behind it and discovered a solid metal door. Milano rattled it to find that it was locked. We listened closely, and I detected seemingly painful groans from behind it. Were there ghouls inside?

We knocked on the door.

"Is anyone in there?" Roger asked. We heard a string of angry growls from within. There were some in there and they were not going to be nice to us.

"Take your shotgun, Roger, and blow the lock," Davies ordered. "The walls of this basement should be able to muffle the sound of the blast."

Roger stood in front of the door, aimed his shotgun at the doorknob and fired. The doorknob was now blown out entirely. We pushed it open and it smoothly creaked back to allow us to get in. We shined the flashlights upon the far wall. There were two creatures chained to the wall, struggling against their bonds to get at us.

"This must be the place where she conditions the ghouls," I said.

Davies walked up to one. Its face was pale and its eyes blank. "What is your name?" It looked at him for several long moments and hesitated, saying nothing. Davies asked it again. Once again it paused, then moved its lips. To our amazement, it spoke!

"My name is Ryan Smith," it said.

"It is actually working. She is actually restoring their reasoning faculties!" Davies said, somewhat surprised. I was shocked and taken aback. Silence fell on our group in surprise from our discovery. Now I knew that these things weren't as dumb as we had thought they were.

We heard a noise from behind as something or someone entered the room.

"Well, I see you fellows are trying to uncover my secret," a woman's voice said. "Didn't think anyone would bother me in this place. I should've locked the front door. I suggest that you lay your weapons on the floor now."

All of us ceased our activities and slowly turned around to face the entrance in utter and complete amazement. A beautiful woman stood before us, almost six feet tall with long dark tresses hanging down, wearing a brown unkempt dress. Her clothes were filthy and it looked as if she hadn't bathed in over two weeks. In her right hand was a Colt .45, loaded with a full clip. We threw our weapons down on the floor as we realized that it was Michelle Ramadan standing before us, armed and dangerous.

"I suggest, gentlemen, that you stay out of my affairs, and drop the briefcase," the young woman said.

"My notes are missing from upstairs. I'm guessing that you have them."

I looked into Ramadan's eyes. There was something wrong with them; they were glazed over and I think she was slightly insane. She took her pistol and aimed it at Davies, poising to fire.

"Put them down!" she ordered. "Right on the floor!" She pointed to the ground in front of Davies with her free hand.

"What are you trying to do, lady? Create a bunch of servants?" I asked.

"Give me my notes! Stop fooling around and give me my notes!" she ordered, with her hand open, dominating with a degree of rage.

Davies walked over to her with the valise in hand.

"Give me the notes!" she said again with her hand still open.

Davies just stood there in front of her, both hands fastened around the handle of the briefcase. He refused to move as if he was planning to do something. At that moment, Davies took his briefcase and then swung it back with all his might, hitting Michelle Ramadan up against the side of the head! She fell to the floor immediately, her gun discharging as she did so, sending a bullet to the far corner of the room. We picked up our weapons, and I kicked her in the stomach. She wrenched in pain, bent over in fetal position as she clutched her gut.

"Let's get out of here now!" Davies ordered.

We all got out of the room quickly. Despite her harmful intentions, I could not bring myself to beat a woman further, much less kill one. We had to leave Markowicz Hall quickly. We ran down the hall of cinderblocks and mounted the stairs as fast as possible. We emerged on the first floor and ran through the messy vestibule, noting the dead body on the floor that tried to attack me earlier. We easily walked to the door and stepped into the dark and dead campus beyond. As we ran across the college center, we saw more of the uncertain shapes stumbling around the dark. They seemed to catch wind of us and stiffly tottered forward with arms outstretched in our direction.

Milano, not looking where he was going, ran into one. It grabbed his wrist and opened up its greedy mouth to take a bite out of his arm and steal his life. In rage he took his pistol, held it to its face and pulled the trigger. A shot rang out in the night as a metal slug went into its brain and destroyed what life it had.

"You shouldn't have done that. You should not have done that!" Davies screamed angrily.

"Did you have a better idea? He was right on me!" Milano retorted.

The campus seemed to come alive as hundreds of obscure shapes came out of the nooks and crannies of the college, trying to find the warm flesh in their midst. Growls and moans filled the air. Roger paused, took aim, and fired his gun. One ghoul was about thirty feet away; it fell over onto the concrete. His efforts were effective but fruitless, for there must have been about two hundred of them closing in to cut off all escape, seeking to consign us to destruction!

"We have to get out of here, now!" Davies said. No one said a word as he led us around the buildings. A mass gathered in front of us, and behind us too! We had no choice but to go to our left in between the two buildings, but they were there as well, waiting for us at the end of the passage. I noticed that the line was thin; maybe we could plow our way through! Milano looked encouraged and confident.

"Let 'em have it!" Milano cried as he led the attack.

Instinctively, we did, guns blazing, fists flying. Davies, being not much of a fighter, managed to get through the line of ghouls, swinging the valise as a club. We followed suit, although Roger was almost bitten in the wrist. He managed to pull his hand away just in time, avoiding a painful demise.

We could see the car up ahead, across the field, and parked on the side of the street. We ran through the overgrown meadow and reached it unimpeded. As Davies pulled the keys out of his pocket, I looked back and saw an unruly howling mob, shambling its way towards us in hot pursuit. Davies unlocked all the doors, and we piled in without wasting a second. We were just in time, for the things neared the car. Davies started the car and backed it around, while the inhuman multitude pursued. He sped off along the road into the town that served as a gravestone for the human race.

Again, we passed the vacant suburban houses amidst the green trees. We approached the center of the town that was marked by the older flat-roofed three story buildings where the old bombed-out cars and trucks predominated. The streets were bristling with activity this time, as a multitude of inhuman figures stumbled out of the buildings and surged towards our speeding car, hobbling through the trash!

"There must be hundreds of 'em!" Milano said, his eyes firmly fixed ahead. Roger, Milano and I quickly reloaded our guns.

Their howls filled the air while Milano and Roger aimed the guns out of the window. Both of them opened fired and many ghouls went down. They were still on the scene though, stumbling over the piles of litter on the street, converging upon our path. Seven or eight now stood on the road, directly in front of the station wagon!

"Brace yourselves!" Davies said, his temples sweating. He plowed through them as the bodies flew across the hood and hit the windshield. We flew through the dead barrier and proceeded down the road. The threat had abated. We had what we came for, or so we thought. All of us sat in the car perspiring, breathing heavily. We were exhausted. The car left the small town and meandered over the bumpy back roads. We drove into the hills and approached our home in Sarkill. I looked to the east and noticed a faint glow on the horizon. The night was almost over and we had achieved a significant victory! Perhaps there will be a solution to this dismal conjecture!

Chapter Twenty-Seven: The Lonely Little Family

We continued through the expanse of dense woods at the foot of the Catskills. Here the population had thinned and wild vegetation took over, dispelling all sense of civilized behavior. The woods were dark, foreboding, uninviting, and cloaking destruction in mystery. After driving several miles, we entered the familiar hamlet of Sarkill, a small slice of safety that was here for one moment and perhaps gone the next. Davies' two-story home was to the left, in the pocket cut into the primitive forest. The woods emanated suggestions of degradation, driving humanity closer and closer to the savagery of the ancient earth.

We pulled into the driveway behind the van, and I noticed that lights were still on in the house. Davies turned the ignition off and the car quietly died. Marcia and Angeline stood in the doorway, with peculiarly long faces, leading me to believe that something was out of place. They did not rush out to greet us, just staying in the entrance watching us. Marcia held the brown bear at her side, apparently for a sense of security. However, Rachel went out to the car to talk to Milano, and they walked toward the house, hand in hand. I hugged Angeline briefly, but for some reason she was not as warm and inviting as she had been in the past. Something was up. Turning from her, I embraced Marcia as well, and stepped into the living room, where Capasso stood with an angry scowl upon his face.

"Our friends with the three whee-luhs were back," Capasso said. "They shot up and raided the general store, and then tore up the rest of the village. Two people are dead and three are injuhed."

I suspected this. We weren't going to be safe here either. We better get out of here and proceed to a more remote area that was completely absent of human habitation. I did not think this was a good time to discuss all that had happened to us, despite the fact we could have been killed out there.

"Yeah," I said.

In about an hour the sun came up and the day began. I talked to Davies and Angeline around the kitchen table about staying in the area. They both agreed to leave. DeVries and his gang were going to continue terrorizing places, pillaging and burning them without mercy until he had violated everything. God knows how many people were in his mob, or how much firepower they packed. It seemed as if the thinning ranks of the law could not stop them one bit.

Angeline and I met in the emptiness of the upstairs hallway of Davies' house. She was full of grace and femininity, yet still saddened. She said nothing, but I knew something bothered her and disturbed the sanctity of her soul. Tears began to well up in her dark brown eyes that seemed to have an infinity of insight.

"Angie, what happened?" I asked.

"I don't wanna talk about it!" she said defiantly. She had gone through some sort of trauma. I let her go and she proceeded downstairs. I walked into a bedroom with a quilted bed, oak desk, and a dresser made out of teakwood. I went up to the window and peered outside. I saw Milano, Bernstein, and Capasso loading up the vehicles with supplies. I figured I'd better help them, so I went down.

As we packed both the van and Davies' station wagon, I noticed the air had grown colder and the ground had begun to freeze, the earth's axis tilting further from the sun. Autumn was coming and Thanksgiving would soon be here, although I did not know what to be thankful for. The heaviness hung in the air no matter where I turned.

For a second, I wondered how my mom was doing. The phone lines were no longer working and I had lost touch with my family in Rome. My heart was pained and I missed both my mother and sister, who seemed to be slipping away into obscurity. We had to get up there soon, but after expending so much fuel on the excursion to the campus, I realized that we had a limited supply of gasoline. Pierce loaned us a little of his, and we left Sarkill as evening fell, no one here wanting to join us. Like the people at Barrett's Hollow, they felt secure in this place and had no desire to leave it. Our troupe seemed to be endless wanderers, in search of an elusive safe haven.

Angeline and Marcia frantically insisted upon going with Davies and me. I wondered what the problem was; I had never seen Marcia this insecure. Did Capasso and Bernstein do something to them? I allowed the thought to slip away. Angeline, Davies, Marcia, and I took Davies' station wagon, while Milano, Rachel, Capasso, Bernstein, and Roger took the rusty van from Handelsman's place. Marcia held the bear tightly in her arms, still longing to feel safe. Both vehicles were in dire need of a tune-up, but they would serve their purpose for now.

Snow fell as we departed over the bumpy roads, covering the landscape in a white blanket that hid the evil and disease. Thankfully, it would not be deep enough to hinder the progress of our travels. The procession journeyed into the pine forests of the surrounding region. We saw a ghoul wandering on the side of the road, getting covered in the snow. The van ahead ignored it, and I guessed Capasso and Bernstein were not interested in destroying the corrupted creature.

The procession had to circumvent Delhi at all costs, since the authorities still kept a heavy presence in the area. We stuck to the more remote routes not serviced by the local municipalities, heading north in the general direction of the Mohawk Valley, not far from where my mom lived. We listened to several radio broadcasts that informed us of a population center near Syracuse that met the needs of over a 100,000 souls. The reports told us that New York City and all of the surrounding areas were now declared non-functioning. We were losing this war. Perhaps we could get my family and carve out a home in the Adirondacks, safe from DeVries' marauding band and the creeping presence of the undead.

It was our desire to reach the Adirondacks, but that would prove difficult since we would eventually run out of gas. Where could we get more? Somehow we would have to press on and hope the situation would resolve itself later. Where, outside of the population centers, would we find the necessary fuel and supplies?

After several hours, we crossed into Herkimer County and headed in the basic direction of Little Falls. We passed many abandoned communities consisting of a few houses and mobile homes, all covered in snow. Other than a few ghouls stiffly wandering about, there were no signs of life, and the landscape breathed a heavy lament. The inhabitants had either fled or were dead. It dawned on me that New York State was becoming a mass tomb, a stack of dead bodies that extended to the very heavens above.

Up ahead, on the side of the road, was an old beige two-story farmhouse with a stone foundation and a long antenna leading upward from the roof. Capasso pulled into the driveway and we followed him. Both vehicles stopped, and everyone subsequently got out to stretch their stiff bodies.

"Maybe we can get the radio to work and find somebody," Capasso said to us.

Capasso, Milano, and Bernstein all walked up to the front porch of the structure, keeping their eyes peeled for enemies, whether they were the living or the dead. All of them had their guns in their hands, ready to shoot before asking questions. They entered the house and found no evidence of anyone living there for months.

There was a ham radio in the building. It was in a room near the back, sitting on a wooden table that had an electronics magazine on top of it, slowly decomposing. After some investigating and snooping around, they found a generator in the shed out back by the barn and wheeled it across the lawn into the back room. Farm families were notorious for keeping such devices in case of an emergency, and we were thankful onc was available to use. Milano siphoned off some gas from the van to the generator in order to power the ham radio. Milano, Capasso, and Bernstein fooled around with it and turned dials, playing around with the switches. To pass the time away, the rest of us sat down on the cold furniture with a frayed deck of cards.

"Goering, get up! We got someone on the radio!" Capasso said standing over me. "Come here!"

I got up from the chair and went into the little room in the back.

"How are you there!" the voice on the radio said.

"We're doin' fine!" Capasso said.

"Where are you headin' to?" the voice asked.

"To the Adirondacks. Can we stay at your place for awhile?"

"Yeah, I think, but only for a few days. We have limited supplies," the man on the radio said.

"What's your name?" Capasso asked.

"Bob Haley. And yours?"

"Bob Capasso."

"You Italian?" the man on the radio asked.

"Yeah!" Capasso answered.

"We're not," Haley said.

It was apparent that Haley wasn't used to dealing with Italian-Americans.

Haley told us that he and his family lived in a farmhouse not too far from Little Falls. There were provisions there and we might find a little solace in the company of other people.

We piled into the vehicles once again and proceeded to Hilton's Corners, where they apparently lived. The house was off the main road, behind a grove of trees where the land rose a bit. We took the road as it was described to us, leading us down to a red brick farmhouse three stories high. I got the impression that the house was a monument to the people who lived inside of it. There was a barn in the back of the farmhouse, and it rested upon an old stone foundation, and in front of the farmhouse was a shiny red pickup truck, most likely owned by Bob Haley. A plume of smoke flowed out of the chimney, and an antenna ran up the side of the house. They had a radio. We pulled into the driveway and stopped the vehicles.

A man with a thick beard walked out of the house. He stood on the front porch dressed in a red plaid hunter's jacket and an orange hat, and he was holding a shotgun. He was tall, solidly built, and seemed to be the type that could not be easily swayed.

"My name is Robert Haley," the man said, as he shook hands with all the men in the group. Rachel, Marcia, and Angeline were passed up.

Another whiskered man followed him, somewhat shorter. He possessed the same solid build and was dressed in camouflaged fatigues, but he was weaponless, carrying the same tough demeanor as Robert Haley.

"My name is Jeff Haley. Glad you could make it!" he said smiling, extending a handshake to Capasso and me. He was Bob's brother.

The Haley brothers took us into their abode and led us to the right, where there was a living room with a stone fireplace in it. A fire blazed, casting off light as it consumed wood. There were some recliners and sofas positioned around the hearth, detracting from the room's inherent emptiness.

"Make yourselves comfortable," Robert Haley said, presenting the room to us with his hand.

A blond woman in her mid-twenties, dressed in blue jeans and a brown and white-checkered shirt, walked in joining all of us.

"Hi, I'm Jennifer," she said, smiling. She struck me as a tomboy with somewhat masculine mannerisms.

"You want some coffee?" Jennifer asked. Most everyone nodded their heads, and our hosts disappeared into the nearby kitchen. A few minutes later, they returned with both hot tea and hot coffee. We drank it to warm our frozen innards.

"We have some food for ya," Jeff Haley said.

They all walked into the kitchen once again and re-emerged bearing biscuits that were topped with long pieces of meat and smothered in brown gravy. I found out that the meat was rabbit, and peas were served on the plate as well.

Apparently, Jeff and Bob liked to hunt the local wildlife and most likely survived on it.

"C'mon, it's good. Eat up!" Bob Haley said with a strange smile.

As we ate the food, the family walked away again. It struck me as being rather rude and odd.

"Roger, where are they goin'?" I asked.

"Have no clue, Andy. Have no clue," he answered eating the rabbit stew.

Strangely, they left us alone just as if they were up to something. A few minutes later, the three appeared once again in the living room, armed with shotguns, barrels toward the floor. All of a sudden, I felt a sudden urge to urinate.

"Okay, everybody, stand still and no one will get hurt. Understand?" Jeff Haley said.

"Just leave your guns where they are. We just don't want no trouble. Comply and everything will be fine," Bob Haley said.

They rounded our firearms up and placed them in some unknown location within the house. I did not like the fact that I had no means of protecting myself.

Later on, after the incident settled, Robert Haley showed us around the farm.

"We've had this place for seven generations," Haley said.

He added that many of their relatives had lived and died here on these premises. Outside, near a grove of trees to the left, was a cemetery. Most of the people buried there were related to the Haley's in one fashion or another. Some fought in the Civil War, others World War I, World War II, and some served in Vietnam. The Haley's were proud of their lineage that came from an English textile worker who left Birmingham for Central New York back in 1825. He became a farmer, cashing in on the profitable tillage of the time.

"We love and respect our family very much, and we don't want nothing to upset or threaten it in any way. We were taught to honor our guests and that's exactly what we're doin' with you," Bob Haley said.

As we stood around the graveyard, unarmed and defenseless, someone showed up on a snowmobile from the woods to the east, behind the house. He was dressed in a thick wool jacket, wearing a baseball cap, and had an unkempt appearance, as though he hadn't shaved for months.

"Who you have here, Bobby?" he asked with a smile that revealed two missing teeth.

"Dey're some visitors, they come from New York City," Bob Haley said.

The man got off the snowmobile. He grinned as he approached us, stepping through the snow that crunched with every footfall.

"My name's Jim Henderson. We're cousins," he said, referring to the Haley's. He extended his hand to all the men and shook hands as he introduced himself.

After the introduction, Bob Haley pointed to the fields to the left of the barn. They were covered in snow.

"We harvest crops in summer and have been able to raise enough food for our own means and that's it!" Bob Haley said. Whatever was left over, they could freeze and store in the basement of the house. They powered the farm using a windmill that converted air velocity into electricity, which was stored in large batteries in the barn. The group could live here indefinitely, and did not want to leave the homestead behind. Periodically, they would make their rounds on dirt bikes, they told us, finding ghouls and killing them as a measure of safety. They seemed happy in their insulated little settlement, miles from nowhere.

"Do you ever see others?" Davies asked Bob.

"Yeah. Dey come in now and then, but we never let 'em stay here long, since we don't have enough supplies," Bob Haley said. I sensed he was trying to make something crystal clear here, in an impolite sort of way.

He told us that many strangers just used this place as a way station to Syracuse or Albany where there were other population centers.

“We ain’t the only ones around here. Dere are a few more,” Haley said. He told us there were about three hundred people left in the vicinity of Little Falls.

“We’ve been listenin’ to the news reports. The authorities say that normal humans are in the minority,” Bob Haley said as he stood in the snow next to Jim.

“We probably number about 30% right about now, and dat ain’t too good!” Jeff Haley said as mist formed at his mouth.

He went on to tell us that many people had gone out west to the Rockies, and that some even went up to Canada to try to survive in the isolated wilds. Others had moved to islands where they could live in impregnable fortresses, trying to weather the storm out. It looked as if humanity may not survive after all. The news destroyed much of the dim hope we still had.

“It will get better,” a voice in my head spoke. I had a hard time believing that voice.

We toured the farm, and they showed us the pigs and cows that lived in the barn. The Haley’s brought up the fact that local families let their animals loose in the wilds and abandoned them then went out west. The livestock earned to survive in the wilds, but others had died, not knowing how to take care of themselves. Some farmers sold their animals to the government, which was raising livestock to feed the dwindling numbers of humanity. They showed us everything on the property except for a certain addition located in the rear of the house.

“What’s in there?” Roger asked Bob Haley.

Haley turned around and took a look at Roger. “None of your business,” he said coldly, in disapproval. A shiver went down my spine at the remark.

At the end of the tour, they brought us back into the brick farmhouse to our beds located in the white rooms upstairs. The women slept in one room. Capasso, Bernstein, and Milano slept in another, and Roger, Davies, and I rested in front of the fireplace, whose glowing embers died down as the darkness expanded into the evening. I missed my guns and wondered what the Haley's had done with them. I also missed my mom, and thought about what might have happened to her. Marcia had not heard from her family for months. She had lost all hope of them surviving some time ago, and realized that she would never see them again.

We woke up the next day like a machine. My sleep was incomplete, interrupted by insecurity. Roger and I prayed together and read a little bit of the Bible as Marcia joined us in the living room. Angeline thought of partaking in the event, but she changed her mind at the last minute. The Haley's, accompanied by Jim Henderson, did not seem to observe any religious faith and skipped out. I think that they were Methodists at one time, but it looked as if they now worshiped each other in some strange way.

Later that morning, Marcia, Roger and I walked about the grounds. We found the area to be extremely remote. There were groves of naked trees of many varieties before us. On the hillsides beyond were distant lifeless houses that had sunk into disrepair. We decided to walk toward the trees to see if the houses were inhabited. Our misty breath formed and vanished in the chilly air as we crunched through the wet snow.

"What wrong wit dese people?" Marcia asked.

"I'm not sure. They don't really care for outsiders, but they're gonna let us stay here for a little while," I stated.

"Maybe they're inbred," Roger said.

"It could be. Hard to say. Something's off and I'm not sure what," I replied.

I did not have much to add, but it was interesting how the Haley's would not let us see what was in the addition in the back of the house, and the whole thing got my curiosity. The three of us walked into the naked woods, only to find it lifeless except for a few squirrels that raced up the trees, running across the boughs. A slight breeze rustled through the leafless branches. We emerged from the woods and crossed a stream that gently ran through a snow-covered pasture. The houses sat on the acclivity perhaps only a half-mile away. They seemed to be empty of all activity, nothing to investigate.

"We'd better get out of here," I said.

The other two agreed and we went back to the house. We sat down in the living room to rest our tired discouraged bones. Robert Haley descended the stairs and walked into the living room, still dressed in his hunter's outfit as if he was lost in a perpetual state of destruction.

"We picked up some broadcasts out of a place called Namibia, which is some African country," Haley explained, not realizing that I heard of the nation before.

"There are some Germans who live there who have built their own city, and they've been keepin' out all of the ghouls. If I were you, I would head there," Haley told us.

He really wanted to get rid of us, as if we were some type of irritant. After he left, I discussed the situation with Capasso and Davies around the fireplace.

"Maybe we should get out of here and head to Africa," I said to Capasso, Milano, and Bernstein.

"I dunno Goering. Not sure if we can make a transatlantic trip. Quite a risk," Capasso said.

"You know how to sail. Right? And Harry can pick locks, right?" I asked.

"Yeah," he answered.

"Then let's go!" I said, practically challenging him.

"It's too much of a risk," Capasso said, declining further discussion about the topic.

He thought that it might be a better idea to head to the Adirondacks or to an island in the Caribbean, but I still wanted to know where my mom was and I was concerned for her safety. I sat in the living room, pondering things for a bit, particularly the idea of wandering the earth in search of a safe haven. Survival seemed to be the only purpose of existence at this point. I remembered that, before the crisis, I was struggling to pay the bills and worrying constantly about where my career was heading. Now all of that was moot, the only thing that mattered was staying alive.

Outside the window, I saw Jeff Haley wandering around in his hunter fatigues, mobile radio in his hand. Robert Haley then joined him, and Henderson came over as well, and all three converged on the spot. They kept on fooling around with the mobile radio, trying to get it to work. To my knowledge, their sister was in the basement of the house and I wondered whom they were talking to.

Marcia came down from the second floor and joined me, looking out the window.

"Who dey talkin' to?" she asked.

"Maybe people from the outside," I said. That was the only explanation I could come up with.

Early that afternoon, Capasso, Milano, and Bernstein, accompanied by two shotguns, took a ride in Haley's pickup to retrieve a deer Jeff Haley had shot earlier. The Haley's seemed to grow antsy at our constant presence. Roger approached me as I sat on the front porch in a folding chair, seemingly contemplating as I stared out at the barren landscape.

"I heard that Robert Haley approached Davies earlier and asked him when he was going to leave. Davies didn't give him a straight answer," he said.

"What's up with these people?" I asked.

"Haley kept on telling Davies, 'You've gotta get out of here! We don't have enough food for all of you!'" Roger exclaimed. They wanted us gone but were trying not to be rude.

The tension mounted throughout the day. Capasso, Bernstein, and Milano were still out in the truck attending to the deer, gone for hours. This left the three women, Davies, Roger, and me alone with the Haley's and Jim Henderson. We were unarmed, unable to defend ourselves, and I felt a little unguarded. We sat in the living room by a lit fire, playing a few hands of poker, occupying the time and trying to relieve the pressure of the situation.

Through the living room window, I could see Robert, Jeff, and Jen Haley standing outside in front of the barn, again talking to their cousin Jim Henderson. All were armed. Robert Haley took out the portable radio again and used it to talk to someone. Then all of them turned and stared at me right through the window! Jeff and Jennifer had revolvers. Robert and Jim had shotguns. A burning sensation materialized in my heart as my thoughts began to race rapidly. The group parted ways as Robert and Jennifer went in one direction and Jim and Jeff went in the other. It was clear that something was up.

A minute later, Robert and Jennifer came through the front door and faced us in the living room, pointing their guns at us! From the rear exit, the other two walked in through the kitchen, aiming their weapons at us as well. My heart beat heavily and Angeline started to cry a little bit. Rachel grew totally still as her face lost all traces of emotion.

"Shut up," Bob Haley said. "You should have left a long time ago and you wouldn't. You don't listen!"

He motioned with his gun for us to get up. We all stood up in total subordination. These were tough times, and law and order was only enforced through the barrel of a gun.

"Hands in the air people," he ordered.

We had no choice but to raise them. Haley had us all move into the pink kitchen, our hands held high to the ceiling.

"We wanted our family to be left alone, and you messed things up! We wanted you out of here, but you wouldn't listen. Someone knows you're here and they want you gone. You wouldn't listen!"

We heard the unmistakable sound of revving three wheelers, a noise I certainly did not want to hear, signaling the return of DeVries! The odds were that the Haley's were talking with DeVries and his gang on the portable radio all along.

Someone knocked on the front door and Jeff Haley let them in. Four men, all dressed up in dark clothing and wearing helmets, walked out of the light of day and into the overcast living room. Jeff Haley shut the door behind them. One of newcomers was a large stocky man who stood over six feet tall and weighed over two hundred pounds. He took his helmet off, revealing his bushy hair and beard.

"Evening folks," he said with a grimacing smile. "I think I have a little score to settle. First, we're gonna take care of you, then we are gonna take care of your friends. I figured this time I'd divide and conquer," DeVries said, referring to Capasso and the others. "Oh, yes, hello, Mr. Goering. I remember you," he said in a tone that was absolutely brutal.

The six of us were led at gunpoint through the kitchen to the addition in the back of the house. Rob Haley opened up a door to the small area and had us step into the room. We found ourselves immersed in darkness, the windows in the room boarded up so little sunlight could get in. The chamber was vacant except for an old rusty milk can that sat doing nothing in the corner. On the dirt floor was a wooden trap door attached to a frame, pegged to four stakes that securely anchored it to the ground.

Jeff and Jim opened up the door and it swung back on hinges. There, in the hole beneath that door, were groping gray hands and faces that reached upward to pull themselves out of the pit. They were ghouls –walking twisted mockeries unable to accomplish any task of reason!

"Meet our parents, fokes, and say 'haillo' to my other sister Jill, Uncle Bill, and our cousin Eddy. This is one big happy family!" Jeff said.

"I was a small man once, but now I'm a big man," DeVries said. He went on to tell us that he was forming a coalition of thousands of people in the Upstate New York area. He would organize an army, and he would be its leader. He wanted to be king, and the Haley's were going to join him, whether they liked it or not. I imagined DeVries had stumbled upon the Haley's earlier and cowed them into submission before our arrival. They were under his thumb and refused to do anything about it, lost in some strange type of ancestor worship.

"Thanks to all this chaos, I have more power than I ever had in my life. This is great!" DeVries said behind us. I imagined his face was beaming brightly.

"You killed Stuart. I don't take stuff like that kindly! You should have left while you had your chance, but you blew it. Too bad, now my mind's made up. You're dead," DeVries ranted.

"We're very hospitable, but we're family. We don't like outsiders staying too long. We just wanted you to leave us alone. Now it's too late," Bob Haley said.

Haley and his brother took me by the arms. They held me at the foot of the pit, the cold steel of a gun barrel against my back. I looked down into the hole before me. It was about eight feet in diameter and about nine feet deep. Gray faces hissed in malignant expectation at the bottom.

"Toss him in, Bobby!" DeVries ordered. "Adios amigo."

The Haley brothers pushed me into the pit, the five ghouls growling like the horrible animals that they were! I landed upon their cold carrion bodies that barely had the energy to move. Hands began to grope upon my back as inhuman moans emanated from horrible throats. They were trying to dig greedily into my living flesh! The two that were under me struggled to get free. I rose to my feet immediately. There were no weapons that I could defend myself with, except for my fists in desperation.

One of the creatures growled and lunged for my neck. I hit it in the jaw, and another grabbed my shoulder. I turned around and slammed it in the face with my elbow. One of the creatures that was on the ground reached out and took my ankle, but I pulled it away. I fought, though it was a futile effort, my energy fading fast.

I heard a ruckus above me as shouts filled the air and echoed around the small room. I looked up, taking notice of the situation, while hitting and kicking like the primitive wildman that I had become! I could see at the top of the pit that Roger was struggling with the woman Jennifer Haley. He viciously yanked the pistol free from her hand and screamed, "Andy, catch!" He tossed it down to me, and it landed upon the cold earthen floor. I hit one of the ghouls in the chin and knocked the damnable creature to the ground. I retrieved the revolver and aimed it at the one that I had just put down. Another one grabbed my arm and tried to take a bite out of it as I squeezed the trigger. I fired off a shot and the one on the ground was now entirely still. I hit the one that tried to bite my arm with my fist and knocked it away. I aimed the pistol again and fired, causing it to sink to the floor.

Above me, the disturbance grew out of hand. I could see from over the top of the pit that Davies and Roger had overwhelmed one of DeVries' men. Gunshots were fired, but I wasn't sure what was happening. Thanks to the pistol, I was able to put slugs into the craniums of the other ghouls. I had one bullet left, and I saw the back of Robert Haley standing at the edge of the pit. I took aim and fired. The bullet went into his head and he fell backwards into the grave-like hole. His body landed on its dorsal side upon the pile of dead corpses. Bob Haley was now deceased.

A rope was dropped down to me, offering temporary salvation. At the top were both Angeline and Marcia, helping me out of the pit. One of DeVries' men was on the floor dead, as were Jennifer Haley and Jim Henderson. They weren't moving, and I concluded that they had most likely been killed.

"Capasso and the others came back at the last minute and interrupted their plans," Angeline said.

All hell broke loose as confusion took over the House of Haley. The subsequent gun battle was taken into the kitchen and somewhere downstairs in the distant basement. We lifted Jim Henderson's gun and took the pistol near DeVries' man. At least we were now armed and equipped to deal with the situation.

We left the dismal room that now served as a mortuary and walked into the kitchen with broken dishes all over the floor. We had to find the others and get out of here. Below me in the basement, I heard more shots being fired.

"Let's try to find the guns," I said to the women. We ran upstairs to the second floor and found Bernstein standing in the hallway, appearing puzzled and uncertain, with his baseball cap on backwards.

"Sasha, where are the others? Do y'know were the guns are?" I asked.

"I have no idea!" he exclaimed as his mild Ukrainian accent slipped out.

I detected movement behind him there at the end of the hall. One of the closet doors slowly opened, and I saw the obscene face that belonged to Jeff Haley. He held a revolver in his hand. The crack was deafening as it hit Sasha Bernstein in the back. He went down and met the unmoving wooden floor. I took my pistol and fired it into the closet, Haley's body collapsing onto the hardwood floor.

I approached Jeff Haley to see if I had killed him. His body was lying on its side in a fetal position. I rolled the corpse on to its back to find Haley's eyes peering blankly into the emptiness before him, motionless. He had been hit in the chest and he was now dead. I looked back and noticed Bernstein lying on the ground, groaning in pain. I momentarily forgot my hatred that I had for him and knelt down, gently turning him over to find out where he was hit. I heard him telling me something low and muffled, but I couldn't make out the weak words. It sounded like, "Look behind you."

Something heavy hit me in the back of the head. I whirled to find out who my attacker was, only to see the bearded face of the big burly and vengeful man named Bruce DeVries! With a furious expression, he took his fist and slammed it into my nose, causing me to fall back against the floor on my buttocks. My gun fell and slid across the wooden planks.

"You people took down a couple of my men Goering, and I'm gonna get you for everything you're worth!"

DeVries crouched over me and hit me again, this time striking me in the mouth. I put my hand up there; I was bleeding. His hands went for my throat and clamped around my neck like a vice, hoping to cut off my lifeline to survival. I felt the pressure tighten upon my windpipe, obstructing all oxygen, and squeezing the very life from me!

"You've caused me enough problems, and now I'm gonna make you pay for everything you've done!" he said, strain in his voice as he spit forth saliva in a rush of madness.

In a spurt of consciousness, I saw Angeline standing over DeVries, poised with the stock of the rifle, ready to deal a crucial blow. She slammed the end of the firearm down upon the back of his head! DeVries cried in pain and stood up, turning to face his attacker. I noticed my gun on the floor and picked it up. I held it to DeVries' back as he grabbed her small wrist. He let her wrist go, turned around, and took the weapon by the barrel to keep me from firing it. I maintained control and pointed the pistol at his abdomen, pulling the trigger. The pistol buried a bullet in his intestines. He looked at me and muttered an expletive, his eyes rolling back into his head in demission. The man fell to the floor, his eyes still open, dead.

The two women were standing at the other end of the hallway, trying to stay out of harm's way. Bernstein was below me, still breathing and looking me over softly with his eyes. I leaned over him. He tried to speak.

"I'm gonna die, and I've been a bad boy. Please ask the Old Man upstairs to forgive me," he pleaded, relinquishing everything to God.

I grabbed his hand and prayed for Jesus to come into his heart. He must have been scared in the last moments of his existence. The life in his eyes ebbed away like the tide rolling out to sea; Sasha Bernstein was dead. I took my pistol and shot Bernstein in the head with it so that he wouldn't revive. I had to do the same with the other two bodies too.

The women and I went down the stairs to the main floor. We ran into Capasso, Milano, Roger and Davies in the living room next to the fireplace, all out of breath. Rachel walked into the living room crying. Apparently, she had escaped outside for the duration of the little gun battle.

Milano went to comfort her, but as he did, I noticed that he was clutching at his shoulder with his other hand. There was blood between his fingers. He had been wounded in the downstairs gun battle with DeVries' two remaining henchmen. Both of them were now dead, with cold bullets for their warm brains. It looked as if the battle at this farmhouse was over.

"We found the weapons downstairs," Capasso told me. "Where's Sasha?"

"Bob, he's dead," I said gravely. A look of sadness came over his face that quickly turned to one of rage. "I want to kill them!" He had lost his friend and stomped about the house, frustrated, unable to bring Sasha Bernstein back from the grave.

Chapter Twenty-Eight: Our Little Hideaway

The next day, we got up and met the brand new morning. All of the men gathered up the corpses, and we took all fourteen of them out to the backyard. We burned them in a pyre, except for Bernstein's body. We dug a shallow and respectable grave for him in the back, but we could only go a few feet deep since the ground was frozen. We gently placed Sasha Bernstein's body in the hole and held a brief religious service for the young man, a secular Ukrainian Jew. Even Capasso was there. After the conclusion of the ceremony, we heaped the cold earth upon the lifeless body. Bernstein stared peacefully up into the overcast sky, with his cap still on backwards.

After Bernstein's burial, we stocked the van with provisions. We also put some in the back of Rob Haley's big bright red truck; he no longer needed it where he was going.

"Let's blow this joint," Capasso said, as we stood around the vehicles in the chilly air.

"I'm gonna ride with you guys," Rachel said to me as we readied to board the van. She would have to remove the buckshot from Milano's arm without drugs to numb the pain that he suffered.

We had to find another safe haven to regroup. We thought about heading to the population center to treat Harry's wound, but since we were still fugitives, we decided against it unless his life was clearly in danger. Capasso, Davies, and Roger rode in the pickup, while Angeline, Milano, Rachel, Marcia, and I took the van, leaving the lonely House of Haley.

Darkness fell, as the iron sky descended upon me once again. We drove into the night and shot through Poland and Newport, finding both communities empty except for an occasional ghoul wandering down the sidewalk. We headed toward the Rome area, hoping to find a remote farmhouse that would offer shelter from the approaching storm. Since we were not too far from the Adirondacks, we expected that the population of ghouls would thin out, just as the living population had. Maybe we could stop in Rome to see if my mother was still alive.

I had Angeline look around the van to find the briefcase where Davies kept Ramadan's critical notes.

"Yeah. Its back here!" she said. I would have to read them soon to get to the bottom of this whole thing.

Marcia sat next to me, bear in hand, and surfed through the radio static to locate broadcasts, though nothing could be found. It was almost as if the government had stopped sending out messages to the straggling remnants of humanity. My guess was that bureaucracy still existed but did not have resources to send anything out on a regular basis, our civilization fading into nothingness. Humanity was starting to disappear altogether.

We continued on back roads, making slow progress since roads, like everything else, fell into disrepair. We passed communities that were becoming more and more dilapidated. Shutters dangled on a single hinge while paint peeled and exposed the outside walls, leaving them naked and vulnerable. Cars sat rusting in the snow and other elements, decaying by the second. The world was being depopulated without mercy. Was there any hope at all?

"Read her notes," a voice in my head seemed to say.

This area, nestled between the Adirondacks and the Mohawk Valley, was characterized by smooth hills clothed in dark green firs and naked brown deciduous. The barbed-wire fences that served to keep the cattle were in disrepair, and strands of the dangerous metal sat ripped, neglected as they hung down to the snow-covered ground.

We pulled over to the side of the road. Capasso got out of Haley's truck and spoke.

"Y'know of a place where we can go?" he asked. He knew I was familiar with the area.

I knew, through endless sessions of joy riding, of some distant houses north of a little hamlet called Steuben Corners. We got back into the vehicles and continued on more rural roads, not a single car passing us as solitude and loneliness predominated and continued into the night. We found an old three-story wooden farmhouse overlooking what I knew to be a picturesque white valley near the small hamlet, Steuben Corners. We parked our vehicles in the driveway and got out to find that the red door was locked. Milano, although wounded, managed to pick the lock of the dwelling. The man had a plethora of skills, and they proved to be a great boon to us. Once inside, we found the house empty, devoid of life. We stood in a living room complete with recliners and glass cabinets full of dishes. Beyond that was a kitchen, and it had a kitchen table and cabinets layered in white formica. However, no ghouls were present and that was a little relieving.

The farmhouse had four upstairs bedrooms to it, which made it perfect for us. We quickly made ourselves at home, sleeping on the old dusty beds in the decrepit rooms, the dirty paper peeling off the rotting walls. Morning came and the snow began to melt as a warmer climate drifted in, indicating that spring would someday arrive. We went into the basement, a foundation made of cinderblocks, to find stacks of cardboard boxes along with an old freezer that no longer worked. Spoiled meat was in that freezer and we would have to clean that out later.

There was a trickling stream that ran by the house, not far from the woods that blanketed this area, and it served as a nice clean water supply. The farmhouse even had a gun cabinet full of rifles and buckshot, enabling us to hunt deer and other small animals for some time to come. There was a plot in back of the house that would allow us to grow a variety of vegetables once the spring came. Beyond the garden, the property sloped downward into the secluded valley. This was not a bad place to hole up for awhile.

There was a gas drum in back of the barn, and when we found the keys, it yielded forth a worthy supply of fuel. Within the garage, we found a large generator. We wheeled it into the kitchen, down the stairs, and into the basement. We used it to power lights and the electric stove, and this enabled us to have a hot and welcoming meal consisting of canned soup and dry biscuits. Rachel and Marcia removed the buckshot from Harry Milano's shoulder as he howled in pain, his screams sailing out over the dark and peaceful valley.

In spite of the security, something weighed heavy on my heart. Where was my mom? Where was my sister? I tried the phone that hung on the wall of the kitchen. As I expected, it would not work. I resolved to do something about the dismal circumstances and entertained the idea of driving to my mom's house to see if she was alive. Maybe there was some small hope that she would be there, or at least that there would be a clue to her whereabouts. Part of me didn't want to go. I might find out that she was not alive, and I really did not want to face that. I wandered about the house then found Roger and Angeline in the backyard conversing as the gentle breeze swept through the naked trees.

"Roger, it's important for me to find out where my mom is, and I've gotta do it. Can you go with me?" I asked.

"Yeah, I'll go," he said. I sensed that he wanted to be supportive. It was good to have someone who would stick to you like glue.

"You might as well count me in too. I'd rather be with you guys than here alone," Angeline said. Her statement didn't quite make sense, pointing to some inconsistency.

We approached Marcia later, who was still clutching that bear for dear life, as she lay upon one of the beds, but we found her a bit timid at this point and she opted not to come along. I think this whole crisis was really wearing on her fragile nerves, which had already been severely frayed. We made plans to leave at nightfall and head off towards Rome.

The fateful sun began to set in the distant sky as we collected two flashlights, two pistols, a rifle, and plenty of rounds for the trip. While everyone else just hung out in the house, cleaning out weapons and so forth, Roger, Angeline and I got into the van and started it up. We backed down the farmhouse driveway onto the isolated country route and drove the long, winding line of rural roads that led into the swallowing darkness. The houses and mobile homes were lifeless and still in the heavy gray air.

The gray colors darkened and turned black as they swirled about like a whirlpool, sucking everything inward like a cosmic vortex that annihilated all matter. I sensed that the spinning shadow would take us to a place where existence ceased and all time stopped as the universe broke down and reconstituted itself. I felt as though I had died behind the wheel several times, only to be resurrected over and over again, trying to understand what my life was all about.

The sun continued to sink into the horizon as the atmosphere turned a deathly shade of black. All of my childhood memories were clearly coming back to me now. I remembered how I grew up in my home with my sister, amidst the laughter and, at times, the tears. I recalled the past moments spent with my parents, engaged in all sorts of boyhood activities and learning about the fascinating world around me. This trip was going to be a season of solemn reflection and not one of rejoicing.

Chapter Twenty-Nine: Childhood Revisited

My home lay somewhere beyond in the dark haze, amongst a housing development three miles north of Rome. It sat in an area amidst woodland and dead fields of clover, peaceful farms not too far away. On the roadside were shadows that seemed to run and jump for the van as it traversed the bumpy tarmac, like monsters lurking behind the cover of some deadly gauntlet.

After about an hour in the suffocating darkness, the road terminated at a route running perpendicular to it. We opted to take a right, and on the left side of the lane there was a cow pasture shrouded in nigrescence. To the rear of the field was a dim, foreboding wood that I could barely see and wanted to avoid, not sure if I wanted to face what lay beyond it. It was there where we had to go, however, and I would have to face down my fears. I pulled the van over and shut the thing off. We had to park way out here so we wouldn't attract attention.

"Ready?" Roger asked.

"Yeah," I answered with a sigh. God, I did not want to go through with this. As we got out, I looked up at the night sky and noticed how innumerable the stars were. I wondered how many of them had fallen over the past several months. We stood at the edge of the wet field, and I noticed a small clearing near a dead and twisted tree that I could barely make out in the heavy night. The clearing led to a path worn by forty years of adolescent ventures, leading down near the lake that sat in back of the housing development. From here, another trail awaited, and that would lead us through the woods and to the empty houses.

My mom's home was near the trees off the trail, and I paused for a minute, asking Roger to pray with me. Angeline, to my surprise, joined in.

"Dear God, I ask you for your protection as we embark upon this journey to find my mom. May we get back safe and sound. In the name of Jesus, we pray. Amen." I felt God's favor shining down despite the dreary darkness, my petition flying upward.

We crossed the field without incident. No ghouls were in the vicinity, and a low noise arose from the cry of a solitary wolf. I had never seen wolves in this area before, and I concluded that the primitive wilds were taking over as humanity disappeared. Shining the electric torches, we managed to find the old gnarled tree that marked the clearing to the path beyond. We took the path, entering the dark and gloomy woods, and detected an owl hoot in some distant tree. I remembered years before when I used to meet my friends back here to sit and drink beer by firelight under the trees, unable to guess as to what the future would bring. Those were the days, the days gone by.

We continued to walk through the darkness, our way quaintly illuminated before us. Shadowy monsters again seemed to jump out at us from the trees as the jittery darkness danced in the beams of the flashlights. The three of us crossed a little gully that led down to the lake as we walked into the winter air.

There was a pine nearby with some low branches, and I immediately recognized it. I stopped and cast the flashlight beam up at it, trying to capture another piece of my childhood. Up in the branches was a large piece of painted plywood that a boy named John Patterson nailed to a bough when I was younger. It was still there after all these years, rotting away. Where was John Patterson now? Where was my childhood? For many years I associated adulthood with a coming time when my life would someday work out. It didn't seem to be working out, and there wasn't much hope that it ever would. I hated this time. "God, where are you? I need you. Please show yourself," I cried in my heart as tears welled up in my eyes. Despair was taking over, consuming the will to go on.

Some sort of presence entered me despite the dismay in my heart. I think it was God, but I wasn't sure, it was so hard to tell in these bleak circumstances. The pervasive confusion made all sensory data so darn uncertain and unreliable. As I pondered these questions, the electric torches revealed birch, elms, sycamores, pines, and even oak here in the forests of Central New York, a confusing tangle of vegetation. Time passed by slowly as I tried to look forward to the hopeless future and forget about the terrible past. What had happened to my mother? Was she alive or dead? I associated my childhood with my mother, and I began to think that, if she was dead, my childhood went with her and life would flow on unresolved.

"Where's your house?" Roger asked.

"Keep going. It's up ahead to the right," I said.

The trail concluded at another path running perpendicular to it, and we made a left at the trail. The weeds on both sides of the pathway were short and brown in the early frost, not quite alive yet. There was a tree-covered grade ahead, and beyond that were the houses that I imagined were both dilapidated and abandoned.

We entered a patch of tall pines that must have been about sixty feet in height, nearing the end of the journey. At the end of the grove was the three-bedroom ranch I once resided in, and my heart seemed to stop beating in anticipation of my mother being alive.

As we neared the edge of the yard, we had to dim the lights so the ghouls would not be able to see us. I could barely make out the outline of the house in the incomplete illumination from the moon that hung above us. The backyard was in shambles. The ceramic birdbath had been tipped over, and one side of the aboveground swimming pool was crushed. A few lawn chairs were sitting in the yard, covered with rust. The place did not look like it had been inhabited for months, empty and neglected. No lights were on in the house — an ungodly sign and my heart began to sink.

We walked up to the extension attached to the back of the garage and I tried the doorknob. It was unlocked, and the door opened unimpeded. We walked through the extension, which was in actuality a tool shop, and noticed the equipment lying around on the floor in disarray. We stepped into the garage and found the truck that my mom owned was gone, but her four-door Toyota was still present, collecting dust. The garage door was closed, and we could not see the street, but that was probably for the better, since a few ghouls might be wandering about on the roadway.

As we stood in front of the entrance to the house, I reached out to test the knob to find that it turned. The door opened, and I pushed the laminated wooden door forward into the dreaded darkness. We stepped into the black interior, flashlights blazing, finding plates and silverware scattered all over the kitchen floor in wanton disregard. It looked as if a group of kids had ransacked the place.

The next chamber was the living room, and clothing was strewn about the area. It may have been the work of looters, motivated by selfish greed, or maybe it was my brother-in-law Pete, trying desperately to find something he needed. Roger went down the hall, pistol in hand, and opened up some of the doors, appearing to have a great deal of courage. He found no one there. I opened up the bedroom where my mother used to sleep, eager to find an answer.

"Mom?" I asked the room. The room did not reply, the dark unmade bed unresponsive. I closed the door, a little disappointed. She did not seem to be here either. Maybe she died and was buried in some nameless grave, in some unknown cemetery. My heart was becoming burdened, saddened at this point.

I began to think. Perhaps my mother was someplace else. Maybe she went to the population center in Syracuse. It was all guesswork at this stage, but it gave me a little hope. We hadn't looked in the basement yet, so I figured that we should investigate it. We went back through the kitchen and found the door to the cellar staircase, not far from where we had first entered. After opening the basement door, I shined a beam into the darkness below. Nothing significant was at the foot of the stairs, and the staircase whined and creaked as we abusively descended it. At the bottom, boxes were piled up in various locations throughout the cellar. A washer and dryer sat next to the wall, clothing tossed around both on the floor and upon the open wooden folding table mounted in the wall.

"Mom?" I asked the darkness. Nothing.

"Mom?" I asked again. I heard something and Roger panned his flashlight beam around the cellar, scanning it from one end to the other to find the source of the noise. He caught an object behind the dusty ping-pong table to the left. There we could see an unclear person with long hair seated with his or her back up against the wall. We got closer to the figure and I recognized it. It was my mom dressed in a tee shirt and a long white skirt!

"Mom, I am so happy that you're alive!" I said almost overjoyed. Then, I noticed something. Her skin, bathed in the yellowish beam of the flashlight, took on a strange cast. It had a grayish color to it, and she moved ever so slowly, like chilled molasses. Her body twitched for a moment, and a long moan emitted from her lips, underneath rumpled blonde hair. The arms stirred, and she stumbled clumsily to her feet. She let out an angry growl and proceeded towards us with a slight stoop in her posture. Her arms reached outward as a hateful expression came across her face.

"Oh God, not you," I cried quietly.

Again, I drifted back to my childhood. I could see my sister and I playing with my mom through the house, running and catching us. I remembered her reading stories to me before I went to bed at night and recalled the pictures in a photo album of my mom proudly posing with me at my high school graduation. Mom, you're dead. The creature that was once my mother stumbled toward me awkwardly, her coordination severely hampered. I did not move away. I could not move, frozen in shock.

I had a rifle in my hand, but I could not bring myself to use it. I pointed the loaded shotgun at her head with no resolve to pull the trigger. Her hand slowly encircled my throat as the mouth opened, displaying an incomplete set of teeth and a mouth that wanted to rip the flesh from my bones. "GRRRAAAAARRR," was all that the thing that used to be my mother could say. She grabbed my wrist and displayed her teeth, threatening to bite me with the lethal, corrupting disease.

"Andy!" screamed Angeline.

Roger hesitated for a moment, and then he took action. There was only one thing for him to do. He took his pistol in his hand and held the barrel up to my mother's head. As time stopped everywhere, he fired a steel-jacketed round into her skull. My mother crumpled to the floor, the sound of discord echoing on forever. I came to the grim realization that he had killed my mom!

"You killed her! YOU KILLED HER!" I screamed with disapproval and hatred.

"I'm sorry, Andy. I had to do it. She was going to kill you," he said apologetically. I stared at the ground with anger and threw the rifle down on the floor in disgust. He was right. He didn't have much choice. If he hadn't acted, I would have been dead. It is strange that I had "killed" his parents so many months before and now the roles had been ironically reversed. In response, I got down on my hands and knees and looked down upon her still face, her blank eyes staring off into space that didn't exist. I cried, my tears flowing like a river that wound through a nebulous ravine into a dark nether-sea, feeding out somewhere into the realm of the uncertain. Angeline put her arms around me and embraced me as I bawled like a little child.

I had always hoped to find my place or time of promise, and now it looked as if I would never find it. My childhood was dead and the hope that things would get better went with it. I could not afford to give up hope, although it seemed to have already rolled away into the waters of a distant sea. We left the house, walking back through the decrepit yard and dark woods. We found the van sitting by the side of the road, undisturbed. My mom was dead. I would have liked to bury her in the backyard, but the ground in the dead of winter was still hard and unyielding. Instead, the three of us drove back towards Steuben Corners in uneasy silence.

Chapter Thirty: Exodus and the Arab Baath

The next day, we had a funeral service for my mom, despite the fact that her body was not present, making due with what we had. She was dead and I wondered where her soul was. Everyone showed up out of respect, except for Capasso, who was off hunting in the countryside. The service concluded half-an-hour later, after I delivered a hastily prepared eulogy.

Life was not bad at our little hideout. The nearest house was about a half-mile away, and we found it uninhabited. Our house did not have running water, but we made frequent trips to the stream that flowed down into the gentle meadows. There was also a wood-burning furnace in the basement that would adequately heat the place as the cold of winter remained.

We plugged the TV into the generator, but it picked up nothing but dead silence. No test pattern. Nothing. Was there anyone left alive? We couldn't be the last ones left, could we? I did not even want to entertain the unthinkable.

Spring had finally arrived, and the trees began to bud back to life. It was April, as I started to piece together all of Ramadan's notes in the warm inviting air. As I pored over them, I began to realize that Michelle Ramadan was a woman whose past lived to haunt her. Her father, Ahmed Ali Ramadan, hailed from the city of Baghdad, in Iraq, and had worked for Hasan al-Bakr, the acting Iraqi president of the late 1960s.

Ahmed Ramadan was a Sunni Arab who embraced the pan-Arab doctrines of Bitar and Aflaq. They were two Arab nationalists who desired to unify all speakers of the Arabic language into one geopolitical unit. The men founded the Arab Baath Resurrection Party in hopes of doing so. It was an organization that believed that the Arab people would once again rise from the ashes of destruction and enlighten the world with the wonders of Arab civilization. The Baath Party took the stage in Iraq as both Hasan al-Bakr and Saddam Hussein consolidated their power. Bakr, Hussein, and the Revolutionary Command Council wanted to de-emphasize Islam and stress Arab cultural achievements, keeping non-Arab elements away from Iraq. The Baath Party sought to make Iraq a powerful entity, so powerful that other Arab states would want to proudly become part of it. It was much like how smaller German municipalities joined Prussia to form the German Empire of the 1870s. However, Iraq would have to have a national consciousness derived from its own history if its natives could respect it, and the state would achieve this by resurrecting Iraq's ancient past.

Starting in the late 1960s, the Baath Party held festivals that emphasized ancient Mesopotamian rites, along with the actual constructing of monuments dedicated to the goddess Ishtar. They used emblems characterizing a bearded man who wore a pointed, almost conical hat in the image of the ancient Chaldean king, Nebuchadnezzar. According to her notes, some paintings existed that featured both Nebuchadnezzar as well as his modern-day successor, Saddam Hussein. The Baath Party also funded the unearthing and reconstruction of the ruins of Mesopotamia, which included a temple dedicated to the goddess Ishtar. It was strange how she reemerged in all of this. It seemed as if Babylon had risen through the art and the building projects strangely designed by Saddam Hussein and the Baath Party. The entity in my dream did tell me that Babylon would rise once again; maybe this was it.

Ahmed Ramadan did not agree with the mass purges conducted by the government during the early 1970s. Ramadan found himself a man without a country, and the Iraqi government ordered him to leave the nation along with his wife, Joumana, and their young daughter. They took up residence in New Haven, Connecticut as political refugees. His daughter, Iman, was renamed Michelle and grew up despising Islam. She embraced the ancient Mesopotamian culture and always hated the regime that ousted her parents from Iraq.

Saddam Hussein, the Iraqi dictator, was defeated in the conflict that ended a few years ago. It was a horrible, bloody war that started when the Americans brazenly invaded Baghdad. Although his military folded quickly, Saddam Hussein remained in the shadows, wreaking havoc upon the American forces that had occupied his land. The operation eventually escalated into a full-scale war that pitted the Islamic nations against the Western World, and several million people had died in the course of the violent and unforgiving conflict. After the Islamic powers were defeated, millions more turned away from the religion of Muhammad to the doctrines of ancient paganism that had fallen into disuse over the centuries. As the ancient paganism was revived, the space probe returned, bringing radiation to earth. Could the gods of old have planted that radiation? I wondered intensely for a few minutes, my mind overwhelmed by all of this; I had to set the notes aside for a little while to digest the magnitude of the information.

By autumn, things were getting kind of difficult. Milano caught a ghoul wandering down a nearby road while hunting for deer and, of course, killed it. The next day, we found two more traveling near a house down in the valley, intruding upon our peaceful haven. Capasso and Roger took care of them. Things were fine for a day, and then I caught six of them tottering around in back of our own home. We had to cut them all down, and we concluded the operation by igniting a pyre in the backyard. It was almost as if they knew that we were up here. I remembered that some of the scientists believed the ghouls had a collective consciousness, and perhaps it was now awakening.

Two days later, there were thirteen, and one of them nearly killed Marcia as she was getting water from the stream. We had to destroy all of them, and even Davies and Angeline helped us annihilate the things into nothingness. I was beginning to think that we better get out of here, but where were we to go? Maybe the distant Adirondacks would be good.

Later that day, I found Marcia in the hallway on the second floor. She appeared glum, made no noise, and her brown skin was a little pale, the teddy bear still at her side. I let the whole thing go by without questioning it. Perhaps I should not have done that, but I was in too much of a hurry to talk with the other guys in the household about the worrisome developments. I remembered catching Rachel in the corridor. She was quiet and moved slowly, barely acknowledging my presence. Something was wrong.

The five of us sat down at the kitchen table and drank coffee that was stored in several cans in the cellar. Capasso, the born leader, or dictator, that he was, was the first to speak.

"It's gettin' worse by the day. I don't think we're gonna be able to stay here much longuh," he said in his Brooklyn accent. He was right. Pretty soon they would be coming from all around until they surrounded this place, leaving us no egress of escape. Capasso and Milano went out in Haley's red truck later on in the afternoon, traversing the countryside. They came back in an hour. I did not like the news that they had to report.

"There are hundreds of them, and they're comin' from miles around," Milano stated. "And they're carryin' bats, shovels, and pieces of wood."

It was an armed uprising of some sort, on the roads and fields coming this way. They would be here in about two hours, Milano guessed. In two hours it would be getting dark, and the sun would sink down into the coming hell.

We called an immediate conference with everyone in the downstairs living room, including the three women. Everybody reposed in chairs, except for the domineering Capasso, who solidly stood in the middle of the floor.

"We have to get outta here as soon as we can," Capasso said.

"You're suggesting that we leave?" Roger asked.

"Do we have much of a choice? They're jus' gonna come back until they wipe us out," Capasso said, in a sarcastic tone.

We made the decision to leave what was left of the United States of America. Capasso knew that there were some sailing vessels on the Hudson River, and he said that we could find a yacht and take it across the Atlantic like Columbus did hundreds of years ago. We couldn't sit around and foolishly debate or argue; there was no time for that.

"Let's get our stuff togethuh! C'mon let's go!" Capasso dictated.

There was a mad scramble of activity, everyone rising from their seats and running helter skelter. Combing the house from the bottom to the top, we placed as much dried and canned food as we could in the spacious back of Haley's truck, adding firearms and ammo to the cargo as well. Everyone joined the effort, including Davies, despite the fact he was about thirty pounds overweight.

Milano stopped what he was doing briefly and walked the length of the driveway to the county route. I saw him stand there, looking down to the right and then peering down to the left. From his body language, I could tell something was wrong. He did not move. Angeline and I stopped loading the truck and approached him at the end of driveway. I watched Milano very closely and noticed that his face carried no expression. Then, I knew why.

We stood on that very same road and looked to the right and then to the left. On both sides of the road were about thirty or forty ghouls, moaning, hobbling forward and brandishing baseball bats! That was not it, though! We looked into the early autumn foliage and could see them tottering through the trees and underbrush! The landscape was crawling with them, and they would be here within minutes!

Milano woke from his trance and declared, "We'd bettuh go! WE'D BETTUH GO!" He broke from us and ran up the driveway to the farmhouse. We ran after him.

Capasso walked out of the farmhouse carrying a cardboard box.

"Get the guns, quick!" Milano said in a panic.

Capasso threw his items in the van and ran inside. Within a minute, Marcia, Davies, and Roger all appeared with rifles and pistols. Milano and Capasso came out with a shotgun and the automatic rifle that was lifted from the cops on the Thruway. We could see the ghouls walking stiffly through the bushes and up the rolling hills, with weapons to be used as clubs. They were groaning, closing in upon the house by the hundreds!

Capasso fired the automatic wildly at the approaching crowd. A few fell, but most were hit either in the torso or in the groin region. He was too excited to aim the weapon carefully and wasted precious ammo. They just continued forward in their resolve. Roger and I went to the right side of the house. There they were, stepping through the weeds and the bushes that grew along the side of the domicile that we lived in. We took our guns and fired at the things, managing to hit a couple in the head.

I looked behind me. All of us were now standing in the front yard armed. Capasso continued to shoot into the trees on the other side of the house as the things closed in. The rest fired upon the advancing multitude that got thicker by the minute. The ghouls that stumbled near the house were cut down like bamboo. Everyone was here outside the farmhouse in defense, except for Rachel. Where was she?

"Harry, where's your girlfriend?" I asked him.

"I dunno," he replied. "She must be in the house somewhere."

Roger, Harry, and I went back into our little abode. We began to hunt all over for the woman, but she could not be found anywhere. We went up to the second floor and opened up all of the rooms to find out that she was not there either. I quickly deduced that she must be in the attic above!

"Let's get to the attic real quick!" I urged.

We ran down the hall and looked for the doorway that led to the third floor. It was a white door that opened outward, revealing a stairway lined with unfinished wood. Running up the stairs, I caught a movement to my side! It was Rachel standing on a chair with a noose around her neck that was tied to a beam. As she saw us, she swung her legs back and kicked the supportive chair out from beneath her, her feet falling towards the distant floor. She was attempting suicide, hoping to never return!

She hung, breathing very heavily, too weak to continue on anymore!

Milano ran up and grabbed both of her legs and lifted her up to relieve the pressure from her neck.

"Don't die, honey! Don't die!" he said practically in tears.

I put my arms around her legs and boosted her up while Roger took a knife from his belt and stood on the chair, cutting the constricting rope down. She collapsed on the floor, and Milano pulled the noose off. She was still moving. She was going to live, but it was obvious that she had been operating on a deficit. I couldn't see the signs, too wrapped up in my own problems.

We heard gunshots as Capasso started up one of the vehicles. The harsh sound of shattered glass could be heard as the windows downstairs gave way to the tide of dead invading the living room. The inconsiderate things had now barged into the building! We ran down the flight to the second floor towards the stairwell. We saw one of the things moving up the staircase somewhat quickly, brandishing a stick of wood. I stood before the creature as it lifted the board in its hand. I took the shotgun in my hand, aimed it at its head, and fired. The side of the skull was taken off, and the thing falling forward onto the staircase. We stepped over it, trying to get to the bottom floor.

I heard Capasso blow the loud horn of the truck. He was obviously growing impatient, and I knew that he would go on without us if given the chance! About half a dozen stood in the living room around us with boards and bats in their hands, seeking to snuff us out. One tottered forward with its baseball bat and swung it, almost hitting Roger! He raised his revolver and fired a steel jacket into its head. The others came forward, swinging like an urban gang! We managed to evade them, but I hit one on the head with the stock of my rifle!

We opened the door and could see Capasso in Haley's red truck, looking as cold as ever. Marcia, Davies, and Angeline were with him in the cab, uncertain expressions on their faces. Capasso stuck his pistol out of the window and fired it as the ghouls surrounded the vehicle, like a noose that slowly tightened. The man was not amused in the slightest. The ghouls swarmed about the van we needed to get to, creating a large obstacle. We would have to shoot and kick our way to get there. If we didn't, we would be finished!

"Ready to do this?" I said to Roger and Milano. They just looked at me, speechless.

Harry ran from the porch with Rachel. Roger was on one side of them and I on the other as we fired our guns at every creature we could, kicking and punching our way through the gauntlet until we finally reached the van. I took the keys out of my pocket and thrust them into the door, unlocking it. I opened my door and then unlocked the others so everyone could pile in, Milano quickly helping Rachel into the car. Roger stayed out and aimed his pistol at one of the things in front of the van. He pulled the trigger and exterminated it!

I wasn't quite in the automobile yet, standing in the open door, ready to get behind the wheel, when something hit me upside the head, the impact ringing incessantly in my skull. I turned around to see one of the creatures with both of its hands gripping a baseball bat, poised to swing it again. I recovered quickly and hit the creature in the head with the butt of my rifle, immediately sending it to the ground. Another one came toward me with its arms outstretched. I reached down and took the baseball bat from the fallen creature and hit the advancing monstrosity repeatedly. Eventually, it too went to the ground.

"Andy, let's go!" Roger said. I immediately got into the van.

Ahead of me, I could see that Capasso was already pulling out of the driveway. The creatures began to surround our vehicle, and one ghoul swung its baseball bat, violently cracking the side window! I floored the pedal, peeling the tires out in the driveway as Capasso sped on before us. I hated the fact that he would not wait. It was almost as if he could care less about our lives. As we left the driveway, I managed to plow through a number of the creatures that were in the way, angry with adrenaline surging. I drove on into the expanse, leaving hundreds of ghouls behind in the setting sun.

Once safe, we had to pull over to the side of the road since Capasso's cab was too crowded. Marcia, Angeline and Davies got out of the truck, Capasso practically pushing them out onto the road. In turn, Milano helped Rachel step out of the vehicle and went to his. It was clear that Davies and the two women felt more comfortable with Roger and me, while Milano and his girlfriend liked Capasso.

Capasso incensed me to the point where everything I saw was bathed in an orange glow of anger! He was so darned inconsiderate and self-centered. Couldn't he realize that Rachel's life was in danger? I stepped out with a pistol in my belt and wanted to put a slug right between Capasso's eyes! As I walked up to the big man in the cab, I nursed that exact intention! He would not hesitate stepping on someone to assume a position of authority, and I hated that. I pulled my gun on the man, but he saw it coming and pulled his out too. He aimed it at me through the truck's open window, sitting there cool and collected, his brown hair flowing. We faced each other down, vicious hatred in our eyes.

"We could have died back there! Don't you care if we die?" I asked.

"I would have died too, so put the gun down and get back in the van!" he said without fear or respect.

"Guys, don't do this. Just put the guns down. We don't have time for this!" Angeline said, shouting from the van.

We lowered the guns, glaring at each other with a hatred that only incubated within our breasts. I walked back to the van, feeling somewhat ashamed for backing down. I began to realize that defending my honor was not worth risking my life, however, and the anger cooled down a bit as I put the miles behind us. But I still wanted to kill the guy. I hated him with a passion. I wondered how Milano could stomach the man and guessed Capasso just "sweet-talked" him to no end.

We continued on the poorly paved rural route. It had probably been over a year since any road crews were out here, their equipment in disrepair and the personnel most likely all dead. We managed to find the New York State Thruway, where we passed the unattended and pointless tollgates and swept over the bumpy tarmac. It too was riddled with potholes, limiting our speed to about thirty miles an hour. We went by the city of Amsterdam, the monolithic mill town that finally gave up the ghost and died. After about five hours, we got off the Thruway somewhere around the town of Hudson, where we hoped to find some isolated port and steal a seaworthy vessel. This boat would have to take us across the Atlantic to distant Namibia.

The procession went through the empty and dead town of Hudson, and we encountered a few ghouls. Some we shot up or drove through, expending our dwindling supply of ammo in defense. Eventually, we located a wharf on the banks of the Hudson River where a few small vessels were conveniently moored. Roger and Capasso took care of the ghouls wandering around the port with a shotgun and the automatic rifle. The rest of us found a large white ketch about seventy feet long, complete with a deckhouse. We thought it might meet our needs, our next home away from home.

"This will have to do," Capasso stated.

I did not want to be anywhere near Capasso. In fact, I purposely stayed out of any of the conversations he had with the others. I stood on the wharf and watched him from a distance. Milano boarded the vessel and got on top of the deckhouse. He picked the lock on the wheel that steered the rudder and liberated the ketch from disuse. He proceeded to remove all the padlocks on the other doors below the deck.

We loaded the vessel with all of our provisions, enough to keep us on a two-month journey far across the sea, and stacked them neatly in an empty cabin. Thankfully, the ketch was equipped with a small generator, giving us a power supply that would contribute a touch of comfort, providing that it worked.

"We should be good to go," Milano said.

Angeline gently helped Rachel to the deck as we all boarded the ketch. Capasso and Milano untied the boat from its moorings and pulled up the anchor. The vessel drifted away from the empty and ruined town, leaving it far behind, as Haley's truck faded away. We sailed down the quiet and majestic Hudson River, past the silent towns that lined the banks toward the harbor, with not even a helicopter or plane passing overhead in the lonesome sky. It no longer mattered if we were fugitives since there were no authorities to arrest us. This once great state was now crumbling into dust, the grand epochs of human history seemingly closed. There was little promise of a future, and maybe that was why Rachel Negron attempted suicide. I wondered how she was faring at this point.

While I stood on the deck of the ketch, Capasso came up from below and said, "The generatuh works. We have powuh."

There was a radio in the boat and we hooked it up to the generator. As far as Milano could tell, the radio was operating, but it picked up no broadcasts. As we realized this, I began to feel trapped, as if there were no places to run to anymore. We had to get to Africa, or we would cease to exist.

"Adios amigos!" Capasso yelled, as we sailed down the Hudson.

Capasso proceeded to steer the vessel down the river and past the dead towns of Haverstraw and Nyack, whose bright lights would no longer blaze. The boat went underneath the Tappan Zee Bridge that used to support the throng of commuting traffic that went into the hustle and bustle of New York City. Several minutes later, we saw the silent

City of New York. Now no one was doing business there anymore, and probably wouldn't be for some time. The Empire State Building still stood, reaching into the sky. I knew that one day it too would fall, just as the Twin Towers did a few years before.

New York City was a gigantic tombstone, a great monument dedicated to the United States of America, as the country crumbled into dust forever. We saw the Statue of Liberty to our left, torch in hand, waving "goodbye," welcoming no one.

Capasso turned east after we sailed past Staten Island, heading to the mysterious coast of Africa. We went far out to sea, and the skyscrapers of Manhattan slipped away into the vast recesses of my memory. That was my home that I had long loved, born and raised there in the country we had just left. I never thought I would live to see it destroyed, but I had witnessed its annihilation. Adios America. I can no longer call you my home. Now, I would have a new home, or so I hoped.

Part III
Afrika

Chapter Thirty-One: The Truth About Capasso

Capasso proved to be very adept at calculating wind direction and positioning the sails of the ketch to gather up speed. He taught Milano to steer the rudder, and Milano ended up, in turn, teaching me how to steer it as well. Capasso said nothing to me, which was not surprising since I almost took the guy's life. He seemed to be a dictator who lived to put people down, as if their feelings meant nothing to him. It would have to come to a stop someday, but I did not know exactly how or what I was going to do about it.

By the first night, we had reached far out to sea. Rachel was standing next to Milano on the top of the deckhouse with his arm around her shoulder. Capasso had left momentarily, and disappeared below the deck.

"Rachel, how're you doin'?" I yelled.

"Okay," she said rather weakly. Milano just stood there rubbing her shoulder, saying nothing as he scrutinized me. It looked as if he was trying to protect her.

Later on, Marcia was in a bad mood and wanted to be by herself up on the deck. She lay down and went to sleep up there, the rest of us reposed in the cabins below. I woke up as the dawn appeared off towards Europe and found Marcia in the small galley in the bow, laying in one of the booths with her head resting upon her brown teddy. I noted to myself that it was peculiar that she was down here. I woke her.

"I didn' sleep too well last na-ihgt," she said in a despondent manner.

"Why?" I asked, intrigued by her admittance. I could tell by her tone that something was wrong. Sitting in the booth, she put her hands up to her face, distraught, and it concerned me.

Her voice began to crack, and then she sobbed, "He raped me. He raped me last na-ight. He and Sasha raped me in de house while you were goone several ta-imes! He did de same ting to Angeline. I didn' wan' tell you, because I was afraid! You and Roger would confront dem and dey'd kill you!"

No wonder the two of them walked around so downcast many months ago! They had been violated, intruded upon several times and made to feel like helpless animals. Bernstein was now dead, but I wanted to make Capasso pay for all that he had done.

When Marcia stood up, I tried to comfort her with an embrace, but she backed away, making me hate Capasso all the more! The desire to right the situation burned in my chest, so I resolved to do something very drastic. As I stewed inwardly and paced back and forth in the galley, I decided upon a course of action. Marcia left and went back to an empty cabin, sobbing.

I went down the hall and knocked on Davies' door, waking him. He came to the opening bleary eyed, with unkempt vanishing hair and fairly long whiskers hanging from his jaw. Like all of the men here, he had a long growth of beard, due to the lack of shaving facilities. Angeline was snoring on the bed, lying on her side, too dead to be concerned.

"Arnold, I have something very, very important to share with you. Come this way please," I beckoned to him in a serious tone.

I had him come into my cabin, where Roger slept innocently. As I walked into the small room with Davies in tow, Roger stirred from his sleep, rolling over at the commotion.

"Capasso raped your daughter," I said to Arnold Davies.

"What!" he exclaimed in wide-eyed disbelief.

I explained to him Marcia's account and it made him furious. "I want to beat everything he has out of him!" Davies said, his voice rising as his face turned red.

He put on his day clothes and took the hallway to a set of stairs, a revolver tucked away in his belt. He meant to kill Capasso, and I was going to stand back and let him do it. He mounted the stairway to the deck with a fury that grew with each step. It was daylight and the sun was coming up over the horizon we were sailing into. Capasso and Milano were sitting in the little console area that sat on top of the deckhouse, not suspecting a thing. They steered the rudder as the sails caught the prevailing wind that took us slowly toward the Old World of ancient evil.

Davies approached both of them, Roger and I close behind him. The two men in the console appeared a little defensive, apparently caught off guard. "What did you do to my daughter?" Davies screamed, his face once again turning beet red. Capasso appeared puzzled and uncertain.

"WHAT DID YOU DO TO MY DAUGHTER?" Davies bellowed again. Capasso still did not seem to understand why Davies was yelling at him. He then stopped, collected himself, and stood confidently with his arms folded in defiance.

"Old man, what are you talkin' about? You're rantin' like a lunatic."

"YOU RAPED MY DAUGHTER!" Davies accused.

"Try to prove it old man. Just try to prove it! There's no couht of law where you can prove anything," Capasso responded.

He was right.

"In fact, in this day and age the one with the most guns wins. You see, Mistah Davies, I am the law here. I have the most power. Whatever I wanna do, I do," Capasso dictated confidently, with so much rebelliousness it actually made me frightened.

Capasso furnished a black Colt .45, pulling it on Davies before the intellectual could react.

"Old man, I'm sick of hearing your mouth at this point." Davies's eyes widened in horror as my own heart palpitated. Then, without remorse, Capasso shot Davies twice in the chest. Arnold Davies fell forward onto the deck like a tree that had been toppled. He lay there unmoving and unresponsive. Capasso had killed him.

Roger pulled his pistol on Capasso. Milano had a rifle under the console, and cocked it, ready to fight. Roger put his hands up in the air. Capasso clearly had an ally.

"Watch them," he told Milano. "I have business to take care of. Gonna put somebody out of my misery now!" Capasso left the command console and went downstairs with his gun in hand to the deck below. I was not sure what he was going to do. I looked at Davies' corpse and noticed that the skin was starting to turn a shade of unreal gray. We knew what would happen next, and we wouldn't like it one bit.

* * *

Capasso banged on Angeline's door with seething anger. He heard her groan something through the door, half-awake. "Wake up little wench. I have something to show you! WAKE UP LITTLE GIRL! COME TO PAPA!" Capasso opened up the door and walked over to Angeline, who was still groggy. He grabbed her by the arm and pulled her out of bed violently, pistol in hand. He yanked her out of the bedroom, down the hallway and up the stairs, dragging her behind him. They emerged on the deck, the breeze blowing back Capasso's long dark brown hair.

* * *

Both of them stepped into the still morning air as the vessel slowly began to veer off course, Milano faithfully held the rifle and forced Roger to throw his gun to the floor of the deck, rooting the resistance out. There was nothing we could do as Capasso pulled Angeline along by her arm. Capasso was a brutal man who obeyed every fickle impulse that shot through his brain.

"Look what we did to daddy, sweetie. LOOK WHAT WE DID TO DADDY! LOOK! C'MON LOOK!" Capasso said as he grabbed Angeline by the hair and pushed her face near the corpse that lay face down on the deck.

Angeline realized that her father was now deceased. "NOOOOO!" she cried. "NOOOOOOOO!" she sobbed in screams, reality now fully set in. Capasso was a sadistic man and had to be stopped, but I did not know how it could be done. I would have to be patient.

Davies had been dead for about ten minutes, but the amount of time it took for a corpse to revive varied. Sometimes it took longer, but usually it would occur within fifteen or sixteen minutes, though in some rare cases it took an hour. Perhaps it depended upon the concentration of radioactive taint in the air. Nonetheless, we waited while Milano pointed the shotgun in our direction, Capasso pressing Angeline's face to the deck. Where were Marcia and Rachel in all of this?

The corpse was turning an unnatural shade of gray, exaggerated and kind of like the primer that is sprayed on cars. The corpse began to stir slightly and the head moved. A short groan emitted from the lips as if in pain. The head turned from left to right and the torso rolled back and forth as if waking from its deathly slumber. It let out a sickening howl, and I began to gasp, my heart beating wildly. The thing turned over on its back and sat straight up.

There it was. Once a man of repute, Davies was now reduced to a thing that struggled to its feet, unable to form sentences or experience patterns of sentience. He stood erect with an angry expression, studying his surroundings.

Capasso, still grasping Angeline by the hair, pulled her to her feet and then took one of her hands and twisted it behind her back. Completely helpless, she could not run or escape. I lurched forward for a second, wanting to help Angeline, but Milano tipped his shotgun at me, threatening to use it. If I did anything, Milano would kill me.

"Capasso let her go! If you want to kill anyone, kill me. It's me who has been giving you problems. She didn't hurt you. Let her go, man! Let her go!" I said in a remarkably bold, confrontational manner.

"Remember, Goering, you're in no position to bargain! I will do whatev-uh I want and kill whomev-uh I want!" he dictated.

The corpse that was once Arnold Davies tottered towards Angeline, arms outstretched, sensing the warm flesh near him. He would sink his teeth into the woman that was once his daughter, all sense of civility gone from him.

"Daddy, its me! It's your daughter, Angie! Please Daddy, don't do this!" Angeline said in a sobbing panic.

What used to be Arnold Davies was not responding. He just kept moving towards his disinherited daughter, placing his one hand upon her face and the other around her right arm! Angeline screamed.

Then a sudden movement from the hatch in the deck caught my eye. It was the young woman from Jamaica, her long braided tresses blowing in the wind, brandishing a pistol in her right hand. Surprisingly, she marched onto the deck without fear.

"Okey, Capasso, let her goo, now! Don' move Milano!" Marcia said as she pointed her gun at Milano who sat with the gun still in his hands.

The corpse that was once Arnold Davies, whirled around to face Marcia, distracted by her disturbance. Roger immediately dived for the discarded pistol on the deck, grabbed it, and fired while still on the floor. He hit the ghoul in the chest, and the travesty of Arnold Davies stumbled away from Angeline. Roger fired again, this time sinking a slug into the head. The ghoul went down to his knees and fell forward, dead for the second time. Marcia still aimed her pistol at Milano and I could tell by the look in her eyes that she'd use it. Roger, sprawled on the deck, pointed his at Capasso, who still had a tight grip on Angeline.

"Let her go now, Capasso!" Roger demanded. Capasso, outgunned, was forced to comply. Angeline ran to me. Her father was no longer here to comfort her. A woman who decided to act beyond the constraints of her fear had thankfully contained a violent crisis. More lives could have been lost, and graciously were not. How I was going to live with Capasso from here on out was not clear, but I had to survive in spite of the tension. We wrapped Arnold Davies' corpse in a white sheet, gave him a short funeral, and committed this agnostic's soul to God, although I was not sure if he was going to be with him. The corpse was dropped into the rolling waves and swallowed up by the eternal sea.

Chapter Thirty-Two: The Voyage Across the Sea

We were strangers going to a strange land, seeking refuge in a world that could not be. Milano, Rachel, and Capasso refused to cook or eat with us, the ongoing conflict dragging out over the weeks. I knew that I would have to keep a gun with me and look over my shoulder at all times, a nagging insecurity I could do without. At any moment, Robert Capasso might want to have his revenge, shooting us in the head when we least expect it. Maybe he let us live because he needed a kingdom to rule.

One evening, I sat at the back of the ketch, noting the moon's reflection upon the dark waves that obscured the Stygian depths below. Angeline sat beside me, her arm around my waist, head against my cheek. She was comfortable and secure and began to fall asleep. I enjoyed this little moment of physical intimacy, and it helped me to forget the trauma of the past several days. I hoped that God would give her the most pleasant of dreams.

The next day, we sailed through a storm that lasted about two hours, sweeping water into the boat but not enough to sink it. We all had to ride below, except for Capasso, who steered the rudder and kept the vessel on course, getting drenched all the while. Harry Milano comforted Rachel in one of the cabins, who was still traumatized from her attempted suicide many weeks ago. The rest of us talked and played cards in the galley at the bow. The storm eventually cleared and we went back up to the deck to observe the now still and peaceful waters of the open ocean.

Far away, on the golden waves that shimmered in the autumn sun, I saw whales surface and spout water into the air. Perhaps they were blue or finback, but from this distance I could not tell. Whatever the case, their chief predator, mankind, was nearly eliminated, enabling these animals to thrive. They were no longer hunted for their oil that would be turned into soaps, glycerin, and used for other purposes. The creatures submerged, disappearing below, off to strain the abundant plankton from the fertile waters.

On another day, the boat was surrounded by a school of dolphins that rode the wave of the bow, like freeloaders trying to take advantage of the situation. They would surface for air and dive back down, frolicking in the water as the ketch continued on its journey. I have heard that many sailors abandoned sinking vessel to find themselves in a school of dolphins that pushed them inland, saving them from drowning. On the flipside of that, I had heard other tales of sailors nudged further out to sea by dolphins to most likely suffer the horrible fate of death by drowning. Some of the creatures here dove up into the air and would arc back down as they disappeared altogether, going off to other cetaceous pursuits. As fast as they arrived they were gone, seemingly bored with us as we sped across the vast expanse of water to the dry and mysterious land that lay beyond.

We continued to sail the spectral sea. It had been about four weeks since we left the graveyard of New York City, with those things wailing to the heavens, having no purpose but to wander endlessly searching for human flesh. Since we could only rely upon the power of the wind, I knew the journey would take some time, feeling like Thor Heyerdahl as he traveled around the world in a primitive boat. We sailed through a few more storms, the fiberglass hull proving seaworthy, the ketch journeying on.

Capasso and Milano had a hard time determining the exact direction the boat was taking, as the storms had blown us off course. Looking at the positions of the stars in the night sky, they figured that we were going to end up on the coast of Sierra Leone or Liberia and had to reposition the sails to catch the winds blowing from the northwest. Perhaps we would reach Africa in another three weeks.

Although we had plenty of provisions, we left plastic tubs out to collect the rainwater that fell from the sky. This could be used for drinking, cooking and taking very short showers. Sometimes, Capasso would let down the sails when the ocean was calm and take out the heavy fishing pole to catch a large bluefish or some sea bass. We could prepare and cook the catch in the galley downstairs. It always made good eating. We were fine for now, doing well despite the fact that I hated Capasso's guts.

One day, I noticed something out on the water's surface while talking to Angeline on the deck. Way out beyond the bow, a mile away perhaps, was a large cream-colored body of land, about an eighth-of-a-mile wide and about half-a-mile long. At first I thought we had reached the shores of Africa, but as we got closer I found that it had a strange glistening and slippery surface that just didn't seem right. I went up to the console and brought it to the attention of Milano, who was steering the boat. He stared at it for a moment and then grabbed a set of field glasses. He viewed it through them.

"There's somethin' wrong with it. The back is way too slippery," he commented. "I don't think it's an island. I think it's something alive!" I stepped back from Milano in both shock and revulsion. We got the others to come up from the cabins to behold the weird object floating on the surface of the ocean. As the boat neared it, the entire island submerged under the water, leaving behind large waves. The women gasped, somewhat startled and unnerved. The ketch continued on with its journey and we never saw the bizarre island in the middle of the sea again. Perhaps that was the ancient *Kraken* many sea legends spoke about.

The *Kraken* was supposedly a giant tentacled monster that was able to grasp the mast of a ship in its arms and drag it under the waves. Some theorized that it was more than a legend perhaps an extremely large squid. Giant squid have washed ashore upon the coasts of Newfoundland and New Zealand over the centuries, but these were creatures probably no more than sixty or seventy feet long at best, and too small to attack a sailing vessel or pull it under. Seafarers have said that there are much larger creatures, perhaps hundreds of feet long and certainly capable of pulling a ship down! Some scientists had theorized that these creatures were big enough to catch whales and devour them for sustenance. I could not wait for the journey to be finally over and done with, to be safe and sound on dry land. At least we would not have to worry about becoming fodder for a giant squid. At this point, anything was possible, even sea monsters.

We sailed on for weeks through storms, time, and tide. Finally, after crossing an endless expanse of waves, Capasso came down to the galley where most of us were sitting. He had something to share that was both exciting and encouraging.

"Land! We found land! Get ready, cuz we are goin' home!" he exclaimed.

We went up to the deck to look out beyond the bow. There they were, the outlines of majestic mountains in the distance, offering limited salvation! Land! Now we could find a refuge from this crisis and a place to replenish lost humanity. Things never looked so good, and the sun never shined so bright! We could see it before us, a limitless sandy ribbon that went on forever along the coast, backed by a green blanket of vegetation, towering mountains resting behind. There was a small coastal town there with several houses along the shore. I studied them for a few minutes and recognized the architecture as unmistakably Dutch. It was now clear we had reached the turbulent and chaotic shores of South Africa. We were almost there!

Chapter Thirty-Three: The Other Lonely Family

Cape Town was to the south of us. Being a large community, ghouls most likely overran the city, and we had to stay clear of it. Capasso turned the ketch to the north to find an isolated wharf where we could safely land. We found one away from the town that we had first seen, a collection of approximately twenty buildings that may have been a small fishing community at one time.

The coastal town waited patiently on the shore for us. We found an empty spot on the wharf to dock the boat. As we unloaded the ketch, a group of ghouls began to congregate a short distance away. However, we were armed and it didn't take long to wipe the mob out, further depleting our ammo.

With Milano's ability to repossess vehicles, we went into the small community, killing a few more ghouls. We found a black pickup truck and a navy blue suburban, as well as some new provisions. We loaded up the trucks and brought along the generator from the ship. The seven of us boarded the vehicles after Roger found a road map in one of the offices. We proceeded northward, where we would hopefully get to the Namibian border and find our way to safety in distant Windhoek. How long it would take to get there was not clear. I hated these uncertain moments that constantly thrust forth obstacles.

We were most likely in the northern part of the Cape Province, an area almost entirely grassland, arid and certainly remote. At one time, it was inhabited by Hottentots, who lived here long before the Bantu came down from the north about five hundred years ago and took away their land.

Where were the people? Was anyone left alive in this nation? How would we find them if there were survivors? These questions continued to haunt me as they raked across my brain. We made our way through the dry grasslands, dotted by fan-like trees that had spreads of foliage on the top of their trunks. We approached some hills as we journeyed on, but I was not sure if we had reached Namibia. In many cases, road signs were knocked down, leaving us guessing as to where we were.

We ventured on into the desolate grasslands. The fan-like trees became more common, and I was not certain if we were still in the Cape Province anymore, we might have been in the Transvaal for all I knew. Dutch-style architecture dominated the area, indicating the Afrikaner culture was still strong in this location. Since the southeastern coast of South Africa was more British, I suspected we were still in the north of the country. In the distance to the south was a range of mountains topped by wisps of clouds. They may have been the Drakensbergs, but I couldn't be sure.

I thought that we were going in the wrong direction. If those mountains were the Drakensbergs, it meant that we were way out of line. None of us knew South Africa, and all we managed to do was get ourselves lost. We approached a solitary Dutch-style house on the roadside somewhere near a town called Roosendaal. The area surrounding the home was mostly a plain, although hills loomed in the background, seeming to hold up the dark sky as storm clouds congregated and spun. There was an antenna shooting up from the back of the dismal house, indicating a radio inside. Perhaps, we could hook the generator up to it and get it to work. We pulled the vehicles over to the side of the road and got out, seeking shelter from the potential storm.

We walked across the lawn and entered the structure. It was a two-story home, empty, and devoid of all life. The inhabitants had either died or fled somewhere far away. This area was not heavily populated, so we had no worries about attracting the attention of an army of ghouls. We all stood in what used to be a living room, the stuffing now torn out of the furniture, magazines strewn all over the floor. Marcia held her bear up to her chest like a little girl. I picked up one of the publications and noticed that it was written in Afrikaans, leading me to believe that the owners must have been Afrikaners, or possibly the Coloured people.

The men walked up and down the halls to make sure that it was safe and concealed no threats in the woodwork, while the three women stayed amongst the disheveled couches and chairs. I walked up the stairway to the second floor to find four doors all shut along a short and abrupt hallway. Mustering up a little courage, I opened up one and found nothing except for an empty mattress with the sheets torn off, looking as if it hadn't been used in a long while. I left that room and went back to the hallway.

I opened up the next one and found it brightly lit, the sun's warm rays gladly shining through the window as the storm approached in the background. There was something else in here that was interesting. There was an actual boy, sitting high on the bed! There was definite human life here in this remote corner of the continent! The kid had blond hair and rested on the mattress, diligently looking at a magazine. He seemed to be absorbed in the periodical as he turned its pages, completely uninterested in me.

"Hello," I said.

The boy continued to peer at the publication in his lap, still turning the pages, almost as if he was autistic. I looked again; taking note that his skin color was off. The boy's dermis had turned a sickening shade of gray and it became apparent to me that he was a ghoulish travesty and nothing more! It looked at me for a moment, staring blankly into my eyes. The empty expression reverted to one of anger as the creature growled at me and climbed off the bed. The ghoul went for my leg and I swung the butt of my rifle, hitting it in the hand and knocking it away without mercy. I pointed the barrel of my gun at the creature and fired it, buckshot flying into its skull. The corpse fell backwards and ceased to move.

Roger appeared in the doorway. "What's going on in here?" he asked.

I looked down at the creature's face. "I thought he was a normal kid, guess not," I answered. I had to do what I had to do, but it didn't mean I liked it.

Roger told me that Capasso and Milano might be able to get the ham radio in the basement to work, if we hooked it up to the generator that we took from the ketch. After making rounds to secure the whole perimeter, Milano actually got the radio to function. Capasso sent out many messages, getting nothing in reply. Maybe the signal from the antenna was not strong enough to broadcast many miles away, and we had no clue as to what to do next. I fell asleep in one of the bedrooms upstairs, and darkness took over my thoughts. Slumber overwhelmed me, as rain began to pour from the sky.

The next morning I was awakened by loud whoops from the basement. I quickly pulled clothes over my body and ran to the kitchen and down to the musty basement with its damp stone foundation. The two men were to my right, seated in front of the ham radio that sat upon a table against the dark wall. They were jubilant, beaming grins a mile wide and practically dancing in the aisles, which I found rather amusing. The amusement was short lived and I remembered that recently I wanted to kill both of them.

"We found some people man," Milano said, grinning. "Listen."

I heard a guttural accent come over the radio's speaker.

"How many people are with you?" the voice asked.

"There are seven of us," Capasso said.

"*Dit is wonderlik! Wat is jou naam?*"

"Can't understand you," Capasso said.

"You don't speak Afrikaans?" the voice asked.

"No, I speak English," Capasso said.

"I asked, 'What is your name?'" the guttural voice said.

"My name is Bob Capasso."

"My name is Andries DeKuyper."

We learned there was a small group of people in a village called Willebroek, to thc northwest of us. There were six living there, and one happened to be a little girl who was wounded. We arranged to meet forty miles from here.

Capasso cried out to everyone at the top of his deep lungs: "WE'RE GETTIN' OUTTAA HERE!" And, surely, we would. Andries DeKuyper gave us the directions we needed and we packed up provisions that afternoon, leaving the abandoned Dutch-style house. We went off into the northwest to find the area mostly hilly with groves of African trees here and there. A few houses could be seen in the distance.

We drove deeper into the grasslands. Capasso told me the Afrikaner and his people lived in a medical building near Willebroek. After making a series of turns, we came to a smaller road lined with a great number of trees. We took that road and found a clearing at the end of the drive accompanied by a two-story plain building. In front was a parking lot with a few cars in it, and Capasso turned his vehicle in like a bullet into the chamber of a revolver. I placed mine along side of his, following his lead.

As we got out of our vehicles, a man stood in the doorway of the building, wearing a tan outfit that consisted of shorts, long socks that nearly went to the knees, along with short boots. I recognized his costume as traditional Afrikaner attire. He walked over to us with a serious expression on his face, and a number of people accompanied him. At first I thought the people were dwarves since most were much shorter than the approaching figure, but then I realized that the man was over six-and-a-half feet tall! He towered and imposed, even over Capasso. The man stood there in a sturdy fashion and said in his guttural accent, "Welcome to South Africa." He was Andries DeKuyper, the man we talked to on the radio. I noticed that most of his group was armed with rifles.

One of the men behind him was dressed in a similar fashion, but balding, in spite of his long hair and beard. He extended his hand out and shook with Capasso and me. He was Johannes LaFontaine.

Next to LaFontaine was a man who wore shorts and a tan shirt. He was shorter, with dark skin, a beard, and wild kinky hair. He shook hands with the group and introduced himself as Abel Van Den Heuvel.

Two women were here as well. Both were black Africans about thirty years of age and were wearing sleeveless dresses with bracelets on their arms and ankles. One of them was a little heavy, with her hair tied in several long braids. Her name was Judith Luthuli. The other woman was a little shorter and thinner; her long hair was tied up on the back of her head. She was introduced as Amanda Dingane. I noticed both women wore belts with revolvers in the holsters, and looked as if they were no strangers to this violent new world.

I looked down at Amanda's weapon. She peered down in response, then looked back up at me, and silently smiled. There was a little blond girl named Elizabeth who stood next to Amanda, an innocent expression upon her face. "Hello," the little girl said, in a distinct South African accent.

"You must be hungry from your long trip," DeKuyper said in a forceful sort-of-way.

"Very," Capasso said.

"We have food inside," Amanda said with a smile. The two African women led us into the brown sterile building, formerly a medical complex when society was still functioning. Everyone followed them, toting their firearms.

We went into the dark, dismal complex and headed down a couple of hallways until we stood in a large dining room with expansive windows that looked out upon the hills outside. There was a large table with places set and everyone sat down for a prepared meal of pasta with tomato sauce seasoned with garlic.

"Where are all of you from?" DeKuyper asked.

"We're from New Yohk," Capasso answered.

"New York at one time was Dutch. Are you part Dutch, Mr. Capasso?" DeKuyper asked.

"All my great-grand parents are from It-lee," he answered.

"I am trying to find some people of Dutch background. How about you Mr. Goering?" he asked me.

"No, I don't have any Dutch in me. Just German, Irish and English. Why do you want to know?" I asked the Afrikaner.

"Just an obsession that I have, I guess," he responded.

"Where is your family from, Andries?" I asked.

"My family came from the Netherlands in the 1850s and settled in the Transvaal as farmers. Their fortunes grew, as they became successful cattle ranchers. My great grandfather fought against the British in the Boer War," he replied.

I found this interesting. I never had a chance to probe into the Afrikaner identity before.

"Johannes, your name is French, but you're an Afrikaner. Why is that?" I asked him.

"That is because the original LaFontaine came from France after 1685, when Louis XIV revoked the Edict of Nantes. My ancestor settled in the Cape Colony seeking protection, and his family later became successful merchants there. Many of the LaFontaine's left the Cape Colony and helped found the Boer republics after the English became too dictatorial," LaFontaine said.

He also had ancestors that fought in the Boer War, and recalled it as if it happened to him yesterday. I gathered that they wanted to make the Afrikaners a strong people once again.

We found out that Abel Van Den Heuvel was from the Cape Province, and he gave a proud spiel about the Coloured people.

"Like other Coloureds, I can trace my ancestry back to Dutch nobility that settled the Cape Colony back in the 1690s," he said, adding he had Zulu in his lineage, with a bit of Javanese tossed in.

"We're from the Zulu nation in the Natal Province," Amanda said, referring to herself and Judith. She mentioned the many tales of the courageous exploits of Shaka Zulu, the great Zulu king killed by insurgents in 1828. "Shaka is my hero," Amanda admitted while shoveling spaghetti into her mouth. Despite the inherent nationalism of the women, the Coloured and the two Afrikaners readily accepted them.

"We found Elizabeth in a suburb of Durban. Her parents disappeared, and we decided to adopt her," Amanda continued. I sensed that Elizabeth was very much attached to Amanda, like mother and daughter all over again.

I asked the people if they had ever heard of the settlement in Windhoek. DeKuyper answered, "Yes." He said nothing else as he stuffed a forkful of pasta into his mouth. I asked him if he had thought about going up there. He sternly replied, "No," and I could feel his cold eyes upon me. The huge Afrikaner exhibited little emotion and divulged as little information as possible. He was a man who didn't care if people liked him or not, very much like Capasso.

"Andries, why don't you wanna go to Windhoek? It would be safer there and you would be able to get medical attention."

"There's a reason, Mr. Goering. If you want to know so badly, I will show it to you," he told me as lukewarm food was passed around the table.

"Elizabeth, come here honey. Let the man see your arm," he said to the little girl. She came over to him carefully, somewhat afraid, standing very still. He had her roll up the sleeve on her arm, and it revealed a circular scar on her bicep.

"She was bitten by a ghoul several months ago and the wound miraculously healed up," DeKuyper said.

I was astounded! The girl should have been infected, but clearly she was not! She was somehow immune to the plague and resisted the undead virus. Somewhere in her veins coursed the cure to this disease that had ravaged the entire human race!

"Andries, do you realize what you have here?" I asked him.

"Yes, and we told the people in Windhoek, but there is a problem. They told me they want to come and take her away. I can't allow that," he said. "They would turn her into a lab animal and try to extract serums from her blood.

These are my people here, and I won't see any harm come to them," DeKuyper stated.

I wondered if it would be worth giving up a child for this type of cause. I could see from his response that DeKuyper was a tough man and would do whatever he wanted to do. He might not listen to reason, except for his own. I already despised Capasso, and I was beginning to hate DeKuyper. Both of them liked to have authority and would trample upon the rights of others to keep it.

After the dinner was over, Van Den Heuvel and Judith showed us to our rooms. Roger and I took a large windowless medical chamber with a bed on each side of the room. He decided to lie down, and I took the other cot and stretched out upon it.

"Rog, what do think about this whole thing with the little girl?" I asked, lying on the bed.

"I think we should take her to Windhoek, but I don't know how we are going to pull it off," he said matter-of-factly. "The thing is, we don't know the roads, and looking at the way we got lost earlier, it might be stupid."

We were uncertain as to what to do, so Roger and I prayed in the stifling chamber, asking God to radically manipulate events and show us an answer.

Finally, I went to sleep on the hospital beds amidst the stands full of operating utensils. I awoke just as fast as I had fallen asleep. It was strange that I hadn't had one of those dreams about Babylon for some time, but I shrugged the thought off and wanted to finish reading Ramadan's notes, although I continued to blow the whole project off. It was easy to get caught up in this pointless life of playing bridge with Marcia, Roger, and Angeline, which is what I did for the rest of the day.

That evening, after a quiet meal with DeKuyper and his "family," Roger and I went up to the second floor in a room that overlooked a thin wood of African deciduous trees. Beyond the trees were hills and grasslands that sloped upward into the background, absent of the presence of humanity, painting a picture of a civilized wasteland. It made me wonder if human extinction was near. I believed that we were very close to being snuffed out like a lone candle on a dark and rainy autumn night.

"We're going to have to make up our minds here," I said.

"Yeah, I know," Roger responded.

At that moment, I saw some movement through the window outside on the ground, in the orange glow of the twilight sun. There I looked down amidst the trees to find tottering shapes wandering toward the medical building. The ghouls were organizing themselves again and were now closing in. Clearly, we were going to have a fight on our hands!

We ran through the dim hallways with rifles in our fists, beneath the yellow fluorescent lights and down to the first level. Roger and I found most of the people in the lounge area talking, not aware of what had been happening.

"Get the guns! Don't just sit around doing nothing! Get the guns!" I said.

DeKuyper, LaFontaine, Van Den Heuvel, and Capasso all picked up their weapons, which were lying against the walls at rest.

DeKuyper led the men through the dark halls and located a rear exit that went outside the medical building. We found ourselves in the back of the complex, in a barren yard that met the trees on the slopes. The ghouls tottered and hobbled out of the forest, some armed with clubs just as they were back in Steuben Corners, giving the impression that this was a coordinated attack. They advanced with groans and animalistic growls, groping with their outstretched arms.

"Okay," DeKuyper said. "Let the lead fly!" We fired our weapons and began to cut them down, pumping bullets into their heads. The two Afrikaners had AK-47s and Capasso had his automatic, keeping the threat in check. Dozens of them congregated to our right. I noticed that most of them were blacks in contemporary clothing, raising their clubs and boards as they hobbled towards us. They charged us in waves, attacking by the dozens, reminding me of the *laager* situation in the

Battle of Blood River, where the Boers were surrounded by Zulu warriors. They placed their wagons in a circle and fired until they had driven off their attackers. We fired and fired until our ammunition was nearly spent. We cut them down as they surged forth, eliminating the contagious threat by leaps and bounds. After all was said and done, there were about eighty laying dead with lead bullets buried in their skulls. We had won. However, I knew that there would be hundreds more tomorrow, and thousands them after that. We had better fly out of here, to a place where no one would bother us.

After the attack, all of the men had a conference at the dinner table in the room with the large windows which looked out to the hills beyond.

"Andries, they'll keep on coming until they overwhelm us. We can't stay here," I said at the dinner table.

It became obvious that something was happening to these creatures, though I did not know precisely what. It was almost as if some unseen intelligence was guiding and directing them. We had to pack up right after the meal. I did not like leaving so fast, but we had to, despite some protests from LaFontaine and the two Zulu women, who were happy right here in this building. DeKuyper had his people load up both a jeep and a truck, while Capasso and the rest of us placed provisions in the back of a jeep and the pickup truck that carried the generator from the ketch. As we loaded up the automobiles, DeKuyper told me in passing that he knew a safe place in Namibia where we could escape the reaches of this decrepit multitude. Hopefully, it would be remote enough that the ghouls would not be able locate us. I decided to travel with the two Afrikaners as the procession coldly left the old medical complex behind. No one would ever use it again.

Chapter Thirty-Four: Namibia

Namibia was a sparsely populated place and we might fare better there. I was beginning to think that the ghouls had the ability to isolate human beings and then move in for the kill. There was something sinister about this whole thing, but I could not put my finger on it.

After traversing a series of roads amongst the plateaus of this region, we made it over the Namibian border. We would be heading to the Keetmanshoop area, an even more isolated place than where we had just been. DeKuyper used to serve in the South African Defense Force when Namibia was still controlled by South Africa. He also worked for the government as an administrator and had connections with his "old life" that would give us access to the place.

As we drove through the grassy highlands of Namibia, I could see hyenas frolicking and running about, playing amongst the deserted huts with cone-shaped roofs. There were probably cheetahs out there, diligently stalking prey as herds of elephants grazed peacefully in fields of grass.

For a few moments, I began to think about the human history of the area. Many centuries ago, the Khoikhoi, or Nama people, originally lived in this country. They were a short people with yellowish skin and unusual tufts of hair, unlike the Bantu that later moved into the area. Their language was characterized by series of clicks that the original Dutch settlers had trouble understanding.

The Herero people of the Bantu race were a taller, stockier folk than the diminutive Khoikhoi. They moved into the land, pushing the Khoikhoi south. The descendants of the Dutch colonists, the Boers, moved up from the Cape Colony in the 1800s and forced many of the Khoisan people, who were also from the Cape, into the region of Namibia. The Khoisan people eventually fought against the Herero several times. After the Congress of Berlin in 1884, the history of Namibia was violently interrupted when the European powers decided to carve up Africa like a giant cake. Germany took the area referred to as South-West Africa, which later became known as Namibia.

Europe came in like a vengeance as the Deutschlanders arrived in Windhoek and set up shop. After suppressing the Herero rebellion in 1904, the Germans moved in more colonists to further establish their presence. Fortunes were reversed in 1915, when the British-led South African force defeated the German army in South-West Africa. The German community continued to keep its identity despite the influx of Afrikaners, which explained the current German presence in Windhoek. It was strange how the Deutsch culture had emerged strong here in this sparsely populated land, so far removed from the Fatherland itself.

"We'll be there in about forty-five minutes," DeKuyper told me as the wind blew back his long hair.

The road met an intersection and a blue sign was there that read, "Keetmanshoop 10km." The procession stopped for a few minutes, and I asked LaFontaine how far away Windhoek was. He said it was about two hundred and twenty kilometers and would probably take about four hours to get there on wheels, so long as the roads were not in need of repairs. We turned right at an intersection and continued on, heading north.

After passing expanses of brown and arid wasteland, there was a complex of white and gray edifices to our right. There were probably about seventeen buildings in all. It looked very much like a college campus, so I raised the point.

"You are correct in your assumption, Andy," LaFontaine said.

"The South African government was working in tandem with the Namibians, trying to complete this complex in the 1980s," DeKuyper told me. "However, as American sanctions began to take affect, all construction was halted. The Namibians put a *heining* (fence) around it to keep it from harm."

The convoy stopped at the gate that barred the entrance to the college campus. As I looked around me, I saw nothing but grassland as far as the eye could see. DeKuyper actually had keys to the place and said he was close to the man in charge of the project.

"I figured that this would be a good back-up plan, in case things went awry," DeKuyper admitted.

Both Afrikaners got out and unlocked the gate, then got back into the vehicles to lead the convoy in. The procession went to a building in the center of the campus that was six stories high. I figured it was intended to be the college's administration building, if the place ever functioned. Milano picked the lock, and we all walked inside the large building to find ourselves standing in a lifeless vestibule. Roger eagerly tried the elevators, only to find that they did not work, since there was no power. The building did nothing but house an endless supply of pens, documents, and typing paper. However, DeKuyper knew of a windmill located on the periphery of the campus, which could be attached to an apparatus that would give us all the electricity we would need. We looked around the inside of the building and found it totally unused. There was no litter or garbage strewn about, indicating that humanity had never quite settled here. This place was untouched and untainted.

In back of the administrative center was a brick building, also six stories high, a student dormitory that could be used as living space. All of us left the vestibule, went back to our vehicles and drove to the dormitory, where we faithfully unloaded the provisions that were packed in the automobiles. Milano picked the locks and allowed us to enter the dormitory. Milano was worth his weight in gold these days.

Once we got past the front vestibule, we located a lounge in the back with stuffed gold-colored sofas, a great place for us to repose and use for meetings. Upstairs on the next floor were the sleeping quarters, and each of us could choose our own bedroom. DeKuyper insisted we all sleep on the same floor for security purposes. DeKuyper seemed to be playing the role of the father figure for this "family."

I chose my room, and Roger took one down the hallway. Angeline and Marcia both got rooms on the other side of the building, and the others slept in various locations. This reminded me of the days when I was a college student, somehow hoping life would one day work out. Now that whole notion was in question. Strangely, as I sat down at the desk, I felt a supernatural peace that told me that everything in my life was truly going to resolve itself. Perhaps, I was not adrift on the ocean of circumstances without rhyme or reason.

The next day, Johannes LaFontaine wanted to take Roger and me around to show us the various campus facilities. We stood outside the residence hall and he pointed to a large building with a rounded roof he felt was pertinent to our cause.

"That is the athletic center. There you'll find squash courts and weight-training facilities. The other buildings are residence halls," LaFontaine said.

"There are some petrol pumps down the road. We found the key to them, so we now have a fuel supply." Gasoline was a necessity at this point in time.

He told us that there was even a broadcasting station on the campus that had a working radio. A few of the buildings served as administrative offices, while others were meant to be lecture halls once the campus was up and running. Behind the residence hall where we lived was a flat-roofed library that I could use to look up much-needed information. The campus sat on the empty savannah, unfulfilled, never realizing the purpose for which it was originally designed, and I felt it could be put to better use for as long as we were here.

The campus was complete with a two-story brown science building on the periphery. Behind the science building was an overgrown plot of weeds that could be converted into a large garden. The long Namibian growing season would enable us to raise a large amount of vegetables that should prove sufficient for our needs. For a source of protein, DeKuyper, Van Den Heuvel, or LaFontaine would have to go out on a safari and kill some water buffalo or catch some fish in one of the tributaries of Fish River.

As we weeded out the garden and made the place "livable," I noticed the gathering tension between DeKuyper and Capasso. They were unusually stiff and silent when they were around me. Perhaps both of them wanted to rule this little nation starting to take shape. I almost wanted to see DeKuyper beat up Capasso without mercy.

After several days, the place became more habitable. We did not have running water yet, but there were some large basins that could be used to collect the rain. We managed, through a pulley system, to get the basins up on the roof of the dormitories. This allowed water to be conveniently dispensed from a faucet, enabling us to take showers, albeit cold ones, once Milano found supplies and installed the plumbing.

From DeKuyper's apparatus, we had Milano put together an electrical mainline that ran to the dormitory, powering the stoves and the lights. Thanks to the device, we were able to hook up some freezers in the dining facility that would preserve the wild game we hunted. Later on, all of us went over to the structure next to the dormitories. Here our hosts served up prime rib carved from Cape buffalo. Included in the meal were canned potatoes and carrots, and Judith even found some raw greens and converted them into salad. It was all quite good, and I momentarily forgot all the carnage and destruction I had witnessed over the past several months.

Capasso sat at the table and continued to down food, as did DeKuyper, both keeping the silence as the tension grew. I looked around the table in the large room with tall windows and high ceilings and noticed that everyone devoured their meals voraciously. I made up my mind to say a few things to break the delicate silence.

"Andries?" I asked.

"Ya?" he answered.

"I think we should all get out of here and get to Windhoek, maybe in a week. We'll be safer there. Not only that, but we could give to them the girl to fight this plague with. We're gonna have to survive somehow," I said.

The big Afrikaner told Elizabeth to leave this large cavernous room. The girl left, accompanied by Amanda Dingane, and DeKuyper just sat steel-like, without motion.

"*Nee. Nee. Nee*," he said rubbing his eyes. "I have told you already, they will hurt her and probably kill her. I can't allow that, so don't bring it up again," he said without once looking me in the eyes. His coldness frightened me.

"Andries," Capasso said. "I think it's a good idea that we all head to Windhoek with the girl. It's saf-uh there and we could get rid a' all these rotten things!"

"Aren't you listening? The girl does not leave the premises! And that's it!" he said in his intense guttural accent.

"I think she should, Mr. DeKuypuh. I think she should," Capasso said with brazen assertion.

I wanted to join Capasso and pound some reasoning into the head of this stubborn Afrikaner. A voice in my head dictated, "Tone it down," so I shut up, realizing the whole thing was at risk of blowing sky-high. No one said a word after that. Out of chaos emerged many to take control, but only one would dominate. I was beginning to see how that worked, and dreaded the anticipated climax.

That evening, Roger, Angeline, Marcia, and I took a walk along the edge of the garden plot to discuss what we had just seen. Marcia held the stuffed bear in her right hand.

"Capasso is a man who likes to boss other people around. He wants power, period," I said. "If he can get the girl, he'll be the one in control, and then DeKuyper and his group will kiss up to him."

"What aboot de people in Windhoek?" Marcia asked.

"They don't know where we are. If they did, they would probably be here by now," I said. "Besides, if he gives the girl to the people there, DeKuyper would lose all bargaining chips. Elizabeth has the cure, and as long as she is in his possession, DeKuyper can get others to do what he wants. With Elizabeth in his grasp, he feels important. He, like Capasso, is born to dominate, and will do anything to make sure he stays on top."

It was all about power. Capasso wanted it, DeKuyper wanted to keep his. Both knew they were enemies of each other. If everyone joined forces and cooperated to begin with, the human race would not be in the sorry condition it was in now. Capasso's and DeKuyper's conflict served as a reminder that humanity had gone downhill and would continue to slide in that direction. We were on the brink of destruction and I knew it.

That night, I reposed in my bedroom and went to sleep, falling into a dream. A bearded man came to me, dressed in an ancient Middle Eastern robe and possessing short hair. His wrists were bleeding from some large puncture wounds that had been sustained to them. He looked at me and said, "I have a reason for you. The entire world is going to know about that reason, and it will be I who will lead you to that victory, Andy. You will overcome." Abruptly I awoke, not sure of its significance. Would it come to pass? I hoped to God that the suggestion would.

I could sleep no longer. It seemed as if I needed to do something. I went to the window and looked up at the clear night sky. Everything appeared so placid and non-threatening. The stars were out, neatly arranged in their constellations of animals, mythological creatures, and cooking utensils. For some reason, my mind turned to the subject of shooting stars. I had never seen one, but I had once witnessed a comet that came close to the earth back in 1986.

Shooting stars are meteors. They are chunks of rock propelled across the heavens to pierce the earth's atmosphere. At that moment, for the first time in my life, I actually saw one! A white line of light passed in front of the constellations, falling down to the earth in a gradually arcing path like a beautiful angel descending from the heavens. It cut a swath through the night sky, coming down to land and bringing a caustic pestilence with it. As I reflected for a moment upon the occurrence, a bad feeling infected the inner recesses of my heart. Something just happened.

Roger and I met at the dining hall the next morning to pray, eat, and read the Bible. We sat at the tables sipping our coffee and eating cold cereal that swam in a sea of water and powdered milk.

"Have you ever seen a falling star?" I asked him.

"Yeah," he answered with a mouth full of cereal. "How 'bout you?"

"Saw one last night," I answered.

"What time?"

"I think it was close to 11:00. Not sure though," I said.

"Saw the same thing," Roger commented. Both of us were staring up into the sky at the same exact moment as the other. Peculiar.

Chapter Thirty-Five: Miss Bergmann

That day, I had to go on the necessary "ghoul patrol" with Abel Van Den Heuvel and hunt around the perimeter. I got behind the wheel, on the right side of the jeep, and flew out into the wild, circling the area about two miles from the campus. All about us were grasslands, and in the distance we could see the rocky hills that were so common to these highlands. We noticed a figure up ahead on the side of the road.

Kind of surprised to see more human life, or that which was remotely human, we approached it to find out whether or if it was fish or foul. As we got closer to the figure, we realized that is was a black African wearing a red shirt, blue jeans, and a pair of sneakers, but his skin was gray. He, or it, just walked on, lurching forward with something strange in its hand. I wanted to dismiss it as an optical illusion, but looking closer, I realized that it held a black .45! I had a hard time believing that ghouls had the sentience to do this, but at this point I had seen everything.

Van Den Heuvel ordered me to stop the jeep out of sheer disbelief. We just stared at the creature, and it just stared back with no emotion. Then something happened. Its mouth started moving as it formed what sounded like words with great difficulty. Speech fell from lips that once had little intelligence, but now the intelligence had strangely returned! I shouldn't be so surprised. Didn't I see this sort of thing back at that campus in Upstate New York, when Davies was still alive?

We listened closely and I could have sworn I heard a phrase clearly articulated. I dismissed the fact in disbelief.

"I want both of you dead!" it said. The creature raised the pistol and aimed it at the Coloured. Van Den Heuvel took his AK-47 and fired it without hesitation, hitting it in six places, including the head. It fell backwards and landed on the ground, unmoving. The pistol flew out of its hand and landed on the grass at the side of the road. We left the corpse there, rotting on the ground.

After the experience, we went back to the campus and found Capasso out in front of the dormitory, cleaning his firearms with rags. We explained to him what had just transpired.

"You heard what sounded like words," Capasso told us.

He suggested that they were no more than grunts or ordinary sounds a beast would make; however, we knew we had heard it clearly. Capasso was a doubter in denial and probably would be for the rest of his life. Something had happened to the cosmos, but still I was not sure what it was.

The next day came, and as Milano and LaFontaine were getting ready for the patrol, I went out to help load the ammo. At that moment, LaFontaine looked up the main road and spied a distant figure walking briskly towards us. I too, saw the figure and we all got into the jeep with our weapons to meet it.

As we got closer, we noticed that the figure was a quickly-moving female. The young blond-haired woman approached, and I noticed her skin was strangely discolored. We stopped the jeep and looked at the woman, who smiled in a non-threatening way. She was dressed in a denim skirt and a cream–colored shirt, her exposed skin coated in the light red resin that the Himba women wore to protect themselves from the sun.

"Don't shoot! Don't shoot! I'm a friend!" she said smiling. "*Meine Name ist Kari Bergmann,* and I'm from Windhoek."

After we checked her for weapons, she boarded the jeep and sat next to me in the vehicle. She told us she wanted to invite us back with her to the northern settlement.

"How did you find out about us?" I asked.

"You radioed to us yesterday and you told us where you lived," she answered.

When LaFontaine stopped the jeep, Bergmann got out, full of vitality, and vivaciously sprinted towards De-

Kuyper and Van Den Heuvel. I noticed that there was something peculiar about her gait, almost as if she had a small degree of cerebral palsy. Both of them drew their assault rifles and prepared to open fire without asking any questions.

"Guys! Stop! She's safe. She's from Windhoek!" Milano said.

With that, they put their guns back. Everyone gathered about her in front of the dormitory, including Rachel, Marcia, and the two Zulu women. Strangely, she refused to take any handshakes.

"Why?" I asked.

"I am forbidden to," the woman answered under the morning sky. She claimed she was part of some sort of new religious order that believed that personal contact was to be avoided except between husband and wife. That puzzled me because I had never heard of such a thing. Maybe this was a particular modern-day creed that evolved out of Windhoek.

"You wanna take a showuh?" Milano asked.

"*Nein.* I am quite all right, but thank you anyways," Bergmann said.

We invited her to partake in activities with us. While we worked outside of the dormitory, she kept busy and tried to help us out, moving tools around. She still refused to wash the reddish resin off of her exposed skin, which I thought was kind of odd. I knew that the sun was hot, but did she have to be so attached to the stuff?

Once again, I noticed how Kari's locomotion was off as she helped move things about the campus. She seemed a little clumsy, as if drugs had impaired her motor skills. Despite the ineptitude, she moved with feminine delicacy, and almost had as much womanly charm as Angeline. Still, there was something peculiar about her I couldn't quite place. As we were all washing up and getting ready for the dinner, Marcia disclosed to me something about Kari that made her uncomfortable.

"Dat Kari a strange woman," Marcia remarked. "She don' wan' be near water."

Marcia went on to explain that the unusual woman had no problem lifting items up and taking them to the dining area. The resin would get on the dishes and the women would have to constantly wipe them off. Marcia and I wondered if she had some sort of infectious disease. She left the room and took her place at the table.

I noticed Rachel standing there at the basin, rinsing her hands under the faucet. She seemed to have more energy, but her face was still downcast. I wondered how well she was recuperating from her attempted suicide.

"How're you doin'? Okay?"

She looked at me with a half-hearted smile. "Everything's fine," she said. She dried her hands off, took her seat at the table, and said nothing more.

It was time for dinner and everyone gathered around the table. DeKuyper always insisted that we ate together. Even though he was no more than ten years my senior, he was like a father figure. He wanted to be in control, and he certainly did not want people to go separate ways. I suspected that DeKuyper wished to preside over us with his fist.

We all ate, famished from the day's labor, diving into all of the food around the long table. I was at one end of the table and DeKuyper was at the other. To my left was Roger, and next to him was Kari Bergmann. Milano flanked her and nonchalantly shoved food into his mouth.

"We would like to invite you to our home in Windhoek. Everyone's needs will be met in our new community," Kari Bergmann said as she forced the meal into her mouth.

DeKuyper told her about the history of the group and how they came about, and he explained how my group had met them. Kari listened to DeKuyper intently. She seemed to wait on every word that came out of the Afrikaner's mouth, particularly when he described to her the whole situation about Elizabeth, especially the fact that in her bloodstream coursed the key to the whole crisis. It must have been a genetic anomaly of some sort.

"We invite you back to the settlement. The girl will be fine. I promise," she said.

I noticed more peculiarities in her movement. Her speech was slurred and hampered, almost as if her neurons weren't firing right.

Milano had laid his revolver on the table beside Kari. She looked at it strangely; something was going on in her mind as she continued to talk. I looked at her hands and her arms and noticed that her clothes covered a lot of her flesh. Was she Amish or something like that? She studied Elizabeth with careful scrutiny, the resin still lightly caked on her face. Bergmann looked at the gun and then toward Elizabeth. This erratic behavior was real unusual. I saw her take her silverware and cut a piece of the meat that was on the plate before her. She put it in her mouth and chewed it, but she seemed to be disgusted with that chunk of flesh. Maybe she didn't like Cape buffalo.

Roger brought up the concept of God to the group, which was totally consistent with his personality.

"So what do you think about Jesus, Kari? Do you think he's God in the flesh?" he asked.

"What a time for this question," I thought!

"Possibly," she said. "He showed us what was in his heart. It serves as a reminder of what we should do for each other on a daily basis. Life is a constant sacrifice," she went on to say.

"We should be constantly looking towards the Deity. We are to honor him by sacrificing our time and we should dedicate our service to him. This is an ongoing, daily ritual," she stated.

Bergmann sounded remotely like a pagan, and I wondered what type of belief system she adhered to. She continued to eye Milano's gun as well as Elizabeth, who sat next to Amanda across the table. Her voice started to slur a bit as she ranted about giving your heart, soul, and mind to the Deity above.

Everyone was starting to appear a little uncomfortable, and Kari began fidgeting around. I looked at my own gun, before me on the table. Most of the men had a habit of laying their weapons next to the meal, out of a sense of security I suppose, and I always did the same.

"How did you find out about us?" DeKuyper asked.

"We picked up some of your radio broadcasts," she responded.

DeKuyper was strangely silent for a moment. He looked down at his meal of Cape buffalo and potatoes, appearing somewhat troubled.

"We haven't used the broadcasting facilities yet," DeKuyper declared, a puzzled expression upon his face.

Something was clearly wrong with the scenario. Bergmann sat next to Milano, continually eyeing the gun and watching Elizabeth. I noticed once again that her coordination was still off.

"Young lady, how could you pick up a signal if we haven't used the equipment?" DeKuyper inquired, leaning forward.

She just cut another piece of buffalo meat and put it in her mouth, chewing it quickly with a rash of impatience. Suddenly, she got up from her seat swiftly and hit Milano in the head with her open hand! Bergmann snatched the gun from the table and drew it on Elizabeth! Harry recovered from the shock of the sudden attack and grabbed her wrist. A struggle ensued and the gun went off! Another shot was squeezed off and I saw a person on the other side of the table go down! As quickly as I could, I grabbed my pistol. One of the Zulu women screamed as Milano and the woman struggled. She lunged for him and tried to bite his wrist, but Harry shoved her down upon the table, scattering the dishes and all of the silverware. That was enough to give me a clear shot. I pulled the trigger and I hit her in the forehead. Her body lay there motionless amongst the spilled food and cracked glass. Clearly, Bergmann was dead and gone.

We walked over to the corpse amongst the plates and silverware. Immediately, I felt its wrist and found that the skin was stone cold. I rubbed the red resin off of its outer dermis to find that the skin had a gray color to it. No wonder she did not wash up; the resin and the clothes hid the gray skin! She was a ghoul, but clearly she had a consciousness and a purpose to boot. Bergmann could move freely with grace, and I knew that something was afoot. Afterward, we took the body outside and had it burned, the black smoke rising into the blue sky to be dissipated by the eternal wind.

There was one casualty, though. Rachel Negron was hit in the chest fatally during the struggle and put Harry Milano to tears. DeKuyper had to fire a slug through the brain of her corpse, and did so without showing any sense of remorse whatsoever, doing it out of a sense of duty. Her corpse was dragged out of the well-lit dining hall, and we hastily dug a hole for her body near the edge of the campus. She tried to take herself out a long time ago, but the circumstances had changed, unfortunately removing her from the picture. We held a brief Catholic funeral as we laid the body into the shallow hole. I came to the disturbing realization that the number of us that left Rockland County was dwindling, and that we may be the last Americans left alive anywhere in this vast world.

After Rachel's burial, I had the urge to read the rest of Michelle Ramadan's notes. I thought God wanted me to get to the bottom of the whole conundrum, and it would take a degree of commitment. The ghouls would be back, and it was obvious that they knew we were here. If we ended up in Windhoek, they'd show up there in greater numbers until everyone was wiped out. I had to try and unravel this mystery before it was too late.

The next day, I walked out to the library on the campus. I went through the doors, found some lights, and turned them on. I stood in the middle of a large room with an arrangement of bookshelves on the peripheries and a number of tables in the center with cobwebs strewn about the place. I went over to one of the tables and took a seat, reading Ramadan's notes and digesting the information in slow increments. The whole concept of Ishtar and the significance of the Gilgamesh legend were still unclear. I scanned over her notes, combing over the information again and again, hoping to make sense out of this grim fable.

I read things I did not want to know or to face, and it unnerved me, making me want to go up to a mountaintop and waste away. These creatures had a collective consciousness, as if something was controlling them from afar, and that control became more manifest by the day. They were dim-witted at first, but they grew more sentient as time went on. Apparently, Ramadan could facilitate the process by brainwashing the ghouls. One of the creatures finally spoke, and it told her that its name was Ryan Smith. We "met" Ryan Smith some time ago. She then asked who had sent it. Eventually, after several attempts, the ghoul admitted that it did the will of Ishtar. Ramadan continued to question the ghoul, and she learned about the story of the ancient Sumerian hero, Gilgamesh.

She found out from the ghoul that the goddess Ishtar was a fallen star, very popular and adored by the gods around her. The Mesopotamians regarded the unstable goddess as the most beautiful creature in the entire universe, and they loved her greatly. She and the rest of the pantheon continued to keep humanity enthralled, getting them to carry out her fickle will in the region that was known as Iraq.

The Persians eventually overran the territory and Ishtar lost her hold upon the people. However, she stayed around, dwelling in the recesses of the subconscious while the Mesopotamians drifted towards the Zoroastrian gods. She was not as powerful as she once was, and her people did not pay the honor that she was so eager for. Then came the God of the Romans followed by the god of the Arabian Peninsula, Allah, who finally took root and destroyed the Iraqi pantheons, nearly erasing Christianity from the Middle Eastern lands.

The gods no longer had a following, and the forces of the universe banished them to the planet Venus, where they spent eternity wandering over the surface of the hot, dry planet. They waited, biding their time beneath the cloud cover for an age where both Islam and Christianity would be discredited and paganism could be exalted.

Ishtar came back, not as a beautiful goddess that she was, but as a created infection that made the dead rise up and eat the living, just as outlined in the legend of Gilgamesh. She destroyed humanity, reviling it out of anger, enraged after being banished for well over a millennium.

Ramadan continued to subject the ghouls to brainwashing techniques, until she conditioned a handful to obey her sole command. They, in turn, could go out and condition others, creating an army of dead servants. Ishtar, Ramadan believed, could also guide them in a vague sort of manner. She could make them aware of their surroundings and stimulate their brains to follow orders. They were her eyes and her ears. It was suggested that, once she returned to earth, she would be able to control their minds and bodies directly, making them do her bidding. Along with that, she could restore the decayed flesh and regenerate the bodies, explaining the Bergmann incident along with the armed African we encountered the day before. This was terrifying, for what I read indicated that a whole army of those undead things could assemble and annihilate fragile humanity. It looked as if we were going to be irrevocably wiped out, the human race swallowed up by the dark earth, never to return.

I did not know what to do with the information in front of me. Here I was, an evangelical Christian, questioning my own faith. We believed that, once people are deceased, they immediately go into some sort of waiting period, where God judges their souls and sends them to either eternal life or eternal contempt. I never, for one minute, believed that Ishtar could let people in and out of heaven or hell, but it was clear that she could somehow revive the dead and restore their consciousnesses. Chances are, she was here, or soon would be, and would wreak the ultimate havoc. What was I going to do about it?

I ran out of the library and back to the dormitory and into the vestibule that led me upstairs. I knocked on Roger's door frantically, and he let me in, I noticed he was a little aggravated and his hair was rumpled, apparently jolted out of sleep. I worked up the nerve to tell him about my findings.

"You've gotta be kidding me. This is a real serious problem. Way too serious," he said.

Roger and I prayed for about two hours on the cold industrial tiles on the floor of the dormitory room, seeking the perfect will of God. Surely humanity would fall unless God did something. Through the long moments in prayer, we got the sense that we were being preserved for a purpose that would soon arrive and present itself to us. God had raised me up for such a time as this. He wanted someone who would be able to deal with the problem at hand, and I was that person whether I liked it or not.

"You will know what to do when the time comes," a voice in my mind told me. Roger admitted that he heard the same thing in his mind too. I began to feel extremely confident that God had not abandoned the human race, or me, altogether. Intuitively, I knew that there was order to the universe, one that would manifest itself with a vengeance.

Chapter Thirty-Six: Little Afrika

That night, as I stared into the sky, a strange sensation came over me. It was almost as if I was standing at the edge of a precipice, at the end of the world. Humanity was poised at the brink of extinction, ready to fall in. Windhoek was probably the last outpost left. It looked as if the forces of evil were closing in and the forces of order and harmony were nowhere to be seen. When the space probe came back, a star fell from the sky. Ishtar had fallen from God's grace thousands of years ago, but she was just now enacting her revenge. I felt like breaking the news to Capasso but decided against it. He was not a man you could count on for empathy.

I went to Angeline, who was in her own private room at the time, sitting at her desk. She ended up with her knees to the floor, in tears.

"I always wanted to believe that there was a reason for this whole thing, and now I'm starting to understand. Daddy was right the whole time." This revelation made it obvious to her that there was only one way out.

"I need a change. I really need a change," she said.

"Maybe you need to know Jesus," I said.

"Maybe I do."

We prayed, and she came to know Jesus Christ right then and there, in a college dorm room. She did so eagerly on the cold vinyl tiles, and it was clear that we had to get out of this place. I would have to talk to DeKuyper and try to persuade him to move from his stubborn position and get out of this place.

I found DeKuyper, locked away in his own room. He opened the door and said, "What do you want, Goering?" I could see that he had converted his quarters into his own private arsenal, with two AK-47s, a shotgun, two Colt .45s, and three hand grenades, all displayed on the desk. He had me step in, and as I did I felt a sense of domination in the room that overwhelmed me to the point that I wanted to leave. I had a mission though and could not neglect it. I had to try to get him to change his mind about this place, or it would be suicide.

He stood there and cleaned the guns, looking down at me periodically, as if my presence scarcely mattered to him. There were old black and white pictures on the desk next to the guns. They were photographs of men wearing a style of hat that folded the brim to one side, the kind worn by Teddy Roosevelt and the Rough Riders. The men also sported long full beards. These were the heroes of the Boer War of 1899-1902, and I remembered that DeKuyper had said that his great grandfather had fought in it. I proceeded to ask him why that conflict was so special to him, in order to find out why he was so stubborn and pig-headed. He towered over me with a gleam of arrogance in his eyes, his arms folded over on his chest.

"The Boer republics eventually had to surrender and submit to British rule, but the Afrikaners came back when Malan had won," he began to tell me. He further explained that the Afrikaner race had dominated South Africa until the western-imposed sanctions brought them down, eventually turning the reigns of the government over to Mandela and his people.

DeKuyper was a man to be pitied, I realized. He was one of the last Afrikaners alive. If his group kept itself apart from the one in Windhoek, the two Afrikaners, DeKuyper and LaFontaine, would be on top, ruling over the Coloured man and the two Zulu women. If he stays here, he will at least go to his grave knowing that he took Afikaner pride with him. This whole struggle, I began to realize, was about human dignity, the passing out of existence with or without proper respect.

"All of Europe had its chance to dominate the globe, but it fell apart after the rise and fall of the Third Reich," he went on to say. "The French had their influence, the Russians reigned supreme, the British ruled over hundreds of millions, and even the Dutch had a significant trading empire. Everything has now crumbled into *stof* (dust). Everyone had his place in the sun. We had our place. We want it again. We will not be absorbed. The Afrikaner nation will flourish, even if we have to impregnate the two Zulu women to restore it," he said.

I thought that was preposterous, since the two Afrikaners, the Coloured, the two Zulu women, along with Elizabeth Brady hardly constituted a gene pool. He tenaciously clung to such a small hope despite the fact that his dream of the Afrikaner race rising phoenix-like from the ashes was unlikely. His best bet would be to go to Windhoek and live there.

"We should go to Windhoek, Andries. At least that way we would have a fighting chance," I told him.

"No! How many times do I have to tell you! I said 'no' and that is final! This is our place and these are my people!" the big man said.

"Are there Afrikaners there?" I asked him.

"Ya," he replied.

"What you're doing is stupid! It's suicidal!" I told him practically in a rage. "Since there are Afrikaners in Windhoek, we can join them and try to weather this whole thing out. Alright?"

He reached over and picked up one of the .45s from the table, aiming it at me. Time stopped as I began to hyperventilate.

"Get out," he said with malice. "Don't bother me again, or I will not hesitate to use this."

I rushed out of the room. It was obvious that he wasn't about to change, dooming himself for destruction. We would have to find a way to get to Windhoek ourselves and leave this man and those who followed him behind to crumble into dust.

That night, I lay in bed under the blankets to warm myself in the cool African night. I fell into the eternal abyss of sleep and the same dream came again. It was the strange one in that bleak gray landscape that I had so many times before. I looked about this desert and noticed clusters of palm trees around several oases. The dead landscape of ignorance was coming alive with understanding. The terrain around me was a despondent gray, but I looked up at the sun and it gave me hope. The jeep came by and stopped. I boarded it as the talons broke through the soil. The dead were rising as they had so many times before.

On the distant horizon was that galloping figure, the epitome of ancient Babylon. The driverless jeep picked up the speed and gained on the figure with the long braids and beard. The dead bodies worked themselves free from the dirt and sand that confined them and stumbled along, raking the air in my direction, homing in on my warm flesh.

At the very edge of that cliff, the Sumerian with the sword dismounted. He looked out onto that decrepit city, full of terraced, flat-roofed buildings that rose from the ancient sands of time. The jeep came to a halt at the top of the hill. I got out and stood near the man, looking out upon the vista with him. Then the dream changed. There was a ripple in the entire landscape, a fluctuation manifesting in my vision that undulated in everything eerie and unearthly. An eternity went by as I beheld the ancient Iraqi city, feeling as if something was invading my subconscious, slicing into it like a knife and holding all of my thoughts captive.

In the distance, I saw a lovely, glittering female figure emerge from one of the ancient buildings, striding across the sands and reaching the foot of the cliff. Then, with one hand in front of the other, she delicately ascended the precipice with the utmost grace and skill. When she reached the top of the cliff, the big Sumerian assisted her with his hand. I looked behind me and saw the ghoulish dead stagger toward us up the grade. I wanted to flee. I ran back and boarded the jeep, jumping behind the wheel, but the jeep would not budge. I turned my head behind me to witness the alluring woman's arrival.

"Babylon is rising, Andrew Frank Goering. You can be part of it, or die," she said, standing in all of her gorgeous splendor. It was she, that lovely woman who was the harbinger of pestilence and annihilation. It was the Queen of Heaven, and I approached her to find out what she wanted.

"What are you talking about?" I asked.

"The old gods are returning to earth," Ishtar said, her long tresses flowing in the strange breeze of this bleak place. She was beautiful, one of the most attractive creatures I had ever seen, but she reeked of destruction and death.

"They sent me here because they want to take the world for themselves and rule it. They will take humanity and transform it. We want to create a new race, one more perfect than the former. The old gods would rule this new species. The old race is imperfect; it is feeble, subject to diseases and a short lifespan. I will make one that is new, more intelligent, durable, and it will live much longer," Ishtar decreed.

"I have returned to the earth, and I am creating an army of men without souls. They will march across the length and breadth of this world and will surround the last significant stronghold of the living and subjugate it."

"What does this all have to do with me?" I asked.

She momentarily broke from her soliloquy and smirked, chilling me.

"I need breeding stock. You have been a very resourceful man. You have an enormous independent will to survive and I can use you," she said.

"For what?"

"The gods can have posterity. We have reproductive facilities. Our genetic information is compatible with yours, and you can impregnate me. I will give birth to all of your wonderful children. Your line will extend forever, and it will be perfectly divine. I am here Andy, for you," she said with a smile that was so inviting. Her eyes were hypnotic, captivating, and her figure was so voluptuous. I wanted so badly to hold her.

"Say 'yes' and I will come to you and you will be spared all of this," she said.

It sounded good to me. I would have sex with this female before me, and she would give birth to this strange offspring. Wasn't Gilgamesh part god, as well? My line would be like his. There was a problem with this scenario, and I thought about it as I stood on the hillside. The legend articulated the truth behind these divine creatures. Ishtar never failed to kill all the men that she had intercourse with. Gilgamesh, in the story, realized this and refused to have anything to do with her. She grew extremely agitated, and it revealed the true nature of her character. If she allowed me to impregnate her, she would give birth to this offspring and then kill me and all the other humans that would help re-populate the world with this demonic race. We would just end up dead when all was said and done. "To hell with your proposition," I said. She was taken aback by that and grew vindictive.

I turned behind me to notice the crowd of stiffly tottering ghouls was closing in. I wanted to flee in the jeep but knew it was not going to move. I had an impulse prompting me to look in back of the jeep, which was covered with a conspicuous brown tarp. The ghouls hobbled towards me up the grade. The Sumerian and the goddess held their heads back and laughed, as I found myself caught between a rock and a hard place.

I pulled the tarp off the back of the jeep and unveiled a large machine gun with hundreds, possibly thousands, of rounds of ammunition on a band that fed into the weapon. A tripod stand for the gun was also located in the back of the jeep and I mounted the gun. It was secure. Looking behind me, I noticed that the Sumerian king and the goddess had stopped laughing. It wasn't funny anymore.

Sitting in back of the jeep, I put my hands around the trigger of the huge and potent weapon. It made me feel strong, as if I had power, as if I had control of my own destiny. I squeezed it and opened fire on the ghouls, mowing them down by the scores and cutting them to pieces! They fell in waves as I exterminated that which wanted to exterminate me. The bodies toppled like monuments to destruction as I annihilated them all, a sadistic glee coming over me. As the dust settled, there was nothing but bodies littered on the sand before me, practically piled on top of one another.

I lifted the machine gun off the tripod and turned around to face the two entities behind me. The Sumerian drew his curved sword from his scabbard and charged me, roaring at the top of his lungs! I opened fire upon him and riddled his body with the heavy lead shells. He fell and dropped his sword to the ground, a commemoration to the destruction. Apparently, Ishtar had control of the entities here in the domain of the subconscious. The entity was now dead and only Ishtar remained. She stood before me, unable to do anything about the fact that I had the gun. I pointed the deadly instrument at her, ready to consume her with its power and violence.

"No!" she said. "I can give you anything! Gold, riches, jewels, women, anything! Just put it down!"

She would kill me if I let her go, and I knew it. She would have me destroyed like she did to so many others. She was a capricious liar from the very beginning, and that was all she would ever be.

"No. You deserve everything that's comin' to you," I said. "You've caused the human race enough problems and heartaches, and I'm getting sick and tired of it! It's payback time, lady!"

I let the bullets fly. She staggered backwards as the rounds pierced her flesh. Blood oozed out of the wounds I inflicted, and she fell down upon her back on the sandy surface. She laid there, arms and legs spread-eagled, lifeless and unmoving. Her eyes, however, remained open, staring into the emptiness of the gray sky above. I walked up and stood over the corpse, scrutinizing my own handiwork. I had to make sure she was deceased.

I pointed the barrel of the gun to her face. All of a sudden, she abruptly sat straight up, getting right back up on her feet, unexpectedly. Obviously, ordinary conventional weapons could not destroy her in this strange place. The pupils in her eyes dilated out of sheer and naked rage. Ishtar faced me with an intense hatred that could burn a hole right through my physical being. She stood, dress stained with blood, and bellowed in a voice that I could not say was human.

"I WILL KILL YOU! AND I WILL SPIT ON YOUR NAMELESS GRAVE!"

She pointed her finger to me and the winds on that grade grew to the intensity of a tempest, and I knew that I was in a heap of trouble. My dream ended and I woke up, the phantasm revealing the true intentions of my heart.

Chapter Thirty-Seven: The Little Excursion

As I went about my morning ranting, I began to wonder about the current circumstances. Ishtar was coming with her legions of the undead, and it was only a matter of time before they found us. She would wipe us out and destroy the settlement in Windhoek. On top of that, any other remaining outposts would be eliminated and the earth would be hers. Perhaps, we should grab the girl and leave DeKuyper, La-Fontaine and Van Den Heuvel far behind, but DeKuyper might very well kill us if we attempted to do so.

Later on, I began to talk to Roger, Capasso, and Milano about the whole subject, outside of the dormitory and in front of the vehicles.

"It might be a good idea to take Elizabeth right out from under DeKuyper's nose and see if we can talk to the Germans in Windhoek," I said to the other three.

"Yeah, sounds good to me. Maybe we should get outta this hellhole," Capasso said.

We decided to leave for the length of the day. The four of us packed up one of the trucks with provisions without DeKuyper knowing. Toward the middle of the morning, we all went out in the vehicle to hunt for wild springbok. This would be a good time to make plans freely out on the remote savannah, away from DeKuyper's prying eyes.

As the sun rose in the sky, Capasso stopped the truck and killed the engine.

"We should go out there," I said to Capasso and Milano.

"It'll take about four hours," Capasso said, with no expression on his face.

I wondered if we had much of a choice.

"Yeah, I think it's a good idea, too. We have to do somethin'," Roger said.

"Yeah, Rog. I agree," Capasso concurred.

"Why not?" said Harry Milano, in a nonchalant fashion.

We decided to do it the next day and went back towards the campus.

That night, I went to sleep and had a very simple dream, but one of great significance. In my vision, I was sitting on the couch in my living room back in Southold, in another place, another time. I was watching TV when I heard a light tapping at the door downstairs. I left my seat and descended the discordant stairs to answer it. I opened the door and found that it was a man wearing ancient Middle Eastern robes who possessed short wiry hair and a beard. I had seen him in a dream before.

The man walked past me and up the flight of stairs. I walked back up the whining steps and found him in the living room relaxing in one of the chairs. I, of course, followed him. He got up from the chair and proceeded to pace and use gestures as he spoke. The man kept on referring to the concept of the essence of timing, over and over again, but it was difficult to comprehend exactly what he was referring to. He paused for several moments, and then spoke slowly with great warmth and utmost clarity: "Trust in the Lord with all your heart and don't lean on your own understanding. I have allowed this to happen so that mankind can start over." I was to remember this. I then woke up.

After packing the truck with provisions and fuel, we all decided to leave the compound early, about 7:00 a.m. For some reason, DeKuyper was not out of bed yet, maybe depressed over the loss of Afrikaner pride and glory. The truck passed through the gates and rumbled into the Namibian grasslands after Roger locked up the compound behind us. In the distance, we could see the fan-shaped trees along with the forests of teak and acacia wood, which at times would be plentiful, giving me the sense that the landscape was not completely dead and sterile.

Capasso drove the truck on. We knew we were going to the north, and if we continued on in that direction, we would run into Windhoek. My group encountered no one on the road at all. There was no ghoulish activity or human activity. Namibia was a dead expanse of land, or so it seemed, going nowhere, and we drove deeper into the nothingness.

We entered the highlands, the hills craggy and hard. We saw many rock badgers waddling around, foraging for food. The sun was up in the sky, distant and uncaring, and it looked as if it might be about noon. Capasso saw something in the distant highlands. It was the glint of something metal, reflecting light off the sun. He blocked the glare with one of his hands.

We continued on, not suspecting anything. Without warning, a whistling sound interrupted the dead terrain, destroying the silence as something heavy sailed through the air. BOOOOOOM! An explosion was seen and heard about twenty feet away! It was an artillery shell! We heard another bomb whizz through the air once again! BOOOOOOM! It went off!

"We have to take covuh! They're shellin' us!" Capasso said. He quickly pulled the truck to the side and stopped it. Another shell landed about thirty feet away, blowing the dirt and sand high into the sky! We all ran over to a nearby hill. Capasso found a broken twig on the ground and then tore some fabric from the white shirt that he was wearing. He tied the rag to the stick and created the benign flag of surrender. He went to the edge of the hill and waved the little banner into the air for several long minutes. Soon a green helicopter appeared overhead, hovering above us about thirty feet. The pilot and his assistant just stared down at us for a few minutes, trying to determine if we were a threat or not. They landed the chopper nearby, and the rotor blades swept away the loose dirt and rock.

Four men armed with automatic rifles got out of the helicopter, all dressed in brown uniforms, brown-billed caps, and black boots. They approached us. One of them wore dark goggles, and we could not see what was in his eyes.

"You speak English, Deutsch, or Afrikaans?" the man asked.

"We speak English," said Capasso. "We don't know nothing about this Africans stuff."

"We need to see the man in charge," I said.

Capasso's head snapped towards me in anger. He did not like me asserting myself and taking control. He could have cracked glass with that intense glare of his.

"The howitzer boys in the hills saw you and they had to defend the perimeter. They were just doing their job. My apologies," the man said. The rest of the guys looked at him without expression.

"By the way, *mein Name ist Matthias Burghoff,*" he said. "Follow us."

Capasso and the rest of us piled back into the truck, and the helicopter lifted off and led the way overhead to Windhoek. After about twenty minutes, a fortress appeared at the end of a dry plain that had some vegetation sprouting on it. It was a compound, entirely surrounded by walls, with towers placed on each corner and a thick gaggle of teak and acacia flanking both sides of the fortress. In the back of the compound was a long, distant acclivity that stretched on for some distance, possibly a mile, topped by a castle-like structure that presided over everything below.

In the foreground was a wire-mesh fence with two armed guards standing at its gate. The helicopter hovered overhead for a few moments, and the sentries looked up at it. It appeared as if Burghoff was communicating using facial expressions. The attendants obediently and mechanically pulled back both sides of the entrance, allowing our vehicle to pass unobstructed.

There was a crowd of men gathered on the road that led to the compound. As the truck got closer, I could tell that they were of many races and varieties, some being black, a few Oriental, but the majority was white. They all wore tattered and dirty clothing, and most of them had full beards. I laughed to myself, "Guess razors were in short supply."

We were led up to the gates of the large compound, the walls about ten feet high and made of solid concrete, firmly set in the ground. There was a metal gate up ahead with a design on it of some sort. I wasn't sure how to describe it, but it resembled a lightning bolt or a Hebrew letter, kind of like a "Z" lying on its side, and I wondered what its significance was. The metal gate slid back as I heard the hum of machinery, allowing the truck to go in.

We found ourselves in the middle of a huge enclosure that sheltered this rag-tag multitude. On the right were garages that must have housed various types of equipment. In the background were large barrack-like structures, two and three stories high. Other edifices were here as well, particularly a large round structure in the center surrounded by white domes that resembled a nuclear facility, some distance away.

In the foreground were hastily constructed shacks made of plywood and particleboard that numbered in the hundreds. Children, many blond-haired and blue-eyed yet slovenly looking and dirty, ran through the streets practically dressed in rags.

There were also members of the Himba, Herero, and Ovambo people mixing with the whites in conversation. The African tribal children played with the white German children seemingly without the burden of racial distinctions. I knew there were some Afrikaners here as well, along with a sprinkling of East Indians and Chinese. This was humanity's last stand. Everyone had to band together if they wanted to survive, even if they at one time were bitter enemies.

We came to a flat-roofed, two-story brick building. It was extremely large and could have housed a number of personnel. There were four fully armed white men wearing torn and disheveled clothing standing guard in front of the entrance of this complex. They approached our vehicle expressionless and forced us all to get out. They led us into the building with little conversation and we found ourselves in a reception room.

"*Legen Sie sofort Ihrer Waffen nieder!* Lay your arms down, now!" one of the men said. We complied without hesitating. One man, surprisingly clean-shaven, and wearing a brown hat, brown field jacket, and black boots who reminded me of a desert Nazi led the way.

"You are going to see our *fuhrer* and his name is Franz Reichard Krebs. He is the man for all seasons who will light the way for the people," the clean-shaven man said in a guttural accent.

This man, Krebs, must have been the director of what may be humanity's last viable outpost. The guards herded us into a freight elevator made up of wire-mesh walls, and we descended two levels within it. This place was like a dark bunker in a war-torn city, and I had no idea how many sublevels were in the structure.

After we got off the elevator, we were led through a series of hallways. There, the commandant and tattered guards led us through a maze of dark passageways, choked with boxes and paraphernalia. At the end of a gray hallway was an open door leading to a lighted room. In that chamber, we could see the silhouette of a man sitting behind a desk, a light dangling from a cord overhead. His silhouette did something to my subconscious mind. I got the sense that the figure emanated both hopelessness and promise at the same time.

Chapter Thirty-Eight: Mr. Germany

The Germans escorted us into the somber office as the storm clouds gathered within, the winds of Wilhelm raging. We stood in front of a man who sat in a gray military uniform under the glow of the hanging lamp. He was a tall, muscular individual with short gray hair and a closely cropped mustache, his age about 50. He exuded power and wore a black Prussian cross on his jacket. It was as if he stood for a new order of things, a harbinger of a world where man would overcome all challenges and emerge victorious as the supreme conqueror of the cosmic maelstrom. This was Franz Reichard Krebs. He smiled calmly and motioned with his hand for all of us to sit in the brown folding chairs that faced the desk. Behind him, on the wall, hung an ovular woodcarving that displayed that same strange sideways "Z" that I had seen on the gates. The clean-shaven guard stayed within, while the others left the overcast chamber. This commandant was armed with a pistol and probably served as Krebs' bodyguard.

Krebs sat before us grinning, and for some reason, I did not like the man. I sensed he was calm and in control and did not appreciate arguments or disputes. He gave the impression that he knew what he was doing, and I bet that he could probably defend himself well if he got into trouble. The commandant introduced us to the imposing *Herr Krebs*.

"Welcome to New Valhalla," Krebs said smoothly, elbows on the top of the table, holding his palms together. He exhibited no fear and I did not even think of challenging him at this point.

"Where are you from?" Krebs asked in a slow, calculated manner.

"Keetmanshoop," Capasso answered, his voice wavering a bit.

"How may I help you?" he asked coldly, palms still together, ruthless and almost sinister. Not one of us, including Capasso, dared utter a sound. There was no gun around him, or weapon of any sort, only an iron presence of submission and destruction.

Finally, someone roused the courage to speak.

"We have a girl," Capasso said. "She was bitten by one of those things. She suhvived. She might have a cure for all of this. Maybe we can cut a deal."

"Deal? What type of deal are you referring to?" Krebs asked with a hint of anger. His voice was so frigid, like an ice floe from the cold Norwegian mountains.

"Maybe I can help run this place here," Capasso said.

"*Nein.* You are my guests here, and I don't want you to feel unwelcome. I am proud of my settlement and would like to keep it in my own hands. Let me show you what I have built, so you can appreciate what I've done," Krebs answered with a calm demeanor. There was no indication that he was threatened, or even challenged, by Bob Capasso's mouth.

Krebs continued to speak, presenting the story of the expansive complex of New Valhalla. "This is named after the place in Norse legend where Teutonic warriors go when they die," he explained. "Do you know what this is behind me?" Krebs said as he pointed to the sideways "Z" on the back wall. No one knew.

"It is the rune *Sugil.* It represented the sun in ancient Norse thought. For me, it stands for the birth of a new age, where I will reshape humanity into something better than it was ever before," Krebs declared.

"There are about 10,000 German Namibians living in this compound constructed around an energy-research facility here," he said. "They are one of the most resourceful groups of people that has ever existed."

Krebs went on to explain that, under his direction, he being an ex-police chief from Luderitz, the South-Westers had erected a fence around the entire area for about a mile, killing every ghoul inside. The German Namibians later moved in and constructed dwellings within the complex. Germans weren't the only group here, though. Herero,

Himba, Ovambo, Basters, and Afrikaners all lived in the fortress, their numbers totaling over 2,000. They were needed here to give the gene pool diversification. Altogether, there were about 12,000 people in Krebs' neo-nation.

Krebs went on, referring to the sterile arrangement of buildings on the dry surface above.

"The compound doubles as an armed fortress. Machine guns are mounted all around the redoubt on concrete walls, and anti-aircraft batteries can be set up in minutes. In the center of the compound are energy research facilities, including a nuclear reactor."

Krebs admitted that he was trying to find a way to end this horrible disease, hoping to destroy the radiation that plagued the planet and made dead corpses rise.

"I am the man who organized this assortment of humanity and turned them into a force that would survive at all costs," Krebs said.

"I must tell about my birth and the great man that I have become. You must know about Franz Reichard Krebs. This is a story in the making, and I will have victory." His boastful attitude was making me sick.

He offered us his history in the despondent chamber with the rune. Krebs was very proud of his accomplishments and felt that everything that he did was part of the cosmic scheme of things, and perhaps that was true. He told us about what had happened here in Namibia sometime in the seemingly very distant past.

"Two years ago, before the crisis came, there was a Lutheran pastor about who believed God had told him that a great disease was coming. Almost all of humanity would be wiped out from this pestilence and it would usher in the end of the world. He had a habit of speaking the message to mostly German-speaking congregations, and for some reason, they seemed to be the only ones who listened. Many blacks rejected the message; they were nationalists who rejected many things that came from the white man and their Christian God. The Germans in Namibia, the South-Westers, soon developed a national consciousness and saw themselves as the guardians of the Deutsch culture. I did not believe in God then, nor do I now, but I identified with them," Krebs continued.

"Then, of course, the space probe was destroyed, and that radiation made the dead rise. Windhoek, Luderitz, and Grootfontein were overwhelmed by the oncoming chaos.

Government troops were deployed in these areas, leaving the Namibian army heavily overtaxed. The complex was lightly guarded, and I, an ex-police chief, led two hundred-and-fifty South-Westers to seize this place. The government, already spread too thin, actually allowed us to walk in and occupy it. Once concrete ramparts were built up around it, I found the facility large enough to house over 10,000," Krebs continued. In essence, he stole the place from the Namibian government. The guy had a lot to say; his explanation became quite involved.

It was here where they would live and survive, divorcing all of Africa, both white and black, in order to become Germans once again. If the Herero, the Ovambos, the Basters, and the Afrikaners wanted to perpetuate themselves, they would have to join the group, give up their culture, and accept the German tongue and all of its mannerisms, culture, and implications, listening to Wagner and Beethoven.

Capasso started to look agitated, as if his desires were not realized. He tapped his fingers on his knee and fidgeted a bit. Something was wrong with Capasso. Appearing increasingly discontented, he suddenly interrupted Krebs with no tact or consideration.

"We have the girl. She can help you stop this whole thing!" Capasso said.

"I'm not finished yet! Don't interrupt me when I'm talking!" Krebs stated, continuing with his soliloquy. I gathered he was a man who thought highly of himself and would not allow anyone to stop him. Krebs loved German culture and his settlement. He was determined to preserve both at all costs.

Krebs spoke endlessly, seemingly charmed by his own elegance as he explained his story, his love, and his power. The German race would survive, although watered down a bit by the black and the Afrikaner presence. Still, the culture would live on; the German people would inherit the earth. It would be the Fourth Reich, the rule of rules, and under Krebs as the leader of leaders, the pinnacle of human achievement. It was the Order of the Sacred Rune.

"Are you the only ones left?" I asked.

"*Nein.* There are others," he answered.

"Some Orthodox Jews have holed themselves up in the highlands around Masada in Israel. They number about 4,000," Krebs said. Immediately, visions of Passover at Barrett's Corners came to mind.

"There are also about 1,000 Maori that left New Zealand and settled upon an island near Fiji. Altogether there is roughly 17,000," the dictator stated grimly.

"That's it?" I asked, not accepting the figures.

"Yes, that's it," Krebs shot back.

The notion overwhelmed me, "There've gotta be others."

"I don't think so," Krebs answered coldly.

My heart sank to the dark ground.

As Krebs paused in his narration, everyone became deathly still. The repercussions of what he said were too much for the four of us to bear. The numbers of humanity had grown for centuries, seemingly without end. The population of Europe exploded in the 1800s, and the governments fostered imperialistic tendencies with a desire for living space. After World War II, with the availability of immunizations, the number of people in the Third World began to multiply until national borders burst at the seams. The world's population had recently exceeded six billion. Then the plague came, corrupting men and turning them into engines of hate and destruction, severely reducing the world's numbers. The disease killed more than the Black Death of the 1300s ever did!

As Krebs boasted about German cultural achievements, I calculated in my head the actual ratio of humans to ghouls in the world. We were outnumbered by approximately 350,000 to one, and I realized the odds of surviving this whole ordeal were extremely small! If all of those creatures in sub-Saharan Africa decided to organize and equip themselves with firearms, we were finished. An army of tens of millions could be found on the doorstep of this place and we would all be gone, adios muchachos! Did Krebs realize this?

Krebs wasn't actually a madman, but he was not too far removed either. He was a man who emerged from the prevalent chaos to establish a new order. He was a man confident in his own abilities who believed that humanity's salvation was within its own resourcefulness. Krebs was proud of his own ethnicity, personal origins, and accomplishments, and for good reason. He forged this settlement from scratch that may hopefully repopulate a dying world some day. He was a man for all seasons that seemed to have all of the answers. It was as if he alone would be the savior of mankind.

"I would like to take you on a little tour, to show you what I have built," Krebs said as he rose from his desk.

He led us from the despondent office, smoothly through the dank hallways and back to the freight elevator, the brown-garbed commandant in tow. It was obvious that Krebs had some things to disclose. We boarded the elevator, and it ascended back into the heavens, emerging in the main room. Ragtag guards sat lazily, reclining in chairs and smoking cigarettes profusely. They immediately rose to attention as Krebs walked by. I imagined they did so out of fear, apprehensive of his wrath, rather than out of respect.

We walked through the door and stepped out to a large open area bathed in sunlight. As Krebs strode through the camp, all the children stopped playing in the large yard, their attention focused upon the man. Someone yelled, "*Achtung!*" and the rest of the people ceased talking and moving. They stared at the *fuhrer* and quickly got out of their master's way.

Krebs and the commandant led us around the building we emerged from and to the shiny domed buildings in back, around the circular structure. He explained the whole arrangement of edifices, and pointed to it while readying himself to make another speech.

"Those are our nuclear facilities. In there we have a cyclotron to create radioactive particles that may counteract the radiation in the air. We are also making nuclear weapons. This facility was set up by South Africans to allow the white population to rule from a position of power. When South-West Africa gained its independence, the project was discontinued, but there were nuclear fuel rods, uranium, and other elements stored nearby, which are being used now."

He also explained that there were laboratories for chemical and biological research in this very compound. "Eventually, we will have to discuss the girl. She would be a great boon to the research community here," he said.

Dazed and uncertain as to what to do with this information, I conversed with the Almighty for direction. I received the impression that I should pick the mind of Franz Reichard Krebs. There was something more to him than meets the eye and I had to find out what it was.

"Most of the German Namibians used to consider themselves Africans. You consider yourself a German. Why, Krebs?" I asked, as we stood outside the nuclear facilities.

"It all began with my grandfather," he said with a gleam of confidence in his eye. "My grandfather was a significant man. He dedicated himself to the survival of the Kaiser's Empire," Krebs said.

"South-West Africa was an area taken by the Germans in 1884, and later opened up to colonization. However, the Germans encroached upon the lands of the native Herero people, who needed the territory for their buffalo herds. In 1904, tensions erupted between the two groups and Kaiser Wilhelm II, Emperor of Germany, called for volunteers to put down the Herero revolt. The Germans brought in both their artillery and their machine guns, and it nearly spelled out the annihilation of the Hereros."

"I remember that from my college days," I said.

"Let me finish," Krebs said disrespectfully. I wanted to hit him.

"A German officer, Udo Matthias Krebs, carried out the destruction of the Herero rebels with glee. A young man from Danzig, Germany, he was eager to see the newly created German Reich thrive. He did so in 1904, for the glory of the Kaiser. In the years before World War I, Germany got its act together; it was a united nation and strong. Germany would begin to take the high seas, supplant the British navy, and dominate the world's commerce. Many young men landed in Luderitz and zealously fought against the forces of Samuel Maherero, subsequently defeating him," Krebs continued. None of us dared utter a sound or interrupt him.

"Udo Matthias Krebs brought his wife and four children along to the fledgling colony in order to establish roots. In a few years, the German army lost South-West Africa to the invading South African forces. Krebs lost his life trying to defend German honor on the plains of what later was renamed Namibia. His sacrifice has been duly noted."

Krebs, long-winded, continued. "Udo Krebs' eldest son, Axel Dieter Krebs, was twelve years old when his father was killed in World War I, and he remembered the loss well. He hated the English who had led the South Africans to destroy him, and he adopted a sense of German nationalism. Despite his objections against British Rule, Axel Krebs remained in the colony even while it was under South African control. He fell into the lucrative diamond trade that burgeoned after the war, and he stayed there, employed as a manager for one of the mining companies. He took a wife, Monika Bremer, a native South-Wester, and had three children." Krebs orated tirelessly.

Krebs told us that Axel Krebs publicly stayed loyal to the British during World War II, but secretly he admired Hitler and the Nazi party's ardent nationalism. Krebs wanted Germany to rise from the ashes of the Great War. His wife, Monika Bremer Krebs, died of colon cancer in 1946 and left him a widower. At that point, Axel Krebs went through a change. He had some sort of conversion experience and became an Evangelical Protestant. He got involved in missionary pursuits and went off to Germany, the country he loved, to "preach the gospel," neglecting the family he had left behind in Africa.

At the age of forty-seven, Axel Krebs took another wife, fifteen years his junior, named Ingrid Schwarzkopf, from Berlin, a German nationalist. She, like her husband, adored Germany for its many cultural achievements. He had two children by her, Adolf and then Franz. Franz was taught to consider himself an ethnic German, although he lived on African soil. He knew that his father loved Germany as well, although he was often away, involved in missionary pursuits in the Fatherland.

A change took place in Franz during his adolescent years. He loved Germany and German civilization, as his mother had always taught him to. However, Franz became angry with his father for abandoning him "to serve God" (as his mother had put it). He grew to hate God for taking his father away from him. His hatred consumed him, and he hated the Deity so much that he rationalized that he didn't exist, since God could not be measured. He loved Germany, though, it could be seen, felt, and experienced. To Krebs, God was some entity that must have faded away into nothingness. In time, he came to resent both his genitor and his God. German culture became Franz's God. He wanted German society to supplant everything and rule it all. His mother, who died young in 1969, taught him to always respect the nation that his family came from. Franz wanted to make the German people great once again and lived to see that dream come to pass. He disrespected his father, yet he carried out his desires and ambitions directly.

As the crisis exploded two years ago, Krebs, a law enforcement official, made arrangements with several Lutheran ministers to seize control of this part of Windhoek, so he could ensure the survival of the German race. He would do so at any cost. One of the pastors he worked with felt that he acted too tyrannical, and the man was shot for insubordination by Krebs' band. Another woman in the compound was a feminist and wanted all of his power. She threatened the little colony with an uprising of supporters. She was shot along with a handful of her people. A few others suspected of undermining Krebs' authority were also killed, all in the unintentional imitation of Nazi purges. Scores were dragged from their beds in the middle of the night and summarily executed. Krebs was a brutal man who stopped at nothing to guarantee the survival of his race. According to him, a few people were expendable for the good of the many and this would enable German culture to live on.

He was the man that rose above the discord to reshape the universe in his own making. He would impose order where there was no order and create something that the world had never seen before. He was the *obermensch* that Nietzsche spoke about; he was the man who would recreate society and recreate mankind. He was the superman the Nazis talked about, that Hitler and the other German supremacy advocates wanted to emulate. He was the one who would preside over the Order of the Sacred Rune.

"This is an arrangement where the man of great ability, who surpasses all standards and expectations, will reign, while the Judeo-Christian God is ignored and falls into obscurity," Krebs said. It was clear that he rejected the concept of God outright.

According to Krebs, billions had now died and now they walked about as shambling things with little reasoning left, grotesque mockeries of what they once were. If he truly existed, God could not allow this whole thing to occur, his creation violated and smeared upon the face of the world.

"Either God was not there, or God left humanity to fend for itself," he said to us, standing in front of the nuclear complex.

If that were the case, then Krebs was God and did all that he could to ensure the survival of the German people. When these ghouls stop functioning, the Germans would emerge the triumphant super-race that Hitler and many others had always sought.

"Do you see that house on the hill behind the compound?" Krebs asked while pointing to the smooth acclivity beyond. We could see it in the distance, reaching to heaven as it stood against the orange sky. It was more like a small Bavarian castle than anything else, and it sat here in Africa of all places.

"That building is full of Lutheran hymnals, Bibles, and other Christian objects that I have collected from the suburbs of Windhoek and other parts of Namibia. I will eventually destroy that house with a small but powerful nuclear device, erasing the old order and ushering in the new. I want nothing to do with God. I shall be God, the savior humanity has always wanted!" He was the man of lawlessness and destruction who hated everything that God represented, and he would destroy God if he could get his hands upon him. A chill went up my spine at the annihilative tendencies so prevalent and embodied in Franz Krebs. Most of the people in the fortress were not around, seemingly afraid of interfering with the progress of Franz Reichard Krebs. They stood at a distance, looking on.

"What happened to your siblings?" I asked, rather curious.

"I had to put bullets in their brains. They were casualties in this great war."

"What are you going to do about all these ghouls? Do you have a solution?" I asked Krebs.

Krebs stood there, a towering and powerful man, resting his arms at his side. "They are things that are driven by some sort of destructive purpose. We have performed experiments on them here in this complex. Once they have been resuscitated, it is clear that they have little mind left, but through the constant repetition of stimuli they can regain their formal identities, but they still want to destroy. Why they exist is beyond any suggestion my scientists can come up with."

I thought about what Krebs had said. He did not see the supernatural as a legitimate force and would not consult it for information or explanations. He was a man that remained blind to many truths, and to me it was clear that a sentient force planted that radiation upon the probe. This entity, or entities, wanted to wreak havoc upon humanity and reviled everything that was dear to God. Perhaps the girl's physiology was the solution to the crisis, or maybe the solution was in the spiritual. Or perhaps it was in both the material and the spiritual.

"I will find a way to annihilate them! I will find the answer and I will succeed at every cost," Krebs stated, as we walked throughout the streets of the complex. Strangely, he did not sound that confident.

The people all paused as Krebs walked by, ranting, raving, gesturing up a storm, as he led us through the sturdy redoubt with carvings of that strange rune appearing everywhere. Some of the men who wore brown uniforms like the commandant stood at attention. The children, once again, stopped playing, and stared at him silently with apprehension. As Krebs passed into the crowd, the people parted their way before him like the Red Sea, and I sensed it was out of fear and not exactly love. Krebs had killed people before, and he would do it again and they knew it.

We followed the silent man to his office below the same brown brick building. The commandant once again brought up our rear. Not one single word was exchanged, revealing the tense nature of the situation. I imagined that Capasso was seething under Krebs' dominance, and I knew that he wanted to assert himself so badly. We headed for that underground office in that winding maze of despondent passageways. The six of us, including the commandant, stepped into the dimly lit chamber at its end. We sat down once again, the four of us at our chairs, while Krebs sat at his table under that dismal hanging lamp, the eerie carving of the rune behind him.

"We have the girl, Krebs," Capasso stated. "With her you can cure the infection stahted by those things. If we can get her here, this place will thrive and you'll be on top."

"And, Mr. Capasso?" Krebs asked without fear, sensing ulterior motives I imagined.

"Let's make a bargain. We can get her here. We just need to make some arrangements."

"What sort of arrangements?" Krebs asked very slowly and quite coldly.

"You run this place? Right?"

"Ya," Krebs answered, staring at Capasso with suspicion.

"Give me my nation. I will give you 70% of the people. Let me have the rest. This way I can help you run things, leaving you to do other stuff!" Capasso stated rather bluntly.

"I told you before, Mr. Capasso, this is my settlement. I helped build this place and I will not bargain its sovereignty!"

"Look, you need the girl, and we are the only ones who can give her to you! You have to give us what we want because you don't have a choice!" Capasso ordered.

"Yes, you are correct Mr. Capasso, we do need the girl. I am questioning if we need you!" Krebs said. "This is what I am going to do. I will have one of you stay here as a hostage, and the others will go back and get the girl. When she is finally here, the hostage will be released. *Verstehst du*?"

"I have what you need and I'm gonna give the orduhs around here! This is gonna be my piece of territory and no one's gonna stand in my way to stop me!" Capasso said in a voice that mounted to a cresendo. "YOU DON'T BOSS ME AROUND, KREBS! NO ONE DOES THAT TO ME, EVUH! DO YOU HEAR ME?" Capasso roared, pointing his finger at Krebs as his face became red with rage.

Capasso stood up suddenly, and everyone became deathly still, including Krebs at his desk. Capasso quickly grabbed a nearby metal chair by the legs and swung it at the commandant who was leaning up against the wall. Stunning the man, Capasso used it to his advantage. He bounded over the row of chairs and confronted the armed soldier. The commandant fumbled for his gun, but Bob Capasso was quicker. Capasso pummeled the man several times in the head and also in the jaw, until he slinked to the ground in unconsciousness.

Capasso took the .45, from the battered commandant, while Krebs, the agile man that he was, emerged from the shock and leapt over his desk, suddenly standing in front of Robert Capasso! Capasso stood there petrified over the sudden speed of the big man. He hesitated before firing, and that was just enough time for Krebs to grab the .45 and yank it out of Capasso's hands.

The two men stood there, both large and imposing, one trying to control the other. I looked at Capasso, and he seemed to be frightened. I suspected he was losing.

"You and I could be a good team. I could get the girl here, and I could help you run this place. Don't you realize that you need me, Krebs? You need me! You can't do this on your own!" Capasso weakly demanded, while sweat beaded and fell from his forehead.

"Mr. Capasso, I have built this place with my bare hands, and no one threatens me and no one takes it from me!" Krebs said and took his free fist and slammed it into Capasso's jaw. Capasso staggered back as Krebs tossed the pistol to the floor.

Krebs laid into Capasso several times with his closed hand. Capasso tried to strike back, but Krebs, the *ober-mensch,* was too fast! Capasso managed to catch Krebs in the jaw, but Krebs beat him without mercy, and Capasso fell upon his back! Capasso looked up at the dictator, stunned and disoriented.

Krebs took something from his belt. It was a knife, probably used in the Herero rebellion by German troops, about a century ago. "*Auf Wiedersehen, Herr Capasso.* See you in the next life!" He said, smiling downward. He drove the knife right into Capasso's heart. Capasso gurgled in terror and in pain as his chest heaved. Blood oozed from his torso and he cried softly, "Goering, help me." He turned his head to look at me and stretched out his hand in my direction. I knew by the sad expresson in his eyes that he was afraid and he did not want to die. The light of life faded from his orbs and he went silent. It was clear that he was dead.

Krebs stood over Capasso in triumph, as he looked down at his handiwork. He grinned at the victory and picked up the .45 that was on the floor. Krebs fired two rounds into Capasso's head. Capasso was essentially a murderer, very much like Bruce DeVries, but I did not like what Krebs had done to him. I hated Capasso, but I hated the brutal man that killed him even more. For a moment, I actually mourned the passing of Bob Capasso. The commandant came to and picked himself off of the floor. Capasso's corpse would be removed and subsequently burned. Just as he lived by the sword, he died by it as well.

Chapter Thirty-Nine: Regeneration

Krebs eventually called up security and four men with brown uniforms like the commandant, all possessing AK-47s, ran in. They saluted Krebs and then conversed with him for several moments in German, and I could not understand a single word said. Krebs turned to us as the discussion concluded.

"Mr. Milano," Krebs said. "We would like you to stay with us." They held a gun to his chest and he had to step back.

"Guys, don't let me down," Harry said with a look of fear in his eyes.

Roger and I had to somehow find our way back to the campus without assistance. If we weren't back in seventy-two hours, Harry Milano would be shot dead without mercy, another casualty of this horrid little war.

The Germans escorted us out of the cellar, leaving Krebs and the commandant behind with an insecure Milano. They led us up the freight elevator and took us out of the building to our transportation. We found the truck still sitting there where we had left it, near the spacious garages that housed all sorts of equipment. We refilled the truck and boarded it, and they gave us general directions back to the campus. The New Valhallans opened up the gates to let us go on our way, and we rode out, onto the savannah, and back towards the distant town of Keetmanshoop.

"Do you think he'll kill Milano?" Roger asked.

"Yeah. Krebs has done it before. He'll do it again," I answered, taking my eyes off of the road to look at him.

After driving for several hours, we could see the campus in the distance, shimmering like a mirage in the empty wasteland. The windmill was spinning, and the aluminum on the roofs cast a glare from the bright sun. We went up to the gates. Van Den Heuvel was there and let us in. LaFontaine ran to us, coming from the direction of the administration building and carrying his AK-47 in his capable hands.

"We were looking all over for you," he said in his guttural accent. "Where have you been?"

"We went off to Windhoek," I answered.

"You shouldn't have done that! Andries doesn't like it! You are putting everyone's life at risk here!" LaFontaine stated with disapproval.

"Where are Capasso and Milano?" Van Den Heuvel asked.

"Capasso's dead and Harry's back in the compound that's out there," Roger answered. I was not sure if Roger should have been so direct about that, but I guess it was too late to retract.

"Andries is going to be absolutely furious!" LaFontaine retorted.

Once again I was reminded of DeKuyper's autocratic tendencies and I became angry at it.

"Why do we have to live and die by what Andries says and does?" I stated.

"You live under his roof, you obey the rules. It's that simple," LaFontaine said. The Coloured was smugly silent. The people here agreed to follow the laws that DeKuyper set forth and they would not challenge his authority. Both men pointed their guns at Roger and me; they forced us to leave the truck. We had to keep our hands up, while the two men pushed us to the dormitory at gunpoint.

They escorted us into the large building and forced us up the stairs into the lobby. Standing in the vestibule, in front of a glass door, was the hulking man with a pistol in his hand. He looked angry, locked into silence.

"I don't want people to leave this place without me knowing about it. I should kill you for that!" DeKuyper said angrily, staring at us. "You do it again and I will kill you!" Looking at his eyes, I knew he meant it. He would end my life without thinking twice about it. He pulled the pistol upon me and I wanted to urinate.

"I should put you out of my misery now, *uitlander!* If I did that I wouldn't have anyone to punish!" he said as he lowered the gun to his side. There was some truth to what he spoke. A king is worthless without his subjects, and he considered me one of his. He came to his senses, and I certainly was relieved. For the rest of the day there was tension.

The next day, I watched Elizabeth Brady play with Amanda and Judith on the concrete walkway outside the dorm. Amanda smiled with sparkling delight in her eyes. Elizabeth seemed to be at home with the two Zulu women. I wondered if she realized that something in her blood held the key to humanity's possible redemption. Could she ever understand? She was no longer regarded as a human being by the powers that be, but as a thing to be tested in the laboratory or used as a bargaining chip. I looked up in the second story window where the TV lounge was and saw DeKuyper looking down at me, watching my every move like a hawk. He did not trust me, and I wasn't too fond of him either. We would have to design a scheme to take the girl.

After our dinner, when everyone else had gone, Roger and I stayed behind to tell him about Milano's predicament as we sat in our places at the table.

"If we don't get Elizabeth to Windhoek, Krebs will kill Harry by the day after tomorrow," I said. DeKuyper's face was expressionless, and I feared his response.

"Mr. Milano has gotten himself into a lot of trouble. He should not have gone on that little adventure of yours. That is his problem; he will have to get himself out. I'm not going to help him," DeKuper said without compassion. Amanda walked in to clear the table of the remaining dishes. She looked somewhat timid as she did so. It was clear from DeKuyper's response that he would let Milano rot. After nearly wasting me back in the Atlantic, it was tempting to let Harry fend for himself, but I had to be merciful.

"You're a sick man, Andries. Don't you care about Harry?" I asked.

"No, not really. Your group decided to join us and not the other way around," the big man said.

I walked away from DeKuyper disgusted, realizing his mind was muddled with hatred. He wanted the Afrikaner race to rule over all other people groups, and he would do whatever he could in order to achieve this. With Elizabeth in his possession, the people in Windhoek would jump as high as he would want them to, making him feel important. We would have to take the girl away from DeKuyper by tomorrow morning or Krebs would kill Milano and that was it. I began to put together a brief plan with Roger, Angeline, and Marcia in the back living room of the dormitory.

The four of us began to come up with some sort of awkward strategy wherein we would take her from the two Zulu women at gunpoint, but I wasn't sure if it would work. We sat around the lobby, while DeKuyper was somewhere else in the dormitory. The Zulu women were down the hall with the little girl. The place was quiet, and maybe this would be a good time to pull it off, but that wouldn't give us any time to flesh out a plan. From out of the blue came an interruption.

LaFontaine ran in from outside with an automatic rifle in his hand and entered the living room, panting and out of breath.

"There are a score of them out there and they have guns!" he said. I grew extremely frightened at the moment. An undead army was clearly forming, and my worst fears were being realized.

"Marcia, go get DeKuyper!" I said. The Jamaican woman got up from the floor and began to search the dormitory.

"We have to get as many rifles as possible. They have actually fired back with weapons of their own. Abel is fighting them now," LaFontaine said.

A minute later, DeKuyper appeared in the living room with the diminutive Marcia behind him.

"Get the guns now!" DeKuyper ordered, somewhat alarmed by the events. The Zulu women appeared promptly, pistols in their holsters. Everyone, except for the Coloured, was now on deck making sure their weapons were locked and loaded.

"We have to go out there and help him!" DeKuyper stated.

He led us through the vestibule and out of the dormitory. Only Amanda and Elizabeth remained inside. DeKuyper yelled for Abel Van Den Heuvel as we stood outside the residence hall. We heard the Coloured answer from some distance away, but his whereabouts were unknown. DeKuyper panned the buildings before us and he found him up against the wall of a cream-colored building about two hundred feet away, firing at something around its corner, out of sight. DeKuyper ran up ahead of the group and talked to him alone. The Afrikaner looked back towards us and motioned for us all to come over.

We joined Van Den Heuvel and DeKuyper a moment later, the sound of gunshots filling the air.

"There are nearly twenty of them out in the *veld*. They are armed! We'll have to take them all out!" DeKuyper said.

Roger, Angeline, and I went around to the front of the building. I peered around the corner and could see a group of ten ghouls, all with gray skin and dressed in contemporary clothing with cold and expressionless faces. They moved very quickly with pistols in hand, hiding behind the low hummocks of the yard. I took one of the automatic rifles and began to fire it. One I hit in the chest, but that did not kill it. I continued to fire at the thing and a bullet eventually imbedded itself in the brain! It fell and ceased moving.

The other ghouls began to open fire! I had to withdraw from the corner to get out of the way of the oncoming bullets. Roger, armed with a shotgun, went up to the edge and emptied some shells. Angeline knelt beneath him and aimed her pistol, squeezing off a few rounds. The woman was becoming more violent as the crisis wore on, but so was I. I peered around the edge to find that three of the creatures were now on the ground. Clearly, we were winning.

I fired the AK-47 several more times. The ghouls continued to advance, ducking behind the small hummocks of earth. We kept on firing, riddling their torsos with bullets, but this did not stop them. I had to remember that they did not rely upon internal organs. They did not groan; they only shot their pistols at us without noise and emotion. We hit them in the brains, and they went to the ground, dropping their weapons. We paused to reload.

Suddenly, a ghoul with gray skin came out from behind a low mound and rushed me with an unmoving face that did not yield! The thing grabbed my throat with both of its hands, opened its mouth and threatened to bite my neck! Angeline pointed the barrel of her pistol at the thing and pulled the trigger. Its fingers went limp and then let go, entirely slumping to the ground. The threat had abated, and we had clearly won this deadly round. We joined the others in the front of the science building, and we cleaned our guns leisurely.

"Andries, we almost bought it. Tomorrow there'll be hundreds, if not thousands, around this place. We're going to have to go to Windhoek or die," I said. DeKuyper just stood there and said nothing, and his face did not move. He looked confused.

It was at dinner, as we all sat around silently feasting upon broiled springbok, when he finally opened up his mouth.

"We'll have to leave *moreoggend* (tomorrow morning). It is going to be very, very bad. We will have to make sure we have all of our stuff together by tonight," he said.

After the dinner was done with, we all cleaned up after ourselves and got ready to depart. The group worked around the clock. We packed together provisions, made sure our guns were clean, and collected plenty of ammunition. We sat around the dormitory living area, thinking about our circumstances, and few words were spoken.

"Goering, you patrol the area tonight," DeKuyper said, standing in the middle of the room with an oppressive presence. I did not have the will to challenge him, and would have to circle around the entire campus three times an hour to make sure we were not infiltrated.

The sun went down, and everybody went upstairs, leaving me alone in the room. It was time for me to make my rounds, so I walked out of the residence hall and into the darkness. I strolled around the campus, which was no more than a square half-mile in area, with flashlight in hand. As I made the circuit, I heard animals moving around in the bush, but it left me a little jumpy. I moved on, hoping to keep my composure throughout the night. To the right of the campus, I saw a hill, and I figured that if I were to climb it I would be able to look out upon the entire savannah to keep watch.

I mounted that hill, clambered up through both the weeds and the rocks to the apex. Standing upon a pile of stones, I could barely make out the bleak and empty plain in front of me due to the pervasive darkness. I saw nothing but the glow of the distant sinking sun, leaving me in sagging blackness.

"God, are you there?" I asked. Nothing responded.

"God, it's lonely here. Are you there?" I asked again.

"I am here, Andy," I thought I heard in my head.

"I am going to take care of you. Don't be afraid," the voice said. "Make sure you are up and out of here before the dawn." And that was it. That was all the voice said, and I heard nothing for the rest of the night. Several times over the next few hours, I paused nervously to see if there was something out there in the darkness as I circled the silent dead buildings. Tension burned in my chest, and I felt the urine press against the walls of my bladder. They could strike at anytime, like a sniper in the streets of Baghdad, firing on an unsuspecting patrolman.

I continued my rounds throughout the haunted campus for several hours, then I decided to check out the scene of yesterday's crime. There, in back of the cream-colored building, with the help of the flashlight, I found a hole in the fence that must have been made. The ghouls took some sort of device and managed to cut the mesh of wire, enabling them to infiltrate. Beyond the fence was a long field that stretched out for over a mile. I could see the sun begin to come up over that plain in the east, towards the Kalahari.

I stared into the landscape that was half-immersed in darkness and remembered what the voice told me. It said to get everyone up and out of bed before dawn! I looked over the forlorn and barren field as the sun poked its head over the horizon, and I could see malignant clusters of figures in the distance. They would be here in minutes!

I ran through the campus back to the dormitory. I had to get them up before the oncoming army arrived. I booked into the building, bounded through the vestibule, and went upstairs where everyone was sleeping.

I ran through the halls and screamed, "Wake up! Everybody get up! They're gonna be here in a matter of minutes! Get up!"

Van Den Heuvel and Roger immediately jumped out of their beds and ran into the hall, armed and dangerous. Everyone was in their day clothes, ready to leave at a moment's notice, running around trying to find their belongings. Roger, Van Den Heuvel, and I descended the stairs. We went out through the lobby, and emerged from the building.

"How many of them are there?" Van Den Heuvel asked.

"I have no idea!" I answered.

We got into the jeep and headed to the area where the hole was made in the fence.

There we could see well over a hundred of the things standing on the other side of the fence and making their way through the opening. We drove the jeep to where they were congregating and Van Den Heuvel, a little trigger happy, opened fire. Their heads shot up and looked at us, and they raised their guns and attacked, spitting forth lead. I swept the jeep before them in an arc, and Van Den Heuvel shot them up with his assault rifle, momentarily halting the invasion. I turned the jeep around and headed back towards the dormitory. DeKuyper, Angeline, and the others were packing up the trucks with some final items.

"They're almost in the perimeter," I said to DeKuyper.

"We have to get out of this place!" DeKuyper said and then shouted some orders to LaFontaine in Afrikaans. LaFontaine jumped into a jeep with DeKuyper at the wheel. Roger, Van Den Heuvel and I decided to take the jeep we were using, while Marcia and Angeline rode together in the black pickup that we lifted while back in South Africa. The generator from the ketch was placed in its backend. Judith and Amanda took a truck with Elizabeth in the back seat. We started up the vehicles and approached the gate.

I looked back towards the fence that surrounded the campus and could see the ghouls inside the perimeter, running toward us at a good pace with that strange impaired coordination, reminding me of the Kari Bergmann incident. LaFontaine got out of his jeep and unlocked the gate. The ghouls began to pour forth from between the buildings, firing upon us with their guns. The four vehicles quickly left the compound. The ghouls would overwhelm the entire area within minutes.

We fled on the road for a few hundred yards. As DeKuyper and LaFontaine approached a grade in the lane, I detected a dust cloud forming on the other side of it in the morning sun. At that moment, I realized that there was a vehicle coming up over the crest of that hill! Could it be Krebs and his men? A blue suburban vehicle drove over the grade with three gray-skinned people in it, all armed. The suburban, at a speed of about fifty miles and hour, headed right for the two Afrikaners! DeKuyper swerved the jeep out of the way, but the vehicle just continued, heading straight for us! Thankfully, my reactions were quick, and I turned the jeep off to the left, totally avoiding the oncoming vehicle. As my jeep collected dust on the side of the road, I heard a large crash from behind me. Immediately, I turned around to find that the suburban filled with ghouls had collided with the passenger's side of Angeline's vehicle! The scream of a woman in pain came from the pickup, along with the hiss of a dying radiator. The occupants of the suburban rolled down the windows and pointed their gun barrels at us. I could see their gray and dead expressionless faces within the shadows of that truck.

Van Den Heuvel and DeKuyper both opened fire with their AK-47s upon the suburban, and I joined them, riddling it with bullets. After a minute of the continual onslaught, the vehicle was reduced to a smoking mess and nothing stirred there any longer. We walked over to the vehicle to check out the ghouls within the haze of the battle. After perusing them from head to toe, we determined that every one had been shot in the head and rendered inactive.

It occurred to me that something was not quite right about this scenario. I looked about me and noticed that someone was missing. Marcia! She was not walking around with everyone else. Oh no, where was she? Angeline was at my side with a bloodied forehead.

"Andy, you've got to come here," she said pulling me by the arm.

We looked inside of Angeline's truck and found Marcia sitting in the passenger's seat, limp, and somewhat lifeless, the stuffed bear at her side. Both the entire dashboard and the door had been pushed into her abdomen and she sat there bleeding profusely. Her eyes opened very slowly, and she noticed me. Her lips began to form words that were so light and so soft that I had to lean over just to hear them.

"Hold my hand, Andy. I startin' to go numb. God, I'm so sceered!" she cried.

Her chest heaved up and down. I reached in and grabbed her by the hand, hoping to comfort the woman I once hoped would be my wife. I realized that she was going to die.

"Andy, put your head up against mine. Please!"

"Honey, remember where you're going when you die. You're gonna be with Jesus! He's up there, honey. He's up there waiting for you!" I could feel her pulse as tears formed in her eyes. They began to roll down her face and disappeared beneath her chin.

"Andy, please hold me!"

She closed her eyes for several moments, her lips silently moving, petitioning to God. Then her eyes opened abruptly, as if her body was going through a physiological change. First, she began to shake, and then she hyperventilated like mad as her body went into shock. She vibrated and her eyes peered at the ceiling. She shook and shook, crimson saliva running from her mouth. Then, the whole thing stopped and her body did nothing. I squeezed her wrist to search for a pulse, but it had faded. It was obvious that Marcia Clarke was now dead. The last of a race of people had slipped into oblivion. I had to bring myself to put a bullet through her skull, as tears fell from my eyes. I knew that I was going to miss this woman.

We lifted the guns from the creatures in the vehicle. We took a shovel out from the back of one of the jeeps and quickly laid Marcia in a two-foot deep hole. We placed the smiling bear at her side, a faithful companion to her for so long. There was no time for a eulogy. Marcia Clarke found me on that street so long ago, several worlds away. She saved me from harm, took me into her home, and made me feel as if I were her brother. We heaped the earth upon her lifeless body and the stuffed bear, while their eyes gazed into the blue sky above them. She was dead and would return no more.

We looked back at the camp. They were still there, moving around, somehow organizing themselves. Many of them were starting to head through the gates toward us with their weapons drawn. Thankfully, we were well over a thousand feet away and it would take them several minutes to get here. We all got into our vehicles and sped on, having paid our respects to the departed Jamaican woman with such a big heart. Angeline had to ride with both Amanda and Judith since the black pickup was now totaled, the generator from the ketch still in its back.

We headed over the savannah, passing grasslands and teak forests, but seeing no other living persons. As the procession advanced towards the settlement in Windhoek, I began to realize something. Somehow those things were able to figure out where we lived and could easily surround us! They drove us out of Steuben Corners, out of South Africa, and even inflicted some casualties in Keetmanshoop. It was only a matter of time before they get to Windhoek, where they'd meet us by the hundreds of thousands!

We continued on as the road wound like a serpent through a teak forest. Judging by a swath cut through the trees some distance away, there was a river nearby. Maybe we could rest here and get some much-needed water. The procession suddenly came to a halt.

"Let's stop here for a little while. We can't stay long. They'll be all around us quite soon." DeKuyper said to the group. We had to watch and be ready to fly at a moment's notice!

Angeline and I climbed down to the stream in the ravine that ran through the teak forest. The waters were bubbling with life, as fish swam through a creek that must have been about fifteen feet wide. We took out our canteens, unscrewed the tops, and dipped them into the brook, filling them with life-giving water.

"Andy, do you think we're going to get through this thing?" she asked.

I paused for several long moments, trying to see beyond the grim scenario. I found myself in a state of uncertainty.

"I….I hope so," I said, while looking into her melancholic eyes.

"You're lying. You just want me to feel better," she said, kind of angrily.

"Yeah. I don't see any way out. I don't know what to tell you. We'll have to go down fighting, and that's it. We got nothing better to hope for." Angeline fell silent. She looked away to the top of the ravine. I sensed a thick despondency emanating from her in waves.

"Look, I'm scared...real scared. There's no hope. Where's God? Why is this happening? Andy, please hold me. I just need you to hold me." She walked over to me and

I put my arms around her for several long moments, kissing her in the embrace.

Gunshots rang out, shattering the last moment of ecstasy that I may ever have with a woman. I looked up and could see ghouls peering down at us with dark faces. I unfastened the AK-47 from my shoulder, and another shot rang out from the top of the gap. I aimed my assault rifle in the direction and fired off a few short bursts. The dark faces were no longer there. It looked as if I chased them away. Angeline and I climbed up to the edge of the ravine.

We got to the top a few minutes later.

"What took you so long?" Van Den Heuvel rushed toward us. "We have been trying to find you! They're all over the place! We've got to get out of here!" he screamed in a panic.

We followed him as he broke into a light jog, running towards the three vehicles. DeKuyper was standing there with a serious expression upon his bearded face.

"They are all over the place. They'll have us surrounded in a couple of minutes," he said with a look of concern.

I looked around into the nearby teaks and noticed several armed figures hidden in the shadows, creeping beneath the overhanging branches. Angeline went to the truck, and I jumped into the jeep, while both Van Den Heuvel and LaFontaine opened fire upon the crouching silhouettes. The things fell back, and the two men ran to the vehicles. Roger and Van Den Heuvel climbed aboard the jeep and joined me as LaFontaine took to DeKuyper. The procession started up again, and DeKuyper led the way.

"There must be hundreds," Van Den Heuvel stated as the jeep sped on. They seemed to be gradually surrounding us.

If Ishtar was truly behind the whole thing, and if she could actually raise the dead, she could put together an army numbering in the tens of millions. If all that were left was about 17,000, the human race didn't stand much of a chance.

We continued on for another hour. How close we were to Windhoek I didn't know, but we were getting there, and that was what counted. On the savannah, we could see a few manmade structures, and judging by the Dutch architecture, they were probably built by Afrikaners. The sky overhead was blue, seemingly filled with promise, but where was the redemption? Was it in Windhoek? If it were in Windhoek, we would all be dead before long. The landscape to the east was sandy and barren, and I wagered that we were near the edge of the dry Kalahari.

My jeep was the last in the procession, with DeKuyper and Angeline in front of us. I looked behind me to see if there were any problems. On the long flat stretch of plain, I saw large hills that looked like mountains in the distance. Back towards those hills, I saw something materialize on the length. It was a vehicle, and another one was following right behind it, leaving a dust cloud in back of it.

They came at a great speed, armed heavily. They approached in two topless convertibles, about two hundred yards off and closing. I could barely make out their faces, but I detected that something was wrong with their skin. They were ghouls and they were coming at a breakneck speed, dust kicking up in their wake.

"Rog, Abel, get your guns ready!" I said.

Both men turned around and aimed their weapons at the approaching cars. The two convertibles were about one hundred feet away when they opened fire! The air was full of lead, and I heard a round ricochet off the back of the jeep! Roger and Van Den Heuvel continued with their barrage, but the ghouls just drove on with blank faces, undaunted by the counterattack! I could have sworn their eyes bore traces of mischievousness in them. The race of one driver was white and the other was black, but they were both united by the same destructive purpose — the annihilation of the human race!

I turned around to look at the sky in front of me. An olive-green helicopter approached us. It swooped down and fired missiles out from near the landing gear. One of the missiles hit the car driven by the white man, causing it to burst into flame. It veered off the road and into the savannah, flames consuming the wreckage. The helicopter fired another round of missiles at the tarmac behind me, destroying the convertible driven by the black ghoul. It swerved off into the scrub on the side of the road and began to catch fire. The occupants of both vehicles were incinerated and would not be coming back.

With the presence of the helicopter, I determined that we must be near Krebs' compound, New Valhalla. The chopper landed, and we pulled over in front of it, leaving our vehicles. A man stepped out of from the bird and walked over to our group. He wore a brown hat and a brown uniform with black boots, very much like the commandant. He was the same man who greeted us the first time that we came out here.

"Welcome again to New Valhalla," he said. It was Burghoff.

DeKuyper walked over to him and told him with no emotion, "There are thousands of those things following us."

"Ya. We know. We can see them from the air. There are much more than that. They cover the hills and the open plains. There must be three or four hundred thousand of them," Burghoff said.

Three or four hundred thousand? How the heck are we going to fight that? "God, wherever you are, please help us," I asked silently. I knew God was still with me, even though the situation was bleak, hopeless and getting out of control, fast.

Chapter Forty: Ragnarok

Within minutes we all left. Burghoff flew the chopper off ahead of us to the compound two miles down the road, and we followed by land. We came to that gate in the wire mesh fence that surrounded Krebs' settlement. The guards stood there, unwilling to let us in. The chopper hovered over us, and Burghoff gestured something to one of the sentries. In response, the guards opened the gate, and the chopper flew off. As we approached the gates to the fortress, we sped by all the people, who busily occupied themselves. The concrete portal with the rune rolled back and we drove into the large space with the little shanties, where Bantu and Boer frolicked alike. The gates shut behind us to the sound of humming machinery.

DeKuyper got out of his jeep and everyone else followed suit, lifting our arms from the vehicles. Amanda stood behind little Elizabeth, who looked absolutely frightened. The little girl knew bad things were happening and probably wished that her parents were still around, but they were not. They were not.

"What is happening?" Judith Luthuli said in a distressed tone. Both of them moved in to protect the girl, dedicated to the preservation of life.

I looked up at the sky. The sun was beginning to set in the west. Burghoff approached the group and immediately conferred with DeKuyper. Then someone else approached from the buildings, and I recognized him immediately. It was the commandant, wearing the brown uniform.

"Did *Herr Krebs* give you an invitation?" he asked DeKuyper.

"He gave us no invitation. They are coming by the hundreds of thousands," DeKuyper said as he looked down at the man.

"*Was?*" the commandant asked, looking surprised.

"It is true," Burghoff said. "They will be here in less than an hour." The commandant stood there for several long moments, astounded and appearing troubled. He vacillated in indecision, and then he barked out orders.

"Sound the alarm! *Geben Sie Alarm-Signal!*" he shouted while walking back near the nuclear facilities. Several minutes went by as we started to unpack the trucks. The children, both black and white, began to mill about us, studying their new visitors. The silence broke as the blare of an air raid siren filled the crowded space around us. All of the children began to run away, scrambling to find their parents. The gates opened again to let the outsiders in who desperately sought cover!

The air raid sirens began to fade as a voice was heard over a distant loudspeaker. It was the commandant. "Everyone take their stations! *Achtung! Jeder nehmen Ihr Positionen!*" His voice was filled with urgency.

From out of the garages, on the backs of open flatbed trucks with boom cranes, came the anti-aircraft batteries. The booms would be used to position the batteries. Another truck rolled into the area where a multitude of rag-tag settlers congregated. The driver got out and opened up doors to the side of the truck, revealing stacks of firearms. The people eagerly lined up to receive them. Both men and women, German Namibian and African black, were side by side ready to defend their lives, Franz Krebs, and the thinning remnants of humanity.

My little group stayed intact and waited while people lined up trying to get their firearms. The voice of the commandant could still be heard over the loudspeaker, barking out orders in both English and German. I saw the big man, Krebs, wading through the parting crowd, looking slightly agitated and insecure. Everything that he had built was now at risk, and I could tell it bothered him to no end.

"Is the girl here?" he asked.

Without opening my mouth, I pointed to Elizabeth, who was standing in front of Amanda.

Krebs turned around to another man who wore a brown uniform similar to the commandant.

"Go and release Mr. Milano." Krebs, thankfully, was a man of his word.

He took the girl from the Zulu woman and led her away. Elizabeth looked back at Amanda, very frightened. I wondered what Krebs would do to the girl. Amanda trailed along after the two, just as devoted to Elizabeth as her own mother would be. Krebs motioned with his hand to have her stay put, and Amanda had no choice but to comply. The two walked through the camp and disappeared somewhere past the familiar brown complex, obscured by the crowd.

The concrete walls making up the enclosure had heavy pegs installed in them about six feet from the ground. Planks were quickly placed upon those pegs, forming catwalks, and the people mounted them with the help of ladders, armed, and poised to defend. I took my assault rifle and ascended a ladder to one of the planks, peering out over the dismal plain as the sun began to set. On the horizon, I detected something stirring. Perhaps a mile away, I spied a group of small vehicles quickly approaching! I counted eight of them coming towards the fortress at breakneck speeds. As they got closer, I could see the passengers hanging out the windows, aiming rifles, and pistols at the walls.

They were about two hundred feet away when they started to open fire.

"*Schiessen!*" Someone yelled from behind the fortifications, and a volley of rocket-propelled grenades rained down upon the nearing vehicles. The cars were reduced to flaming wrecks. We looked ahead on the darkening horizon and beheld an approaching mass that must have numbered in the tens of thousands! An army of ghouls slowly advanced upon the fortress, moving steadily without fear, without emotion. A young unshaven man with long hair stood next to me and viewed the spectacle through a pair of field glasses.

"Do you mind if I have a look?" I asked the man.

"Not at all," he said in his German accent as he handed them to me.

As I peered through the binoculars, I noticed that over half of the ghouls moved in a sluggish manner, tottering across the savannah with guns in their hands. The rest were partially regenerated and moved swiftly, forming the front guard. The multitude parted, forming a channel for more vehicles to drive down. Ten to twelve automobiles came forward and sped down the partition. They got to within about two hundred feet of the gate when the New Valhallans opened fire. From the wall, the rocket-propelled grenades, automatic rifles, and turreted machine guns went off like mad, blowing the vehicles to pieces. I looked to the dark horizon and estimated that there were over two hundred thousand of those things coming this way! They could keep this up for hours, and it was just a matter of time before they got through.

Without the help of automobiles, the shuffling gray monstrosities advanced en masse, their weapons down at their sides, coming in clusters and waves. They moved closer to the huge compound, past the burning autos, continually building up their forces. They were preparing to roll upon the fortress by the thousands, hoping to overwhelm us by sheer numbers!

I heard a voice out on the savannah that was surprisingly familiar. It belonged to a woman booming something through a megaphone in English. I panned over the dark *veld* with the field glasses and detected a truck with large speakers on it. A woman stood upon that truck speaking into the microphone. I checked her out for a moment and realized that it was none other than Michelle Ramadan! She was guiding and directing the vast army of ghouls. Somehow she had made it across the Atlantic too.

The ghouls continued to congregate, ready to charge the fortress that surrounded the last significant aggregate of humanity. A number of them stood upright along the entire length of the front wall. Another group knelt down before them and I realized that they were forming a line, attempting to get inside.

"When I give the order to fire, shoot at everything in the fortress," Ramadan said over the loudspeaker. The creatures remained with blank expressions, ready to do the will of the tall woman with the microphone.

There was a rush of activity on the ground behind me. I heard orders shouted in both English and German as men, both black and white, ran around the area below me trying to position themselves. An open truck drove up from deep within the compound, bearing what looked like flame-throwers and other heavy weapons on its back. A group of men came out of nowhere and began to distribute them to the frightened crowd.

The ghouls opened fire on Ramadan's orders. Automatics sprayed the walls with bullets, hitting many of the New Valhallans in the process. In response, the flame-throwers spat forth the burning napalm and covered the creatures on the front lines, causing them to burn and scream. The ghouls always hated fire, though I did not know precisely why. Maybe it was because they were creatures of darkness and the fire represented something warm, holy, and consuming. Scores of ghouls were burned, some running into the mass making others erupt into flame. The people of New Valhalla managed to repel an enemy attack once again, a hopeful sign that we might make it till morning.

"Get away from the burning bodies!" Ramadan ordered through the speaker. The ghouls seemed to obey her every command as they shuffled away from the flaming corpses.

"Move away from the middle channel," she said. I did not know what was happening, but I watched as the mass of ghouls parted further, forming a swath one hundred feet wide. The gap stretched on as far back as I could see under the ominous twilight sky.

I heard the distant sound of engines revving. Sixteen automobiles, both trucks and cars, drove down that path at a speed of forty miles an hour and headed straight for the gates of New Valhalla.

I heard more orders yelled in German. A change was taking place amongst the crowd within the compound. I noticed that some trucks began to transport the anti-aircraft batteries perched on the sidewalls.

The cars outside continued forward with gun barrels protruding from the open windows. The gangsters in the cars fired, aiming for the tops of the walls. Some of the people behind the enclosure were starting to go down!

"*Shiessen!*" someone barked. The anti-aircraft guns opened fire at the cars, reducing most to burning wrecks. A few remained and continued to drive forward, colliding with the front wall of the compound, and were met by a barrage of lead. One car rushed to the foot of the compound and stopped before the gate. A ghoul tossed something through its open window and it sailed over the wall behind the fortifications. It exploded on the other side, inflicting some casualties. In response, automatic fire rendered the car a smoking hulk. I began to realize that, once the anti-aircraft weapons went dead, that would be it.

"Make more room! Make more room!" I heard Ramadan speak.

The crowd continued to part, making the avenue much wider than before. I could hear the loud rumbling of vehicles somewhere in the approaching darkness as the sun sank below the horizon.

"*Stellen Sie die Lampen in position!*" the commandant ordered. Bright lamps, the type used to illuminate stadiums, were transported in on the backs of large trucks and were set up appropriately. They bathed the landscape before us in an artificial glow, causing the ghouls to back away, shielding their eyes with their hands from the intense light.

The wrecked hulks of all the cars were still on fire, burning away. Several ghouls, maybe one hundred and fifty, had fallen in the waves of attacks. I looked back upon the floor of the compound, realizing that we had lost perhaps a dozen or so. We did not have the numbers to keep this up! The rumblings in the distance got louder, and I realized that they were moving in for the kill! Judging by the sound they made, they were heavy, armored, and most likely tanks! One appeared about three hundred feet away, moving into view with its huge cannon pointed at the walls of the compound. Behind it were more tanks, about seven in all. They started forming a line behind the burning wrecks, getting ready to fire. Masses of ghouls gathered in back of the tanks, and it became evident that an attack was being coordinated!

"*Shiessen!*" I heard the commandant's voice once again. The batteries barraged the tanks with missiles. Most were destroyed, but one managed to pump out a shell into the wall of the compound, causing damage. One of the remaining tanks sent out another shell, and it hit part of the fortress near the gate, threatening to penetrate it! The mass of ghouls surged forth from behind the armored vehicles. It was strange that no sound could be heard from them and no war cries were uttered. They perished silently in the barrage of anti-aircraft missiles that wiped out the last two remaining tanks.

Machine guns on turrets went off from the walls of the fortress, mowing the mass of silent creatures down. In response, the creatures fired upon the fort but were cut down as well. More bodies and destruction littered the savannah before us. Ramadan barked out a series of orders, telling the ghouls to make way. The part between the two multitudes became ever wider as I heard more vehicles rumble in from some distance away. Lights came toward us down that ever-widening channel. They were sending in more automobiles, maybe twenty-five or thirty, with rifles protruding from the windows, threatening to take down the cracking fortress. Pickups carried personnel armed with rocket-propelled grenades.

They drove along the length of the front wall, going in many different directions at once, crossing paths and making it extremely difficult for us to get a bead on them. They opened fire with their machine guns and rocket launchers, striking the tops of the walls. The walls crumbled under the onslaught as more bodies went down! The anti-aircraft batteries fired back, destroying some while the machine guns cut down the rest!

I heard the whipping of helicopter blades slicing through the evening air overhead. I looked up to notice two olive-green choppers in the sky above me, shining their floodlights down upon the dead mass. They hovered in the air for long moments and then took to their positions. Suddenly, they fired their mobile missile batteries at the remaining tangle of vehicles, annihilating many of them. Mobile rocket-launchers from behind the walls took out more, but we had suffered some casualties. They were slowly whittling away at our ranks and soon there would be no one left. The helicopters gave up their position in the sky and returned to the compound.

I was beginning to wonder what they were going to throw at us next. After handing back the field glasses to their rightful owner, I descended the ladder to find Krebs. I had to let him know that this whole thing was going to spiral out of control. People were running around me under the artificial lights with weapons in hand in a state of panic.

I looked above me again, and I watched one of the choppers shoot through the sky, ready to go off to war and annihilate more of those things. It went up about thirty or forty feet over the savannah, sailing above the undead multitude. It hovered there for a minute as if it was waiting for orders. In the next moment the chopper exploded and burst into flame! The ghouls had some sort of anti-aircraft device! I knew this was going to get worse, and I desperately had to find Krebs!

I turned around to face the confusion of people running about in a scattered and confused manner. Rising above the crowd, I saw the large speakers mounted on the back of a large flatbed truck. There was the brown-garbed commandant with a microphone in his hand standing next to them. I made my way through the crowd toward the man.

"Where's Krebs?" I asked the commandant.

"I can't tell you. He does not want anyone to know," he said.

"We just lost a chopper. The more we throw at them, the more they return it. And this whole thing's gonna get worse! Where is he?" I asked.

"I told you before, I cannot disclose that!" the commandant insisted.

At that moment, we heard it, the sound of helicopter blades spinning, cutting up the air. The noise had an ominous effect, and I felt tension burn in my chest once again. I looked up overhead into the night sky and beheld another helicopter, *but this time it was theirs!* They had aerial support! The people in the compound below fired upon the chopper. It just circled around and around and flew out above the inhuman multitude. It hovered for a moment or two, waiting patiently for something to happen. Suddenly fire shot forth from under its landing gear, and one of the anti-aircraft batteries in the compound exploded! They were going to match us piece for piece, weapon for weapon, man for man!

"Get Krebs up here on the double!" I told the man. The commandant bolted from his post and ran to the low flat building that housed Krebs' office!

I found Roger and Angeline by my side, disoriented from the growing chaos. Van Den Heuvel, LaFontaine, and DeKuyper appeared as well, trying to get their bearings!

"This is going to get *mal!*" the huge Afrikaner said.

Around us, in the fortress, all the bodies of the fallen were gathered into a pile. The corpses would be lined up and slugs would be sent into their craniums. It made this battle all the harder.

In the smoke of the conflict, an explosion rocked one of the anti-aircraft batteries. Krebs appeared, and behind him was Harry Milano and five armed guards. We walked up to him as one of our choppers passed overhead, drawing machine gun fire from the inhuman mass outside.

Harry ran over to us, smiling. He was elated, but I greeted him with nothing more than a handshake. I did not care for the man, remembering the incident on the ketch where we almost killed each other.

I looked up at Krebs and said to him, "This place is not gonna to be standing here in another two hours."

He looked at me confidently, despite the mounting chaos all around us.

"I have an ace up my sleeve. Come with me. I have to show you this," he said.

The commandant and five guards, all dressed in the same brown uniforms, surrounded Krebs. Angeline, Roger, DeKuyper, Van Den Heuvel, LaFontaine, and I joined them. Milano ducked out, and I had no idea where he had gone. Krebs and his contingent led the rest of us between the shanties, through the nuclear and laboratory facilities, to the rear of the sprawling complex. After a few minutes, amidst the sounds of the chaotic battle around, we neared the rear of the redoubt. I could see a small door in the surrounding wall of the compound that was guarded by three troops, all clothed in tattered uniforms.

"*Oeffnen Sie die Tuer!*" he told them. The men unfastened the door, loyally unlocking a series of deadbolts.

The door opened out to the hills beyond, and I could see the silhouette of the castle-like building mounted on the proclivity, a little over a mile away. There was a clearing in front of us where an empty truck sat before a road that wound its way through the trees. As Krebs and company approached the vehicle, there was a rustle of activity from the right. Two figures dressed in dark clothing emerged from the woods holding sub-machine guns, spraying the entire area with bullets. Some of our people fell and Krebs, his guards, and DeKuyper, returned fire. Both figures were subsequently cut down. They must have been part of a small party that had stumbled through the woods to investigate the area.

There were casualties. One of Krebs guards, Wiedemann, was hit fatally, lying motionless upon the ground. The other one was Johannes LaFontaine, who also lay there on the cold earth, not moving. He was dead. Tears welled up in DeKuyper's eyes. The big man drew a pistol from his belt and fingered it in remorse.

"*Ek moet dit doen* (I have to do this)," I heard him say as he fired the gun into LaFontaine's skull. He had to do what he had to do, and the man would not rise again. DeKuyper was saddened and cried lightly as part of his nation fell to the land of shades.

Krebs and another soldier got into the cab of the truck along with the commandant. The rest of us piled into the back of the open vehicle. Krebs started the truck up, and it rumbled up the tree-flanked road to the castle on the hill. It stopped, and we all bounded out of the back.

Before us sat a four-story mansion that had two cylindrical columns full of windows on its face. In between the two columns was a large solid double door, which would allow us to enter the structure. Most of the ground floor windows were narrow and slit-like, and the building could probably withstand a mounting attack for hours.

"This place was built for some of the scientists who would have worked in the complex," Krebs said. "The man who designed it was a native South-Wester."

Before the mansion was a piece of artillery that overlooked the distant complex of New Valhalla, and behind the cannon on the ground was a cache of ten black shells that sat upright. I turned around and could see the lights coming from the huge compound. Both sides of the fortress were enveloped by the tangle of teak forest, which made it almost impenetrable from either side. Helicopters sailed through the air over the compound, ready to discharge heavy explosives.

Krebs walked over to the howitzer and motioned for us to follow him. He said something to the guards in German that produced a quick rush of activity. One of the men wheeled a large set of floodlights into place and another brought forth a large generator that chugged to life and pumped out power for the lamps. They lit up the yard before the large house, and we could now easily see what we were doing. Krebs took out a mobile radio and spoke to someone on it in the German language.

"Okay," he told the group. "Burghoff knows that we are back here in case something bad happens. He will check on us in sixty minutes with *der Hubschrauber* (helicopter)."

He ordered the commandant over to the large metal shells, and the remaining guards accompanied him.

"I do have an ace up my sleeve, and it is my pleasure to show you this. The complex below has proven to be very useful. A number of South African and Russian nuclear physicists have joined us here, and they have produced six small thermonuclear devices from a certain isotope of hydrogen. When they explode, they give off mostly neutrons and little radiation will be released. The blast will not harm my people. One is in the house. The others are here in these shells. *Ich habe an alles gedacht,* I have thought of everything," he said smiling. "This is better than Wagner-Appreciation Day." I wondered if he was only delaying the inevitable. His men readied one of the large shells and loaded it from the rear of the howitzer.

"The bomb will explode on impact," Krebs said.

I could see that multitude on the great plain beyond the complex bathed in the glow of the powerful floodlights. There were probably three or four hundred thousand strong, but that was only a guess, due to the thick pervading darkness that obscured everything. All the ghouls of Namibia may be here. Was this humanity's last stand? Somewhere out beyond the fortress, out upon that savannah, I could see a strange light materialize there, resembling a lantern approaching the compound. I could not be certain if it was a person or not. The light was no more than a mile-and-half away and closing.

"*Schiessen!*" Krebs ordered.

The artillery shell was launched. It went through the air, whistling as it sailed over the fortress. It landed several miles away on the savannah, producing a beautiful orange mushroom cloud with a widening bottom that swallowed the writhing multitude below it. I hoped that it annihilated thousands of those things.

"*Wunderbar. Wunderbar. Wunderbar,*" Krebs said. "We must have eliminated tens of thousands. Launch another," he said to the commandant.

The commandant barked orders in German to the men.

"*Schiessen!*" Krebs ordered again.

The howitzer lobbed the shell over the distant fortress, and like the first, it also landed several miles away upon the dark savannah. The explosion was a little bit smaller than the original, but still devastated a significant number of the enormous army in a mushroom cloud that lit up the flat plain. Hopefully, we had wrecked all of the military equipment that they had.

Krebs had his men fire two more atomic devices. Like the ones previously, they hit the mass multitude, incinerating them in the orange glow. Perhaps we had cut their numbers by a third. I looked out upon that same vista, and I noticed that there were still a few helicopters flying over the complex and discharging missiles. I hoped that Burghoff had somehow managed to hide his chopper. Down towards the side of the fortress, to the right within the teak forest, I could see that same strange light, glowing like a lantern and making its way here. It was getting closer. What was it?

I noticed Krebs on the mobile radio once again. His face did not look so good as his men prepared the next nuclear weapon.

He looked at DeKuyper and me.

"Burghoff just told me a number of them are coming around the sides of the complex, through the forest. They are heading straight toward us," he said. Apparently, they knew that we were throwing the atomic weapons at them from here and wanted to put a stop to it.

The final nuclear weapon was fired through the barrel of the howitzer. It landed off to the right, near the hills on the outer edges of the plain. Like before, I saw an orange cloud light up the sky and offer a temporary solution, much smaller than the prior ones. I remembered Krebs said that the radioactive fallout was miniscule. Radiation poisoning would be kept to an absolute minimum.

The sound of automatic weapons fire ripped through the night. Down the hill to the left, a number of figures emerged from the teak forest. Judging by the swift speed of their ascent, they were ghouls that had been completely regenerated. The glowing light in the woods grew brighter as it got closer. To the right, on the other side of the road, a group of ghouls stepped out of the teak forest. They were all armed and led by Michelle Ramadan!

There must have been fifty of these creatures, and they raked the area near the howitzer with automatic fire. My entire group backed towards the house, Krebs firing his pistol in retreat. The ghouls moved with speed as they surged up the hill, firing wildly with shotguns and automatics. One of Krebs men was struck in the abdomen and immediately fell backwards. Another one of Krebs's men attended to him, but the man who had fallen looked as if he was dead. Krebs' soldier pulled his pistol from his holster, shot the person in the brain, and joined us as we fell back to the castle-like house.

Krebs took a set of keys out of his pocket that jingled in the night air. He thrust them into the double door and pushed it open. The barrier swung into the empty darkness inside.

Chapter Forty-One: The Dead Man Runs

"Everyone get inside quickly! *Gehen Sie Schnell!*" he said.

We ran over the threshold. I turned around to notice a number of gray faces under the moonlight staring at us. They were expressionless and blank as they rushed the door. Krebs shut the door and locked it. The glass covering the narrow windows of the edifice shattered as machine gun bullets and buckshot went through them. We had to back further away from the door into the living room. The double door rattled as we heard them try the lock. We heard bullets fire from the other side of the door, slowly splintering away the timber.

"We have to get to the cellar of this house," Krebs said. We stumbled deeper into the dark structure, and the commandant found a hallway that led further into the dark expanse.

"There are some rooms on the other side of the hallway with furniture. We have to take them and form a barricade to slow them down," Krebs said.

To the left, I walked into a room that had a solitary narrow window in it, Van Den Heuvel and DeKuyper accompanied me. We found a couch and decided to move it out into the corridor. DeKuyper took one end and Van Den Heuvel and I took the other. All of a sudden, a gray face appeared outside the small window behind me. It opened fire, shattering the glass. Van Den Heuvel was caught in the barrage and fell backwards, dropping his corner of the couch. DeKuyper and I set down the couch and returned fire upon the ghoul. The thing fell back from the broken window and did not return. We dragged Van Den Heuvel near the doorway of the chamber, away from the open casement. He was groaning in pain.

A man appeared in the doorway to the room, and I recognized him immediately. It was the commandant. "We have to get to the cellar now! They are almost here!" He shouted.

The big Afrikaner swung the wounded man over his shoulder, and we made our exit from the room. The commandant took us down a passageway to the right, but before I went around the bend, I paused and looked behind me. The front door had finally opened and the hallway was filled with bullets. Several pieces of furniture were laid out in the corridor, forming a barrier to obstruct the intruders. A strange light outside the house accompanied the machine gun bursts and lit up the windows, producing an eerie glow. Whatever was causing that luminescence was now right outside this building. The light was neither warm nor comforting and dimmed my hopes of getting out of this thing alive.

I ducked into the hallway and followed the commandant. He opened up a door that led down a set of dark stone stairs. DeKuyper and I walked past him as the commandant turned the deadbolt on the cellar door. We descended the wide stone staircase that led to a landing. The stairs turned to the left at the landing, and we went down accordingly. The steps concluded at the bottom, and we stood in a stone room filled with shadow.

Once in the room, I heard the hum of a distant generator and the lights flicked on overhead, illuminating the dank cellar. We found ourselves in a spacious and windowless chamber, complete with columns that supported a vaulted ceiling, reminding me of a crypt below an ancient English cathedral. Stacks of boxes and piles of old furniture sat upon a floor composed of cement. Roger and Angeline were standing here as well, previously surrounded in darkness. It was like an impregnable fortress and would make it difficult for them to get down here. Krebs knew what he was doing when he chose this place.

DeKuyper laid the Coloured man on the cement floor and scanned his limp body from head to toe. His eyes stared blankly at the ceiling, and his chest no longer moved up and down. Abel Van Den Heuvel was dead. DeKuyper paused and once again a sad look came over his countenance. He pointed the pistol to Abel's head, ready to pull the trigger.

"*Vaarwel vriend,*" he said. That was it, the Coloured man would not revive to wander after expiration.

We ran further back into the cavernous old cellar, the high arching ceilings and walls made up of silent brown and gray stone. The commandant took us into a passageway that turned and twisted this way and that. It terminated in a large room that was a repository for cardboard boxes. On the floor of this chamber sat several paintings of Jesus hanging from a cross. On the wooden tables about the place were small heaps of crucifixes. I remembered that Krebs wanted to supplant Christianity and replace it with a new order reminiscent of old Norse paganism. Krebs and his men were gathered at the back of this room, their attention on an object placed upon a brown table that sat against the moist and dank stonewall.

Curious, I had to walk over and find out what was going on. Looking behind me, I noticed that Angeline and Roger had followed me into the room, apparently lending strong support. The five men were huddled around a rectangular device about the size of a football. I studied it, not sure what it was.

"What is it?" I asked Krebs.

"It is a small nuclear device. I wanted to use it to annihilate every last trace of God I could find. Most of the Bibles, crucifixes, and Protestant crosses from the suburbs of Windhoek are here in this building. I am going to detonate it before they get here. That way I can go down in flames like a true Teutonic warrior," Krebs said.

"You're going to murder us all? Just like that?" I asked him, slightly angry.

"There is no hope. We don't have enough atomic bombs to wipe them all out, and they have an endless supply of soldiers. If we destroy the ones outside the compound, they will just regroup in the millions. We are finished," he said.

He was right, and I said nothing in resignation. Where was God at a moment like this? He seemed to be a million miles away, preoccupied with the affairs of some remote corner of the universe. With a sharp stab of his index finger, Krebs hit a button on the side of the box. A small door slid back in the device, revealing a keypad. Krebs took his left index finger and diligently pushed the buttons on the number pad, entering a cryptic code.

"All I have to do is press one more button and the bomb goes off within thirty seconds," Krebs announced.

The man wanted to die and did not think twice about taking the lives of the rest of us. Krebs' men silently looked on, completely subordinate.

To the back of the table, against the wall, there was a gray rectangular shaft leading from the ceiling to the floor with some sort of purpose. It looked like part of a ventilation system. A hole was cut in the top of the table to make room for it to pass freely.

"Where does this go, Krebs?" I asked.

"To below," he said.

"What's down there?" I asked.

"That is an air shaft. There is a small sublevel below this place. It can be accessed from a stairway in the hall that led to this chamber," he said. "If we have to, we can hide there. They will be here soon."

A ruckus could be heard from the cavernous main room, echoing into infinity, an incessant pounding that wouldn't stop.

DeKuyper ran into the unholy chamber, exhausted and out of breath.

"The door! *Die Deur!*" he shouted, pointing in the direction of the large tomb-like room.

Everyone left the sacrilegious room full of paintings and crucifixes to follow the big Afrikaner. The dark winding passageways spread out like a catacomb beneath this house-like castle. In a few seconds, we emerged in the same vacuous main room that we were in earlier, gathered silently, waiting for something to happen. I heard an explosion where the cellar door was. The entrance to the basement stairwell began to glow brilliantly as something strange and out of place descended it. Two black Africans in brown uniforms emerged from the doorway. They fired their automatic rifles, and we answered back with a hail of bullets as we ducked behind the piles of furniture and stone pylons, trying to take cover.

Two more joined them, trying to obtain entrance into this large room. DeKuyper let out a burst of bullets from his assault rifle. It hit one of the ghouls in the chest several times, but he failed to pierce its skull. Another one of the figures threw a canister into the main room. It landed with a metallic clank, belching forth a thick vapor, obscuring everything in sight. It was a military-style smoke bomb.

Roger, Angeline, DeKuyper, and I drew back to another pile of furniture. Krebs, the commandant, and the three remaining soldiers were on the other side of the room, backing away from the billowing cloud, moving from pile to pylon. They wasted their ammunition, firing blindly and haphazardly into the smoky haze, hoping to hit the ghouls concealed within. About a dozen of obscured figures advanced toward us through the dark smog. DeKuyper and the commandant managed to cut some of them down as the rest of us crouched behind old furniture and cardboard boxes, keeping clear of the bullets that went forth. My group fired their weapons as well, destroying more, but they outnumbered us, driving us back to the very edges of the vaulted chamber that we were in.

The smoky gas cloud finally began to dissipate. As it cleared, we noticed that two of Krebs' men had gone down, leaving very few of us standing to stem the threat before us. The strange glow that I saw walking through the teak forest earlier had now entered the cellar. As it did, I felt a strong despair and gloom that made me want to give up and die, but I kept on firing the AK-47 with resolution. There was a flurry of activity in front of me as the ghouls fanned out to hold the crypt. The glowing figure got closer, and the smoke thinned out, pulling despondency in with it.

“What’s going on?” Angeline asked, just after firing her pistol.

“I’ve no clue darlin’. Have no clue,” I answered, squeezing off a few more rounds.

The bright light grew brighter until I clearly realized the shimmering figure in a phosphorescent glow. It brought to remembrance Davies’ tale of the advancing female recorded by the Venus probe, harboring the horrid destruction that held the earth captive. Before me, bathed in unnatural light, was a beautiful woman clothed in a blue dress, wearing a strange and ancient funnel-like hat. She had flowing elegant tresses and held a curved Middle Eastern sword in her hand.

I had seen that figure before in my dreams. It was her, the legendary Queen of Heaven who was loved and feared by the Mesopotamian masses, who had come to reclaim the abode that rudely and coldly rejected her. She was Ishtar, the untamed goddess of eroticism and violence. There was another figure to her right, nearly as tall and majestic as the goddess herself, in unkempt garb and looking like the queen of the derelicts. It was none other that Michelle Ramadan, and the color of her skin had become a pallid gray.

There was some activity on the other side of the chamber with Krebs and his two remaining men, who were lost in the flurry of rebellion.

“*Schiessen*!” he ordered.

He and his men cut down a few more of the ghouls but suddenly stopped firing. Krebs and some of his men desperately and frantically looked at their weapons. Their magazines had been spent and they were running out of bullets. In response, I aimed my assault rifle at the majestic goddess and her cold entourage. A couple of bullets were fired as I squeezed the trigger! Then my rifle ceased as my ammunition was depleted. DeKuyper still had ammunition left in his, and he emptied it at the glowing woman in our midst. The barrel belched forth lead without effect. The goddess took the sword and swung it over her head in circles, charging the hulking Afrikaner who had no means to defend himself.

"AAAAAAAAAAAAAAH!" she screamed as her sword descended upon DeKuyper's brittle collarbone. A gush of blood came forth from the mortal wound as DeKuyper screamed in protest. His eyes rolled back in his sockets as if he was unable to accept his own mortality. His corpse slid to the floor silently, life ebbing from it! The man was dead and his soul escaped to the land of no return! Angeline, Roger, and I threw our guns to the floor and put our hands up in surrender. There was nothing to fight back with, and we could do nothing about the circumstances!

Ramadan came forth confidently, with a pistol firmly in her hand. Surrounding us were over thirty ghouls, mostly black, and all wearing tan uniforms like the desert legions of Erwin Rommel. Their faces were expressionless, yet they bore a trace of mischievousness, imps brandishing assault rifles, pistols, and shotguns. The goddess, with both of her hands on the bloodied sword, looked at all of us. Her eyes were angry and deeply evil, no redemption in them at all.

"I sense there is a nuclear device in the vicinity. It must be neutralized," the goddess said.

Ramadan stood next to her, pointing the pistol at us. "She wants all of you to get over to the center of the floor," she said, motioning with the barrel of her lethal sidearm. Everyone moved to the middle of the room with their hands up, including me. The ghouls, with a trace of malice in their eyes, surrounded us like puppets on a string.

"Think we're in a lot of trouble!" I said to Roger.

"Andy, he'll get us out of this problem. God is real good. I know he will," Roger said with limitless confidence. I thought the man was absolutely crazy.

"All of you have been excellent fighters, and the goddess is pleased. She has a proposition for you," Ramadan said.

Silence fell, and the luminescent goddess, Ishtar, sheathed her sword in her scabbard as she scanned all of us from head to toe. I felt like I was a rat in a cage.

"I want to begin a new race," she said. "I have been on Venus, imprisoned by the persistent unbelief of the human race, but the world again began to have faith in me, empowering me to make the dead rise. The pantheon sent me here to soften all resistance. As I neared the earth, my power over the ghouls grew. Now I have the ability to restore the dead and regenerate their physical bodies, leaving their souls for the afterlife. The dead have annihilated and devoured the living, fulfilling the dream I have harbored for many centuries. The gods want to return to earth from Venus and will make it their home once again."

She continued to speak from a position of arrogant power, not fearing a single thing.

"We will use the remnants of the settlement that *Herr Krebs* so valiantly calls 'New Valhalla' to repopulate the earth. From you will come more perfect beings. Andy, this I told you, many nights ago. I was mad at you, but I will forgive you if you accept the proposition. I like you. You are an independent thinker, and you are a survivor. Those are good traits to have. I will use you for breeding stock, and you can be my collaborator and friend. We will use all of you as breeding stock," the glowing goddess said with a smile that had gone awry.

"You will all make love to the gods, and from them will come a new super race. Do you want this?" she asked, as the shadows of the crypt distorted her face.

Krebs stood there for a moment, looking at De-Kuyper's fallen corpse and the blatant destruction around the room. He looked down at his own open hands, and then his eyes met the eyes of both the faithful commandant and the remaining soldier. They were going to act in unison.

"You are going to destroy everything that I have built! You will kill my people! YOU ARE AN ABOMINATION!" he screamed at the top of his lungs, charging the angry goddess with his bare hands. The commandant and the remaining soldier began to attack the congregating ghouls with their fists, the hopeless charge of the doomed light brigade. The glowing goddess reached out with her right hand and grabbed Krebs by the neck with a grip of steel. With one hand, she effortlessly picked the large man up off the ground and applied pressure to his throat ever so slowly. Automatic fire filled the chamber as the other two remaining men were sacrificed in a hail of bullets.

Krebs struggled to break free from her iron grip as her fingers drew tighter and cut off his air.

"I will kill you if it's the last thing I do!" he said, struggling to get the words out of his constricted passageway.

Krebs died from suffocation in one last sudden gasp; his once powerful body now limp. She let go of his feeble corpse, and it flopped to the floor of the vaulted cellar. "It is a pity he rebelled. I could have used his genetic material. That is what will happen to you if you don't do what I ask. You will be killed. Then you will be mine. Now that I am here on the earth, I can restore the consciousness of many and neglect the soul. These are men without spirits, subject to my command," the goddess spoke.

I began to pray. I was not sure what was happening, but I began to sense God's presence amidst the despair and gloom that emanated from the Queen of Heaven.

A voice suddenly rubbed across my thoughts, slightly irritating me. "The dead man will run. Just speak to him and he will run," it said. This information made no sense, but I had to believe that it was from God.

"Ishtar and I worked together," Ramadan said. "I knew how the radiation worked. It stimulated a certain part of the brain and caused the body to reanimate. Ishtar could guide them and direct them to a degree, but her power is limited. She cannot be everywhere at once. I found that, by reconditioning a ghoul and reminding it of its past life, I could induce it to regain some of its past consciousness. With Ishtar now present, her power is stronger; the decay can be reversed and the body can be restored, though the soul is long gone," the beautiful dead gray woman said.

"Look what I can do, Andy Goering. Look at how powerful I am. I can destroy God's creation and make it mine. Watch!" the goddess ordered.

She walked over to the body that was Franz Reichard Krebs. She touched it, placing her hands upon its head. Her glowing fingers glowed much brighter now as the corpse began to stir. Its head began to move from side to side slowly, as if it had a stiff neck. Its eyes snapped open as it pushed itself up with powerful hands. The corpse struggled to its feet and regained its footing like a little child learning how to walk. The gray reanimated corpse stood with a blank look upon its face and opened its dead mouth to speak.

"Was ist passiert (what is happening)?*"* Franz Krebs said. He appeared somewhat disoriented.

"This is what I can do! This is my power!" the goddess ranted.

Then, at that moment, I gathered the courage to speak with a question that probed into the depths of the unknown.

"If you can revive him, can you also make him inactive?" I asked.

"Yes," the beautiful goddess replied. "However, there are limitations."

"What sort of limitations?" I asked.

"If I render him inactive, I render all of them inactive. I will lose my army. I need more power."

"More power?" I questioned.

"Yes. There are energies that float about the universe, waiting .to be possessed and manipulated. Through certain rights, incantations, and sacrifices I can take them and make them mine. I want to gather more, so that I can challenge the Almighty God who exists inside and outside of the cosmos."

She wanted to challenge Jehovah himself? Was this woman insane? She was like Captain Ahab, trying to destroy the white whale and all he represented. Another question entered my mind and it sunk there, taking root.

"Ishtar," I said. The goddess continued to face me. "Tell me. Where is Michelle Ramadan's soul?"

"Michelle Ramadan's soul is in the afterlife, but her consciousness remains here under my control," the goddess answered. "She has no will of her own and gave it to me when she injected the ghoulish blood into her own system."

For some reason, my mind was bombarded by another idea. The concept screamed into my brain until it overwhelmed every pattern of sense and emotion. It swam around in my head and circulated, trying to find a place to land. The thought articulated itself as it spoke to my brain:

"Ask her about God. She will tell you. Remember, speak to the dead man. He will run." It was God. It had to be, but I still did not know what he meant by that meaningless phrase.

"Ishtar, are you angry?" I asked the long and flowing goddess.

"Angry at what?" she asked, appearing puzzled.

"At God."

"Yes. Yes. Yes. I hate God," she said as she closed her eyes for a moment. "He created me, and I was his prize creation. He showed me to the other beings, and they honored me to no end. I wanted more than what he would give me; I wanted all of the cosmos to bow down to me, but he would not allow it. He threw me to earth, where I was at humanity's whim, trying to please them and coax them to do my bidding, but they rejected me. Now, I shall have my revenge! I will destroy his precious little creation, and that is the human race itself."

I looked at the face of the man that was once Franz Reichard Krebs. He stared at the floor and then peered about the room. He saw the heavily armed ghouls and noticed Michelle Ramadan to his left. He saw the bodies of the commandant and the fallen soldiers, and a grievous expression came over his face. Something was happening to the man who had just recently died.

"So, you believe that there is a God, Ishtar? Did he make you?" I asked.

"Oh, yes!" she said with a strange look in her eye.

"I am living proof that he exists! He knew I could supplant him and he would lose his place in the universe, so he threw me to earth. He is like an overgrown child, given to temper tantrums. I will repay him for everything that he has done to me! To hell with God! To hell with the human race! I will rise above it all, all the chaos, all the disease, all the destruction! I WILL BECOME THE UNDISPUTED MASTER OVER ALL OF THE EARTH AND THE ENTIRE UNIVERSE WILL BE MINE!"

Looking at what she said, she was clearly the bringer of doom and destruction. Then I got this idea to say something.

"Krebs! She's going to destroy your people! Krebs do something! Snap out of it, now!" I shouted to the corpse.

The gray-skinned man looked at Ishtar and studied his hands, noting the strange color. He flipped over the hands again slowly, and meticulously studied their backs. He placed his hands to the side of his face and carefully examined it with his cold, dead fingertips. A look of uncontrolled anger came over his pallid countenance as hatred and remorse consumed him totally. He screamed at the top of his lungs the battle cry of a Teutonic warrior: "*MEIN GOTT*, FORGIVE ME!"

All eyes fell upon the man that was once Franz Reichard Krebs. Hesitation and shock seemed to ripple through the collection of animated corpses. One of the regenerated ghouls stood next to Krebs, looking uncertain as to what to do next, lost in confusion. Krebs violently yanked the AK-47 out of its hands and fired it without hesitation, hitting several of the ghouls that lethargically collapsed to the floor. He panned his gun in and arc and hit Ramadan in the torso several times, her body jerking from the impact of the bullets. He mercilessly pumped several slugs into her brain, causing her to fall backwards on the floor behind her.

"YAAAAAAAAAAH!" he screamed as he opened fire upon the other ghouls with precision, hitting about ten of them in the cranium. They toppled to the floor like dominoes.

"C'mon guys, quick, while they're distracted!" I said.

Angeline, Roger, and I picked up some of the live weapons from the fallen ghouls. Krebs continued to fire with incredible accuracy as the ghouls took cover behind piles of old furniture. Ishtar stood there, dazed and confused in the enveloping chaos. I cocked the shotgun and fired at her point blank. The buckshot did nothing to the creature. I took a grenade from one of the fallen ghouls, pulled out the pin, and tossed it near the majestic goddess. It went off, exploding and enveloping her in a cloud of smoke, hiding the entity from view. For a second or two, there was silence amidst the haze, but she emerged from the cloud furious, unsheathing her sword viciously.

She lunged at me, swinging the blade wildly above her head! I immediately fell back, but she came at me again, swirling the sword with great accuracy and skill. "I WILL CUT YOUR HEAD OFF AND SPIT ON YOUR NAME-LESS GRAVE! GRAAAAAAAAAAAAAAA-AAAAAAA!" She cried out as she charged me.

"God, if I ever needed you, now is the time! Please be with me!" She came towards me with the sword circling in the air. I fell backwards, her sword striking the concrete floor as I managed to roll out of the way! While I was still on the ground, she whirled the sword over her head again. The blade descended over my torso, and I once again moved out of its lethal path! I stood up and found my back against the unyielding wall. Realizing that I had no place to go, she sheathed the sword and came forward.

"I will eliminate you, crush you like the worthless insect that you are, and you will not have a chance to impregnate anyone!" She advanced, threatening to strangle the life out of me! Then there was a sudden movement to the right of us. A figure sat up, causing a disturbance that could be felt in the far reaches of the cosmos. She turned to look at it and found DeKuyper back from the grave! Quickly, while her attention was elsewhere, I slinked away from the wall and escaped from the mad goddess.

Krebs, Angeline, and Roger were firing at the remaining ghouls, crouched behind two piles of equipment in the cellar. The ghouls' numbers were reduced to about seven, but they still blocked the path to the stairwell. At that moment, my mind flashed back to the events of the past two years. I could see the figure on horseback amongst the gray sands of time in the dream. The scene of my mother lying there on the floor of the basement behind a ping-pong table surged through my mind. I recalled the Jamaican woman dying at my side in a wrecked vehicle, accompanied by a brown teddy bear. I got the sense that the next moment would be one of the most important junctures I would ever have.

Looking over at the entrance to the stairwell, I could have sworn that I saw Jesus peering at me, leaning up against the threshold still clothed in his brown Middle Eastern garment. He shined forth hope and encouragement. Suddenly, it became very clear to me what I was supposed to say and do.

"Krebs! Blow up the house. Finish what you were going to do and blow up the house! Now! Save your people, Krebs. Save your people before it's too late!" The man stopped firing and turned to look at me. He reflected and peered behind him at the doorway that led back to the sacrilegious room with the bomb. He dropped the gun to the floor and took off running into the twisting hallway at an unstoppable speed.

Ishtar saw the whole thing as it played out. She screamed in fury, "NOOOOOOOO!"

She lost all interest in me and then flew into the hallway to pursue Krebs. As the mad goddess turned down that hallway, the other seven ghouls broke from their positions and followed her, locked into a macabre chase. I could hear them firing their assault rifles at the living corpse that was once Franz Reichard Krebs, the frustrated and rejected son of a mistaken missionary.

I picked up the radio that was not too far from where DeKuyper had lain. His corpse was a few feet away and whirled around at the sound of my voice, and he growled with a twisted expression! I picked up a .45 that was lying near me and fired a slug into his brain. The corpse fell to the floor, and with it, the Afrikaner dream of domination.

"Angeline! Roger! Let's get out of here now! This whole place is going to go sky high!" I said, realizing we might not even make it. We immediately left the cellar and ascended the cold and dank stairs. We only had seconds to act! I took the mobile radio in my hand and turned it on. I managed to get Burghoff.

"Matthias, we're up at the house! Get us quick!" I told him.

"I'm almost there!" he said with his raspy voice echoing metallically from the radio.

* * *

Franz Reichard Krebs sped down the corridor with all of his might. He could hear the ranting goddess behind him as her expressionless henchmen fired their weapons. He knew what he had to do. She had turned him into an undead mockery of all that he once was. Now he was going to try with all of his strength to repay her in kind. He could see a man in a brown robe and beard before him, leading him to the thermonuclear device in the room full of articles. A bullet went into his back but caused no pain, his nervous system already non-functional. He ran down the convoluted corridor to the right, to the left, and then to the right again. The man in the robe was always ahead, guiding him and directing him with eyes of forgiveness.

"YOU STOP! YOU OBEY ME!" the goddess cried, her voice having no weight in his spirit.

He strained his legs with everything he had as more shots rang out, this time hitting him in the calf. He pushed on, racing to cross the finish line into the room before him. Krebs ran into that chamber with the crucifixes and Bibles quaintly stored in contempt. The gracious man with the beard and the robe stared at him and pointed to the rectangular device on the table.

"You must do what you were created to do. You will join me very shortly!" he declared.

Krebs stumbled towards the tables at the end of the room, nearly falling to the floor.

"GRAAAAAAAH! STOP! OBEY!" Ishtar desperately screamed as she entered the room.

"YOU OBEY ME! NO ONE ELSE! ME!"

Another shot rang out as a bullet pierced Kreb's torso again! He fell against the table and managed to pick himself up quickly! The rectangular box sat before him, perched majestically upon the wooden table. Automatic fire filled the room and Ishtar screamed again. His gray index finger shot out and hit a button on the box of atomic fire. The little door in the device rolled back and revealed a numbered pad. There was just one final button to push, and then he pressed it! In thirty seconds it would all be oblivion and emptiness.

"NOOOOOOOOOOO!" the goddess shrieked.

The bomb had to be placed out of her reach or she would destroy it. His eyes caught the airshaft that led through the table to the floor below. There was a small vent in the shaft, and he pulled it out in desperation. Krebs took the bomb firmly with his other hand! Automatic fire continued to erupt around the room and struck him in the neck, damaging one of the tendons, causing his head to flop to the right. Krebs heard a long metallic rasping sound from behind him. He looked to the left, his head hanging limp, and saw the bearded man several feet away, smiling in mercy, as he thrust the atomic device down the shaft. He felt nothing as the sharp blade cleaved into his skull. His vision went black…

* * *

We clambered over the barrier of furniture and entered the living room, running towards the lead riddled double door. A brown figure suddenly stood and obstructed the doorway! It was a ghoul holding an assault rifle, and it annoyingly shot off a short burst of bullets. Angeline squeezed her AK-47 and filled it with shells. It fell to the ground and did not rise.

I knew we only had precious seconds in which to act. Stepping over the corpse, we emerged from the house, and I looked into the hopeful sky above. Burghoff was approaching in the chopper, like an angel from the heavens.

"He'd better get here fast," I said. Burghoff landed the chopper and we all ran to its door in a mad scramble to escape.

“Matthias, get us out of here, now!” He lifted the helicopter off the ground and flew into the night sky.

“They’re starting to get into the complex! They’re surrounding the entire place!” he said to the three of us.

“Matthias, step on it!” I said. Within a few seconds the chopper lurched, hundreds of feet into the air. It was just a matter of time now. We could see the compound loom below us, and I knew we were safe.

Behind us, on the hill, was a wonderfully bright orange explosion; it gave way to a small mushroom cloud rising to the heavens, completely enveloping the castle-like house below. The blast continued in slow motion, consuming everything inside. All the books, Protestant crosses, the bodies of Michelle Ramadan, Andries DeKuyper, Abel Van Den Heuvel, Krebs’ men, and Krebs himself were vaporized. I hoped to God that the glowing goddess was destroyed as well. It was a wonderfully hopeful explosion, bringing forth the fires of redemption.

Chapter Forty-Two: The End of an Age

As we circled the sky above the complex, I noticed that the undead multitude below started behaving very strangely. They seemed to be slowing down as they milled around in front of the compound, bathed in fluorescence. They suddenly went still, faltering in their tracks, collapsing in waves. One of the helicopters that was aloft came crashing to the ground and burst into flames. The creatures continued to crumple to the ground in pulses that radiated from the central explosion in concentric circles. It made me smile, Ishtar perishing in the atomic blast that vaporized the house. There was no power to maintain the animated corpses anymore, and they were all dying!

Burghoff landed the helicopter skillfully in the middle of the expansive compound. People started to file out of their hiding places as we all exited the chopper. It was over, the plague had vanished.

I met the New Valhallans, black, white, and Asian with handshakes and beaming smiles. I was elated, relishing in the victory of the millennium. Elizabeth, the girl who may have been the solution, approached us along with Amanda Dingane and Judith Luthuli behind her. Dingane smiled and Milano was in back of them. I was no longer angry with the man, and I shook his hand and embraced him.

"Sorry about Rachel," I said. "I forgive you. I really do."

"Yeah, thanks," he said. He was smiling.

Looking at the delighted faces, I knew everyone was relieved. I peered at the sky and realized how good God was, took Angeline and kissed her like a sailor returning home from World War II. I hugged Roger as well.

We stood in the middle of the complex as everyone started to nurse their wounds from the final attack of the dead. Just before the atomic blast, the ghouls had managed to surround the compound and pierced some of the barricades. Ammunition was running low, and the place would have been overrun in another half-an-hour. The human race was so close to extinction. They counted the bodies to find that about five hundred of the New Valhallans had lost their lives in what was humanity's last stand.

*   *   *

As the sun rose up in the blue sky above, Roger, Angeline, and I stood on top of the hill near where the house of sacrilege once was. We overlooked a crater about twenty feet deep and four hundred wide. Utilizing a Geiger counter, we found that the radiation readings were very low. I remembered that Krebs said that the fallout from the blast would be almost nonexistent. He was right, and hardly anyone would die from the radioactivity. We looked beyond the compound and could see corpses stretching on for miles, birds circling about in the sky overhead. It would take us weeks, if not months, to destroy all of the bodies and burn them in a pyre that would reach for infinity.

"How are the Israelis doing?" Roger asked.

"They're doing fine. Apparently, they were never attacked. They'll be sending a group to meet us on a jet within the next twenty four hours," I said.

"How about the Maori?" Angeline asked.

"They're fine too," I said.

There were Germans in Africa. There were Jews in Israel, along with Maori in Fiji. Would these final outposts of humanity thrive, flourish, and live to challenge each other again? Only time would tell.

Ishtar had sent a great plague to the earth in her anger towards humanity, and billions perished as a result. My mom lost her life. Robert Capasso, Rachel Negron, Sasha Bernstein, Arnold Davies, Andries DeKuyper, Johannes LaFontaine, Abel Van Den Heuvel, Franz Krebs, and Marcia Clarke also lost theirs, but there was hope. We would start over, and we would teach our children to love God, to love his Word and never turn their backs upon people again. We would abolish the Order of the Sacred Rune that Krebs so innocently, or maybe not so innocently, created. Old ways die hard, and I had a world to rebuild.

"Andy, why do you think God allowed this whole thing to happen?" Angeline asked.

"Not sure. I remember that I read something in the Bible that said that God would allow evil to rise to the surface so that it could be skimmed off. Ishtar was certainly evil, and she had to be taken out of the picture. Also, we were the only ones who would continue to move from place to place. Most everyone wanted to stay put, so that they would not have to face change. As a result, they died like dinosaurs in an avalanche of sliding mud," I said.

"One thing," Roger said. "Why did Franz Krebs detonate the bomb? Wasn't his mind under Ishtar's control? He shouldn't have been able to rebel like that."

"Yeah. I thought about that one too. Remember, she revived him awfully fast. He had barely been dead by the time she did it," I said.

"So, what are you getting at?" Roger asked.

"Some say that the soul hovers around the body for several minutes before passing on into the afterlife. Maybe his soul never really left his physical self," I said. "He just woke up and realized what had happened to him, totally aware of the circumstances and wanting to undo all the damage he had done. He was redeemed in the last act of his life, if you wanna call it that."

Roger said nothing as his dark brown beard hung from his jaw, desperately needing to be trimmed.

I looked at Angeline and she smiled. She appeared very beautiful in spite of the fact that she was dirty and covered in welts and cuts, her character shining so much more than her physical body ever could. Perhaps Angeline and I would get married and have children, allowing humanity to survive and repopulate the earth. God was good, and I knew he was smiling down on us. I looked up at the sky and noticed the sun that hung there, suspended by gravity. It emanated the hope and warmth that would help us all go on.

My life had emerged significant as I understood that it was God's plan for me to piece humanity back together.

"The sun is pretty bright up there," I said to Angeline as we held hands.

"Yeah, it is," she replied.

Roger let out a heavy sigh as he looked onto the expanse of corpses. He stood there for several long moments, lost in contemplation. He ran his fingers over his lips and closed his eyes tightly for a few seconds.

He turned to us with a smile. "Guess we have a lot of work ahead of us."

"Yep," I answered. "A whole lotta work…"